The Borgia Bride

Also by Jeanne Kalogridis

The Burning Times

The Borgia Bride

Jeanne Kalogridis

St. Martin's Griffin New York

 Printed in the United States of America. For inform
ation, address St. Martin's Press, 175 Fifth Avenue, New York, N.Y. 10010.

Map and family trees drawn by Leslie Robinson

www.stmartins.com

Library of Congress Cataloging-in-Publication Data

Kalogridis, Jeanne.
The Borgia bride / Jeanne Kalogridis.—1st U.S. ed.
p. cm.
ISBN 0-312-34138-5
EAN 978-0312-34138-1
1. Italy—History—1492–1559—Fiction. 2. Female friendship—Fiction. 3. Married women—Fiction. 4. Borgia family—Fiction. 5. Rome (Italy)—Fiction. I. Title.

PS3561.A41675B67 2005
813'.54—dc22

2004066433

First published in Great Britain by HarperCollins*Publishers*

20 19 18 17 16 15 14

ACKNOWLEDGEMENTS

This novel centres around a woman thrust into the role of a hero. Heroes are uncommon, but I have been blessed to come across more than a few in my life, and I would like to name some of them here.

First, I am indebted to Jane Johnson—especially for her extreme patience, her keen, boundless talent as an editor, and her refusal to accept less than my best. Without her inspired comments and suggestions, this book simply would not be. Thanks must also go to her associate at HarperCollins UK, Emma Coode, for all her wise input. Both have, in no small way, helped to shape this novel for the better.

I am also deeply grateful to my heroic U.S. agent, Russell Galen, for his saintly tolerance, his unwavering support, and his constant hand-holding; in addition I wish to thank my foreign agent, Danny Baror, for his unparalleled tenacity as my advocate. Both of these gentlemen are brilliant negotiators; I'm fortunate to have them on my side.

Now, the greatest hero of all: my husband, George. George has endured with good humour what no partner should have to—helping an extremely cranky novelist edit her bulky manuscript.

His eye for spotting repetitious phrases and logical gaps is unmatched, and he offered up numerous ideas (which I cheerfully stole) for making dull scenes in this novel come to life. (His suggestions for Sancha and Jofre's wedding night helped make the encounter far more poignant.) Over the twenty-odd years I've been writing, George has been pressed into service countless times during every stage of the book. Here are heartfelt thanks for you, sweetheart, though I know they do little to ease the pain.

For Jane Johnson
For the chance

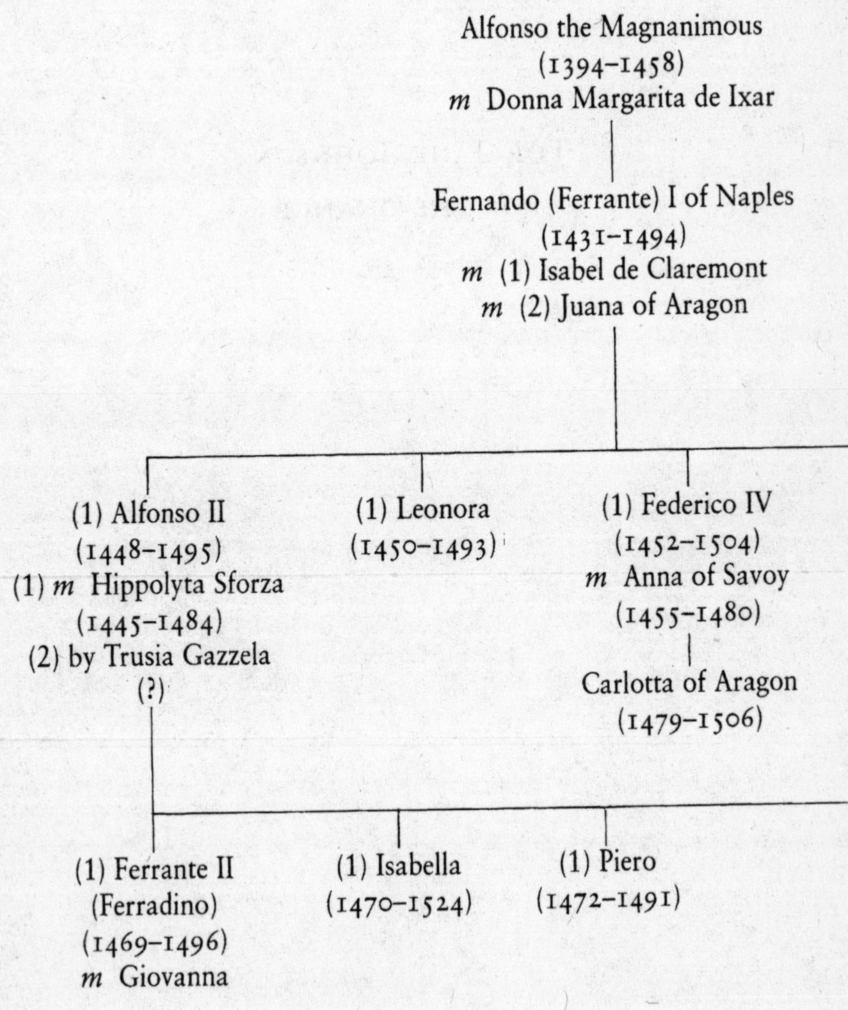
Alfonso the Magnanimous
(1394–1458)
m Donna Margarita de Ixar
Fernando (Ferrante) I of Naples
(1431–1494)
m (1) Isabel de Claremont
m (2) Juana of Aragon
(1) Alfonso II
(1448–1495)
(1) m Hippolyta Sforza
(1445–1484)
(2) by Trusia Gazzela
(?)
(1) Leonora
(1450–1493)
(1) Federico IV
(1452–1504)
m Anna of Savoy
(1455–1480)
Carlotta of Aragon
(1479–1506)
(1) Ferrante II
(Ferradino)
(1469–1496)
m Giovanna
(1) Isabella
(1470–1524)
(1) Piero
(1472–1491)

THE HOUSE OF ARAGON

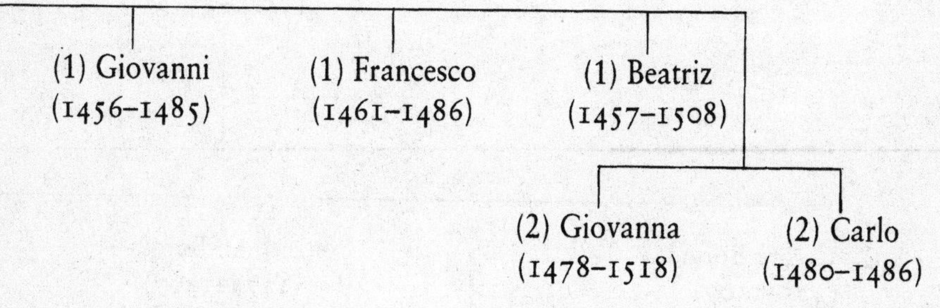

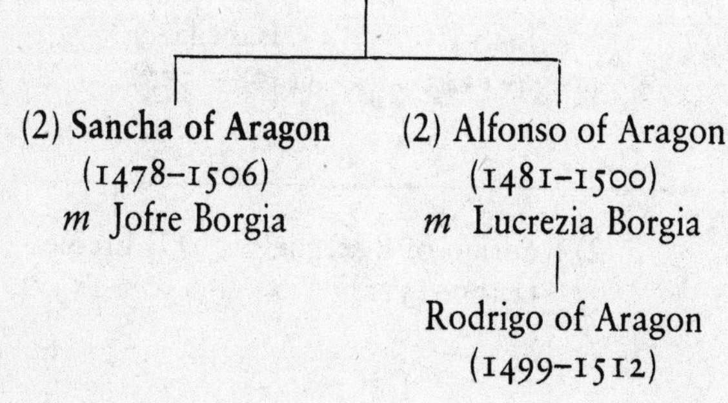

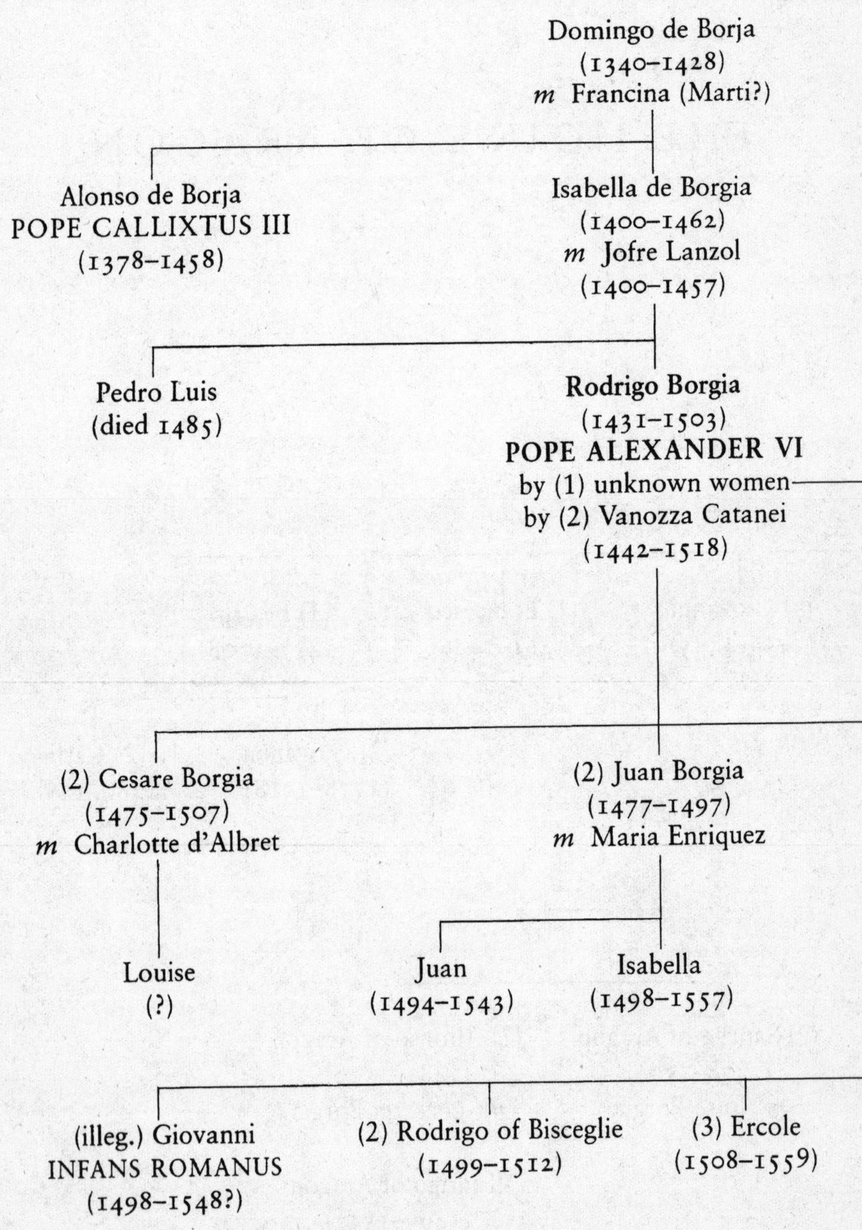

Domingo de Borja
(1340–1428)
m Francina (Marti?)
Alonso de Borja
POPE CALLIXTUS III
(1378–1458)
Isabella de Borgia
(1400–1462)
m Jofre Lanzol
(1400–1457)
Pedro Luis
(died 1485)
Rodrigo Borgia
(1431–1503)
POPE ALEXANDER VI
by (1) unknown women
by (2) Vanozza Catanei
(1442–1518)
(2) Cesare Borgia
(1475–1507)
m Charlotte d'Albret
(2) Juan Borgia
(1477–1497)
m Maria Enriquez
Louise
(?)
Juan
(1494–1543)
Isabella
(1498–1557)
(illeg.) Giovanni
INFANS ROMANUS
(1498–1548?)
(2) Rodrigo of Bisceglie
(1499–1512)
(3) Ercole
(1508–1559)

THE HOUSE OF BORGIA

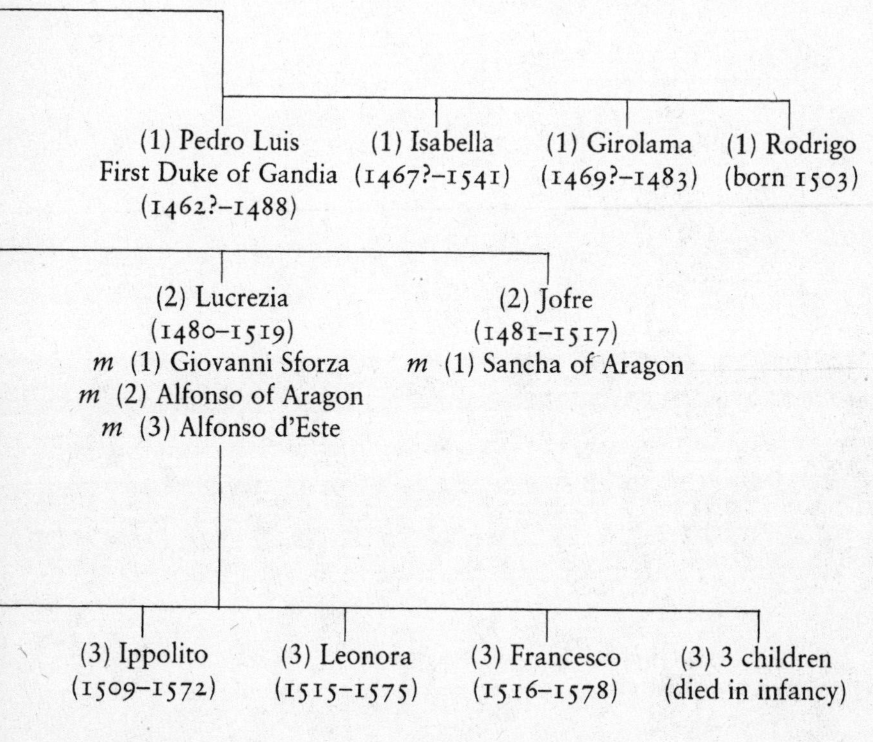

Bologna
Imola
Ravenna
Faenza
Forli
Cesena
ROMAGNA
Pesaro
Senigallia
Florence
Pisa
Arno
THE MARCHES
Siena
Tiber
ELBA
UMBRIA
Spoleto
TYRRHENIAN
SEA
Soriano
PATRIMONY
OF ST PETER
Nepi
SABINA
Trevignano
L. Bracciano
Bracciano
Rome
CAMPAGNA &
MARITTIMA
Milan
VENICE
Venice
Po
Genoa
Taro
Ferrara
Bologna
Ravenna
ROMAGNA
Pisa
Arno
Florence
FLORENCE
ADRIATIC
SEA
PAPAL
STATES
Siena
SIENA
TUSCANY
Elba
ABRUZZI
Pescara
TYRRHENIAN
SEA
Tiber
Rome
KINGDOM
OF NAPLES
Garigliano
Volturno
Bisceglie
Naples
Ischia
APULIA
SALERNO
Otranto
MEDITERRANEAN
SEA
Squillace
N
Messina
CALABRIA
KINGDOM
OF
SICILY
San Lorenzo

PROLOGUE

The *canterella*, it is called: a poison powder so deadly a mere sprinkling of it can kill a man, strike him down in a matter of days. The effects are ghastly. One's head aches as if in a vice; the vision blurs; the body quakes with fever. The bowels release a bloody flux, and the gut clamps tight in an agony that makes the victim howl.

Rumour says only the Borgias know its secret: how to compound it, store it, administer it so as to hide the taste. Rodrigo Borgia—or shall I say, His Holiness Alexander VI—learned the secret from his favourite mistress, the fiery-haired Vannozza Cattanei, when he was still a cardinal. Rodrigo's elder brother, Pedro Luis, would undoubtedly have been elected pope . . . were it not for subtle and well-timed administration of the canterella.

Being generous parents, Rodrigo and Vannozza shared the recipe with their offspring—at the very least with their sweet-faced daughter, Lucrezia. Who better to lull the wary into carelessness than she with the demure smile and the soft voice? Who better to murder and betray than she who is hailed as Rome's greatest innocent?

The 'Borgia fever' has decimated Rome like the plague, thinning the ranks of prelates until every cardinal with land and a bit of wealth lives in terror. After all, when a cardinal dies, his riches go at once to the Church.

And it takes a great deal of wealth to fund a war. A great deal of wealth to amass an army large enough to capture every city-state in all of Italy, and declare oneself leader not only of things spiritual, but of things secular. This pope and his bastard son, Cesare, want more than Heaven; they will have Earth, as well.

In the meantime, I sit in the Castel Sant'Angelo with the other women. From my chamber window, I can see the Vatican nearby, the papal apartments, and the Palazzo Santa Maria where I once lived with my husband. I am allowed to roam the grounds and am accorded courtesy, but there is no more status, and I am under guard, a prisoner. I curse the day I first heard the name Borgia; I pray for the day when I hear the bells toll for the old man's death.

But there is freedom to be had. At this very moment, I hold the vial up to the bright Roman sun that streams into my generously-appointed apartment. The container is Venetian glass, emerald-coloured, shining like a gem: the powder inside is drab bluish-grey, opaque.

Canterella, I whisper. *Beautiful, beautiful canterella, rescue me . . .*

Autumn 1488

I

I am Sancha of Aragon, natural daughter of the man who became Alfonso II, King of Naples, for a year and a day. Like the Borgias, my people came to the Italian peninsula by way of Spain, and like them, I spoke Spanish at home and Italian in public.

My most vivid childhood memory was formed at the end of my eleventh summer, on the nineteenth of September, the year of our Lord 1488. It was the Feast Day of San Gennaro, patron saint of Naples. My grandfather, King Ferrante, had chosen that particular date to celebrate the thirtieth anniversary of his ascension to the Neapolitan throne.

Normally, we royals did not attend the event held in Gennaro's grand Duomo, the cathedral built in his honour. We preferred to celebrate in the comfort of the Chiesa Santa Barbara, the church enclosed within the magnificent walled grounds of the royal palace, the Castel Nuovo. But that year, my grandfather deemed it politic to attend the public ceremony, given the anniversary. Thus, our large entourage processed into the Duomo, watched at some distance by the *zie*, the aunts, *di San Gennaro*, the wailing, black-clad women who pleaded with the Saint to protect and bless Naples.

Naples needed blessing. It had been the site of many wars; my family of Aragonese royalty had won the city through bloody battle only forty-six years prior. Although my grandfather was peacefully handed his throne by his father, the revered Alfonso the Magnanimous, Alfonso had violently wrested Naples from the Angevins, supporters of the Frenchman Charles of Anjou. King Alfonso was beloved for rebuilding the city, for constructing grand palaces and piazzas, strengthening the walls, restocking the royal library. My grandfather was less loved. He was more interested in maintaining a strong hold on the local nobles whose veins held Angevin blood. He spent years in petty wars against different barons, and never came to trust his own people. In turn, they never came to trust him.

Naples had also been the site of earthquakes, including one witnessed in 1343 by the poet Petrarch, which razed half the city and sank every ship in the normally placid harbour. There was also Monte Vesuvio, which was still prone to eruptions.

For these reasons, we had come to beseech San Gennaro that day, and, with luck, to witness a miracle.

The procession into the Duomo was no less than grand. We royal women and children entered first, escorted by blue-and-gold clad guards to the front of the sanctuary, past the black-clad commoners who bowed before us like wheat beneath the wind. Ferrante's Queen, the nubile Juana of Aragon, led us, followed by my aunts Beatriz and Leonora. They were followed by my then-unmarried half-sister Isabella, who had been assigned the care of myself and my eight-year-old brother, Alfonso, as well as Ferrante's youngest daughter, my aunt Giovanna, born the same year as I.

The older females were dressed in the traditional garb of the Neapolitan noblewoman: black gowns with full skirts, tightly-laced bodices, and sleeves narrow at the shoulders then blossoming to the width of church bells at the wrist, so that they draped downward well past the hip. We children were allowed colour: I wore a gown of bright green silk with a brocade bodice laced tightly against absent breasts. Around my neck hung pearls from the sea, and a small gold cross; on my head was a veil of black gossamer. Alfonso wore a pale blue velvet tunic and breeches.

My brother and I walked hand-in-hand just behind my half-sister, careful not to trip on her voluminous skirts. I did my best to look proud and self-assured, my gaze restricted to the back of Isabella's gown, while my brother stared freely out at the assembly. I allowed myself one sidewise glance, at the great cracks in an archway between two large marble columns; above it, a round portrait of Saint Dominic had split in two. A scaffolding stood just beneath it, marking the last of the repairs from an earthquake that had ravaged the Duomo two years before Ferrante came to power.

I was disappointed to have been left in Isabella's care, and not my mother's. My father usually invited my mother, Madonna Trusia Gazullo, a ravishing golden-haired noblewoman, to all functions. He particularly delighted in her company. I believe my father was incapable of love, but certainly he must have come close to it in my gentle mother's arms.

King Ferrante, however, declared it unseemly to bring my father's mistress as part of the royal entourage inside a church. Just as strongly, my grandfather insisted that my brother Alfonso and I come. We were children, not to be blamed for the accident of our parentage. After all, Ferrante himself was of illegitimate birth.

For that reason, my brother and I had been raised as royal children, with all rights and privileges, in the Castel Nuovo, the king's palace. My mother was free to come and go as my father wished, and often stayed at the palace with him. Only subtle reminders from our half-siblings and more pointed ones from our father reminded us that we were lesser creations. I did not play with my father's legitimate children, as they were several years older, or with my Aunt Giovanna or Uncle Carlo, both close to my own age. Instead, my little brother Alfonso and I were inseparable companions. Though my father's namesake, he was the opposite: golden-curled, sweet-faced, good-natured, his sharp intelligence remarkably free of guile. He had Madonna Trusia's pale blue eyes, while I resembled our father to such a striking degree that, had I been a son, we would have been twins separated by a generation.

Isabella led us to an aisle at the front of the sanctuary which had been roped off; even after we had settled into our place in the Duomo, my brother and I continued to clasp hands. The great cathedral dwarfed us. High overhead, the distance of several Heavens, was the massive, gilded cupola, rendered dazzling by the sunlight that streamed in through its arching windows.

The royal men came next. My father—Alfonso, Duke of Calabria, that sprawling, rustic region far to the south, on the eastern coast—led the way. Heir to the throne, he was renowned for his ferocity in battle; in his youth, he had wrested the Strait of Otranto from the Turks in a victory that brought him glory, if not the people's love. His every move, every glance and gesture, was imperious and forbidding, an effect accentuated by his severe costume of crimson and black. He was more beautiful than any woman present, with a perfect straight, thin nose and high, upward-slanting cheekbones. His lips were red, full, sensuous beneath his thin moustache, his dark blue eyes large and arresting beneath a crown of shining jet hair.

Only one thing marred his handsomeness: the coldness in his expression and eyes. His wife, Hippolyta Sforza, had died four years before; the servants and our female relatives whispered she had given up in order to escape her husband's cruelty. I remembered her vaguely as frail with bulging eyes, an unhappy woman; my father never failed to remind her of her failings, or the fact that theirs was a marriage of convenience because she came from one of Italy's most ancient and powerful families. He also assured poor Hippolyta that he took far greater pleasure in my mother's embrace than in hers.

I watched as he moved in front of us women and children,

forming a row directly in front of the altar, to one side of th empty throne that awaited the arrival of his father, the King.

Behind him came my uncles: Federico and Francesco. Then came my father's eldest son, named for his grandfather, but affectionately called Ferrandino, 'little Ferrante'. He was nineteen then, second in line to the throne, the second most handsome man in Naples but the most attractive, for he possessed a warm, outgoing nature. As he passed the worshipers, feminine sighs echoed in his wake. He was followed by his younger brother Piero, who had the misfortune to resemble his mother.

King Ferrante entered last, in breeches and a cape of black velvet, and a tunic of silver brocade embroidered with fine gold thread. At his hip was the sheathed, jewelled sword given him upon his coronation. Though I knew him as an old man with a limp exacerbated by gout, on this day he moved gracefully, without any hesitation in his gait. His good looks had been eroded by age and indulgence. His hair was white, thinning, revealing a scalp burned pink by the sun; he had a ponderous double chin beneath his trimmed beard. His eyebrows were dark and startling, especially in profile, due to each thick hair's attempt to launch itself in a different direction. These stood above eyes strikingly like mine and my father's—an intense blue with hints of green, capable of changing colour depending on the light and hues surrounding him. His nose was red, pock-marked, his cheeks covered with broken veins. But his bearing was straight, and he was still capable of silencing a crowd simply by walking into a room.

His solemn expression, upon entering the Duomo San Gennaro, generated pure ferocity. The crowd knelt even lower, and waited for the King to settle himself upon a throne near the altar.

Only then did they dare rise; only then did the choir begin to sing.

I craned my neck and caught a glimpse of the altar, where a silver bust of San Gennaro wearing his bishop's mitre had been placed in front of burning tapers. Nearby stood a marble statue,

n life, of Gennaro in full regalia, two fingers of
d in blessing, a crosier resting in the crook of his arm.
he King was situated and the choir had fallen silent, the
of Naples emerged and gave the invocation; his assistant
n appeared, bearing a silver reliquary in the shape of a lantern. Behind the glass was something small and dark: I could not see clearly from my position, being too short—my view was blocked by the backs of my black silk-clad aunts and the men's velvet capes, but I peeped in between. I knew it was a vial containing the dried blood of the martyred San Gennaro, tortured, then brutally beheaded on the orders of the Emperor Diocletian over a thousand years before.

Our bishop and the priest prayed. The *zie di San Gennaro* let out sonorous wails, beseeching the saint. Carefully, the priest, without touching the glass, turned the reliquary end-over-end, one time, then two.

An eternity seemed to pass. Beside me, Isabella had lowered her head and shut her eyes, her lips moving in a silent prayer. On my other flank, little Alfonso had lowered his head solemnly, but was peering out from beneath his curls in fascination at the priest.

I believed fervently in the power of God and the saints to intervene in the affairs of men. Deeming it safest to follow Isabella's example, I bowed my head, squeezed my eyes closed, and whispered a prayer to Naples' patron saint: *Bless our beloved city, and keep it safe. Protect the King and my father and mother and Alfonso. Amen.*

A murmur of awe passed through the crowd. I caught a glimpse of the altar, of the priest proudly displaying the silver reliquary, holding it up for the crowd's scrutiny. *'Il miracolo e fatto,'* he proclaimed.

The miracle is accomplished.

The choir led the congregation in singing the *Te Deum*, praising God for bestowing this blessing.

From my vantage point I could not see what had occurred, but Isabella whispered in my ear: the dark, dried substance in the vial had begun to melt, then bubble, as the ancient blood once again became liquid. San Gennaro signified that he had heard our prayers, and was pleased; he would protect the city which he had served as bishop during his mortal years.

It was a good omen, she murmured, especially for the King on his anniversary. San Gennaro would protect him from all enemies.

The current Bishop of Naples took the reliquary from the priest and stepped down from the altar to the throne. He held the square, silver-and-glass box before King Ferrante and waited for the monarch to unseat himself and approach.

My grandfather neither rose nor knelt in the presence of such a marvel. He remained settled on his throne, forcing the bishop to bring the reliquary to him. Only then did Ferrante yield to ancient custom and press his lips to the glass, beneath which lay the sacred blood.

The bishop retreated to the altar. The royal males of Aragon then approached one by one, my father first, and kissed the holy relic in turn. We women and children followed—I and my brother still firmly clinging to each other. I pursed my mouth against the glass, warmed by the breath of my relatives, and stared at the dark liquid housed inside. I had heard of miracles, but never before seen one; I was amazed.

I stood beside Alfonso as he took his turn; afterwards, we processed back to our assigned places.

The bishop handed the reliquary back to the priest and made the sign of blessing, two fingers of his right hand slicing a cross through the air, first over my grandfather, then over the assembled royal family.

The choir broke into song. The old King rose, a bit stiffly. The guards left their positions about the throne and preceded him outside the church, where carriages waited. As always, we followed.

Custom required the entire congregation, including royals, to remain in place during the ceremony, while each member came forward to kiss the relic—but Ferrante was too impatient to be kept waiting for commoners.

· · ·

We returned directly to the Castel Nuovo, the trapezoidal hulk of mud-coloured brick built two hundred years earlier by Charles of Anjou to serve as his palace. He had first removed the crumbling remnants of a Franciscan convent dedicated to the Virgin Mary. Charles had valued protection over elegance: each corner of the castle, which he called the *Maschio Angiono*, the Angevin Keep, was reinforced by vast cylindrical towers, their toothy merlons jutting against the sky.

The palace stood directly on the bay, so close to the shore that, as a child, I often stuck an arm through a window and imagined I caressed the sea. On that morning a breeze rose off the water, and as I rode in the open carriage between Alfonso and Isabella, I inhaled with pleasure the scent of brine. One could not live in Naples without being in constant sight of the water, without coming to love it. The ancient Greeks had named the city Parthenope for the ancient siren, half-woman, half-bird, who for unrequited love of Odysseus had cast herself into the sea. According to legend, she had washed up on Naples's shore; even as girl, I knew it was not for love of a man that she had been lured into the waves.

I pulled off my veil to better enjoy the air. To get an improved view—of the concave lunar crescent of coastline, with dusky violet Vesuvio to the east, and the oval-shaped fortress, Castel dell'Ovo, just to our west—I rose in the carriage and turned round. Isabella reseated me at once with a harsh tug, though her expression remained composed and regal, for the benefit of the crowd.

Our carriage rumbled through the castle's main gate, flanked by the Guard Tower and the Middle Tower. Connecting the two was the white marble Triumphal Arch of Alfonso the Magnanimous, erected by my great-grandfather to commemorate his victorious entry into Naples as its new ruler. It marked the first of many renovations he made to the crumbling palace, and once the arch was in place, he rechristened his new residence the Castel Nuovo.

I rode beneath the lower of the two arches, and stared up at the bas relief of Alfonso in his carriage, accompanied by welcoming nobles. Far above, his hand reaching beyond the towers, an exuberant, larger-than-life statue of Alfonso gestured toward the sky. I felt exuberant, too. I was in Naples, with the sun and the sea and my brother, and I was happy.

I could not imagine that such joy could ever be taken from me.

Once inside the inner courtyard with the main gate closed, we climbed from the carriages and entered the Great Hall. There, the longest table in the world held a feast: bowls of olives and fruit, all manner of breads, two roast boars, their jaws propped open with oranges, roast stuffed fowl, and seafood, including succulent little crayfish. There was much wine, too—the *Lachrima Christi*, the tears of Christ, made from Greco grapes cultivated on the fertile slopes of Vesuvio. Alfonso and I took ours diluted with water. The Hall was adorned with flowers of every variety; the vast marble columns were draped with swags of gold brocade, trimmed in blue velvet, to which were fastened wreaths of blood-coloured roses.

Our mother, Madonna Trusia, was there to greet us; we ran to her. Old Ferrante liked her, and cared not a whit that she had borne two children to my father without the benefit of wedlock. As always, she greeted each of us with a kiss on the lips, and a warm embrace; I thought she was the loveliest woman there. She glowed, an innocent golden-haired goddess amidst a flock of scheming ravens. Like her son, she was simply good, and spent her days worrying not about what political advantage she might gain, but what love she might give, what comfort. She sat between me and Alfonso, while Isabella sat to my right.

Ferrante presided over the feast at the head of the table. In the distance behind him stood a great archway which led to his throne room, then his private apartments. Over it hung a huge tapestry of Naples' royal insignia, gold lilies against a deep blue background, a *fleur-de-lis* legacy from the days of Angevin rule.

That archway held special fascination for me that day; that archway was to be my passage to discovery.

When the feast ended, musicians were brought in and dancing began, which the old King watched from a throne. Without so much as a sidelong glance at us children, my father took my mother's hand and led her away to dance. I took advantage of the merriment to slip from Isabella's half-attentive gaze and make a confession to my brother.

'I am going to find Ferrante's dead men,' I told him. I intended to enter the King's private chambers without his permission, an unforgivable violation of protocol even for a family member. For a stranger, it would be a treasonous act.

Above his goblet, Alfonso's eyes grew wide. 'Sancha, don't. If they catch you—there is no telling what Father will do.'

But I had been struggling with unbearable curiosity for days, and could no longer repress it. I had heard one of the servant girls tell Donna Esmeralda—my nursemaid and an avid collector of royal gossip, that it was true: the old man had a secret 'chamber of the dead', which he regularly visited. The servant had been ordered to dust the bodies and sweep the floor. Until then I had, along with the rest of the family, believed this to be a rumour fuelled by my grandfather's enemies.

I was known for my daring. Unlike my younger brother, who wished only to please his elders, I had committed numerous childhood crimes. I had climbed trees to spy upon relatives engaged in the marriage act—once during the consummation of a noble marriage witnessed by the King and the Bishop, both of whom saw me staring through the window. I had smuggled toads inside my bodice and released them on the table during a royal banquet. And I had, in retaliation for previous punishment, stolen a jug of olive oil from the kitchen and emptied its contents across the threshold of my father's bedchamber. It was not the olive oil that worried my parents so much as the fact that I had, at the age of ten, used my best jewellery to bribe the guard in attendance to leave.

Always I was scolded and confined to the nursery for lengths of time that varied with the misdeed's audacity. I did not care. Alfonso was willing to remain a prisoner with me, to keep me comforted and entertained. This knowledge left me incorrigible. The portly Donna Esmeralda, though a servant, neither feared nor respected me. She was unimpressed by royalty. Though she was of common blood, both her father and mother had served in Alfonso the Magnanimous' household, then in Ferrante's. Before I was born, she had tended my father.

At the time, she was in the midst of her fourth decade, an imposing figure: large boned, stout, broad of hip and jaw. Her raven hair, heavily streaked with grey, was pulled back tautly beneath a dark veil; she wore the black dress of perpetual mourning, though her husband had died almost a quarter of a century before, a young soldier in Ferrante's army. Afterwards, Donna Esmeralda had become devoutly religious; a gold crucifix rested upon her prominent bosom.

She had never had children. And while she had never taken to my father—indeed, she could scarcely hide her contempt for him—when Trusia gave birth to me, Esmeralda behaved as though I was her own daughter.

Although she loved me, and tried her best to protect me, my behaviour always prompted her reproach. She would narrow her eyes, lips tugged downward with disapproval, and shake her head. 'Why can you not behave like your brother?'

That question never hurt; I loved my brother. In fact, I wished to be more like him and my mother, but I could not repress what I was. Then Esmeralda would make the statement that cut deeply.

'As bad as your father was at that age . . . '

In the great dining hall, I looked back at my little brother and said, 'Father will never know. Look at them . . . ' I gestured at the adults, laughing and dancing. 'No one will notice I'm gone.' I paused. 'How can you *stand* it, Alfonso? Don't you want to know if it is true?'

'No,' he answered soberly.

'Why not?'

'Because it might be.'

I did not understand until later what he meant. Instead, I gave him a look of frustration, then, with a whirl of my green silk skirts, turned and threaded my way through the throng.

Unseen, I slipped beneath the archway and its grand tapestry of gold and blue. I believed myself to be the only one to escape the party; I was wrong.

To my surprise, the huge panelled door to the King's throne room stood barely ajar, as if someone had meant to close it but had not quite succeeded. I quietly pulled it open just enough to permit my entry, then shut it behind me.

The room was empty, since the guards were busy eyeing their charges out in the Great Hall. Though not quite as imposing as the Hall in size, the room inspired respect: against the central wall sat Ferrante's throne: a structure of ornately carved dark wood cushioned in crimson velvet, set upon a short dais with two steps. Above it, a canopy bore Naples' insignia of the lilies, and on either side, arched windows stretched from floor to ceiling, framing a glorious view of the bay. Sunlight streamed through the unshuttered windows, reflecting off the white marble floors and the whitewashed walls, giving a dazzling, airy effect.

It seemed too open, too bright a place to hold any secrets. I paused for a moment, examining my surroundings, my exhilaration and dread both growing. I was afraid—but, as always, my curiosity overpowered my fear.

I faced the door leading to my grandfather's private apartments.

I had entered them only once before, a few years earlier when Ferrante was stricken by a dangerous fever. Convinced he was dying, his doctors summoned the family to make their farewells. I was not sure the King would even remember me—but he had laid his hand on my head and graced me with a smile.

I had been astonished. For my entire life, he had greeted me and my brother perfunctorily, then looked away, his gaze distant, troubled by more important matters. He was not given to socializing, but I caught him at odd moments watching his children and grandchildren with sharp eyes, judging, weighing, missing no detail. His manner was not unkind or rude, but distracted. When he spoke, even during the most social of family events, it was usually to my father, and then only of political affairs. His late marriage to Juana of Aragon, his third wife, had been a love match—he had no need to further his political advantage, to produce more heirs. But he'd long ago spent his lust; the King and Queen moved in separate circles and now spoke only when occasion demanded it.

When he had lain in his bed, supposedly dying, and put his hand upon my head and smiled, I had decided then that he was kind.

Back in the throne room, I drew a breath for courage, then moved swiftly toward Ferrante's private chambers. I did not expect to find any dead men; my anxiety sprang from the consequences of my actions were I caught.

On the other side of the heavy throne room door, the sound of the revellers and music grew fainter; alone, I could hear the sweep of my silk skirts against marble.

Tentatively, I opened the door leading to the King's outer chamber. I recognized the room, having passed this way when Ferrante had been sick. Here was an office, with four chairs, a large desk, tables, many sconces for late-night illumination, a map of Naples and the Papal States upon the wall. There was also a portrait of my great-grandfather Alfonso wearing the jewelled sword he had brought from Spain, which Ferrante had worn earlier in the Duomo.

Daringly, I pressed against walls, thinking of hidden compartments, of passageways; I scanned the marble floor for cracks that hinted at staircases leading down to dungeons, but found nothing.

I continued on through an archway into a second room furnished for the taking of private meals; here again, there was nothing of note.

All that remained was Ferrante's bedchamber. This was sealed off by a heavy door. Squashing all thoughts of capture and punishment, I boldly opened it, and made my way into the most interior and private of the royal chambers.

Unlike the other bright, cheerful rooms, this one was oppressive and dark. The windows were covered with hangings of deep green velvet, blotting out the sun and the air. A large throw of the same green covered most of the bed, accompanied by numerous blankets of fur; apparently, Ferrante suffered from chills.

The chamber was fairly unadorned given the status of its resident. The only signs of grandeur were a golden bust of King Alfonso on the mantel, and gold candelabra flanking either side of the bed.

My gaze was drawn to an interior wall, where another door stood fully opened. Beyond it lay a small, windowless closet, outfitted with a wooden altar, candles, rosary, a statuette of San Gennaro, and a cushioned prayer bench.

Yet at the termination of that tiny chamber, past the humble altar, was another portal—this one closed. It led further inward, its edges limned with a faint, flickering light.

I experienced excitement mixed with dread. Had the maidservant told the truth, then? I had seen death before. The extended royal family had suffered loss, and I had been paraded past the pale, posed bodies of infants, children, and adults. But the thought of what might lie beyond that interior door taxed my imagination. Would I find skeletons stacked atop each other? Mounds of decomposing flesh? Rows of coffins?

Or had the servant's confession to my nursemaid sprung from a desire to keep the rumour alive?

My anticipation rose to near-unbearable levels. I passed quickly through the narrow altar room, and placed unsteady fingers on the bronze latch leading to the unknown. Unlike all the other doors, which were ten times my girlish width and four times my height, this one was scarcely large enough to admit a man. I pulled it open.

Only the cold arrogance conferred by my father's blood allowed me to repress a shriek of terror.

Shrouded in gloom, the chamber did not easily reveal its dimensions. To my childish eyes, it seemed vast, limitless, due in part to the darkness of unfinished stone. Only three tapers lit the windowless walls: one some distance from me, and two on large iron sconces flanking the entrance.

Just beyond them, his face lit by the candles' wavering golden glow, stood my welcoming host. Or rather, he did not stand, but was propped against a vertical beam extending just past the crown of his head. He wore a blue cape, attached to the shoulders of his gold tunic with *fleur de lis* medallions. At breast and hip, ropes bound him fast to his support. A wire connected to one arm raised it away from his body, and bent it out at the elbow, the palm turned slightly upward in a beckoning gesture.

Enter, Your Majesty.

His skin looked like lacquered sienna parchment, glossy in the light. It had been stretched taut across his cheekbones, baring his brown teeth in a gruesome grin. His hair, perhaps luxuriant in life, consisted of a few dull auburn hanks hung from a shrivelled scalp. And his eyes . . .

Ah, his eyes. His other features had been allowed to shrink gruesomely. His lips had altogether disappeared, his ears become thick, tiny flaps stuck to his skull. His nose, half as thin as my little finger, had lost its fleshy nostrils and now terminated in two gaping holes, enhancing his skeletal appearance. But the disappearance of the eyes had not been tolerated; in the sockets rested two well-fitting, highly-polished orbs of white marble, on which were carefully painted green irises, with black pupils. The marble gleamed in the light, making me feel I was being watched.

I swallowed; I trembled. Up to that moment, I had been a child on a silly quest, thinking she was playing a game, having an adventure. But there was no thrill in this discovery, no precocious joy, no naughty glee—only the knowledge that I had stumbled onto something very adult and terrible.

I stepped up to the creature before me, hoping that what I saw was somehow false, that it had never been human. I pressed a tentative finger against its satin-breeched thigh and felt tanned hide over bone. The legs terminated in thin, stockinged calves, and fine, tufted silk slippers that bore no weight.

I drew my hand away, convinced.

How can you stand it, Alfonso? Don't you want to know if it is true?

No. Because it might be.

How wise my little brother was: I wished more than anything to disremember what I had just learned. Everything I had believed about my grandfather shifted then. I had thought him a kindly old man, stern, but forced to be so by the burden of rulership. I had believed the barons who rebelled against him to be bad men, lovers of violence for no reason save the fact they were French. I had believed the servants who said the people despised Ferrante to be liars. I had heard Ferrante's chambermaid whisper to Donna Esmeralda that the King was going mad, and I had scoffed.

Faced with an unthinkable monstrosity, I did not laugh now. I trembled, not at the ghastly sight before me, but at the realization that Ferrante's blood flowed through my veins.

I stumbled forward in the twilight past the chamber's sentry, and saw perhaps ten more bodies in the shadows, all propped and bound, marble-eyed and motionless. All save one.

Some six dead men's distance, a figure bearing a lit taper turned to face me. I recognized my grandfather, his white-bearded visage rendered pale and spectral in the flickering glow.

'Sancha, is it?' He smiled faintly. 'So. We both took advantage of the celebration to slip away from the crowd. Welcome to my museum of the dead.'

I expected him to be furious, but his demeanour was that of one greeting guests at an intimate party. 'You did well,' he said. 'Not a peep, and you even touched old Robert.' He inclined his head at the corpse nearest the entrance. 'Very bold. Your father was much older than you when he first entered this place; he screamed, then burst into tears like a girl.'

'Who are they?' I asked. I was repelled—but curiosity demanded that I know the entire truth.

Ferrante spat on the floor. 'Angevins,' he answered. 'Enemies. That one'—he pointed to Robert—'he was a count, a distant cousin of Charles d'Anjou. He swore to me he'd have my throne.' My grandfather let go a satisfied chuckle. 'You can see who had what.' Ferrante moved stiffly over to his former rival. 'Eh, Robert? Who's laughing now?' He gestured at the macabre assembly, his tone growing suddenly heated. 'Counts and marquis, and even dukes. All of them traitors. All of them yearning to see me dead.' He paused to calm himself. 'I come here when I need to remember my victories. To remember I am stronger than my foes.'

I gazed out at the men. Apparently the museum had been assembled over a period of time. Some bodies still had full, thick heads of hair, and stiff beards; others, like Robert, looked slightly tattered. But all were dressed in finery befitting their noble rank, in silks and brocades and velvets. Some had gold-hilted swords at their hips; others wore capes lined with ermine, and precious stones. One had a black velvet cap with a white ostrich plume, tilted at a jocular angle. Some simply stood. Others struck various poses: one propped a wrist on his hip, another reached for the hilt of his sword; a third held out a palm, gesturing at his fellows.

All of them stared ahead blankly.

'The eyes,' I said. It was a question.

Ferrante blinked down at me. 'Pity you're a female. You'd make a good king. Of all his children, you're most like your father. You're proud and hard—much more so than he. But unlike him, you'd have the nerves to do whatever's necessary for the kingdom.' He sighed. 'Not like that fool Ferrandino. All he wants are pretty girls to admire him and a soft bed. No backbone, no brains.'

'The eyes,' I repeated. They troubled me; there was a perversity to them that I had to understand. I had heard what he had just told me—words I had not wanted to hear. I wanted to distract myself, to forget them. I wanted to be nothing like the King, like my father.

'Persistent little thing,' he said. 'The eyes dissolve when a body is mummified—no way around it. The first ones had shut eyelids over empty sockets. They looked like they were sleeping. I wanted them to hear me when I spoke to them. I wanted to be able to see them listening.' He laughed again. 'Besides, it was more effective that way. My last "guest"—how it terrified him, to see his missing compatriots staring back at him!'

I tried to make sense of it all from my naive perspective. 'God made you King. So if these men were traitors, they went against God. It was no sin to kill them.'

My remark disgusted him. 'There is no such thing as sin!' He paused; his manner turned instructive. 'Sancha, the miracle of San Gennaro . . . it almost always occurs in May and September. But when the priest emerges with the reliquary in December, why do you think the miracle so often fails?'

The question took me by surprise; I had no inkling of the answer.

'Think, girl!'

'I don't know, Your Majesty . . . '

'Because the weather is warmer in May and September.'

I still did not understand. My confusion registered on my face.

'It's time you stopped subscribing to this foolishness about God and the saints. There's only one power on earth—the power over life and death. For the time being, in Naples at least, I possess it.' Once more, he prodded me. 'Now, think. The substance in the vial is at first solid. Consider the fat on a pig, or a lamb. What happens to that fat if you roast the animal on a spit—that is, expose it to warmth?'

'It drips down into the fire.'

'Heat turns the solid into a liquid. So perhaps, if you took the reliquary of San Gennaro from its cool, dark closet out into the Duomo on a warm, sunny day and wait for a while . . . *il miracolo e fatto*. Solid to liquid.'

I was already shocked; my grandfather's heresy only deepened that sensation. I recalled Ferrante's cursory attitude towards all things religious, his eagerness either to absent himself from or to be done swiftly with Mass. I doubted he ever knelt at the little altar which led to the chamber housing his true convictions.

Yet I was simultaneously intrigued by his explanation of the miracle; my faith was now imperfect, threaded with doubt. Even so, habit was strong. I prayed silently, speedily to God to forgive the King, and for San Gennaro to protect him despite his sins. For the second time that day, I prayed for Gennaro to protect Naples—though not necessarily from crimes wrought by nature or disloyal barons.

Ferrante reached with his bony, blue-veined hand for my smaller one, and squeezed it in a grip that allowed no dissent. 'Come, child. They will wonder where we are. Besides, you have seen enough.'

I thought of each man within the museum of the dead—how they must have been introduced by my gloating grandfather to the fate awaiting them, how the weaker ones must have wept and pleaded to be spared. I wondered how they had been killed; certainly by a method that left no trace.

Ferrante held the taper high and led me from his soulless gallery. While I waited inside the altar room as he closed the little door, I reflected on the clear pleasure he took from the company of his victims. He was capable of killing without compunction, capable of savouring the act. Perhaps I should have feared for my own life, being an unnecessary female, yet I could not. This was my grandfather. I studied his face in the golden light: it wore the same benign expression, possessed the same ruddy cheeks with their latticework of tiny broken veins that I had always known. I searched his eyes, so like mine, for signs of the cruelty and madness that had inspired the museum.

Those eyes scrutinized me back, piercing, frighteningly lucid. He blew out the taper and set it upon the little altar, then retook my hand.

'I will not tell, Your Majesty.' I uttered the words not out of fright or a wish to protect myself, but out of a desire to let Ferrante know my loyalty to my family was complete.

He let go a soft laugh. 'My dear, I care not. All the better if you do. My enemies will fear me all the more.'

Back through the King's bedchamber we went, through the sitting room, the outer office, then last of all the throne room. Before he pushed open the door, he turned to regard me. 'It's not easy for us, being the stronger ones, is it?'

I tilted my chin to look up at him.

'I'm old, and there are those who will tell you I'm becoming feeble-minded. But I still notice most things. I know how you love your brother.' His gaze focused inward. 'I loved Juana because she was good-natured and loyal; I knew she would never betray me. I like your mother for the same reason—a sweet woman.' He drew his attention outward to study me. 'Your little brother takes after her; a generous soul. Worthless when it comes to politics. I've seen how devoted you are to him. If you love him, look out for him. We strong have to take care of the weak, you know. They haven't the heart to do what's necessary to survive.'

'I'll take care of him,' I said stoutly. But I would never subscribe to my grandfather's notion that killing and cruelty were a necessary part of protecting Alfonso.

Ferrante pushed open the door. We walked hand-in-hand back into the Great Hall, where the musicians played. I scanned the crowd for Alfonso, and saw him standing off in a far corner, staring owl-eyed at us both. My mother and Isabella were both dancing, and had for the moment altogether forgotten us children.

But my father, the Duke of Calabria, had apparently taken note of the King's disappearance. I glanced up, startled, as he stepped in front of us and stopped our progress with a single question.

'Your Majesty. Is the girl annoying you?' During my brief lifetime, I had never heard the Duke address his father in any other fashion. He looked down at me, his expression hostile, suspicious.

I tried to summon the mannerisms of pure innocence, but after what I had seen, I could not hide the fact I had been shaken to the core.

'Not in the least,' Ferrante replied, with good humour. 'We've just been exploring, that's all.'

Revelation, then fury, flashed in my father's beautiful, heartless eyes. He understood exactly where my grandfather and I had been—and, given my reputation as a miscreant, realized I had not been invited.

'I will deal with her,' the Duke said, in a tone of great menace. He was famous for his vicious treatment of his enemies, the Turks; he had insisted on personally torturing and killing those captured in the Battle of Otranto, by methods so inhuman we children were not permitted to hear of them. I told myself I was not afraid. It was unseemly for him to have me, a royal, thrashed. He did not realize that he already imposed on me the worst punishment possible: he did not love me, and made no secret of the fact.

And I, proud as he, would never admit my desperate desire to gain his affection.

'Don't punish her, Alfonso,' Ferrante said. 'She has spirit, that's all.'

'Girls ought not to have spirit,' my father countered. 'This one least of all. My other children are tolerable, but *she* has done nothing but vex me since the day of her birth—a day I deeply regret.' He glared down at me. 'Go. His Majesty and I have matters to discuss. You and I will speak about this later.'

Ferrante let go my hand. I made a little curtsy and said, 'Your Majesty.' I would have run full tilt had the Hall not been filled with adults who all would have turned and demanded decorum; as it was, I walked as swiftly as possible over to my waiting brother.

He took a single glimpse at my face and threw his arms about me. 'Oh, Sancha! So it *is* true . . . I am so sorry you had to see. Were you frightened?'

My heart, which had grown so chilled in the presence of my

two elders, thawed in Alfonso's presence. He did not want to know the details of what I had witnessed; he wanted only to know how I had fared. I was a bit surprised that my little brother was not more shocked to learn that the rumour was true. Perhaps he understood the King better than I did.

I drew back, but kept my arms entwined with his. 'It was not so bad,' I lied.

'Father looked angry; I fear he will punish you.'

I shrugged. 'Maybe he won't. Ferrante didn't care a whit.' I paused, then added with childish bravado, 'Besides, what will Father do? Make me stay in my room? Make me go without supper?'

'If he does,' Alfonso whispered, 'I will come to you, and we can play quietly. If you're hungry, I can bring you food.'

I smiled and laid a palm on his cheek. 'The point is, you mustn't worry. There's nothing Father can do that will really hurt me.'

How very wrong I was.

Donna Esmeralda was waiting outside the Great Hall to lead us back to the nursery. Alfonso and I were in a jolly mood, especially as we moved past the classroom where, had this not been a holiday, we would have been studying Latin under the uninspired tutelage of Fra Giuseppe Maria. Fra Giuseppe was a sad-faced Dominican monk from the nearby monastery of San Domenico Maggiore, famed as the site where a crucifix had spoken to Thomas Aquinas two centuries earlier. Fra Giuseppe was so exceedingly corpulent that both Alfonso and I had christened him in Latin *Fra Cena*, Father Supper. As we passed by the classroom, I solemnly began the declension of our current favourite verb. '*Ceno,*' I said. I dine.

Alfonso finished, *sotto voce*. '*Cenare,*' he said. '*Cenavi. Cenatus.*'

Donna Esmeralda rolled her eyes, but said nothing.

I giggled at the joke on Fra Giuseppe, but at the same time, I recalled a phrase he had used in our last lesson to teach us the dative case. *Deo et homnibus peccavit.*

He has sinned against God and men.

I thought of Robert's marble eyes, staring at me. *I wanted to know they were listening.*

Once we were in the nursery, the chambermaid joined Esmeralda in carefully removing our dress clothes while we wriggled impatiently. We were then dressed in less restrictive clothing—a loose, drab gown for me, a plain tunic and breeches for Alfonso.

The door to the nursery opened, and we turned to see our mother, Madonna Trusia, accompanied by her lady-in-waiting, Donna Elena, a Spanish noblewoman. The latter had brought her son, our favourite playmate: Arturo, a bony, long-limbed hellion who excelled at chases and tree-climbing, both sports I enjoyed. My mother had changed from her formal black into a pale yellow gown; looking at her smiling face, I thought of the Neapolitan sun.

'Little ones,' she announced. 'I have a surprise. We are going on a picnic.'

Alfonso and I whooped our approval. We each grasped one of Madonna Trusia's soft hands. She led us from the nursery into the castle corridors, Donna Elena and Arturo in tow.

But before we reached freedom, we had an unfortunate encounter.

We passed my father. Beneath his blue-black moustache, his lips were grim with purpose, his brow furrowed. I surmised he was headed for the nursery to inflict my punishment. Given the current circumstances, I could also guess what it would be.

We came to an abrupt stop.

'Your Highness,' my mother said sweetly, and bowed. Donna Elena followed suit.

He acknowledged Trusia with a curt question. 'Where are you going?'

'I am taking the children on a picnic.'

The Duke's gaze flickered over our little assembly, then settled on me. I squared my shoulders and lifted my chin, defiant, resolved to show no sign of disappointment at his next utterance.

'Not her.'

'But Your Highness, it is a holiday . . . '

'Not *her*. She misbehaved abominably today. It must be dealt with at once.' He paused and gave my mother a look that made her wilt like a blossom in scorching heat. 'Now *go*.'

Madonna Trusia and Elena bowed again to the Duke; my mother and Alfonso both shot me sorrowful little glances before moving on.

'Come,' my father said.

We walked in silence to the nursery. Once we arrived, Donna Esmeralda was summoned to witness my father's formal address.

'I should not be required to waste an instant of my attention on a useless girl child with no hope of ascending to the throne—much less such a child who is a bastard.'

He had not finished, but his cursory dismissal so stung that I could not let an opportunity to retaliate pass. 'What difference does it make? The King is a bastard,' I interrupted swiftly, 'which makes you the son of a bastard.'

He slapped my cheek so hard it brought tears to my eyes, but I refused to let them spill. Donna Esmeralda started slightly when he struck me, but managed to keep herself in check.

'You are incorrigible,' he said. 'But I cannot permit you to further waste my time. You are not worth even a moment of my attention. Discipline should be the province of nursemaids, not princes. I have denied you food, I have closeted you in your room—yet none of this has done anything to calm you. And you are almost old enough to be married. How shall I turn you into a proper young woman?'

He fell silent and thought a long moment. After a time, I saw his eyes narrow, then gleam with understanding. A slight, cold smile played on his lips. 'I have denied you the wrong things, haven't I? You're a hard-headed child. You can do without food or the outdoors for a while, because while you *like* those things, they are not what you love most.' He nodded, becoming ever more pleased with his plan. 'That is what I must do, then. You will not change until you are denied the one thing that you love above all else.'

I felt the first pangs of real fear.

'Two weeks,' he said, then turned and addressed Donna Esmeralda. 'She is to have no contact with her brother for the next two weeks. They are not permitted to eat, to play, to speak with each other—not even permitted to catch a glimpse of each other. Your future rests on this. Do you understand?'

'I understand, Your Highness,' Donna Esmeralda replied tautly, her eyes narrowed and her gaze averted. I began to wail.

'You cannot take Alfonso from me!'

'It is done.' In my father's hard, heartless expression, I detected traces of pleasure. *Filius Patri similis est.* The Son is like the Father.

I flailed about for reasons; the tears that had gathered on the rims of my eyes were now in true danger of cascading onto my cheeks. 'But . . . but Alfonso loves me! It will hurt *him* if he can't see me, and he's been a good son, a perfect son. It's not fair—you'll be punishing Alfonso for something he didn't do!'

'How does it feel, Sancha?' my father taunted softly. 'How does it feel to know you are responsible for hurting the one you love the most?'

I looked on the one who had sired me—one who so cruelly relished hurting a child. Had I been a man, and not a young girl, had I borne a blade, anger would have overtaken me and I would have slit his throat where he stood. In that instant, I knew what it was like to feel infinite, irrevocable hatred for one I helplessly loved. I wanted to hurt him as he had me, and take pleasure in it.

When he left, I at last wept; but even as I spilt angry tears, I swore I would never again permit any man, least of all the Duke of Calabria, to make me cry.

I spent the next two weeks in torment. I saw only the servants. Though I was allowed outside to play if I wished, I refused, just as

I petulantly refused most of my meals. I slept poorly and dreamed of Ferrante's spectral gallery.

My mood was so dark, my behaviour so difficult that Donna Esmeralda, who had never lifted a finger against me, slapped me twice in exasperation. I kept ruminating over my sudden impulse to kill my father; it had terrified me. I became convinced that without Alfonso's gentle influence, I should become a cruel, half-crazed tyrant like the father and grandfather I so resembled.

When the two weeks finally passed, I seized my little brother and embraced him with a ferocity that left us both breathless.

When at last I could speak, I said, 'Alfonso, we must take a solemn oath never to be apart again. Even when we are married, we must stay in Naples, near each other, for without you, I will go mad.'

'I swear,' Alfonso said. 'But Sancha, your mind is perfectly sound. With or without me, you need never fear madness.'

My lower lip trembled as I answered him. 'I am too much like Father—cold and cruel. Even Grandfather said it—I am hard, like him.'

For the first time, I saw real anger flare in my brother's eyes. 'You are anything but cruel; you are kind and good. And the King is wrong. You aren't hard, just . . . stubborn.'

'I want to be like you,' I said. 'You are the only person who makes me happy.'

From that time on, I never once gave our father cause to punish me.

Late Spring 1492

II

Slightly more than three years passed. The year 1492 arrived, and with it a new pope: Rodrigo Borgia, who took the name Alexander VI. Ferrante was eager to establish good relations with him, especially since previous pontiffs had looked unkindly on the House of Aragon.

Alfonso and I grew too old to share the nursery and moved into separate chambers, but we were apart only when sleep and the divergence in our education required it. I studied poetry and dance while Alfonso perfected his swordsmanship; we never discussed our foremost concern—that I was now fifteen, of marriageable age, and would soon move to a different household. I comforted myself with the thought that Alfonso would become fast friends with my future husband and would visit daily.

At last, a morning dawned when I was summoned to the King's throne room. Donna Esmeralda, could not entirely hide her excitement. She dressed me in a modest black gown of elegant cut and fine silk, with a satin brocade stomacher laced so tightly I gasped for air.

Flanked by her, Madonna Trusia, and Donna Elena, I crossed the palace courtyard. The sun was obscured by heavy fog; it dripped onto us like soft, slow rain, spotting my gown, covering my face and carefully arranged hair with mist.

At last we arrived at Ferrante's wing. When the doors opened onto the throne room, I saw my grandfather sitting regally on his crimson cushions; beside him stood a stranger—an acceptable-looking man of stocky, muscular build. Next to him was my father.

Time had not bettered Alfonso, Duke of Calabria. If anything, my father was more temperamental—indeed, vicious. Recently, he had called for a whip and flogged a cook for serving his soup cold; he beat the poor woman until she fainted from loss of blood. Only Ferrante was able to stay his hand. He had also dismissed, with much cursing and shouting, an aged servant from the household for failing to properly shine his boots. To quote my grandfather, 'Wherever my eldest son goes, the sun retreats behind the clouds in fear.'

His face, while still handsome, was a portrait in misery; his lips twitched with barely-repressed indiscriminate anger, his eyes emanated an unhappiness he delighted in sharing. He could no longer bear the sound of childish laughter; Alfonso and I were required to maintain silence in his presence. One day I forgot myself, and let loose a giggle. He reached down and struck me with such force, I stumbled and almost fell. It was not the blow that hurt as much as the realization that he had never lifted a hand against any of his other children—only me.

Once, when Trusia had believed me to be preoccupied, she had confided to Esmeralda that she had gone one night to my father's chambers only to find it in total darkness. When she had fumbled about for a taper, my father's voice emerged from the blackness: 'Leave it so.' When my mother moved towards the door, he commanded: 'Sit!' And so she was compelled to sit before him, on the floor. When she began to speak, in her soft, gentle voice, he shouted: 'Hold your tongue!'

He wanted only silence and darkness, and the knowledge that she was there.

I bowed gracefully before the King, knowing my every action

was being sized up by the common-looking, brown-haired stranger beside the throne. I was a woman now, and had learned to funnel all my childish stubbornness and mischief into a sense of pride. Others might have called it arrogance—but ever since the day my father had wounded me, I had vowed never to let myself show hurt or any sign of weakness. I was perpetually poised, unshakable, strong.

'Princess Sancha of Aragon,' Ferrante said formally. 'This is Count Onorato Caetani, a nobleman of good character. He has asked for your hand, and your father and I have granted it.'

I lowered my face modestly and caught a second glimpse of the Count from beneath my lowered eyelashes. An ordinary man of some thirty summers, and only a count—and I a princess. I had been preparing myself to leave Alfonso for a husband—but not one so undistinguished as this. I was too distraught for a gracious, appropriate reply to spring quickly to my lips. Fortunately, Onorato spoke first.

'You have lied to me, Your Majesty,' he said, in a deep, clear voice.

Ferrante turned in surprise at once; my father looked as though he might strangle the Count. The King's courtiers suppressed a gasp at his audacity, until he spoke again.

'You said your granddaughter was lovely. But such a word does no justice to the exquisite creature who stands before us. I had thought I was fortunate enough to gain the hand of a princess of the realm; I had not realized I was gaining Naples' most precious work of art as well.' He pressed his palm against his chest, then held out his hand as he looked into my eyes. 'Your Highness,' he said. 'My heart is yours. I beg you, accept such a humble gift, though it be unworthy of you.'

Perhaps, I mused, *this Caetani fellow will not make such a bad husband after all.*

Onorato, I learned, was quite wealthy, and continued to be outspoken concerning my beauty. His manner towards Alfonso was warm and jovial, and I had no doubt he would welcome my brother into our home whenever I wished. As our courtship proceeded rapidly, he surprised me with gifts. One morning as we stood on the balcony looking out at the calm glassy bay, he moved as if to embrace me—and instead slipped a necklace over my head.

I drew back, eager to examine this new trinket—and discovered, hung on a satin cord, a polished ruby half the size of my fist.

'For the fire in your soul,' he said, and kissed me. Whatever resistance remained in my heart melted at that moment. I had seen enough wealth, taken its constant presence for granted long enough, to be unimpressed by it. It was not the jewel, but the gesture.

I enjoyed my first embrace. Onorato's trimmed golden-brown beard pleasantly caressed my cheek and smelled of rosemary-water and wine, and I responded to the passion with which he pressed his strong body against mine.

He knew how to pleasure a woman. We were betrothed, so it was expected that we would yield to nature when alone. After a month of courting, we did. He was skilled at finding his way beneath my overskirt, my dress, my chemise. He used his fingers first, then thumb, slipped between my legs, and rubbed a spot that left me quite surprised at my own reaction. This he did until I was brought to a spasm of most astounding delight; then he showed me how to favour him. I felt no embarrassment, no shame; indeed, I decided this was truly one of the greatest joys of life. My faith in the teaching of priests was weakened. How could anyone deem such a miracle a sin?

This behaviour occurred on several occasions until, at last, he mounted me, and inserted himself; prepared, I felt no pain, only enjoyment, and once he had emptied himself in me, he took care afterwards to bring me pleasure as well. I so delighted in the act, and so often demanded it, Onorato would laugh and call me insatiable.

I suppose I am not the only adolescent to mistake lust for love, but I was so taken by my future husband that, during the last days of summer, as a whim, I visited a woman known for seeing the future. A *strega*, the people called her, a witch, but though she garnered respect and a certain amount of fear, she was never accused of evil and on occasion did good.

Flanked by two horsemen for protection, I travelled from the Castel Nuovo in an open carriage with my favourite three ladies-in-waiting: Donna Esmeralda, who was a widow, Donna Maria, a married woman, and Donna Inez, a young virgin. Donna Maria and I joked about the act of love and laughed all the way, while Donna Esmeralda pursed her lips at such scandalous talk. We passed beneath the glinting white Triumphal Arch of the Castel Nuovo, with Falcon's Peak, the *Pizzofalcone*, serving as its inland backdrop. The air was damp and cool and smelled of the sea; the unobstructed sun was warm. We made our way past the harbour along the coast of the Bay of Naples, so bright blue and reflective of the sky that the horizon between the two blurred. We headed toward Monte Vesuvio to the east. Behind us, to the west, the fortress of Castel dell'Ovo stood guard over the water.

Rather than ride through the city gates and attract attention from commoners, I directed the driver to take us through the armoury, with its great cannons, then alongside the old Angevin city walls that ran parallel to the shoreline.

I was besotted with love, so giddy with happiness that my native Naples seemed even more beautiful than ever, with sunlight gleaming off the white castles and smaller stucco homes built on the rises. Though the date had not been set for the nuptials, I was already dreaming of my wedding day, of myself presiding as mistress of my husband's household, smiling at him across a laden table surrounded by guests, of the children that would come and call out for their Uncle Alfonso. This was all I required of the strega—that she confirm my wishes, that she tell me the names of my sons, that she give me and my ladies something fresh to laugh and gossip about. I was happy because Onorato seemed a kind, pleasant man. Away from Ferrante and my father, in the company of Onorato and my brother, I would never become like the men I so resembled, but rather like the men I loved.

In the midst of my girlish giggling my eye caught sight of

Vesuvio, destroyer of civilizations. Massive, serene, grey-violet against the sky, it had always seemed benign and beautiful. But that day, the shadow it cast on us grew deeper the closer we moved towards it.

A greater chill rode upon the breeze. I fell silent; so in turn did each of my companions. We rumbled away from the city proper, past vineyards and olive orchards, into an area of softly rolling hills.

By the time we arrived at the strega's house—a crumbling ruin of a house built against a cavern—sombreness had overtaken us. One of the guards dismounted and announced my arrival with a shout at the open front door, while the other assisted me and my attendants from the carriage. Chickens scattered; a donkey tethered to a porch beam brayed.

From within, a woman's voice called. 'Send her in.' It was, to my surprise, strong, not frail and reedy, as I had imagined.

My ladies gasped. Indignant, the first guard drew his sword, and stepped upon the threshold of the house-cave.

'Insolent crone! Come out and beg Her Highness Sancha of Aragon for forgiveness! You will receive her properly.'

I motioned for the guard to lower his sword, and moved beside him. Try as I might, I could see nothing but shadow inside the doorway.

The woman spoke again, unseen. 'She must come in alone.'

Again my man instinctively raised his sword and took a step forward; I thrust an arm into the air at his chest level, holding him back. An odd dread overtook me, a pricking of the skin at the nape of my neck, but I ordered calmly, 'Go back to the carriage and wait for me. I shall go in unaccompanied.'

His eyes narrowed in disapproval, but I was the future King's daughter and he dared not contradict me. Behind me, my ladies murmured in dismay, but I ignored them and entered the strega's cave.

It was unthinkable for a princess to go anywhere alone. I was at all times attended by my ladies or by guards, except for those rare moments when I saw Onorato alone—and he was a noble, known to my family. I ate attended by family and ladies, I slept attended by my ladies; when I was a young girl, I had shared a bed with Alfonso. I did not know what it meant to be alone.

Yet the strega's presumptuous request did not offend me. Perhaps I understood instinctively that her news would not be good, and wished only my own ears to receive it.

I recall what I wore that day: a deep blue velvet tabard, since it was cool, and beneath, a stomacher and underskirt of pale grey-blue silk trimmed with silver ribbon, covered by a split overskirt of the same blue velvet as the tabard. I gathered the folds of my own garments as best I could, drew a breath, and entered the seer's house.

A sense of oppression overtook me. I had never been inside a peasant's house, certainly never as dismal a dwelling as this. The ceiling was low, the walls crumbling and stained with filth; the floor was dirt and smelled of chicken dung—facts that augured the ruination of my silk slippers and hems. The entire house consisted of one tiny room, lit only by the sun that streamed through the unshuttered windows. The furnishings consisted of a small, crude table, a stool, a jug, a hearth with a cauldron, and a heap of straw in one corner.

Yet there was no one inside.

'Come,' the strega said, in a voice as beautiful, as melodious as one of Odysseus' sirens. It was then I saw her: standing in a far, shadowed corner of the hovel, in a narrow archway behind which lay darkness. She was clad entirely in black, her face hidden by a dark veil. She was tall for a woman, straight and slender, and she lifted a beckoning arm with peculiar grace.

I followed, too mesmerized to remark on the lack of proper courtesy toward a royal. I had expected a hunchbacked, toothless crone, not this woman who moved as though she herself were the highest-born nobility. Into the dark passageway I went, and when the strega and I emerged, we were in a cave with a vast, high ceiling. The air was dank, making me grateful for the warmth of my tabard; there was no hearth here, no place for a fire. On the wall was a solitary torch—a rag soaked in olive oil—which provided barely enough light for me to find my way. The witch stopped at the torch briefly to light a lamp, then we proceeded further, past a feather bed appointed in green velvet, a fine, stuffed chair, and a shrine with a large, painted statue of the Virgin on an altar adorned with wildflowers.

She motioned for me to sit at a table much more accommodating than the one in the outer room. It was covered with a large square of black silk. I sat upon a chair of sturdy wood—finely crafted by an artisan, not made for a commoner—and carefully spread my skirts. The strega set the oil lamp down beside us, then sat across from me. Her face was still veiled in black gauze, but I could make out her features after a fashion. She was a matron of some forty years, dark-haired and complected; age had not erased her beauty. She spoke, revealing the pretty curves made by the bow of her upper lip, the handsome fullness of the lower.

'Sancha,' she said. It was familiar in the most insulting way, addressing me without my title, speaking without being spoken to first, sitting without permission, without genuflecting. Yet I was flattered; she uttered my name as if it were a caress. She was not speaking to me, but rather releasing my name upon the ether, sensing the emanations it produced. She savoured it, tasted it, her face tilted upwards as if watching the sound dissolve in the air above.

Then she looked back down at me; under the veil, amber-brown eyes reflected the lamplight. 'Your Highness,' she addressed me at last. 'You have come to know something of your future.'

'Yes,' I answered eagerly.

She gave a single, grave nod. From a compartment beneath the table, she produced a deck of cards. She set them on the black silk between us, pressed her palms against them, and prayed softly in a language I did not understand; in a practised gesture, she fanned them out.

'Young Sancha. Choose your fate.'

I felt exhilaration mixed with fear. I peered down at the cards with trepidation, moved an uncertain hand over them—then touched one with my forefinger and recoiled as though scalded.

I did not want that card—yet I knew that fate had chosen it for me. I let my hand waver above the spread a few moments more, then yielded, slid the card from the deck and turned it over.

The sight of it filled me with dread: I wanted to shut my eyes, to blot out the image, yet I could not tear my gaze from it. It was a heart, impaled by two blades, which together made a great silver X.

The witch regarded the card calmly. 'The heart pierced by two swords.'

I began to tremble.

She picked the card up, gathered the deck and returned it to its hiding place beneath the table. 'Give me your palm,' she said. 'No, the left one; it is closer to your heart.'

She took my hand between both of hers. Her touch was quite warm, despite the chill, and I began to relax. She hummed to herself, a soft, tuneless melody, her gaze fixed on my palm for some time.

Abruptly, she straightened, still clasping my palm, and stared directly into my eyes. 'The majority of men are mostly good, or mostly evil, but you have within you the power of both. You wish to speak to me of insignificant things, of marriage and children. I speak to you now of far greater things.

'For in your hands lie the fates of men and nations. These weapons within you—the good, and the evil—must each be wielded, and at the proper time, for they will change the course of events.'

As she spoke, I was seized by terrifying images: my father, sitting alone in darkness. I saw old Ferrante, whispering into the shrunken ears of the Angevins in his museum, staring into their sightless eyes . . . and his face, his form, changed to become mine. I stood on tiptoe, my firm flesh pressed against mummified leather, whispering . . .

I thought of the instant I had longed for a sword, that I might cut my own father's throat. I did not want power. I feared what I might do with it.

'I will never resort to evil!' I protested.

Her voice held an edge of hardness. 'Then you condemn to death those whom you most love.'

I refused to acknowledge the terrifying statement. Instead I clung to my naive little dream. 'But what of marriage? Will I be happy with my husband, Onorato?'

'You will never marry your Onorato.'

When she saw my trembling lip, she added, 'You will be wed to the son of the most powerful man in Italy.'

My mind raced. Who, then? Italy had no king; the land was divided into countless factions, and no one man held sway over all the city-states. Venice? Milan? Unrivalled Florence? Alliances between such states and Naples seemed unlikely . . .

'But will I love him?' I pressed. 'Will we have many children?'

'No to both,' she replied, with a vehemence approaching ferocity. 'Take great care, Sancha, or your heart will destroy all that you love.'

I rode back to the castle in silence, frozen, shocked into stillness like a victim caught unawares, buried in a heartbeat by the ash of Vesuvio.

Late Summer 1492–Winter 1494

III

A week after my visit with the strega, I was summoned from breakfast to an audience with the King. The urgent command came as such a surprise that Donna Esmeralda dressed me hastily—though I insisted on wearing Onorato's ruby round my throat, a touch of grandeur despite my dishevelment—and we two appeared alone before my grandfather. The rising sun streamed through the arched windows on either side of the throne where Ferrante sat; the effect on the marble floor was so dazzling that I did not see my father until he took a step forward. Only he stood in attendance; the vast chamber was otherwise empty.

Ferrante's health had been failing of late, and his normally ruddy complexion had taken on a dark crimson hue, leaving him in foul spirits. But this morning he was smiling as I curtsied.

'Sancha, I have wonderful news.' His words echoed off the vaulted ceiling. 'You know that your father and I have been trying for some time to strengthen Naples' ties to the Papacy . . . '

I knew. I had been told since childhood that the papacy was our best protection against the French, who had never forgiven my great-grandfather for defeating Charles of Anjou.

'The problem has been that His Holiness, Pope Alexander, dedicated both his sons to the priesthood . . . eh, what are their names?' Ferrante scowled and turned to my father. I knew them before the Duke had a chance to reply; I even knew the given name of the Pope, who before his election had been Cardinal Rodrigo Borgia.

'Cesare, sixteen, and Jofre, eleven.'

'Yes, Cesare and Jofre.' The King's expression lightened. 'Well, at long last, we have succeeded in convincing His Holiness that it would be wise to tie himself to Naples.' He beamed proudly. 'You are betrothed to the son of the Pope.'

I paled; my lips parted. As I fought to control myself, my father remarked with cruel delight, 'She is upset. She thinks she has feelings for this Caetani fellow.'

'Sancha, Sancha,' my grandfather said, not unkindly. 'We have already informed Caetani of the arrangements; in fact, we have already found him a suitable wife. But you must do what is best for the Crown. And this is an infinitely better match. The Borgias are wealthy beyond anything you have ever seen. Best of all, the marriage contract states you will both live in Naples.' He gave me a small wink, to show that he had done this for my benefit; he had not forgotten my attachment to Alfonso.

I stared at my father, my heartbreak spilling forth as fury. '*You* have done this,' I charged, 'because you knew I loved Onorato. You could not stand to see me happy. I will not marry your Cesare Borgia; I spit on the name.'

Rendered graceful by rage, Ferrante rose to his feet with the speed of a falcon diving for prey. 'Sancha of Aragon! You will not speak to the Duke of Calabria in that tone!'

Hot-cheeked, I bowed my head and glared down at the floor.

My father was laughing.

'Spit on the name of Cesare Borgia all you like,' he said. 'You are to be married to the younger one, Jofre.'

Unable to contain my temper, I swept from the King's throne room and headed back to my own suite. So rapid was my pace that Donna Esmeralda, who had awaited me outside, fell behind.

Such was my intent. For when I reached the balcony where Onorato had presented me with the ruby, I tore the great jewel from my neck. Briefly, I held it up to the sky; for an instant, my world was bathed red.

I clenched my fist over the gem and cast it down into the placid bay.

Behind me, Donna Esmeralda let go a shriek of pure horror. '*Madonna!*'

I cared not. Imperious, tormented, I strode away. I could think only of Onorato, agreeing all too swiftly to take a different bride. I had allowed myself to love him, to trust another man besides my brother—yet my heart was of no consequence to him, to Ferrante, to my father. To them I was chattel, a pawn to be used for political gain.

Only when I arrived at my bedchamber and banished all the ladies did I fling myself upon my pillows. But I did not permit myself to weep.

Alfonso came as soon as he was free from his lessons. Donna Esmeralda silently let him enter, knowing he alone had the ability to soothe me. Morose and self-pitying, I lay facing the wall.

The instant I felt Alfonso's gentle hand upon my shoulder, I turned.

He was still a boy of twelve, but already showed the signs of approaching adulthood. Over the past three-and-a-half years, he had shot up a forearm in height; he now stood slightly taller than me. His voice had not changed completely, but it had lost all trace of childish falsetto. His face now revealed a blend of the best of his father's and mother's features: he would grow into a strikingly handsome man.

Despite his increased exposure to our father and his study of politics, his eyes were still gentle, untainted by selfishness or guile. I gazed up into them.

'Duty is a hard thing,' he said softly. 'I'm so sorry, Sancha.'

'I love Onorato,' I murmured.

'I know. There is nothing that can be done. The King has made up his mind. He is right that it is to Naples' advantage.' Somehow, hearing the words from my brother's lips was not as painful as hearing them from Ferrante's. Alfonso would tell me only the truth, and that lovingly. He paused. 'They did not do this to intentionally hurt you, Sancha.'

So; my heated outburst at my father was no secret. I scowled, too full of rancour to agree with the latter statement. 'But Jofre Borgia is only *eleven*, Alfonso! He is a *child!*'

'Only a year my junior,' Alfonso said lightly. 'He *will* grow older.'

'Onorato was a *man*. He knew how to treat a woman.'

My little brother actually blushed; I suppose it was uncomfortable for him to imagine me in the nuptial embrace. But he collected himself and responded, 'Jofre may be young—but he can be taught. And for all you know, he might be quite personable. You might like him. I will certainly do everything in my power to make friends with him.'

I scoffed. 'How can I possibly like him? He is a Borgia!' His father, Rodrigo Borgia, supposedly achieved the position of pontiff not through piety, but through guile and bribery. His efforts to buy the papacy were rumoured to be so blatant that, soon after his election, certain members within the College of Cardinals called for an investigation. Mysteriously, their objections soon ceased, and the man who christened himself Pope Alexander VI now enjoyed the full support of the College. It had even been said that Rodrigo had poisoned the likeliest contender for the papal tiara: his own brother.

Alfonso eyed me sombrely. 'We have never met the Borgias, so we cannot judge them. And even if every word of gossip about His Holiness is true, you are not being fair to Jofre. Sons are not always like their fathers.'

His latter statement silenced my objections. Even so, I had to ask, in the most dolorous tone, 'Why must there be marriage? It only takes us away from those we love.'

But for Alfonso's sake, I vowed to myself, I would not be selfish. I would try to be like him—brave and good, and willing to do what was best for the realm.

Many months passed, and 1493 arrived. The more I contemplated marriage to a Borgia, the more concerned I became. King Ferrante could insist that Jofre and I maintain a household in Naples, and could commit it to writing. But a pope's word held more authority than a king's. What if Alexander changed his mind, and called his son back to Rome? What if he demanded a separate kingdom for Jofre elsewhere? I would be bound to accompany my husband. Only a Neapolitan husband would do, one who would never have reason to take me from my native city.

Since the day I had discovered Ferrante's leering mummies, my religious faith had been tentative, half-hearted. Now I embraced it full force, in a desperate test. I called one morning for a private carriage and slipped away, accompanied by a single guard and a driver.

I headed for the Duomo, startling the stray worshipers inside, who were abruptly herded out by my guard.

At the altar where the miracle had occurred, I knelt. There, with all my sincerity, I prayed to San Gennaro. I begged him to free me from my engagement to Jofre Borgia, to find me a good Neapolitan husband. Together, I promised, we would donate vast sums of money for the upkeep of the Duomo and for the care of Naples' poor.

When I returned to the castle, I requested and received a painting of the saint. In my bedchamber, I erected a small shrine to Gennaro, where I repeated my promise morning and evening. Once a week, I arranged a private excursion to the Duomo. Esmeralda was pleased.

How nice, everyone said, *that she is calming down and becoming devout. No doubt it is because she is to marry the Pope's son next year.*

. . .

I continued my regular devotions and fought not to become discouraged. The simple act of prayer brought with it a temporary peace, and I found myself adding to my original selfish request. I asked for the continued health of Alfonso, my mother, and Donna Esmeralda; I asked for health to be restored to old Ferrante, who was failing. I even prayed for a miracle so great I dared not believe in its possibility: that my father's heart might be opened, that he might become happy and kind.

One late summer afternoon, a royal aide came to fetch me to Ferrante's chambers. I was confused; I turned to Donna Esmeralda for support. I had done nothing of late to displease my elders; if anything, I had behaved circumspectly. In fact, in my hand was a Latin translation of the Proverbs; before the aide arrived, I had been reading the last one:

> *A perfect wife—who can find her?*
> *She is far beyond the price of pearls.*
> *Her husband's heart has confidence in her,*
> *from her he will derive no little profit.*
> *Advantage and not hurt she brings him*
> *all the days of her life.*

San Gennaro, I had prayed, *grant my petition and I will become thus.*

I was dressed in the black, full-sleeved gown of the southern noblewoman; I had worn no colour since the announcement of my second engagement. Before leaving, I set down the little book, touched the small gold crucifix at my throat, then followed the King's aide. Esmeralda stayed close by my side.

The door to the throne room was flung open; the chamber itself was empty. But as we crossed the marble floor, I heard sounds of agitation and anger coming from the King's office.

The aide opened the door and ushered us inside.

Ferrante sat at his desk, his face starkly scarlet against his white beard. Queen Juana sat beside him, trying to calm him, only occasionally succeeding at capturing one of his wildly gesticulating hands and stroking it in an effort to soothe. Her murmurs were drowned out by my grandfather's shouts. Beside them both stood my grim-faced father.

'Roman son of a sow!' Ferrante caught sight of me, and by way of explanation, waved at a letter on the desk. 'The bastard has appointed his new College of Cardinals. Not a soul from Naples among them, despite the fact we had several qualified candidates. *And* he appointed two Frenchmen. He mocks me!' My grandfather slammed his fist on the desk; Juana tried to clutch it, but he pulled it away. 'The lying son of a whore mocks me!'

He drew a sudden wheezing breath, then put a hand to his brow as if dizzied.

'You must calm yourself,' Juana said with uncharacteristic firmness, 'or I will send for the physician.'

Ferrante paused a moment and forced himself to slow his respiration. When he spoke again, it was more deliberately. 'I will do better than that.' He glanced up at me. 'Sancha. I will not permit the wedding to go through until this situation is rectified. I will not allow a princess of the realm to be married to the son of a man who mocks us.' He glared down at the letter on the desk. 'Alexander must be taught that he cannot extend one hand to us, then betray us with the other.'

My grandfather had not forgotten the crime committed against him decades earlier by Alexander's uncle Alonso, also known as the pontiff Callixtus III. Callixtus, disapproving of an illegitimate commoner like Ferrante taking Naples' throne, had supported the Angevins.

As desperately as Ferrante needed the new Pope's support, he had never entirely forgiven the Borgias.

My father's tone was urgent. 'Your Majesty, you are making a grave mistake. Some of the cardinals are old. They will die soon, and then we can lobby for their replacement with loyal Neapolitans. But the fact that the French now have a voice in the Vatican makes a liaison with the papacy all the more imperative.'

Ferrante turned on him, and with the candour born of ill health and old age, said, 'You were always a coward, Alfonso. I have never liked you.'

An unpleasant silence ensued. At last, my grandfather looked back at me and snapped, 'That's all. Go on, then.'

I curtsied, then left before I betrayed my joy with a smile.

For four months, from the beginning of fall into the depths of winter, I was blissful. I added words of thanksgiving to my daily prayers. San Gennaro, I was convinced, had decided my pious behaviour earned me the right to remain with my brother.

And then something occurred which everyone but I had expected.

Winter and summer in Naples are both temperate, but one rare night in late January 1494, it turned so bitterly cold that I invited Donna Esmeralda and another lady-in-waiting into my bed. We piled fur blankets high, and still shivered.

I slept fitfully, given the cold; or perhaps I sensed evil coming, for I was not as surprised as I should have been when a loud knock came at the door to my outer chamber. A male voice called, 'Your Highness! Your Highness, it is urgent!'

Donna Esmeralda rose. Limned by the fireplace, the soft, downward-sloping curves of her body, covered in a white wool nightgown, took on a coral glow. Shaking with cold, she clasped a fur throw about her; a single thick braid fell forward onto her shoulder, over her breast, past her thick waist. Her expression was one of alarm. An interruption at such an hour could not bring happy news.

I rose from the bed and lit a candle while, in the outer chamber, low voices murmured. Esmeralda returned almost at once; her expression was so stricken that I knew even before she spoke what she would say.

'His Majesty is gravely ill. He has asked for you.'

There was no time to dress properly. Donna Esmeralda fetched a black wool tabard, and held it behind me while I slipped my arms backwards into the opening, then pulled the flowing garment forward and secured it at my breast with a brooch. That, over my silk shift, would have to do. I waited as she then coiled my braid at the nape of my neck and fastened it with a pin.

I went out and followed the grim-faced young guard, who held a lantern to light our way. In silence, he led me to the King's bedchamber.

The door stood wide open. Though it was night and the heavy curtains were drawn, the room was brighter than I had ever seen it. Every taper on the great candelabra was lit, and three oil lamps burned on the night table. Beneath the great gilded mantel, a large fire blazed, casting off enormous heat and glinting off the golden bust of King Alfonso.

Off in one corner, two young physicians conferred sombrely, quietly. I recognized them as Doctors Galeano and Clemente, reputed to be the best in Naples.

The bed-curtains had been pulled back, and in the centre of the bed lay my grandfather. His face was a dark mottled purple, the colour of Lachrima Christi. His eyes were squinted tightly shut, his lips parted; his breath came in short, sharp bursts.

Juana sat on the bed beside him, barefoot and unashamed to be wearing only her nightgown; her hair was loose, and a dark, waving tendril had fallen across her face. She gazed down at her husband with a look of extreme tenderness and compassion that I have witnessed elsewhere only in artists' depictions of saints. The King's left hand was enveloped between both of hers. I wondered at the love inspired by this man, capable of so many atrocities.

In a chair some distance away sat my father. He leaned forward, staring at Ferrante, fingers of both hands spread, pressing into his brow and temples: he wore an entirely unselfconscious look of dismay. His eyes glittered with unshed tears, reflecting countless tiny flames. He glanced up when I entered, then quickly turned away.

Next to him stood the royal brothers: Federico and Francesco, both of whom grieved openly; Federico sobbed without restraint.

The doctors acknowledged me at last. 'Your Highness,' Clemente said. 'We believe His Majesty suffers from unchecked bleeding of the brain.'

'Is there nothing that can be done?' I asked.

Doctor Clemente shook his head reluctantly. 'I am sorry, Your Highness.' He paused. 'Before he lost the power of speech, he called your name.'

I was too numbed to know how to respond to this, too numbed even to weep at the realization that the King was dying.

Juana lifted her serene face. 'Come,' she said to me. 'He wanted to see you. Come sit next to him.'

I moved to the bed, and with the assistance of one of the doctors, climbed onto it so that I sat on my grandfather's right, while Juana sat on his left.

Gently, I lifted Ferrante's limp hand and squeezed it.

And gasped as his bony fingers gripped mine like talons.

'You see,' Juana whispered. 'He knows you. He knows you have come.'

For the next few hours, Juana and I sat together in a silence broken only by an occasional sob from Federico. I understood why Ferrante, as he was dying, would cling to his wife; her sweet goodness no doubt brought him comfort. But I did not understand, at that moment, why he had called for me.

The King's breathing gradually grew fainter and more irregular. He was gone for minutes before Juana finally realized he had not drawn a breath in some time, and called for the doctors to make a determination.

Even in death, he clung to us; I had to pry my hand loose from his grip.

I half-slid from the bed to my feet, and found myself facing my father. All signs of grief and anxiety had vanished from him; he stood before me, composed, commanding, regal.

He was now King.

My grandfather lay in state for a single day in the cathedral of Santa Chiara, which we royalty preferred for official functions due to its size and grandeur. It had always been used for funerals, as its chapels and naves housed the crypts of Neapolitan royalty. Behind the altar lay the Tomb of Robert the Wise, Naples' first Angevin ruler: the grave site was topped by a towering monument, the top level of which showed the living King Robert, crowned and triumphant, upon his throne. Beneath lay a sculpture of the King in the repose of death, hands piously crossed upon a sceptre. To the right of the altar was the Tomb of Charles, Duke of Calabria, Robert's only son.

In the early hours of pre-dawn, before the rest of the city woke to the news, our family filed past Ferrante's washed, carefully posed corpse in its coffin.

His face was pinched and stern, his body shrunken and frail, with no trace of the leonine spirit that had once filled it. He was at last like the men in his museum: utterly powerless.

All that night, I had considered why my grandfather had liked me while he lived, why he had called for me in death. *Hard and cold*, he had called me proudly, as if these were qualities to be admired.

Perhaps he had needed the comfort of Juana's kindness; perhaps he had also needed my strength.

I knew at once that my marriage to Jofre Borgia was now inevitable. My father had vehemently stated his opinion; the wedding was only a matter of time. There was no point in behaving like a child, in expressing anger over my fate. It was time to accept it, to be strong. I could rely on no one save myself: if God and the saints existed, they did not concern themselves with the petty requests of heartbroken young women.

After the family said its farewells to Ferrante, a feast was held in the Great Hall. There was no music that day, no dancing, but a great deal of talking and distractions.

I passed alone and unseen to Ferrante's bedchamber. The bed-curtains were still pushed back, and the canopy swathed in black; the green velvet hangings were likewise draped in the colour of mourning.

One of the oil lamps on the night table still flickered with a faint, bluish flame. I lifted it, opened the door to the narrow altar room, and from there, passed into the kingdom of the dead.

Little had changed from the way I remembered it; the expired Angevin called Robert still welcomed me with a sweep of his bony arm. This time, I was not alarmed. There was nothing frightening here, I told myself, just a collection of tanned hide and bone propped against iron poles.

But two new corpses had been added to the collection since I last visited, more than four years ago. I walked up to the nearer of them, and held the lamp up to the mummy's face. His marble eyes had dark brown irises painted on them; his beard and moustache were thick, his gleaming black hair luxuriant and curling. This was no fair-haired Angevin, but a Spaniard, or Italian. There was still a slight fullness to his features that spoke of recent demise. Alive, he had no doubt been a handsome man, who had laughed and wept, and perhaps been disappointed in love; he had known, too, what it was to be the victim of relentless cruelty.

Fearlessly, I pressed my fingers against the shining lacquered brown cheek.

It was cold and hard, like my grandfather and father.

Like me.

Winter–Spring 1494

IV

The reparation of the strained relationship between Naples and the papacy took time. I was not surprised when an entire month passed before I received the expected summons from my father.

I had prepared myself for the encounter, and reconciled myself to the thought of marriage to Jofre Borgia. The fact filled me with a strange pride; my father would expect his announcement to wound me, and be disappointed when it did not.

When the guard came to fetch me, he led me to the King's chambers. The throne was draped in black; my father would not ascend it until his formal coronation some months hence.

Ferrante's former office already bore my father's touch: a fine carpet, booty captured during the Battle of Otranto, covered the marble floor; Moorish tiles hung from the walls. I had heard my father had beheaded many Turks; I wondered how many he had killed to obtain these particular trophies. I gazed down at the red-and-gold patterned carpet searching for blood stains, eager to distract myself with odd thoughts in order to maintain my composure during the unpleasant exchange.

The new King was busy, surrounded by advisors; as I entered, he was squinting at several documents scattered on the dark wooden desk. At that instant, I realized that no longer could we Neapolitans simply refer to 'King Alfonso' to mean the Magnanimous. There were now King Alfonsos I and II.

I stared beyond the latter through the unshuttered west-facing windows that looked onto the Castel dell'Ovo and the water beyond. It was said that the great stone fortress, supposedly built by Virgil, rested upon a great magical egg hidden upon the ocean floor. If the egg were ever to crack, Naples herself would crumble and fall into the sea.

I waited in silence until my father glanced up and frowned distractedly; I was an afterthought in the midst of a busy afternoon. His son Ferrandino, now the *de facto* Duke of Calabria, leaned over his shoulder, one hand resting on the desk. Ferrandino looked up at the same time, and gave me a polite but formal nod whose subtext was clear: *I am next in line to the throne, a legitimate heir, and you are not.*

'You are to be married to Jofre Borgia in early May,' my father said curtly.

I bowed graciously from the shoulders in reply, and directed a single thought at him: *You cannot hurt me.*

The King directed his attention back to Ferrandino and one of the advisors; after murmuring a few sentences to them, he looked back up as if surprised to see me still standing before him.

'That is all,' he said.

I curtsied, triumphant over my self-control, but also disappointed that my father seemed too preoccupied to notice. I turned to leave, but before the guard escorted me through the doorway, the King spoke again.

'Oh. To appease His Holiness, I have agreed to make his son Jofre a prince—only fitting, given your rank. Therefore, you will both rule the principality of Squillace, where you will reside.' He gave a curt nod of dismissal, then returned to his work.

I left swiftly, blinded by hurt.

Squillace lay several days to Naples' south, on the opposite coast. It was a far longer journey from Naples to Squillace than from Naples to Rome.

When I returned to my chambers, I tore the portrait of San Gennaro from its place of honour and hurled it against the opposite wall. As it clattered to the floor, Donna Esmeralda let go a shriek and crossed herself, then spun about and followed me out to the balcony, where I stood seething, transforming my grief into rage.

'How dare you! There can be no excuse for such sacrilege!' she scolded, stalwart and glowering.

'You don't understand!' I snapped. 'Jofre Borgia and I are to live in Squillace!'

Her expression softened at once. For a moment, she stood silently, then asked, 'Do you think this will be any easier for Alfonso than for you? Will you force him again to comfort you when his own heart is breaking? You may be more likely to show your temper, Donna Sancha—but do not be fooled. He is the more sensitive soul.'

I turned and stared into Esmeralda's wise, lined face. I wrapped my arms about my ribs, let go a shuddering breath, and forced my internal tempest to ease.

'I must get hold of my emotions,' I said, 'before Alfonso learns of this.'

That evening, I took supper alone with my brother. He spoke animatedly of his training in swordsmanship, and of the fine horse my father had recently purchased for him. I smiled and listened, adding little to the conversation. Afterwards we took a stroll in the palace courtyard, watched by a lone, distant guard. It was the beginning of March, and the night air was brisk but not unpleasant.

Alfonso spoke first. 'You are quiet tonight, Sancha. What troubles you?'

I hesitated before answering. 'I was wondering whether you had heard the news . . . '

My brother gathered himself, and said, with feigned casualness, 'You are to be married to Jofre Borgia, then.' His tone at once turned soothing. 'It won't be bad, Sancha. As I said before, Jofre might be a decent young man. At least, you'll live in Naples; we'll be able to see each other . . . '

I stopped in mid-stride, turned toward him, and rested my fingertips gently on his lips. 'Dear brother.' I fought to keep my voice steady, my tone light. 'Pope Alexander wants not just a princess for his son; he wants his son to be a prince. Jofre and I will go to Squillace to rule.'

Alfonso blinked once, startled. 'But the contract . . . ' he began, then stopped. 'But Father . . . ' He fell silent. For the first time, I focused not on my feelings, but on his. As I saw a wave of pain pass over his fair young features, I thought my heart would melt.

I wrapped an arm about him, and began once more to walk. 'I can always come visit Naples. And you can visit Squillace.'

He was used to being the comforter, not the comforted. 'I will miss you.'

'And I you.' I forced a smile. 'You told me once that duty is not always pleasant. That is true, but we shall make the best of it with visits and letters.'

Alfonso stopped walking, and pressed me to him. 'Sancha,' he said. 'Ah, Sancha . . . ' He was taller, and had to bow his head to rest his cheek against mine.

I stroked his hair. 'It will be all right, little brother,' I said. I held him tightly and did not permit myself to weep. Ferrante, I thought, would have been proud.

The month of May came all too soon, and with it, Jofre Borgia. He arrived in Naples with a large entourage, and was escorted into the Great Hall of the Castel Nuovo by my uncle, Prince Federico, and my brother Alfonso. Once the men had arrived, I made a grand entrance, coming down the staircase in a sea green brocade gown with an emerald choker round my neck.

I could see at once from my bridegroom's slightly slack-jawed reaction that I had made a favourable impression; the reverse was certainly not true.

I had been told Jofre Borgia was 'almost thirteen'—and I expected to encounter a youth resembling my brother. Even in the short span of time since I had told Alfonso of my engagement, his voice had deepened further, his shoulders broadened and become more muscular. He now surpassed me in height by the breadth of a hand.

But Jofre was a child. I had passed my sixteenth birthday since meeting the strega, and I was now a woman with full breasts and hips. I had known sexual ecstasy, known the touch of an experienced man's hands.

As for the youngest Borgia, he stood a full head shorter than me. His face still had a babe's chubbiness, his voice was pitched higher than mine, and his frame was so slight I could well have lifted him off his feet. To make matters worse, he wore his copper blond hair like a girl, in long ringlets that spilled onto his shoulders.

I had heard, as had everyone with ears in Italy, of Alexander's uncontrollable passion for beautiful women. As a young cardinal, Rodrigo Borgia had scandalized his aged uncle, Pope Callixtus, by conducting a baptism, then escorting all the women in the entourage into the walled church courtyard and locking the gate, leaving the enraged men outside to listen to the sounds of giggling and lovemaking for some hours. Even now, Pope Alexander had brought his latest mistress, sixteen-year-old Giulia Orsini, to live with him in the Vatican—and was given to flagrant public displays of affection for her. It was reputed no woman was safe from his advances.

It was impossible to believe that Jofre was the same man's son.

I thought of Onorato's strong hands moving over my body; I thought of how he had mounted me, how I had grasped his powerful back as he rode me, then brought me to pleasure.

Then I looked upon this skinny child and secretly cringed with disgust at the thought of the marriage bed. Onorato had known my body better than I had myself; how could I possibly teach this effeminate young creature all a man should know about the art of love?

My heart despaired. I went through the next several days in stunned misery, performing as best I could the role of the happy bride. Jofre spent his time in the company of his entourage, and made no effort at courtship; he was no Onorato, concerned with my feelings. He had come to Naples for one reason: to gain a princely crown.

The civil ceremony came first, in the Castel Nuovo, presided by the Bishop of Tropea and witnessed by my father and Prince Federico. In his anxiety, little Jofre shouted out his hasty reply to the Bishop's question well before the old man had finished asking, which caused a ripple of amusement to pass through the crowd. I could not smile.

There came afterwards the presentation of gifts from my new husband: rubies, pearls, diamonds, brocades woven with thread of real gold, silks and velvets, all to be made into adornments and gowns for me.

But our union had not yet been blessed by the Church, and so could not be physically consummated; I had a respite of four days before the Mass.

The next day was the Ascension and the Feast of the apparition of the Archangel Michael; it was also proclaimed a day of celebration for the Kingdom of Naples.

The black morning sky released a stinging downpour of rain and gusting winds. Despite the ominous weather, our family followed my father and his barons to the great cathedral of Santa Chiara, where Ferrante had lain in state only months before. There, the altar had been carefully prepared by Alexander's Pontifical Master of Ceremonies, with all the symbols of Neapolitan rulership laid out in the order they would be presented to the new King: the crown, studded with gems and pearls; the royal sword, in a jewelled scabbard; the silver sceptre, topped with the gold Angevin lily; and the imperial globe.

My father led us into the church. He had never seemed more handsome, more regal than he did at that moment. He was dressed grandly in a tightly-fitted tunic and breeches of black satin, over which he wore a robe of shining crimson brocade lined with white ermine. Our family and the courtiers stopped at the designated place, but my father continued alone down the vast aisle.

I stood beside my brother and clutched his hand. Neither of us looked the other in the eye; I knew if I met Alfonso's gaze, I would betray my unhappiness at an hour when I should have felt quite the opposite.

I had learned, shortly after my betrothal to Jofre was renewed, of the deal the new King had struck with Pope Alexander. Alfonso II would grant to Jofre Borgia the principality of Squillace; in return, His Holiness would send a papal legate (in this case, a powerful cardinal from his own family) to crown the King. Thus, Alexander gave his direct, irrevocable blessing and recognition to Alfonso's reign.

The exchange had been the King's idea—not the Pope's, as my father had told me.

He had intentionally purchased his joy at the cost of my sorrow.

The man who would soon be known as Alfonso II stopped at the choir of the canons, where he was greeted by the Archbishop of Naples and the Patriarch of Antiochia. They led him to his seat before the altar, where he listened along with the rest of us as the Papal Bull declaring him undisputed ruler of Naples was read.

My father knelt on a cushion before Cardinal Giovanni Borgia, the papal legate, and carefully repeated the oath after him.

I listened at the same time I contemplated my fate.

Why did my father hate me so? He was indifferent to his other children, save the Crown Prince, Ferrandino—but he showed his eldest son attention only insofar as it was necessary to train him for his position in life. Was it because I had caused more trouble than the others?

Perhaps. But perhaps the answer also lay in old Ferrante's words: *Of all his children, you are most like your father.*

But my father had shrieked when he saw the Angevin mummies; I had not.

You always were a coward, Alfonso.

Was it possible that my father's cruelty sprang from fear? And did he despise me because I possessed the one attribute he did not—courage?

Near the altar, my father had finished swearing his oath. The cardinal handed him a piece of parchment, thus investing him as King, and said, 'By virtue of Apostolic authority.'

Now a prince of the realm by virtue of marriage, Jofre Borgia stepped forward, small and solemn, with the crown. The cardinal took it from him, then placed it upon my father's head. It was heavy and slid a bit; the prelate steadied it with one hand while he and the archbishop buttoned the strap beneath my father's chin, to hold it fast.

The items of rulership were handed to the new King: the sword, the sceptre, the orb. Ceremony dictated that all the Pope's prelates should now form a circle behind my father, but his brothers, sons, and loyal barons surged forward in an abrupt, impetuous show of support.

Laughing, my father sat down on his throne while the assembly cheered.

'Viva Re Alfonso! Viva Re Alfonso!'

Despite my fury and resentment at being his pawn, I looked upon him, crowned and glorious, and was amazed by the sudden welling of loyalty and pride within me. I called out with the others, my voice breaking.

'Viva Re Alfonso!'

. . .

The next three days I spent being fitted for a splendid wedding gown. The stomacher was made of the golden brocade my husband had given me, and the gown itself was of black velvet striped with satin, with a chemise of gold silk; both the gown and stomacher were seeded with Jofre's pearls, and more of his diamonds and pearls were carefully woven into a headdress of the finest gold thread. The sleeves, which tied onto the bodice, were also of striped black velvet and satin, and so voluminous I could have fit my new husband into one. There was a time I would have taken great pride and interest in the gown, and in adorning myself to further enhance my beauty; this was not such a time. I looked upon that gown as a prisoner beholds his chains.

My wedding day dawned crimson, with the sun obscured by clouds. I stood on my balcony at the Castel Nuovo, unable to sleep the long night before, knowing that I was to surrender my home and all I knew to go and live in a strange city. I savoured the scent of the cool sea air and drew it deep into my lungs; would it smell as sweet in Squillace? I stared out at the leaden green bay, presided over by dark Vesuvio, knowing the memory of that moment would never be enough to sustain me. My life revolved around my brother, and his around mine; I conversed with him each morning, supped with him each night, spoke to him throughout the day. He knew and loved me better than my own mother. Jofre seemed a kindly lad, but he was a stranger. How could I cheerfully face life without Alfonso?

Only one thing troubled me more greatly: The knowledge that my little brother would suffer similar loneliness—perhaps worse, since Donna Esmeralda had said he was more sensitive than me. That was the hardest of all to endure.

At last I went inside to my ladies, to begin the preparations for the marriage ceremony, to be held mid-morning.

As the day progressed, the sky grew more dismal and overcast, a perfect reflection of my mood. For Alfonso's sake, I hid my sorrow; I remained gracious, poised.

As a bride, I was magnificent in my gown; when I entered the castle's Royal Chapel, a murmur of awe ran through the waiting assembly. I took no pleasure in such appreciation. I was too preoccupied with avoiding the gaze of my brother, allowing myself only a glimpse of him as I passed. He looked regal and adult in a tunic of dark blue, with a gold-hilted sword at his hip. His expression was taut, grave, without a trace of the radiance he had inherited from our mother. He stared carefully ahead at the altar.

Of the religious ceremony, I can tell you only that it went on interminably, and that poor Jofre bore himself with all the regal grace he could summon. But when the time came for him to pass the Bishop's kiss on to me, he was compelled to stand on tip-toe, and his lips trembled.

Afterwards came a concert, then a lunch that endured for hours, with much drinking of wine and salutes to the new bride and groom. When dusk came, Jofre retired to a nearby palazzo which had been prepared for us. Sunset was entirely hidden by the great, dark storm clouds that had gathered over the bay.

I arrived with the night and the first muted rolls of thunder, accompanied by my father the King, and the Cardinal of Monreale, Giovanni Borgia. The Cardinal was a homely, middle-aged man, with coarse lips and a demeanour to match. His head was shaved in the priest's tonsure, and his bald crown covered with a red satin skullcap; his portly form was covered by a white satin cassock topped by purple velvet robes, and his thick fingers sparkled with diamonds and rubies.

I left the men in the corridor and entered the bedchamber, which my women had readied for us. Donna Esmeralda undressed me, carrying away not just the beautiful wedding gown, but even my silk chemise. Naked, I was led to the nuptial bed, where Jofre waited. At the sight of me, his eyes grew round; he stared with a naive lack of restraint as one of my ladies pulled back the sheet for me, waited for me to lie beside my new husband, then drew the covering up only so far as my waist. There I lay, my full breasts bared to the world.

Jofre was too shy and I too disheartened to make small talk

during this embarrassing ritual—one of the more unpleasant requirements of nobility and power, and there was naught could rescue us from it.

When the King and Cardinal Borgia, whose office it was to witness the nuptial event, entered the chamber, Jofre greeted them with a gracious smile.

It was clear that Cardinal Borgia shared his cousin Rodrigo's appreciation for younger women, for he stared quite pointedly at my bosom and sighed. 'How beautiful they are. Like roses.'

I fought the impulse to cover myself. I seethed with resentment that this old man should be carnally entertained at my expense; nor was I at ease with the fact that my father had never seen me unclothed.

The King's gaze flickered over my nakedness with a detachment that made me shudder; he gave a cold little smile. 'Like all flowers, they will wither quickly enough.' His eyes were no longer troubled; tonight, they were bright. He had achieved all he had ever wanted in this world—he was King, with the Pope's blessing, and such was all the sweeter because he would also soon be rid of his troublesome daughter. This was the moment of his greatest triumph over me; this was the moment of my greatest defeat.

Never did my hatred for my father burn so brightly as it did at that moment; never had my humiliation been so complete. I turned my face away, lest Jofre and the cardinal see the loathing in my eyes. I wanted desperately to pull the sheets around me, to storm from the bed, but the intensity of my anger left me wooden, unable to move.

Jofre broke the brief silence with disarming honesty. 'Forgive me, Your Majesty, Your Holiness, if I find myself at the mercy of nerves.'

The cardinal laughed lecherously. 'You are young, my boy—at your age, all the nerves in Naples cannot impede your performance.'

''Tis not my age that gives me hope of success,' Jofre countered, 'but the dazzling beauty of my bride.'

From any other lips—save perhaps my Alfonso's—such words

would have been a pretty display of courtly wit. But Jofre uttered them with sincerity, and a shy sidewise glance.

Both men laughed—my father derisively, the cardinal appreciatively. The latter slapped his thigh. 'Take her then, boy. Take her! I can see from the rise of the sheet that you are ready!'

Awkwardly, Jofre rolled toward me. At that point, his attention was on me: he could not see our two witnesses lean forward in their chairs, keenly watching his every move.

With my assistance, he managed to climb atop me; he was more slender than I and shorter, so when he pressed his pursed lips against mine, his male member poked hard into my belly. Again he trembled, but this time, not from nerves. Given his feminine appearance, I had earlier feared Jofre might be the sort who preferred boys to women, but such was clearly not the case.

Fighting to ignore the sheer misery of the situation, I steadied him and parted my legs as he slid downward toward his goal. Unfortunately, he began to thrust too soon, into my thigh. Unlike the elder Borgia, this youngest one was entirely uneducated as to the act of love. I reached for him, intending to guide him—but the instant I touched him, he let go a cry, and my hand was filled with his seed.

Instinctively, I pulled the evidence out from beneath the sheets and away, inadvertently revealing the mishap to our witnesses. Jofre let go another groan, this one of pure failure, and rolled onto his back.

My father was smiling as broadly as I had ever seen him. Hand extended, palm up, he turned to the chuckling cardinal and demanded: 'Your purse, Holiness.'

With good humour, the cardinal shook his head, and withdrew from his satin cassock a small purple velvet bag, sagging with coin. This he dropped in the King's hand. 'Pure luck, Your Majesty. Pure luck, and nothing more.'

As one of my ladies hurried into the chamber and cleaned my hand with a damp cloth, Jofre propped himself up on his elbows and stared at the two men. His cheeks flushed bright scarlet at the realization that his performance had been the subject of a wager.

The cardinal registered his discomfort and laughed. 'Don't be embarrassed, boy. I lost because I didn't believe you would get so far. You endured longer than most your age. Now we can all get to the real business at hand.'

But my husband's eyes had filled with mortified tears; he moved away from me and huddled on his side of the bed.

His suffering allowed me to transcend my own shame. My actions did not spring from a desire to be done quickly with this sordid business, but from a desire to free Jofre from his unhappiness. He seemed a gentle soul; he did not deserve such cruelty.

I rolled toward him and whispered in his ear. 'They mock us because they envy us, Jofre. Look at them: they are old. Their time is past. But we are young.' I placed his palms upon my breasts. 'There is no one else in the room. It is only you and I together, here in our marriage bed.'

For pity's sake, I kissed him—softly, with tender passion, as Onorato had once kissed me. I closed my eyes, blotting out the sight of our tormentors, and imagined I was with my former lover. I ran my hands over Jofre's narrow, bony back, then down between his thighs. He shivered, and moaned when I caressed his maleness, just as I had been taught; soon he was firm enough to be guided into me, this time successfully.

I kept my eyes closed. In my mind's eye, there was nothing in the world save me, my new husband, and the approaching thunder.

Jofre was no Onorato. He was small, and I received little stimulation; had it not been for his violent thrusting and the fact I had helped him enter me, I would scarcely have known he penetrated me.

Still, I held on tightly; given the pressure against my chest, I could not help releasing gasps. I only hoped he interpreted them as sounds of pleasure.

After perhaps a minute, the muscles of his legs stiffened; with a howl, he reared his torso backwards. I opened my eyes and saw his own widen with astonishment, then roll upwards, at which point I knew we had met with success.

He collapsed atop me, panting. I felt the subtle sensation of his male organ shrinking inside me, then sliding out altogether; with it came liquid warmth.

I knew that this time, there would be no sexual pleasure for me. Onorato might have cared about satisfying my desire, but it was of no concern to the three men here tonight.

'Well done, well done,' the cardinal said, with a faint note of disappointment that his task was so swiftly completed. He blessed us and the bed.

Just behind him stood my father. With Jofre still lying atop me, I stared up at the man who had betrayed me, keeping my gaze cold, heartless. I did not want him to have the pleasure of seeing the unhappiness he had inflicted.

He wore a small, victorious smile; he did not care that I hated him. He was glad to be done with me, even gladder to have received something of value in exchange.

The two men left, and my new husband and I were finally alone. My ladies would not trouble us until morning, when the sheets would be collected as further evidence of our contract's consummation.

For a long moment, Jofre lay atop me in silence. I did nothing, for after all, he was now my lord and master and it would be rude to interrupt him. And then he pushed my hair behind my ear, and whispered, 'You are so beautiful. They described you to me, but words cannot do you justice. You are the most beautiful woman I have ever seen.'

'You are sweet, Jofre,' I replied sincerely. A boy he might be, but a likeable one, utterly guileless, if lacking in intelligence. I could grow fond of him . . . but never love him. Not the way I had loved Onorato.

'I'm sorry,' he said, with a sudden vehemence. 'I'm so sorry . . . I—I—' Quite abruptly, he burst into tears.

'Oh, Jofre.' I wrapped my arms about him. 'I'm sorry they were horrible to you. What they did was unspeakable. And what you did was—it was perfectly normal.'

'No,' he insisted. 'It's not the bet. It was unkind of them, yes, but I am a terrible lover. I know nothing about pleasuring women. I knew I would disappoint you.'

'Hush,' I said. He tried to pull up and away, onto his elbows, but I pressed him down against me, against my breasts. 'You are simply young. We all begin inexperienced . . . and then we learn.'

'Then I will learn, Sancha,' he promised. 'For your sake, I will learn.'

'Hush,' I said, holding him to me like the child he was, and began to stroke his long, soft hair.

Outside, the storm had finally broken, and the rain came down in sheets.

Summer 1494–Winter 1495

V

Early the next morning, Jofre and I left on the journey to our new home in the southernmost reaches of Calabria. I kept my private vow to be brave: I embraced my brother and mother and kissed them both good-bye without shedding a tear; we all repeated promises to visit, to write.

King Alfonso II, of course, could not be bothered to take his leave.

Squillace was a rock scalded by the sun. The town itself stood perched atop a steep promontory. Our palace, painfully rustic by Neapolitan standards, lay far from the sea, the view partially blocked by the ancient monastery founded by the scholar Cassiodorus. The coastline was stark and spare, lacking Naples' full, graceful curve, and the faded leaves of scraggly, struggling olive orchards constituted the only greenery. The region's greatest contribution to the arts, of which the populace was immensely proud, was its red-brown ceramics.

The palace was a disaster; furniture and shutters were broken, cushions and tapestries torn, walls and ceilings cracked. The temptation to yield to self-pity and to curse my father for sending me to such a dismal place was great. Instead, I occupied myself with making the palace into a suitable dwelling for royalty. I ordered fine velvet to replace the moth-eaten brocade on the aged thrones, had the worn wood refinished, and sent for fine marble to replace the uneven terra cotta floor of the throne room. The private chambers of the royal couple—the prince's to the immediate right of the throne room, the princess' to the left—were in even worse disrepair, and required me to order even more fabrics and hire more craftsmen to set things aright.

Jofre kept himself occupied in quite a different manner. He was young, and away from his domineering family for the first time; now that he was master of his own kingdom, he had no idea how to comport himself properly—and so he did not. Soon after our arrival in Squillace, we were descended upon by a group of Jofre's male friends from Rome, all of them eager to celebrate the new prince's good fortune.

In the first few days after our marriage—including the time spent in our comfortable carriage during our southward journey—Jofre half-heartedly tried to make good on his promise to become a better lover. But he tended towards ineptitude and impatience; his own desire soon overwhelmed him, and he usually fulfilled his own needs without addressing mine. After the tenderness and tears he had displayed on our wedding night, I had hoped that I had found someone as kind as my brother. I soon learned that Jofre's pretty words sprang not so much from compassion as a desire to placate. There was a great difference between goodness and weakness, and Jofre's agreeable nature was born of the latter.

This was made abundantly clear after the appearance of Jofre's friends a week after our arrival in Squillace. All of them were young nobles, some married, most not, none of them older than me. There was a pair of his relatives as well, both recently descended upon Rome in order to make the most of their connections to His Holiness: a Count Ippolito Borja from Spain, who had not yet taken to Italicizing the spelling of his name, and a young cardinal of fifteen, Luis Borgia, whose air of smug self-importance immediately provoked my dislike. The palace was still in chaos—scaffolding was everywhere, and the floors were still cracked terra cotta; the marble had not yet been laid in the throne room. Don Luis did not miss an opportunity to comment on the pathetic nature of our dwelling and our principality, especially compared to the magnificence of Rome.

When the crowd arrived, I played my role of hostess in as decent a fashion as possible, given our rural surroundings. I put on a feast and poured for them our best Lachrima Christi, brought from Naples, since the local wine was unpalatable. I dressed modestly in black, as a good wife ought, and at the feast, Jofre showed me off proudly; the men flattered me with countless toasts to my beauty.

I smiled; I was bright and charming, attentive to the men who wanted to impress me with tales of their valour and their wealth. When the hour grew late and everyone else was inebriated, I retired to my chambers and left my husband and his guests to do as they pleased.

I was awakened in the hours before dawn by the muffled screams of a child. Donna Esmeralda, who slept beside me, heard them too: alarmed, we regarded each other only an instant, then snatched our wrappers and hurried toward the source of the sound. No one of conscience could have ignored anything so heart-rending and pitiful.

We had not far to go. The instant I threw open the door that led from my outer chamber to the throne room, I was greeted by a scene Bacchanalian beyond my imagination.

The unfinished floor was covered with tangled bodies, some writhing in drunken passion, others motionless, snoring from a surfeit of wine. Jofre's friends and whores, I realized with disgust, though as a woman, it was not my place to comment on the peccadilloes of my husband's guests.

But when I glanced at the two thrones, a fury rose in me which would not be ignored.

In the prince's throne sat Jofre, somewhat askew; he was entirely naked from the waist down, and his slippers, stockings and breeches lay in a heap upon the step leading to his throne. His pale, bare legs were wrapped tightly about those of a woman who sat upon his lap. No courtesan of noble blood, she was the coarsest, commonest sort of local whore, perhaps twice Jofre's age, with lips stained an unnatural lurid red and eyes lined heavily with kohl; she was gaunt, poor, unlovely. Her cheap red satin gown had been pulled up to her waist, revealing no undergarment beneath, and her small, sagging breasts had been lifted up from their bodice so that my young husband could clutch them with his hands.

So drunk was he that he failed to notice my entrance and continued to ride his mount, she releasing exaggerated cries with each thrust.

Dalliances were expected of royal men; I had no right to complain, save for the disrespect Jofre now showed the symbol of rulership. Although I had tried to prepare myself for the inevitability of Jofre's unfaithfulness, I still felt the sting of jealousy.

But it was the sacrilege occurring beside my husband that I would not endure.

Cardinal Luis Borgia, he who so worshiped all things Roman, sat upon *my* throne—entirely unclothed, his red robe and cardinal's hat lost somewhere amidst the carnal assembly. Upon his lap was balanced one of our kitchen servants, a boy of perhaps nine years, Matteo, whose breeches had been carelessly pulled down to his knees. Tears streamed down Matteo's cheeks; it was he who had screamed, he whose cries had now turned to moans of pain as the young cardinal entered him vigorously, brutally, clutching him fast by the midsection so that the child would not be thrown to the floor. The boy himself fought the forward momentum by gripping the recently refinished wooden arms of the throne.

'Stop!' I shouted. Incensed by the cardinal's cruelty and irreverence, I forgot all modesty and let go my wrapper; it dropped to the floor. Clad only in my undergarment, I strode directly to Matteo and tried to pull him away.

His face contorted with inebriated fury, the cardinal held onto the child. 'Let him scream! I paid the little bastard!'

I cared not; the boy was too young to know better. I pulled again, harder; sobriety conferred on me a determination Luis lacked. His grip weakened and I led the sobbing boy over to an outraged Donna Esmeralda. She took him away to be looked after.

Indignant, Luis Borgia rose—too swiftly, given his drunkenness. He collapsed, and sat quickly down on the stair leading up to my throne, then rested an arm and his head upon the new velvet cushion covering the seat, stained now by Matteo's blood.

'How dare you,' I said, my voice quavering with anger. 'How dare you harm a child, paid or not, and how dare you disrespect me by performing such an act upon my throne! You are no longer welcome as a guest in this palace. Come morning, you will leave.'

'I am your husband's guest,' he slurred, 'not yours, and you would do well to remember that he rules here.' He turned toward my husband; Jofre's eyes were still closed fast, his lips still parted, as he slapped his body against the whore's. 'Jofre! Your Highness, pay attention! Your new wife is a keening virago!'

Jofre blinked; his thrusting ceased. 'Sancha?' He regarded me uncertainly; he was far too intoxicated to register the implications of the situation, to feel shame.

'These men must leave,' I said, in a clear, strong voice to make sure he heard. 'All of them, in the morning, and the whores must go straightaway.'

'Bitch,' the cardinal said, then leaned his head over my new velvet throne cushion, and emptied the contents of his stomach.

As I insisted, Jofre's guests *did* leave the next afternoon. My husband was indisposed for most of the day; not until evening did I speak to him of the previous night's events. His memory was most spotty. He only remembered his friends urging him to drink. He recalled nothing of the whores, he claimed, and certainly he would never sully the honour of the throne willingly by committing such an act—his friends must have dared him.

'Is such behaviour typical in Rome?' I demanded. 'For it will not do here—or anywhere else I dwell, for that matter.'

'No, no,' Jofre reassured me. 'It was Luis, my cousin—he is a profligate, but I should never have allowed myself to become so drunk that I lost my senses.' He paused. 'Sancha . . . I do not know why I sought comfort in the arms of a whore, when I have the loveliest wife in all Italy. You must know . . . You are the love of my life. I know I am clumsy and thoughtless; I know I am not the shrewdest of men. I do not expect you to return my love. Only have mercy upon me . . . '

He then begged my forgiveness, so pitifully that I gave it, for there was no point in making our lives unpleasant out of resentment.

But I remembered his weakness, and took note of the fact that my husband was easily swayed, and not a man to be relied upon.

Less than two weeks later, we received a new visitor, one sent from His Holiness himself, the Count of Marigliano. He was an older man, prim and stately, with silvering hair and subdued but elegant dress. I welcomed him with a fine supper, relieved that, unlike Jofre's other friends, he did not appear at all interested in revelry.

What he *was* interested in, however, shocked me.

'Madonna Sancha,' he said sternly, as we enjoyed the last of the Lachrima Christi after supper (Jofre's friends had earlier drunk up almost the entire supply brought from Naples). 'I must now bring up a most difficult subject. I am sorry that I must speak of such things to you in the presence of your husband, but you both must be informed of the charges that have been brought against you.'

'Charges?' I studied the old man incredulously; Jofre, too, was startled. 'I'm afraid I don't understand.'

The count's tone struck the perfect balance between firmness and delicacy. 'Certain . . . visitors to your palace have reported witnessing unseemly behaviour.'

I glanced at my husband, who was guiltily studying his goblet, turning it round in its fingers so that its inlaid faceted gems caught the light.

'There *was* unseemly behaviour,' I said, 'but it had naught to do with me.' I had no intention of implicating Jofre; neither did I intend for my accuser to achieve his revenge. 'Tell me, was one of these witnesses Cardinal Luis Borgia?'

The count gave a barely perceptible nod. 'May I ask how you would know this?'

'I discovered the cardinal in a compromising situation,' I replied. 'The situation was such that I demanded he leave the palace as soon as possible. He was not pleased.'

Again, the old man gave a slight nod as he absorbed this information.

Jofre, meantime, was flushed with what seemed a combination of both anger and embarrassment. 'My wife has done nothing wrong. She is a woman of the highest character. What charges have been brought against her?'

The count lowered his gaze in a show of reluctance and modesty. 'That she has entertained not one, but several men at different times in her private chambers.'

I let go a small laugh of disbelief. 'That is absurd!'

Marigliano shrugged. 'Nonetheless, His Holiness is quite distraught over the matter, to the point of recalling both of you to Rome.'

As unhappy as I was in Squillace, I had no desire to go live among the Borgias. At least in Squillace, I was close to the sea. Jofre also looked grim at the thought of returning to his native city. He spoke only in the most passing terms about his family, never at length; from what little he had said, I gathered that he was intimidated by them.

'How can we disprove these charges?' I asked.

'I have been sent on an official investigation,' Marigliano said. Although I was far from comfortable with the notion of being scrutinized by a papal representative, I liked the old count's candour. He was gracious but forthright, a man of integrity. 'I shall require access to all the servants in the household, in order to interview them.'

'Speak to anyone,' Jofre said at once. 'They will be happy to tell you the truth about my wife.' I smiled at my husband, grateful for his support.

The count continued. 'There is also the question of extravagance. His Holiness is not pleased with the amount of money that has been spent upon the Squillace palace.'

'I believe that is a question you can answer with your own eyes,' I told him. 'Simply look about you, and judge whether our surroundings are too lavish.'

At that, even Marigliano had to smile.

The investigation was concluded within two days. By then, the count had spoken with every servant and lord- and lady-in-waiting; I made sure, as well, that he conferred privately with little Matteo. All of our entourage was wise enough not to implicate Jofre in any wrong-doing.

I escorted Marigliano himself to his waiting carriage. He hesitated a moment for his attendant to precede him, so that he and I could speak privately.

'Madonna Sancha,' he said. 'Given what I know about Luis Borgia, I had no doubt when I began this investigation that you were innocent of the charges. Now I know you are not only innocent, but a woman who has inspired great affection and loyalty in all those who surround her.' He glanced about us with a faint furtiveness. 'You are deserving of the full truth. It is not just because of the cardinal's charges that I was sent here.'

I could not imagine what he hinted at. 'Why, then?'

'Because these witnesses also spoke of your great beauty. Your husband described it in letters in the most lyrical terms, which piqued His Holiness' interest. But now it has been said that you are even more beautiful than *La Bella*.'

La Bella, the Beautiful One: This was the nickname given to Giulia Orsini, the Pope's current mistress, for it was claimed she was the most beautiful woman in Rome, and perhaps in all Italy.

'And what will you report to His Holiness?'

'I am an honest man, Madonna. I must tell him that it is true. But I will also tell him that you are the sort of woman who will remain loyal to her husband.' He paused. 'To be frank, Your Highness, I do not believe the latter fact will make any difference.'

This was one time I took no pleasure in flattery. I had not wanted a marriage to Jofre Borgia because I had been in love with another man, because I had wanted to stay in Naples with my brother, and because Jofre had been a mere child. Now I had yet another reason for regret: a father-in-law with lascivious designs—who just happened to be the leader of all Christendom.

'May God bless and keep you, Your Highness,' Marigliano said, then climbed into his carriage, bound for Rome.

I soon had an even greater worry than the thought of an amorous father-in-law, a pope with dreams of making me his new mistress.

Only a month after my wedding, news filtered southward into Calabria: Charles VIII, King of France, was planning to invade Naples.

Re Petito, the people called him, 'The Little King', for he had been born with a short, twisted spine and crooked limbs; he looked more gargoyle than man. He had also been born with a craving for conquest, and it took little for his advisors to convince him that the Angevins in Naples longed for a French king.

His queen, the lovely Anne of Brittany, did her best to dissuade him from his dreams of invasion. She and the rest of France were devoutly Catholic and deeply loyal to the Pope, who would be outraged by an intrusion into Italy.

Concerned, I wrote to my brother Alfonso to learn the truth of the matter. It took weeks to receive a reply which gave little comfort.

> *Have no fear, dearest sister,*
>
> *True, King Charles is hungry for conquest—but at this very moment, our father is meeting with His Holiness Alexander in Vicovaro. They have forged a military alliance, and have carefully planned their strategy; once Charles hears of this, he will be filled with doubts, and will give up his foolish notion of invasion. Besides, with the Pope so strongly on our side, the French people will never support an attack on Naples.*

Alfonso could not help trying to couch everything he told me in the most positive terms, but I understood his letter all too well. The French threat was real—so real that my father and the Pope were drawing up battle plans at a retreat outside Rome.

I read the text aloud to Donna Esmeralda. 'It is just as the priest Savonarola predicted,' she stated darkly. 'It is the end of the world.'

I scoffed. I had no patience for the Florentine fool who fancied himself anointed by God, nor for the masses who flocked to hear his Apocalyptic message. Girolama Savonarola railed against Alexander from the safety of his pulpit in the north and lambasted the ruling family of his own city, the Medicis. The Dominican priest had actually presented himself to Charles of France and claimed that he, Savonarola, was God's own messenger, chosen by Him to reform the church, to cast out the pleasure-loving pagans who had overrun her. 'Savonarola is a raving madman,' I said. 'He thinks that King Charles is a judgment sent by God. He thinks Saint John predicted the invasion of Italy in the Apocalypse.'

She crossed herself at my lack of reverence. 'How can you be sure he is wrong, Madonna?' She lowered her voice, as if concerned that Jofre, on the other side of the palace, might hear. 'It is the wickedness of Pope Alexander and the corruption of his cardinals that has brought this upon us. Unless they repent, we have no hope . . . '

'Why would God punish *Naples* for Alexander's sins?' I demanded.

For that, she had no reply.

Even so, Donna Esmeralda took to praying to San Gennaro; I took to fretting. It was not just that the family throne was threatened; my little brother was no longer considered too young to fight. He was trained in the art of the sword. If the need arose, he would be called upon to wield one.

Life continued for the remainder of the summer in Squillace. I was kind to Jofre, though given his weak character, I could not bring myself to love him. In public we were affectionate with one another, even though he visited my bedchamber less often and spent more nights in the company of local whores. I did my best to show no sign of hurt or jealousy.

September arrived, and brought with it evil news.

> *Dearest sister,* Alfonso wrote,
>
> *Perhaps you have already heard: King Charles has led his troops through the Alps. The feet of French soldiers are planted on Italian soil. The Venetians have struck a bargain with them, and thus caused their city to be spared, but Charles' eye is now on Florence.*
>
> *You must not worry. We have amassed a sizable army under the command of Crown Prince Ferrandino, who will lead his men northward to stop the enemy before it ever arrives in Naples. I am remaining here with Father, so you need have no concern over me. Our army, once joined by papal forces, will be invincible. There is no call for fear, for His Holiness Alexander has publicly stated, 'We would lose our mitre, our lands and our life, rather than fail King Alfonso in his need.'*

I could no longer hide my distress. Jofre tried his best to comfort me. 'They will get no further than Rome,' he promised. 'My father's army will stop them.'

Meanwhile, the French made good time. They sacked Florence, that centre of culture and artistry, then pushed their way relentlessly southward.

Our troops are making progress, Alfonso wrote. *They will soon join up with the papal army and stop Charles' men.*

On the last day of December in the year 1494, my brother's prediction was put to the test. Laden heavily with priceless, stolen goods, the French entered Rome.

Jofre received word of the invasion via a hastily-written letter from his older sister, Lucrezia. It was my turn to comfort him, as we both imagined bloody battles raging in the great piazzas of the Holy City. For days we suffered without word.

One fateful afternoon, as I sat on my balcony composing a long epistle to my brother—the only satisfactory way I could settle my nerves—I heard the thunder of hooves. I ran to the ledge and watched a lone horseman ride up to the castle entrance and dismount.

The style of his dress was Neapolitan; I dropped my quill and ran down the stairs, calling as I did for Donna Esmeralda to summon Jofre.

I hastened into the Great Hall, where the rider already waited. He was young, with black hair, beard and eyes, and dressed in a noble's finery of rich brown colour; he was covered in dust, and exhausted from a hard journey. He carried no letter, as I had hoped; the message he bore was too critical to commit to writing.

I called for wine and food, and he drank and ate greedily while I impatiently awaited my husband. At last, Jofre entered; we gave the poor man leave to sit, and settled ourselves while we listened to his tale.

'I come at the request of your uncle, Prince Federico,' the rider told me. 'He has received direct word from Crown Prince Ferrandino himself, who as you know was in Rome in command of our forces.'

The word *was* immediately provoked my alarm.

'What news of Rome?' Jofre asked, unable to restrain himself. 'My father—His Holiness, Alexander, my sister and brother—are they well?'

'They are,' said the messenger, and Jofre leaned back with a sigh. 'So far as I know, they are safe behind the walls of the Castel Sant'Angelo. It is the situation of Naples itself which is now dire.'

'Speak,' I commanded.

'Prince Federico has bid me to relay the following: Crown Prince Ferrandino's army entered Rome and engaged the French army there. However, King Charles' forces outnumber those of Naples, and Ferrandino therefore was relying on the promised assistance of His Holiness.

'Unbeknownst to the Pope, the Orsini family earlier engaged in a conspiracy with the French and captured Giulia, she who is known as *La Bella*, Alexander's favourite. When His Holiness heard that Madonna Giulia was in danger, he ordered his own army to stand down and commanded Prince Ferrandino to withdraw from the city.

'Prince Ferrandino, facing certain loss, was forced to obey. He now marches homeward, where he will prepare to engage the French army once again.

'His Holiness, in the meantime, received King Charles in the Vatican, and there negotiated with him. In return for Madonna Giulia, he offered up his son Don Cesare—your brother, Prince Jofre—as a hostage to ride with the French. In this way, he has guaranteed *Re Petito* safe passage to Naples.'

I stared at the messenger for a long moment before whispering, 'He has betrayed us. For the sake of a woman, he has betrayed us . . . ' I felt such outrage that I could not move, could only sit and stare in disbelief at the young noble. Despite his speech about first giving up his mitre, lands, and life, Alexander *had* deserted King Alfonso, without surrendering a whit.

The tired nobleman took a long drink of wine before continuing. 'All is not well in Rome, either, Your Highness. The French have plundered the city.' He turned toward Jofre. 'Your mother, Vannozza Cattanei—her palace was ransacked, and it is said . . . ' He lowered his eyes modestly. 'Forgive me, Highness. It is said they committed unseemly acts upon her person.'

Jofre pressed a hand to his lips.

The rider continued. 'Madonna Sancha, your uncle, Prince Federico, sends this urgent message: Naples needs the help of all her citizens. It is feared that the approach of the French will encourage an uprising amongst the Angevin barons. The prince has requested that you and your husband bring whatever men and arms Squillace can render.'

'Why has my uncle, and not my father, the King, sent you?' I demanded. I was convinced that my father had not cared enough to keep me informed, that this was yet another slight.

But the messenger's answer surprised me. 'It has been necessary for Prince Federico to be involved in the day-to-day affairs of the kingdom. I am sorry to be the one to tell you, Your Highness. His Majesty is unwell.'

'Unwell?' I rose, surprised by how greatly this news unsettled me, by the fact that I cared. 'What is wrong with him?'

The young man would not meet my gaze. 'Nothing *physical* afflicts him, Your Highness. Nothing the doctors can help. He . . . he has been deeply shaken by the French threat. He is not himself.'

I sank slowly back into my chair, ignoring the poignant glance my husband directed at me. The image of the rider in front of me disappeared: I saw only my father's face. For the first time, I focused not on the viciousness there, on the mocking expression directed at me. Instead I saw the dark, haunted look in his eyes, and realized I should not have been surprised to hear he was mentally unsound. He was, after all, the son of Ferrante, who had not only killed his enemies, but dressed their tanned hides in glorious costumes and spoke to them like the living.

I should not have been surprised by any of it: I should have realized from the beginning that my father was insane, my father-in-law a traitor. And the French were, despite all of Alfonso's efforts to convince me otherwise, on their way to Naples.

I rose and this time stayed on my feet. 'You may eat and rest as much as you need,' I told the messenger. 'Then, when you again face Prince Federico, tell him that Sancha of Aragon has heeded his call. I will see him in the flesh not long after your return.'

'Sancha!' Jofre protested. 'Have you not paid attention? Charles is leading his army to Naples. It is too dangerous! It makes far more sense to remain here in Squillace; the French have little reason to attack us. Even if they do decide to seize our principality, it will be some months . . . '

Skirts swirling, I turned on him. 'Dear husband,' I countered, in a voice colder and more unyielding than iron, 'have *you* not paid attention? Uncle Federico has asked for help, and I will not deny him. Have you so quickly forgotten that you, by virtue of your marriage to me, are yourself a Prince of Naples? You should not only provide troops, your own sword should be raised in her defence. And if you will not go, I shall take your sword and raise it myself.'

For that, Jofre had no reply; he stared at me, pale and somewhat embarrassed to be chided in front of a stranger for his cowardice.

As for myself, I swept from the room, headed back to my chambers to tell my ladies to commence packing at once.

I was going home.

Winter 1495

VI

The carriage that had borne me and my new husband to Squillace was outfitted for the journey back to Naples. This time we rode with a larger contingent of guards, armed for battle, traversing Italy in a north-easterly diagonal from coast to coast. Given the size of our entourage—three wagons bore our attendants and luggage—the trip required several days.

During that time I contemplated with dread the reunion between myself and my father. *Deeply shaken*, the messenger had said. *Unwell. Not himself*. He had let the running of the kingdom fall to Federico. Was he yielding to the same madness that had claimed Ferrante? Whatever the situation, I vowed I would put all personal hurt and antipathy aside. My father was the King, and during this time of looming war, required total fealty. If he was in any condition to understand me, I would pledge it to him.

On the final morning of our journey, when we saw Vesuvio towering over the landscape, I caught Donna Esmeralda's hand with excitement. Such gladness it was, to at last draw near the city, and see the great cupola of the Duomo, the dark stone of the Castel Nuovo, the hulking fortress of the Castel dell'Ovo; such gladness, and at the same time, sorrow, knowing that my beloved city was endangered.

At last our carriage pulled beneath the Triumphal Arch of Alfonso the Magnanimous into the courtyard of the royal palace. Look-outs had reported our arrival, and my brother was waiting as Jofre and I were assisted from the carriage. I smiled broadly: Alfonso was fourteen; the Neapolitan sun glinted off the beginnings of a blond beard upon his cheeks.

'Brother!' I cried. 'Look at you; you are a man!'

He smiled back, flashing white teeth; we embraced. 'Sancha,' he said, in a voice that had deepened even further, 'how I have missed you!'

We reluctantly let go of one another. Jofre was waiting nearby; Alfonso took his hand. 'Brother, I am grateful you have come.'

'We could do no else,' Jofre replied graciously—a statement which was true, if only because of my insistence.

While the servants dealt with the luggage and our other effects, Alfonso led us toward the palace. As the joy of reunion slowly faded, I noted the tension in my brother's face, his manner, his step. Something evil had just occurred, something so terrible that Alfonso was waiting for the proper moment to tell us. 'We have prepared chambers for both of you,' he said. 'You will want to refresh yourselves before you greet Prince Federico.'

'But what of Father?' I asked. 'Should I not go first to him? Despite his troubles, he is still the King.'

Alfonso hesitated; a ripple of emotion crossed his features before he could suppress it. 'Father is not here.' He faced me and my husband, his tone as sombre as I had ever heard it. 'He fled during the night. Apparently he had been planning this for some time; he took most of his clothing and possessions, and many jewels.' He lowered his face and flushed, mortified. 'We had not deemed him capable of this. He had taken to his bed. We discovered this only a few hours ago, Sancha. I think you can understand why all of the brothers, especially Federico, are preoccupied at the moment.'

'*Fled?*' I was aghast, bitterly ashamed. Up to that moment, I had considered the most treacherous man in Christendom to be the Pope, who had deserted Naples in her hour of greatest need—but my own father had proven capable of even greater betrayal.

'One of his attendants is missing,' my brother added sadly. 'We assume he was part of the plan. We are not certain where Father has headed. They are conducting an investigation at this moment.'

An agonizing hour passed, during which time I paced the elegant guest bedchamber; Giovanna now resided in the one that had once been my own. I walked out onto the balcony; now my view faced east towards Vesuvio and the armoury. I paused to stare out at the water. I remembered how, a very long time ago, I had stood upon my old balcony and hurled Onorato's ruby into the sea. I wished that I could reverse my childish action now; such a gem could purchase rations for countless soldiers, or dozens of cannons from Spain.

At last Alfonso came for me, with Jofre flanking him. Together, we went to the King's office, where Uncle Federico sat dejectedly at the dark wooden desk. He had aged since I had last seen him; his black hair had begun to silver, and the shadows I had seen upon my father's face were now beginning to gather beneath Federico's brown eyes. His features were round and not as handsome, his demeanour stern as old Ferrante's, yet somehow still kindly. Across from him sat his younger brother, Francesco, and his even younger half-sister, Giovanna.

At the sight of us, they rose. Federico had clearly taken charge; he stepped forward first, and embraced Jofre, then me. 'You have your mother's loyal heart, Sancha,' he told me. 'And Jofre, you are a true knight of the realm, to have come to Naples' aid. As Protonotary and Prince, we welcome you.'

'I have told them the news regarding His Majesty,' my brother explained.

Federico nodded. 'I won't soften the truth. Naples is threatened as never before. The barons are in revolt—frankly, with good reason. Against all advice, the King taxed them beyond conscience, appropriated lands unfairly for his own use, then publicly tortured and executed those who dared protest. Now that they know the French are on their way, the barons are heartened. They will fight with Charles to defeat us.'

'But Ferrandino is coming, with our army,' I said.

Prince Federico eyed me wearily. 'Yes, Ferrandino is coming . . . with the French on his heels. Charles has four times the men we have; without the papal army, we are doomed.' This he said without apology, despite the fact that Jofre shifted uneasily at the words. 'That is one reason I sent for you, Jofre. We need your assistance as never before; you must make good on your ties to our kingdom, and convince His Holiness to send military aid as quickly as possible. I realize the safety of your brother Cesare is compromised, but perhaps a solution can be found.' He paused. 'We have sent for help from Spain—but there is no way such assistance, even if it is granted, can arrive in time.' He let go a gusting sigh. 'And now we are without a king.'

'You have a king,' my brother countered swiftly. 'Alfonso II has clearly abdicated his throne in favour of his son, Ferrandino. That is what the barons and the people must be told.'

Federico gazed at him with admiration. 'Shrewd. Very shrewd. They have no cause to hate Ferrandino. He is far more liked than your father ever was.' He began to nod with the first stirrings of enthusiasm. 'The hell with Alfonso. You're right, we should consider this disappearance an abdication. Of course, it will be difficult. The barons don't trust us . . . they might still fight if they believe this is political manoeuvring on our part. But with Ferrandino, we have a better chance of winning popular support.'

My Uncle Francesco spoke at last. 'Ferrandino, and mercenaries. We simply have no choice but to hire help, and quickly, before the French arrive. It's all very well for Prince Jofre to convince Alexander to send papal troops, but we don't have time for such diplomacy. Besides, they're too far north to get here in time.'

Federico scowled. 'Our finances are strained as it is. We can scarcely support our own army, after all of Alfonso's spending on rebuilding the palaces, and commissioning all of that unnecessary artwork . . . '

'We have no choice,' Francesco argued. 'It's that, or lose to the French. We can always borrow money from Spain after the war.'

Federico was still frowning; he opened his mouth to reply, then closed it again at the sound of urgent knocking. 'Come,' he commanded.

I recognized the white-haired, hawk-nosed man whose face appeared in the doorway; it was the seneschal, the man in charge of the royal household—which included the royal jewels and financial matters. His expression was stricken; Federico took one glimpse at it, then forgot all royal protocol and hurried over, bending his head down so that the old man could whisper in his ear.

As Federico listened, his eyes widened, then grew dazed. Finally, the seneschal retreated and the door closed once again. My uncle took a few unsteady steps, then sat heavily upon his chair, lowered his head, and put his hand to his heart. He let go a strangled sound.

I thought, for a terrifying instant, that he was dying.

Uncle Francesco rose at once and went to his brother's side. He knelt and put a hand upon the suffering man's arm. 'Federico! Federico, what is it?'

'He has taken it,' Federico gasped. 'The Crown treasures. He has taken it *all* . . . ' The Crown treasures constituted the majority of Naples' wealth.

It took a moment before I realized the word *he* referred to my father.

I had always imagined that my return home to visit my brother would be one of the happier moments in my life, but the next few days in the Castel Nuovo found us all caught in a special sort of misery. My husband and I spent time in Alfonso's company, but it was scarcely happy; the harm our father had inflicted upon the kingdom left us stunned and sombre. We could do nothing but wait and hope for Ferrandino and his troops to reach Naples ahead of the French.

Even more painful was the discovery that my mother had disappeared as well. This was a hard fact to accept: *you have your mother's loyal heart*, Uncle Federico had said, but I could not accept that Trusia's loyalty to her lover outweighed that to Naples and her own children. The notion was so ghastly that my brother and I could not bear to discuss it; and so my mother's betrayal went unmentioned.

The morning after our arrival at the castle, Donna Esmeralda admitted Alfonso into my chambers. I smiled, faintly, in greeting—but my brother did not. He held a wooden box slightly longer than my hand and half as wide; he proffered it to me as a gift.

'For your protection,' he said, his tone infinitely serious. 'We cannot predict what might happen, and I will not rest until I know that you are capable of defending yourself.'

I laughed, partly from a desire to dismiss such a topic.

'Do not scoff,' Alfonso urged. 'It is no joke: The French are on their way to Naples. Open it.'

Reluctantly, I did as instructed. Inside the box, nestled against black velvet, was a small, long dagger with a narrow silver hilt.

'A stiletto,' my brother explained, as I drew it from its little scabbard. The hilt was quite short; most of the weapon consisted of the triangular blade, of fine, polished steel terminating in a wickedly sharp point. I dared not even touch the tip with my finger to test its keenness; I knew it would draw blood at once.

'I chose this for you because it can be easily concealed in your gown,' Alfonso said. 'We have seamstresses who can set to work immediately. I came this morning because we have no time to waste. I shall instruct you in its use now.'

I let go a clicking sound of scepticism. 'I appreciate your thoughtfulness, brother, but this can hardly do battle against a sword.'

'No,' Alfonso agreed, 'and therein lies its beauty. Any soldier will presume you are unarmed, and will therefore approach you without fear. When your enemy draws close, *that* is when you surprise him. Here.' He took the weapon from me, and showed me how to hold it properly. 'With a dagger like this, the best method of doing damage is underhanded, thrusting upward.' He demonstrated, slitting an imaginary opponent from belly to throat, then handed the little blade to me. 'Take it. You try.'

I copied his movements precisely.

'Good, good,' he murmured approvingly. 'You are a natural fighter.'

'I am a daughter of the House of Aragon.'

He at last smiled faintly, which had been my intent.

I scrutinized the steel in my hand. 'This might be suitable against an Angevin,' I remarked, 'but hardly deadly against an armoured Frenchman.'

'Ah, Sancha, therein lies its power. It is slender enough to pierce chain mail, to slip between spaces in armour—and keen and strong enough, if wielded with sufficient enthusiasm, to penetrate light metal. I know; it was mine.' He paused. 'I only pray you never have to use it.'

For his sake, I pretended not to share his fear. 'It is pretty,' I said, holding it to the sunlight. 'Like jewellery. I shall wear it always, as a keepsake.'

But in the days that followed, after small pockets had been added to my bodice, just above the folds of my skirts, I practised alone: withdrawing the stiletto swiftly, surreptitiously, wielding it underhanded, over and over, slaying invisible foes.

Two more days passed, during which time the royal brothers met constantly to formalize their strategy. An edict was announced in the streets, that King Alfonso II had abdicated in favour of his son, Ferrandino. We hoped this would mollify the barons, and keep them from fighting with the French against the Crown. In the meantime, Jofre wrote an impassioned letter to his father, Alexander, giving the official explanation of the abdication and begging for papal support; Prince Federico edited it heavily, then sent it to Rome via secret courier.

One sun-filled February morning, shortly before noonday, I was dining with Jofre and Alfonso when our quiet, listless conversation was interrupted by a faraway thunder. Three simultaneous thoughts competed for my attention:

It is nothing, a passing storm.

Has Vesuvio come alive?

Dear God, it is the French.

Wide-eyed, I stared in turn at my brother, then husband as the sound came again—this time unmistakably from the northwest—and echoed against nearby Pizzofalcone. No doubt we all shared the last thought, for we rose as one, and together raced upstairs to the floor above, where a balcony offered a view of the city's western horizon. Soon Donna Esmeralda joined us, and pointed due north of Vesuvio, towards Naples' furthermost boundary. I followed the gesture with my gaze, and saw small puffs of dark smoke in the distance. Thunder rolled again.

'Cannon fire,' Esmeralda said with conviction. 'I will never forget the sound. I have heard it in my dreams ever since the baronial uprisings against Ferrante, when I was a young woman.'

We watched, captivated by the horizon, not daring to speak further as we awaited the answer to a single question: Was this Ferrandino being welcomed, or the French announcing themselves?

I stroked my hand lightly over the stiletto hidden in my bodice, reassuring myself it was still there.

'Look!' Jofre shouted, with such abruptness that I started. 'Over there! Soldiers!'

Marching in loose formation, small, dark forms moved on foot over the gently rolling landscape towards the city. It was impossible to distinguish the colour of their uniforms, to ascertain whether they were Neapolitan or French.

Alfonso came to himself. 'Federico must know at once!' he exclaimed, and hastened to leave; Esmeralda called to him.

'Don Alfonso, I think he already does!' She gestured at the walls outside our own palace, where armed guards hurried into defensive positions. Even so, my brother departed to make certain.

For a long, dreadful moment those of us remaining squinted into the distance, not knowing whether we should welcome or fight those who made their way steadily towards the city and the royal palace.

Suddenly, hoisted above the approaching troops, I saw the banner: golden lilies against deep blue.

'Ferrandino!' I cried, then seized my husband and kissed him madly upon the lips and cheeks. 'See, it is our flag!'

Ferrandino's entry into Naples was far from joyous. The cannons I had mistakenly thought were fired by our own soldiers, announcing their arrival, had in fact been fired by angry barons lying in wait to attack the young prince. Although our rebellious nobles lacked the numbers and the weaponry to launch a serious campaign on their own, they managed to kill a few of our men. One of the cannon blasts startled Ferrandino's horse, so that he was almost thrown.

We family awaited him in the Great Hall. There were no flowers on this day, no tapestries or adornments of any kind; everything of value had been packed away in case of the need for swift flight.

Ferrandino was far different from the arrogant young man I had known as a girl. He was still handsome but exhausted and gaunt, humbled and aged by responsibility, war and disappointment. *All he wants are pretty girls to admire him and a soft bed*, old Ferrante had said years ago, but it was clear the prince had had neither for a very long time.

He entered the room. He had changed his tunic and washed

away the dust of travel, but his face was brown from sun, his dark hair and beard unkempt, untrimmed. Ferrante's daughter, Giovanna, then seventeen, dark-haired and voluptuous, threw her arms around him and they kissed with great passion. Despite the fact that she was his aunt, he had long ago fallen in love with her, and she with him; they were betrothed.

'My boy.' Federico was first of the brothers to embrace him warmly.

Ferrandino returned his and Francesco's embraces and kisses a bit wearily, then scanned the assembled group. 'Where is Father?'

'Sit down, Your Highness,' Federico said, his voice tinged with affection and sorrow.

Ferrandino glanced at him with alarm. 'Do not tell me he is dead.' Giovanna, standing on his other side, put a comforting hand upon his arm.

Federico's lips pressed together tightly to form a thin, straight line. 'No.' And as the young prince sat, the older muttered, 'Better though if he were.'

'Tell me,' Ferrandino commanded. He glanced at the rest of us, standing around the table, and said, 'Everyone, sit. And Uncle Federico, you speak.'

With a great sigh, Federico lowered himself onto the chair next to his nephew. 'Your father is gone, boy. Gone and sailed to Sicily, as best we can tell, and taken the Crown treasures with him.'

'Gone?' The prince stared at him, lips parted in disbelief. 'What do you mean? For his safety?' He looked round at our solemn-faced assembly, as if pleading for a word, a sign, to help him understand.

'Gone as in deserted. He left in the middle of the night without telling anyone. And he has left the kingdom without funds.'

Ferrandino turned wooden; for a long moment, he did not speak, did not look at anyone. A muscle in his cheek began to twitch.

Federico broke the silence. 'We told the people that King Alfonso decided to abdicate his throne in favour of you. It is the one way we can regain the trust of the barons.'

'They showed no trust today,' Ferrandino said tightly. 'They fired on us, brought down some men and horses. A few fools with swords even charged our infantry.' He paused. 'My men need food and fresh supplies. They cannot fight on empty bellies. They have been through enough. When they learn—'

He broke off and covered his face with his hands, then bent forward until his brow touched the table. All was silent.

'They will learn that you are the King,' I said, surprising even myself with my sudden, vehement words. 'And you will be a better King by far than my father ever was. You are a good man, Ferrandino. You will treat the people fairly.'

Ferrandino straightened and ran his hands over his face, forcing away his grief; Prince Federico directed a look of profound approval at me.

'Sancha is right,' Federico said, turning back to his nephew. 'Perhaps the barons mistrust us now. But you are the one man who can win their confidence. They will see that you are just, unlike Alfonso.'

'There is no time,' Ferrandino said tiredly. 'The French will soon be here, with an army more than thrice the size of ours. And now there is no money.'

'The French will come,' Federico agreed grimly. 'And we can only do our best when they do. But Jofre Borgia has written to his father, the Pope; we will get you more troops, Your Highness. And if I have to swim to Sicily with these tired old arms'—he held them out dramatically—'I will get you the money. That I swear. All we must do now is find a way to survive.'

Instinct propelled me to rise, to go to Ferrandino's side and kneel. 'Your Majesty,' I said. 'I swear fealty to you, my sovereign lord and master. Whatever I have is yours; I am entirely at your command.'

'Sweet sister,' he whispered, and clutched my hand; he drew

me to my feet, just as old Federico knelt and likewise pledged his loyalty. One by one, each family member followed suit. We were a small group, torn by fear and doubt over what would betide us in the coming days; our voices wavered slightly as we cried out:

Viva Re Ferrante!

But our hearts were never more earnest.

So it was that King Ferrante II of Naples came to power, without ceremony, a crown, or jewels.

VII

From the moment Ferrandino arrived, Naples was overrun by soldiers. The armoury lay just cast of the royal castle, along the shoreline, protected by the ancient Angevin walls and newer, sturdier walls erected by Ferrante and my father. From my bedchamber balcony, I had a direct view: never had I seen so much artillery, so many great heaps of iron balls the size of a man's head. During my lifetime, the armoury had been a mostly deserted place, filled with silent cannons rusted by salt and spray: now it was bustling and noisy as soldiers worked on the equipment, practised drills, and shouted to one another.

Our palace, too, was surrounded by the military. On the winter days when it was not too cool and the sun shone, I liked to take my meals on the balcony—but now I stopped the practice, for it was disheartening to see the soldiers lined up around the castle walls below, their weapons at the ready.

Each morning, Ferrandino was visited by his commanders. He spent his days closeted in the office that had been his grandfather's, then his father's, discussing strategy along with his generals and the royal brothers. He was only twenty-six years of age, but the lines in his brow were those of a man much older.

Of our military plans, I had only the news which Alfonso, who often attended the meetings, shared with me: that Ferrandino had posted royal decrees lowering the taxes on the nobles, promising rewards and the return of lands for those who remained loyal to the Crown and fought with us against the French. Word was spread that our father had willingly abdicated in favour of his son and had left Naples for a monastery, in order to do penance for his many sins. Meanwhile, we waited to hear from the Pope and the Spanish King, hoping for promises of more troops; Ferrandino and the brothers hoped the barons might be swayed by the decrees and send a representative, promising support. What Alfonso did not say—but which was clear to me—was that such expectations were founded on the deepest desperation.

With each passing day, the young King's expression grew more haunted.

In the meantime, Alfonso and Jofre engaged in swordplay as a method of easing the nerves that afflicted us all. Alfonso was the better swordsman, having been schooled in the Spanish fashion as well as being naturally more graceful than my little husband; Jofre was immediately impressed and made fast friends with him. Wishing always to please those in his company—which now included my brother—Jofre treated me with more respect and gave up visiting courtesans. The three of us—Alfonso, Jofre and I—became inseparable; I watched as the two men in my life parried with blunted swords, and cheered for them both.

I treasured those few pleasant days in the Castel Nuovo with a sense of poignancy, knowing they would not last long.

The end came at dawn, with a blast that shook the floor beneath my bed and jolted me awake. I threw off my covers, flung open the doors and ran out onto the balcony, vaguely aware that Donna Esmeralda was beside me.

A hole had been blown in the nearby armoury wall. In the greyish light, men lay half-buried in the rubble; others ran about shouting. A crowd—some of them soldiers, wearing our uniforms, others in commoner's clothing—stormed into the armoury through the breach in the stone and began to hack at the startled victims with swords.

I glanced at once at the horizon, anticipating the French. But there were no invading armies here, no dark figures marching across the sloping hills towards the town, no horses.

'Look!' Donna Esmeralda clutched my arm, then pointed.

Just below us, at the Castel Nuovo walls, the soldiers who had for so long guarded us now unsheathed their sabres. The streets outside the palace came alive with men, who emerged from every door, from behind every wall. They swarmed toward the soldiers, then engaged them; from beneath us came the sharp, high ring of steel against steel.

Worse, some of the soldiers joined with the commoners, and began to fight against their fellows.

'God help us!' Esmeralda whispered, and crossed herself.

'Help me!' I demanded. I dragged her back inside the bedchamber. I pulled on a gown and compelled her to lace it; I did not bother with tying on sleeves, but instead fetched the stiletto, and nestled it carefully into its little sheath on my right side. Deserting all decorum, I helped Esmeralda into a gown, then took a velvet bag and put what jewels I had brought with me into it.

By that time, Alfonso rushed into the chamber; his hair was dishevelled, his clothes hastily donned. 'It does not seem to be the French,' he said swiftly. 'I'm going at once to the King, to get his orders. Keep packing; you women must be sent to a safe place.'

I glanced at him. 'You are unarmed.'

'I will get my sword. First, I must speak with the King.'

'I will go with you. I have packed everything I need.'

He did not argue; there was no time. We ran together through the corridors as, outside, the cannon thundered again, followed by screams and moans. I imagined more of the armoury collapsing, imagined men writhing beneath piles of stones. As I passed the whitewashed walls, their expanse broken by the occasional portrait of an ancestor, the place that I had always considered eternal, mighty, impregnable—the Castel Nuovo—now seemed fragile and ephemeral. The high, vaulted ceilings, the beautiful arched windows latticed with dark Spanish wood, the marble floors—all I had taken for granted could, with the blast of a cannon, be rendered to dust.

We headed for Ferrandino's suite. He had not yet been able to bring himself to sleep in our father's royal bedroom, preferring instead his old chambers. But before we reached them, we found the young King, his nightshirt tucked into his breeches, scowling at Prince Federico in an alcove just outside the throne room. Apparently, the two men had just exchanged unpleasant words.

Federico, bare-legged and unslippered, still in his nightshirt, clutched a formidable-looking Moorish scimitar. Between the two men stood Ferrandino's top captain, Don Inaco d'Avalos, a stout, fierce-eyed man of the highest reputation for bravery; the King himself was flanked by two armed guards.

'They're fighting each other in the garrisons,' Don Inaco was saying, as Alfonso and I approached. 'The barons have reached some of them—bribery, I suppose. I no longer know which men I can trust. I suggest you leave immediately, Your Majesty.'

Ferrandino's expression was set and cold as marble: he had been preparing himself for this, but his dark eyes betrayed a glimmer of pain. 'Have those you deem loyal protect the castle at all costs. Buy us as much time as you can. I need your best men to escort the family to the Castel dell'Ovo. From there, we will need a ship. Once we are gone, give the order to retreat.'

Don Inaco nodded, and went at once to do the King's bidding.

As he did, Federico lifted the scimitar and pointed it accusingly at his nephew; I had never seen the old prince so red-faced with outrage. 'You are handing the city over to the French without a fight! How can we leave Naples at her hour of direst need? She has already been deserted once!'

Ferrandino stepped forward until the weapon's curved tip rested against his breast, as if he dared his uncle to strike. The guards who had flanked the King looked nervously at one another, uncertain as to whether they should intervene.

'Would you have us all stay, old man, and have the House of Aragon die?' Ferrandino demanded passionately. 'Would you have our army remain behind to be slaughtered, so that we never have a chance of reclaiming the throne? Think with your head, not your heart! We have no chance of winning—not without aid. And if we must retreat and wait for that aid, then we will do so. We are only leaving Naples for a time; we will never desert her. I am not my father, Federico. Surely you know me better by now.'

Grudgingly, Federico lowered the weapon; his lips trembled with an inexpressible mix of emotions.

'Am I your King?' Ferrandino pressed. His gaze was ferocious, even threatening.

'You are my King,' Federico allowed hoarsely.

'Then tell your brothers. Pack everything you can. We must leave as swiftly as possible.'

The old prince gave a single nod of assent, then hurried back down the corridor.

Ferrandino turned to Alfonso and me. 'Spread the word to the rest of the family. Take what is of value, but do not tarry.'

I bowed from the shoulders. As I did, the guard closest to me drew his sword and, too swiftly for any of us to impede him, plunged it into the gut of his fellow.

The wounded young soldier was too startled even to reach for his own weapon. He gazed wide-eyed at his attacker, then down at the blade that pierced him through, protruding from his backside, beneath his ribs.

Just as abruptly, the attacker withdrew the weapon; the dying man sank to the ground with a long sigh, and rolled onto his side. Blood rushed crimson onto the white marble.

Alfonso reacted at once. He seized Ferrandino and pushed the King away with great force, using his own body to block the assassin. Unfortunately, the guard had positioned us to his advantage: both Ferrandino and Alfonso were now backed into the alcove, without the opportunity for flight.

I shot a glance at the King, at my brother, and realized with panic that neither was armed. Only the soldier bore a sword—and he had no doubt been waiting for Don Inaco and Federico and his scimitar to leave.

The guard—a blond, scraggly-bearded youth with determination and terror in his eyes—took another step closer to my brother. I moved between them, to add another layer of protection, and faced the murderer directly.

'Leave now,' the guard said. He raised the blade threateningly and tried to affect a harsh tone, but his voice wavered. 'I have no desire to harm a woman.'

'You must,' I replied, 'or I will kill you.' *He is a boy*, I thought, *and afraid*. That realization caused a strange and sudden detachment to arise in me. My fear departed; I felt only a sense of disgust that we should be in this desperate situation, where one of us should have to live and one of us die, all for the sake of politics. At the same time, I was determined in my loyalty to the Crown. I would give my life for Ferrandino if need demanded it.

At my statement, he laughed, albeit nervously; I was a small female, and he a tall lad. I seemed an unlikely threat. He took yet another step, lowering his sword slightly, and reached out for me, thinking to pull me to him and fling me aside.

Something arose in me: something cold and hard, born of instinct rather than will. I moved towards him as if to embrace him—too close for him to strike at me with his long blade, too close for him to see me free the stiletto.

His body was almost pressed to mine, preventing me from launching a proper, underhanded blow. Instead, I raised the stiletto and struck over-handed, downward, slicing across his eye, his cheek, just grazing his chest.

'Run!' I shrieked at the men behind me.

The soldier in front of me roared in pain as he pressed a hand to his eye; blood trickled from between his fingers. Half-blinded, he lifted his sword and reared back, intending to bring it down upon my head, as if to split me in two.

I used the distance between us to find his throat. This was no time for delicacy: I stood on tiptoe and reached up, using my full strength to sink the dagger into the side of his neck. I pushed hard until I reached the centre, only to be stopped by bone and gristle.

Warm blood rained down onto my hair, my face, my breasts; I ran the back of my hand across my eyes in order to see. The young assassin's sword clanged loudly against the marble; his arms gyrated wildly for an instant as he staggered backwards, my dagger still protruding from his throat. The noises he emitted—the desperate wheezing, the frantic suction of flesh against flesh, mixed with bubbling blood, the effort yet inability to release a scream—were the most horrible I had ever heard.

At last he fell hard onto his back, hands clutching at the weapon lodged in his neck. The heels of his boots kicked against the floor, then slid up and down against it, as if he were trying to run. Finally, he let go a retching sound, accompanied by the regurgitation of much blood which spilled from the sides of his gaping mouth, and grew still.

I knelt beside him. His expression was contorted in the most terrifying way, his eyes—one punctured, red and welling with blood—wide and bulging. With difficulty, I pulled the weapon from his torn throat and wiped it on the hem of my gown, then replaced it in my bodice.

'You have saved my life,' Ferrandino said; I looked over to see him kneeling across from me, on the opposite side of the soldier's body, his face revealing both shock and admiration. 'I shall never forget this, Sancha.'

Beside him crouched my brother—pale and silent. That pallor and reticence came not from terror over the incident, I knew, but rather from the most recent event he had just witnessed: my removing the stiletto from my victim's throat, then casually wiping the blood on my gown.

It had been such an easy thing for me, to kill.

I shared a long look with my brother—what a ghastly sight I must have been, head and cheeks and breast soaked crimson—then glanced back down at the failed assassin, who stared up blindly at the ceiling. 'I'm sorry,' I whispered, even though I knew he could not hear me—but Ferrante had been right; it did help when the eyes were open. 'I had to protect the King.'

I reached out then, and placed my palm gently upon his cheek, where my stiletto had left its mark. His skin was soft still, and very warm.

Alfonso and the King armed themselves with swords from Ferrandino's chambers, then escorted me back to my rooms, though I had proven my ability to protect myself.

When Donna Esmeralda saw me—drenched from head to skirt with thickening blood—she screamed, and would have fallen had Alfonso not caught her. Once she learned I had not been harmed, she recovered remarkably. Jofre was there, too, having come searching for me, and he cried out my name with such fear and alarm I was quite gratified. Even after he learned I was well, he clasped my hand—undeterred by its sticky coating—and would not leave my side until the King gave the order.

Once the men had left—promising to return with instructions—Donna Esmeralda brought a basin of water and set to work bathing me.

As she dipped a cloth in the water, rosy and clouded from my victim's blood, she whispered, 'You are so brave, Madonna! His Majesty should give you a medal. What was it like, to kill a man?'

'It was . . . ' I paused, searching for the right words to describe my feelings. 'Necessary. Just something you do because it is necessary.' In truth, it had been remarkably simple. I began to tremble, not because I had taken a man's life, but because I had done so with ease.

'Here, here.' Donna Esmeralda draped a shawl around my

naked shoulders; I had thrown the damp gown on the floor, leaving it for an Angevin traitor or a Frenchman to find later and puzzle over. 'I know you are bold, but it has still been a great shock.'

I had no patience for coddling, however. I dressed again quickly, then rinsed my blade in the bloodied water, wiped it carefully, and resheathed it beneath my clean bodice. Only then did I help Esmeralda gather up our most vital belongings in a trunk. The costliest jewels I hid on my person, wrapping them tightly against my hips, beneath my skirts. Many beautiful things—fine fur coverlets, carpets, silk tapestries and brocade hangings, as well as heavy candelabra of silver and gold, paintings by old masters—had to be left behind for our enemies.

After that, there was nothing more to be done than wait, and calm ourselves each time the cannons roared.

Shortly before noonday, Jofre appeared with servants to carry our trunk, and a pair of armed guards. Out of a habit acquired before appearing in public, I smoothed my hair—only to discover it was stiff from remnants of dried blood.

Once again, I moved swiftly through the corridors of the Castel Nuovo: this time I did not allow myself the luxury of studying the walls and furnishings, of indulging in grief over what I was leaving behind. I kept my mind divorced from my emotions, with the former ascendant. We may have been in the midst of defeat—but I believed that Ferrandino was right, that it was only temporary. I did my best to bear myself with dignity and assurance, for the House of Aragon had never needed it more. Jofre, to his credit, walked beside me, his manner grave and intense, but revealing no fear.

At last, our little party arrived at the double doors leading to the enclosed courtyard, and paused while the guards hurried forward to open them.

Beside me, Donna Esmeralda broke into loud sobs.

I chided her at once. 'Save them for when we are alone,' I commanded. 'Walk with pride. We are not vanquished; we will return. And Naples will welcome us when we come.'

She obeyed, wiping her eyes upon her ample sleeve.

The doors opened onto a scene of the most utter disarray. The courtyard was filled beyond its capacity with people: distant relatives and noble acquaintances who had managed to find sanctuary inside the castle walls when the fighting had first begun, and frantic servants and employees who had deserted their posts and now realized they were about to be left behind at the mercy of the rebels. These two groups had been herded together and were now guarded at sabre-point by a contingent of our soldiers, in order to keep them away from the carriages prepared for our escape.

There were other soldiers as well—some recently expired, dragged off into corners, and some wounded, moaning with pain. Those who were whole surrounded the four enclosed carriages of the sort used for local trips around the city; these vehicles were encircled first by men on horseback, two abreast, then by foot soldiers. Our men were dressed for battle, in Spanish helmets with blue and gold plumes, and engraved plate armour covering their chests and backs.

Every bit of greenery had been trampled, including the first flowers of spring. Even the once-fragrant air was now filled with smoke from burning palazzos and the acrid, sulphurous stench of artillery. The sound of human voices, lifted in a chorus of desperation and terror, drowned out all else save the cannons.

As the guards genuflected, I stepped with the utmost regal bearing into the madness.

'Make way!' they cried out. 'Make way for the Prince and Princess of Squillace!'

A murmur traversed the crowd. Nearby soldiers turned and, with a sincerity and an admiration I did not understand, bowed low. 'Make way for Princess Sancha!'

So large was the gathering and so confined our surroundings that men stood pressed shoulder against shoulder; yet never was I jostled, never once was my personage touched.

A captain emerged from the assembly. 'Your Highnesses,' he said to me and my husband. 'His Majesty has requested that you accompany him.'

The captain himself led us past two of the carriages. Uncle Federico was pushing his brother into the first, with the same ferocity he had used to wield the scimitar earlier that morning. The weapon was in a scabbard at his hip now; every man, royal or not, bore arms.

The foot soldiers surrounding the King's carriage parted to permit us passage, and the horsemen flanking it reined their steeds back so that we could enter. As one of the guards proffered his arm so that I might climb up into the carriage, he said, as I touched him lightly: 'It is an honour, Your Highness. You are Naples' greatest heroine.'

Inside, I found Alfonso, Giovanna, and Ferrandino awaiting us. As dreadful as the situation certainly must have been for him, the young King managed a faint smile; he had overheard the guard's statement. 'Come, sit beside me, Sancha. I will feel safer. As you have no doubt realized, you have earned quite a reputation for your bravery today.'

In the face of such a statement, my composure wavered: I had not thought of my deed as an act of courage, but rather a disturbing symptom of my heritage. I lowered my eyes and stammered, as Jofre and Esmeralda entered the carriage behind me, 'It was mere accident that I was the only one with a weapon, Majesty. Had my brother been armed, he would have been first to defend you; and had you been armed yourself, we would have had no fear, given your skill as a swordsman.' I took my seat beside the King, who was flanked on his other side by Giovanna. Across from her sat Alfonso, then Jofre, with Esmeralda last, opposite me.

'Accident or not, because of you, we are here,' Ferrandino countered, 'and we are grateful. You are my lucky talisman now, Sancha.'

He fell silent as the carriage lurched; with the movement came the shouts of men, as lookouts from the towers above us relayed the circumstances outside the castle gates to the soldiers below. Apparently, our flight from the Castel Nuovo had been anticipated by enemy forces, for a large group of foot soldiers hurried to reinforce those already protecting our front.

Several guards ran to the gates and unbolted them; they swung open onto chaos.

Outside, our men fought traitors within their own ranks, as well as commoners and nobles. Once the gates opened, our reinforcements rushed into the fray with fearsome roars—and were soon engaged in swordplay so rapid my eyes could scarcely follow it.

Our carriage wheels rolled forward just past the archway, then settled with a creak to rest beneath the Triumphal Arch of Alfonso I. We were effectively trapped inside the unbarred courtyard while our protectors tried to hack their way through the enemy line at the gate.

I peered through the carriage window.

'Do not look!' Jofre warned, and Ferrandino echoed him.

'Do not look! I am sorry you women must be exposed to the harshness of war.'

But I was fascinated, just as I had been by Ferrante's museum of mummified corpses. I watched as an unarmoured Angevin nobleman, his fine brocade tunic damp with sweat and blood, his face soot-covered, wielded his sword mercilessly upon the infantryman farthest to my right. The noble was middle-aged, exquisitely trained; our soldier was young and terrified, and not long after being engaged, he stumbled slightly. It was enough for the older Angevin to move in for the kill, which he did, most efficiently: one stroke, two, and the young foot man turned, shrieking, to stare in horror at his right arm—which no longer bore a sword, or a hand, or an elbow. It was no more than a bleeding stump, and the lad fell back in a faint.

The noble parried his way past a second infantryman, then a third, by which time I could hear his victorious shout: 'Death to the House of Aragon! Death to Ferrandino!'

His lips were still rounded in the final 'O' when one of our horsemen—disconcertingly close to the window—leaned down with his sabre and neatly ran the width of his blade along the Angevin's shoulders, severing the head from the body.

The head toppled down, bouncing off the horse's flank, then beneath its hooves, which kicked it beneath our carriage; a swift gush of blood spewed from the decapitated corpse's neck, then its brocade-clad shoulders fell back and away. Our wheels attempted to roll forward and were obstructed as if by a great stone; the driver lashed his steeds until they pulled with all their might. With a great upward lurch, the carriage jolted over the Angevin impediment. Blessedly, the cacophony of battle drowned out the sound.

Across from me, Donna Esmeralda began a tremulous, impassioned prayer to San Gennaro for our safety; white-faced, Giovanna seized Ferrandino's arm and held it fast.

More swords flashed silver in the sun. I saw a commoner engage our men, and get run through for his efforts; I saw another of our foot soldiers wounded, this time in the thigh. He fought as long as he could, then fell for want of blood. Though I could not see his end, given the height of the carriage and the soldiers that blocked my line of sight, I saw the rebel who raised his sword, again and again, and hacked at the fallen man.

After a time, we began to move in earnest, and made our way out onto the street. I turned for a final look at the Castel Nuovo. The gates were still open wide, even though the last of the royal carriages had passed; Angevins and commoners swarmed beneath the Triumphal Arch. In vain, I searched for helmets with plumes of gold and blue.

I craned my neck even more: behind us, the armoury was fully ablaze, its stone walls jagged and gaping. Farther beyond, greyish haze rose from fires dotting the landscape near Vesuvio. One would have thought the volcano had belched smoke and flame on the city, but this time, it bore innocent, silent witness to the destruction wrought by man.

Before I could take in more, Alfonso, seated next to Esmeralda, spoke firmly. 'Leave it, Sancha. There is no point . . . '

He was right, of course. I forced myself to turn round and face forward, to censor the thoughts that tried to rise, of the pitiful people we had left behind in the courtyard, of my childhood home, abandoned to the enemy.

We clattered down the cobblestone streets. Our path took us directly along the coast. To my left lay the placid bay; to my right stood the exterior gardens of the royal palace, now a battlefield, and past them, the Pizzofalcone, on whose slopes Aragonese palaces burned. Behind me lay the city.

Our progress was steady but far from swift, given the size of our military escort. But our destination, the ancient fortress of the Castel dell'Ovo, which guarded the harbour of Santa Lucia, loomed ever closer. Now that we had passed through the thick of the fighting, for the first time I considered not what our family was leaving behind, but where we were going. Ferrandino had called for a ship: had he a destination in mind?

Were I King of a war-torn nation whose treasury had been stripped bare, there was but one place I would go. The notion caused me some trepidation—but I was immediately distracted by a sight that aroused my indignance: two commoners were running away from the royal palace, carrying the rolled-up Turkish carpet that had graced the floor of my father's office. Worse, a third man accompanied them, clutching in his arms the golden bust of Alfonso I from my grandfather's mantel.

My indignance did not last long. My ears filled with a booming, searing blast of wind: at the same instant, the carriage pitched sideways to the left, hurling me against Ferrandino and him against Giovanna; likewise, Esmeralda was thrown against my husband and brother. I cried out involuntarily at the shock, half-deafened, barely able to hear my own voice or the shrieks of the others.

Simultaneously, I was spattered with blood entering the window. For a breathtaking moment, we teetered on two wheels, propped against screaming men and horses. As all of us within the carriage clawed for purchase, soldiers rushed to push it: at last, it settled upright with a jolt.

Once we had collected ourselves, I stared out my window at the source of the commotion: a cannonball. It sat harmlessly now upon the cobblestone, but it had exacted a grisly toll. Beside it lay one of our riders, his thigh and the belly of his hapless mount sheared almost in half; the blood and bones and meat of man and horse mingled, impossible to distinguish.

Only one kindness had been granted them: both appeared to have been struck dead at once, for the young soldier's open eyes and composed expression showed intensity, but no sign of astonishment or fear; he still bore the reins in one clutched fist. The horse's large, handsome head was up, the bit still in his mouth, his eyes intelligent and bright; one of his front hooves was lifted gracefully, in preparation for the next prancing step. Each seemed, with the exception of their horrid, gaping wounds, a beautiful example of youth and strength.

I had wanted to be strong and perfect and brave, for the sake of the others, but I bowed my head, able to bear no more; in that fashion, I travelled the rest of the way to the Castel dell'Ovo. The image of the young rider and his mount accompanied me; indeed, it travels with me still.

I had grown up in Naples, but had never had cause to visit the homely keep named for Virgil's mythical egg. It was scarcely the place for a princess to entertain herself, being a great stone square, wider at the base than at the top, with no furnishings other than military weaponry; it had been constructed to serve as a lookout and first defence against those who invaded by sea, and a last refuge and defence against those who invaded by land. It smelled dank and forbidding; the worn, uneven brick steps were slippery with mildew.

Rather than stay in safer quarters below, I insisted on climbing to the top, where soldiers served as lookouts. Several cannons, accompanied by piles of iron balls, stood at each turret, ready to fire down into the city. All of us who had travelled in the carriages—including those in the family who had preceded and followed us—had been deeply shaken not just by the ignominy of forced retreat, but by the suffering we had witnessed. I could not bear to sit and mourn with Donna Esmeralda as we waited for rescue; instead, I distracted myself by looking out at the sea, for the ship that was to take us away.

There was no sign of it. For hours, there was no sign, and I paced restlessly upon the aged bricks of the terrace while, from time to time, Alfonso emerged from below and asked whether the boat had been spotted.

No, I told him again and again, and each time, he returned to the chamber downstairs, where the King and his general were engaged in discussions of strategy. I stared west, refusing to watch the destruction of the city behind me, and watched as the sun moved lower towards the horizon.

The final time he inquired about the ship, I demanded:

'Where are we going?'

He leaned forward and spoke in my ear, as if relaying a state secret that the soldiers were not to hear, even though his answer seemed so expected and obvious to me, it would have made no difference had he shouted it down into the streets. 'Sicily. They say the King there has granted Father refuge in Messina.'

I gave a single nod.

Soon it was dusk, and I went downstairs to see the family. Given the delay, we had all grown quite nervous as to whether the general had kept his word, and the ship was indeed on its way: but once the sun had completely set, a shout came from one of the lookouts.

We hurried down to the ship without protocol, without elegance, without fanfare. The vessel was small and fleet, designed for speed, not comfort; for safety's sake, she flew the yellow and red Spanish banner instead of the Neapolitan colours.

Despite Donna Esmeralda's urging that I come below, I stood on the deck as we set sail from Santa Lucia's harbour. Although it was night, the city glowed from the blazes that had been set, and the cannons lit up the sky like bursts of lightning, allowing me to pick out landmarks: the armoury and Santa Chiara, where my father had been crowned, were both aflame; the Poggio Reale, a magnificent palace built by my father when he was still Duke, was almost entirely consumed. I was relieved to see that the Duomo had, for the time being, survived.

As for the Castel Nuovo, it burned brightest of all. I could not help wondering how the people had reacted when they discovered Ferrante's museum.

I stood a long time watching on the deck, listening to the lap of the waves as Naples receded, a glittering, angry red jewel.

Spring–Summer 1495

VIII

We sailed due south through the warm waters of the Tyrrhenian Sea, and within a matter of days, arrived in Messina, once called *Zancle*, or 'sickle', by the Greeks due to its scythe-shaped harbour. I was grateful to see land; I did not travel well by sea, and this was the longest journey I had made on a sailing ship. My first two days were spent in misery.

Sicily had been ruled for the past twenty-seven years by King Ferdinand of Aragon, he who had joined his kingdom to that of his wife, Isabella of Castile, with the idea of uniting Spain. Besides his blood ties to my family, Ferdinand had good reason to be kindly to the Borgias. As Jofre explained it, when his father Rodrigo was still Cardinal of Valencia, Ferdinand sought Pope Sixtus IV's formal sanction of an Inquisition, by which he and Isabella hoped to rid their kingdom of all Moors and Jews, Christianized or not.

Sixtus flatly refused. Only after long, intense lobbying by the persuasive and powerful Cardinal Rodrigo Borgia did the Pope slightly relent—allowing the Inquisition to proceed in the province of Castile alone.

'King Ferdinand was so grateful for my father's help,' Jofre told me, with a naiveté that might have been touching had it not chilled me to the bone, 'that he lent his full support to my father's election as Pope.'

Ferdinand the Catholic, Rodrigo Borgia had always referred to the Spanish King thereafter.

After we set foot upon land and news of our flight from Naples had spread, we were welcomed by the Spanish ambassador, Don Jorge Zuniga. We had taken refuge at a barely adequate villa that left us sorely crowded, with the brothers sharing a bedchamber, Alfonso and Jofre another, and Giovanna, Esmeralda and I a third, so that Ferrandino had the privacy befitting a monarch.

Don Jorge appeared the night of our arrival. He cut a dashing figure, in a cape and matching tunic of bright carmine, with a quick, easy smile beneath a drooping black moustache. I believe he had expected a warm welcome from our family, and abject pleas for help; he certainly did not expect what he received.

'Your Highnesses,' he said, bowing low to us all, and removing a feathered velvet cap with a sweep of his arm. 'It is with great sorrow that I learned of the circumstances surrounding your journey to our fair island.' He paused. 'Our agents informed us of the uprising amongst the barons; we assume that they were emboldened by the events at Capua.' The city of Capua lay inland, not far to the north of Naples. 'The citizens there were so frightened by the size of Charles' army that they opened the gates and let the French enter at will.' He paused. 'His Majesty King Ferdinand welcomes you, and stands ready to offer whatever aid you require.'

Ferrandino sat in the centre of our assembled family, in a place of honour, while the rest of us stood out of deference to his rank. Don Jorge, however, failed to notice the significance of this, prompting Uncle Federico to growl at him:

'You will not address Ferrandino as His Highness any longer. He is now King Ferrante II of Naples.'

Don Jorge blinked in utter confusion, and began, 'But King Alfonso . . . ' Then, ever the diplomat, he sensed the disapproval emanating from us, and bowed a second time, directing the gesture at Ferrandino. 'Your Majesty. I humbly beg your pardon.'

'Granted,' Ferrandino said. Like the rest of us, he was exhausted, but projected an admirable air of authority. Even so, no amount of kingliness could erase the lines in his brow or the desperation in his eyes. His appetite remained poor, despite Giovanna's coaxing, and his cheekbones now stood out in startling relief. 'I do not know under what pretext my father came here to Messina; I can only assume that he was not forthcoming concerning the circumstances. I am also sure that you are a man of discretion, who can be trusted with the truth.'

'Of course,' the ambassador replied smoothly.

'My father deserted us in our hour of greatest need,' Ferrandino continued, 'and stole a great deal of money from the state. We are here to retrieve it.'

Uncle Federico, whose indignance had been slowly building, could no longer contain himself. 'You have been hosting a criminal! Is it not bad enough that your king did not supply us with troops in time . . . '

My half-brother turned on him and said sharply, 'That is enough, uncle. You will not interrupt our conversation again.'

Federico pursed his lips.

'We must offer our most abject apologies,' Don Jorge said. 'We assumed, when His Majesty—when His Highness Alfonso arrived, he did so for health reasons, to take advantage of our weather. We thought, most wrongly, that the family was aware of his arrival.' He paused, tilted his head to study us each in turn, then said, 'You are all royals here; I have no doubt you can all be trusted with the most confidential material.'

'They can,' Ferrandino affirmed.

'I bring you very good news for the House of Aragon. Your calls for help have not fallen on deaf ears, Your Majesty. The Pope, the Emperor, King Ferdinand, Milan, Venice and Florence have banded together to form a Holy League. I apologize that we were unable to inform you of this fact earlier; there was too great a danger that the French might have intercepted a message and learned of our plans. But an army surpassing that of Charles' will shortly be marching south from Rome to meet him.'

Ferrandino's expression and eyes softened abruptly, as if he were looking upon something inexpressibly tender, like a newborn son, or a much-adored lover; for an instant, I thought he might weep. Though moved, he collected himself sufficiently to say, in a low voice, 'God bless the Pope and the Emperor; and God bless King Ferdinand.'

Don Jorge arranged for carriages the following morning to take us to my father's refuge. Federico, however, suggested Ferrandino remain behind—'For,' as he said, 'it would not be seemly for the King to go begging for what is rightly his.' The plan was to shame—and if necessary, threaten—my father into coming to his new sovereign, pledging fealty, asking forgiveness, and, most importantly, turning over the Crown treasures, which were still necessary if our troops were to fight alongside the Holy League. Certainly, they would be necessary for the day to day running of the kingdom—a prospect for which we now had real hope.

Ferrandino—transformed into a younger-looking man by what was probably his first night's true rest in a year—agreed to Federico's plan. Our two uncles wanted to go alone on their mission, but my brother convinced them otherwise. 'Sancha and I must accompany you,' Alfonso insisted. 'We have a right to see our father and our mother, and ask them ourselves the reason for their actions.'

Thus, we all descended on the palazzo where the former Alfonso II now resided—a grand structure situated on a gentle slope above the harbour. Curiously, not a single guard stood watch at the unbarred gate; our own driver climbed down and swung it open wide, manoeuvred the carriage inside the courtyard, then secured the gate behind us.

Nor did servants greet us at the door. Don Federico opened it and called out loudly until two feminine voices chorused from a distance: 'Who is there?'

One belonged to Donna Elena, my mother's long-time lady-in-waiting; the other, to Madonna Trusia herself.

Uncle Federico stepped inside the entryway and thundered, 'No less than the House of Aragon! And we have come to set things aright!'

Trusia appeared in the corridor. She had weathered well; being younger than my father, she had at last reached the age where she was at her fullest womanly bloom, with ripe lips and well-sculpted cheeks beneath large eyes. I drew in a small, silent breath; after a time apart, I was amazed by my mother's beauty.

At the sight of us standing in the arching doorway, her face brightened at once, and she half-ran to greet us.

Her expression reflected naught but joy; it dimmed only when she registered our sombre—and in the case of Federico, hostile—demeanour.

'Your Highnesses,' she addressed the brothers, with a curtsy. Then she craned her neck to peer past them, at Alfonso and me. 'And my children! How I have missed you! Sancha—it has been so long!'

She opened her arms to me. Despite my hurt and disapproval, I went to her, and let myself be enfolded by them, let my cheeks be kissed—but I could not return the embrace. 'How?' I asked bitterly. 'How could you let yourself be party to such a terrible thing?'

She drew back, puzzled. 'Your father is ill. How could I abandon him? Besides, his guard compelled me to accompany him.'

Before I could press her further, Alfonso sought out her embrace. His response was more trusting—but still distant. He clearly believed her incapable of wrongdoing, and was waiting for an explanation.

Uncle Federico was disgusted. 'We have not come here for reunions. A crime against the realm has been committed—a crime, Madonna, in which you share complicity.'

My mother paled visibly, and laid a hand to her throat. 'It is true, Alfonso abandoned his throne—but he did not know what he was doing. I swear before God, Your Highness, I was not aware of his intention to flee until the very night I was forced at sword-point to join him.' She paused, then straightened and assumed a slight air of defiance. 'His only crime is madness. He needs my help, Don Federico. In retrospect, I would have come freely with him. If there was any crime, it was mine alone, in not writing to you to explain the circumstances. But until this morning, when the guards fled, I was not at liberty to do so.'

Federico studied her with a hawk-like gaze for a long moment. He had always liked Trusia; indeed, she had never earned the mistrust of anyone in the court. At last he spoke, his tone solemn and calm. 'Donna Trusia, let us go inside, where we can speak privately.'

'Of course.' She led us to a chamber where she was given leave to sit with us. Prince Federico told her the entire sad tale—of the Crown treasures missing, of Ferrandino returning to discover Naples had neither King nor funds for his soldiers, of our perilous flight from the rebels.

Trusia was shocked by our news. When she recovered herself, she said, 'You all know I am not given to deceit. I would never support such heinous thievery. Perhaps I am a fool and alone in my ignorance; this morning I was surprised to find that all the servants, with the exception of Donna Elena, had gone. Last night, we heard the rumour that you had arrived in Messina.'

'They knew,' my brother responded, 'and feared recompense.'

'Indeed,' Federico interjected with vehemence, 'if I find them, I will see them hanged for treason.' He calmed himself. 'For now, we must recover the Crown treasures, assuming that no one has made off with them. They are our only hope; without them, Ferrandino has no chance of recovering and holding the throne.'

My mother's reply was simple. 'Tell me what I must do.'

. . .

We were led to the room where my father now spent his days—alone, Trusia said, save for those few times when he made a request of a servant, or had a peculiar question for his mistress. At the door, my mother turned to Federico and Francesco, her expression pleading. 'You remember how he was in the days before we left . . . '

'Yes,' Francesco replied. His manner was kindlier, more sympathetic than Federico's. 'Bedridden. Confused. But there were times we could consult him on matters, when he was quite lucid.'

'Those times are past,' my mother answered sadly. 'He does not remember coming here, or comprehend his situation. You will need diplomacy and patience if you are to recover the treasure.'

She opened the door.

Inside was a vast chamber, sparsely furnished. Its most notable feature was a very broad arched window, spanning from ceiling to floor, and providing a magnificent view of Messina's harbour.

On the opposite wall stood a very large, ornately carved wooden chair; above it hung a massive wrought iron candelabrum holding some two-score tapers. The combination resembled a throne beneath a canopy; and in the chair sat my father.

His visage startled me. His hair had turned from almost entirely black to mostly grey, and his complexion had taken on the ashen pallor of one who shunned all light. He was noticeably thin, and his royal garb—a blue silk tunic embroidered with gold thread, and a sash decorated with medals from Otranto—hung loosely on his frame.

He had been staring vacantly out the window; when we entered, he gave us the most cursory of glances, as if he still saw us every day, as if he had never left Naples under cover of night.

'Yes?' he demanded imperiously; and when, after a pause, all of us—even the vociferous Federico—remained speechless, he stamped his foot in irritation. 'Do not stand there gaping! Bow, and address me properly!'

Anger flared in Federico's eye. Ignoring Trusia's warning look, he stepped forward. 'I will not bow. But I will address you properly—Your Highness. For that is what you are: a prince who has given up his right to be King.'

My father's face reddened with fury; he pointed accusingly at his brother and exhorted the rest of us: 'Seize that man, and punish him for his impudence!'

Another moment of silence passed; Federico faced my father with a hard little smile. 'Your orders are no good here, Alfonso. Don't you remember? You abandoned your throne. You left us to face the French alone, and sailed here with Trusia. You gave up your right to the Crown when you fled like a coward, and stole the money Ferrandino needed for our troops.'

Eyes ablaze, my father rose. 'I am King of the two Sicilies, and you will show me the proper respect!'

'Stop playing the madman! Naples and Sicily have been separate kingdoms for generations,' Federico countered heatedly. 'Your *son* is now King, and you had best go begging on your knees to him for your life, for you have committed nothing less than treason!'

My father's face contorted with rage. 'Liar!' he screamed. 'Guards—!' He turned to Trusia indignantly. 'Where are the guards? Have them seize this man!'

'The guards are all gone,' Trusia answered softly.

'Listen carefully to me,' Federico said. 'There is only one way you can save your life. Tell us where the Crown treasures are, and we will leave you in peace.'

'Not only a liar, but a thief,' my father sneered. 'You would steal my crown. My sword! Trusia, bring me my sword!' In his agitation, he moved away from his chair and swung a fist at Federico; the latter ducked, missing the blow, but his temper had been ignited. The two brothers locked arms, wrestling, glaring at each other, each panting with the effort to break free from the other's grasp.

'You're as mad as Father!' Federico shouted. 'Even madder!'

'I'll kill you myself!' my father shrieked.

My brother Alfonso stepped into the fray; with the help of Francesco, he prised the two apart.

'Take him from my sight!' my father screamed, and retook his imaginary throne. Madonna Trusia hurried to his side, whispered something in his ear, then made her way over to where Alfonso and Francesco were still trying to calm Federico.

'He is too agitated now,' she said. 'We will need to try a different approach.' She gestured for us to leave, then returned to my father's side and stroked his arm soothingly.

Grudgingly, Federico let himself be led outside, where the rest of us contemplated what to do next.

'Logic holds no sway here,' Alfonso said. 'He cannot be reasoned with. We must play along with his beliefs in order to get what we want.'

'He is weak,' Federico countered. 'Accuse him of treason, show him the rope, and he will break.'

Alfonso shook his head. 'You saw him—you two will only come to blows again. It is time for a different approach.'

'It's true, Federico.' Francesco spoke up, in a rare display of disagreement with his older brother. 'That was no pretence—he has gone mad.'

At that instant, Madonna Trusia emerged from the chamber and quietly shut the door behind her. 'Don Francesco is right. I have calmed him sufficiently, but I think it would be wise for you brothers to remain outside.' She looked at my brother and me. 'Alfonso, Sancha . . . If you go to your father, and tell him the treasures are necessary to save the kingdom— the kingdom he believes he still rules—perhaps he will give them to you. He trusts you.'

I shook my head. 'Let Alfonso go. Father trusts him—but he will not listen to anything I have to say. He despises me.'

She jerked her head slightly, as if my words themselves were a slap, then gazed at me with a disbelief that outweighed my own. 'Your father has always admired you. Why, he has always told me that, had you been born a man, you would be the man he would want to become.'

Anger laced with longing rose in me. *Then why did he never tell me so? Why has he always treated me with the utmost contempt? Why delight in hurting me?*

My emotional struggle must have shown on my face, for my mother came to my side and gently took my hand. 'Come,' she said, in a tone that comforted and conferred courage. 'I will lead you and Alfonso inside. Let your brother do most of the speaking, and all will go well.'

We three returned to the chamber.

'Your Majesty,' my mother said, ignoring my discomfort at her use of the term. 'Look, your children have come to visit you.'

The former King Alfonso II had been regal and controlled when all of us had entered together. But now, as he sat in his phantom throne staring out at Messina's harbour, his shoulders, once so straight, were slightly hunched, and in his eyes was a disturbing vagueness.

'Vesuvio,' he remarked, frowning at the vista. 'This window has a dreadful view; I can't see Vesuvio. We will have to hire an architect to remedy that.'

'Certainly,' Madonna Trusia said. 'Your Majesty, Don Alfonso and Donna Sancha have come to see you.' And she stepped back, directing a nod at my brother.

'Your Majesty,' Alfonso stated, his voice distinct and loud. 'I must speak to you regarding a matter of extreme urgency.'

My father grunted, and at last took his gaze from the window and turned it upon his youngest child. 'Alfonso. You seem to have become a man.'

'Yes, Sire.'

'Have you married yet?'

'No.' My brother paused. 'There is great trouble in Naples, Father. The barons are in revolt, and the French have invaded. Our troops have desperate need of funds; we must borrow from the Crown treasure. It is the only way to keep the throne safe.'

My father's gaze swept over me. 'And Sancha. You married the Pope's little bastard. Tell me, has he yet grown a beard?'

I felt a rush of temper, but guarded my tongue; I also felt sorrow, to see the man reduced thus. My father's cold, unyielding cruelty had destroyed his kingdom, and separated him from his family and his sanity. Only my mother remained loyal.

'He is older,' I replied softly.

My father nodded, then stared back out the window at the foreign coastline. 'How much of it is required?' he asked suddenly.

'A great deal,' my brother replied. 'But I will take only what is needed.'

'There is the matter of a key . . . ' My father murmured. He gestured for Alfonso to approach him—then took notice of me and my mother standing nearby. 'The women must leave,' he commanded.

My mother bowed; I followed suit, then left with her to join the brothers, who waited anxiously out in the corridor.

'He trusts Alfonso,' Trusia told them. 'I think we will meet with success.'

Her instincts were correct. Only a moment later, my brother emerged from the chamber, alone and smiling. In his hand, he held a golden key.

The key did in fact unlock the closet where my father had hidden the treasures; and I reflected on how my mother's and brother's gentleness and patience had led to our salvation, when anger and demands had failed. Once again, I resolved to be less headstrong, to be more like my sweet-natured brother.

Ferrandino and Uncle Federico argued over whether or not to leave sufficient funds to keep my father comfortable in his madness; Federico wanted to leave nothing, but in the end, the King's wishes were obeyed. Ferrandino turned over a reasonable sum to my mother, with instructions to use it frugally.

We spent only a few restless weeks in Messina. During that

time, the Spanish ambassador brought us three separate pieces of amazing news. The first, which we had both expected and dreaded, was that our exhausted forces in the Castel dell'Ovo had finally surrendered to the French: Virgil's egg had cracked.

The second revelation was one that gave Jofre great relief, and put us all in good humour. I had never forgiven Pope Alexander for surrendering to King Charles so easily, or for handing over his son, Cesare, to ride with the French as a hostage. Cesare and Alexander were cunning, however; before the army ever entered Naples, Cesare escaped the French army one night, taking with him as much of the stolen spoils of war as he could manage. This he did by bribing a number of Charles' soldiers to help him.

The third message followed with surprising swiftness on the heels of the second. Hearing of the formation of the Holy League—with its formidable army far outnumbering his own—Charles VIII took fright, and retreated from Naples several weeks after invading it, leaving a single garrison behind. (This news revealed even more of the Pope's and Cesare's shrewdness; the latter had taken care to absent himself before King Charles learned of the League.) It brought Ferrandino no small amount of pleasure to learn that *il Re Petito* was a vicious little man, who treated our rebellious barons so badly that they turned their swords against the French and now called for the return of the House of Aragon.

This inspired Ferrandino to make plans to join his encamped forces, commanded by Captain Don Inaco d'Avalos, on the island of Ischia in the Bay of Naples. Ischia was a short distance from the city's coastline, easily allowing the King to launch attacks on the mainland.

I was determined to go with him, and Jofre dared raise no objections—I was so filled with optimism that I expected we would return home, triumphant, within days. Alfonso also decided to go to Ischia, in case his skill as a fighter was required; Francesco and Federico, chose to remain behind in Sicily until Naples was freed.

The night before we were to set sail, I called upon Madonna Trusia. We sat together in her small antechamber while my father sat in the darkness in his imaginary throne room, staring out at the lights reflecting on the dark waters of Messina's harbour.

'Come with us,' I urged. 'Alfonso and I have missed you terribly. There is nothing here for you anymore; Father is not even aware of who surrounds him. We can hire servants to care for him.'

Wistful, she shook her head, then lowered her face and stared down at her pale, graceful hands, placed one atop the other in her lap. 'I miss you both as well. But I cannot leave him. You do not understand, Sancha.'

'You are right,' I said curtly. I was furious with my father, for the spell he had cast over her, for the fact that, even insane and seemingly helpless, he was able to make such a good person miserable. 'I do not understand. He has betrayed his family and his people, yet you remain loyal to him. Your children adore you, and will do everything possible to make you happy; all he can give you is hurt.' I hesitated, then with great emotion, asked the question that had troubled me my whole life. 'How could you ever have loved a man so cruel?'

Trusia lifted her chin at that, and regarded me intensely; her voice held a trace of indignance, and I understood that the depth of her love for my father transcended all else. 'You speak as though I had a choice,' she said.

We reached Ischia in the fullness of spring; it was round and rugged, covered with olive trees, fragrant pines, and a profusion of flora that had earned it the nickname 'The Green Island'. The landscape was dominated by Monte Epomeo, which erupted every few centuries, rendering the soil dark and fertile.

Jofre, Alfonso and I stayed with Ferrandino in the isolated grand Castello connected to the main island by a bridge built by my great-grandfather, Alfonso the Magnanimous. There was little to do as April bled into May, then May into June, save pray (with a sceptic's faithlessness) for our army as they made forays onto the mainland. The campaigns went well: our losses were few, for we now had the barons' support as well as that of the Holy League. The French were disheartened.

Neither Jofre nor Alfonso were needed to fight—to their disappointment, I suspect, and to my deep relief. We three again became inseparable; we dined together, visited the small towns—Ischia and Sant'Angelo—and the hot mineral springs, reputed to be good for the health.

But I began each morning alone, with a walk down to the beach of fine sand, and stared across the calm waters of the bay. On clear days, Naples' curving coastline was visible; Vesuvio stood like a beacon, and I could just make out the Castel dell'Ovo, a small, dark dot. I stood so long I grew brown from the sun; Donna Esmeralda often came after me, scolding, and forced me to cover my head with a shawl.

On foggy days, I still went out, and like my father, vainly sought a glimpse of Vesuvio.

I had thought myself homesick in Squillace—but then, I had been certain of a home to which I could return. Now I knew not whether the palace in which I had spent my childhood stood. I yearned for Santa Chiara and the Duomo as if they were loved ones, and feared for their safety. I thought of the graceful ships in the harbour with their bright sails, of the courtyard gardens, which—had they not been destroyed—now would have been in full bloom, and my heart ached.

Ferrandino met constantly with his military advisors. We saw almost nothing of him until the month of July, when my husband, brother and I were summoned to his office.

He sat at his desk; beside him stood his Captain, Don Inaco, and I knew from the brilliant, satisfied smiles on the faces of both men what news the King was about to share with us.

Ferrandino could scarcely restrain himself; even before we had finished bowing, he spoke, his tone giddier than I had ever heard it. 'Pack your trunks, Your Highnesses.'

'Mine was never unpacked,' said I.

Summer 1495–
Late Spring 1496

IX

Our journey across the Bay of Naples was swift. Indeed, it took more time for servants to load our ship with provisions and belongings than it took to sail from Ischia into the harbour of Santa Lucia.

Our royal entourage, consisting of His Majesty Ferrandino, his betrothed, Giovanna, Jofre, Alfonso, and me, boarded the vessel in exceedingly high spirits. As the ship launched, Alfonso had bottles of wine and goblets brought, and we repeatedly toasted the King, the House of Aragon, and the city to which we were returning. Those were the most joyous moments of my life; I believe they were for Ferrandino as well, for his eyes had never been so bright, nor his smile so broad. At an impetuous instant, he seized Giovanna round her waist, pulled her to him, and kissed her passionately—much to the delight of our cheering assembly.

Jofre made light of the preacher Savonarola and his dire predictions that Charles VIII would bring about the end of the world. 'My father, His Holiness, has commanded Savonarola to come to Rome and defend his view of the Apocalypse—which seems to have been a bit premature. Savonarola, coward that he is, pleads illness and says he cannot make the journey.'

We roared as Jofre suggested a new toast: 'To Savonarola's continued ill health.' I was glad that Esmeralda was below deck, so that she could not hear the insult to the priest she so revered.

As we drew closer to the Neapolitan coastline, silence overtook us. Vesuvio, which during our exile had come to represent for me a beacon of hope, still held vigil over the city: but its dusky purple was the lone spot of colour in a once-verdant landscape now reduced to cinders. The fields, the slopes, all of which should have been abloom with flowers, bright with ripening crops, were blackened, as though the great mount had erupted once again.

Only Ferrandino still smiled; he had seen this devastation before, in forays with his captains. 'Have no despair,' he told us. 'The French may have ensured we would have no harvest this season—but the fires they set will enrich the soil, and bring us bountiful yield next year.'

Even so, the rest of us remained quiet and disturbed. As we pulled into the harbour alongside the charred skeletons of ships, the Castel dell'Ovo—its solid, ancient stone unmarred—was a reassuring sight. I stared anxiously into the city proper, past the jagged, war-torn walls, and clutched Alfonso's arm excitedly.

'Look!' I cried. 'The Church of Santa Chiara still stands! And the Duomo!' It was true: despite the flames I had seen emerging from her, the exterior of Santa Chiara was nearly unscathed, save for streaks of soot. The Duomo appeared untouched.

But as our little family rode together in a carriage, headed for the Castel Nuovo, I struggled to hide my grief and hatred—nor was I alone. Even Ferrandino's expression had grown grim; Giovanna was fighting tears, and Alfonso kept his face turned to the window.

It was a short ride from the harbour to our destination—but even that brief distance allowed us to view some of the destruction wrought by the French. Palace after palace, commoners' dwellings, all of them had been scorched, reduced to rubble by cannon fire, or both. The armoury, once filled with artillery and soldiers, protected by a double thickness of walls, was nothing more than a blackened heap of stones and trapped, festering corpses.

Giovanna covered her nose. I could not help noticing that, along with the usual perfume of salt water that I so loved, the Bay now released a subtle but ghastly smell—that of rotting flesh. Apparently, it was easier to be rid of the dead by feeding them to the waves instead of the earth.

The walls surrounding the Castel Nuovo wore a madman's uneven, gap-toothed grin. 'No matter,' Ferrandino said, and pointed overhead. 'Look who greets us.' I gazed upward, and for the first time since arriving in Naples, smiled; the Triumphal Arch of Alfonso I still stood proud and unscarred, and our carriage rode beneath it, past the waiting guards who held the gate open for our entry.

Inside the courtyard, now a pile of trampled earth denuded of its gardens, a captain left his contingent of soldiers and ran up to the carriage, opened the door, and bowed. 'Welcome, Your Majesty,' he said, and assisted Ferrandino down. 'We must apologize for the state of the royal palace. We had hoped to have it ready for your arrival today, but unfortunately, most of the servants who worked here were killed. We have been forced to recruit untrained commoners and impoverished nobles, and they have been slow to repair the damage.'

'It matters not,' Ferrandino replied graciously. 'We are glad to be home.'

But any happiness I felt upon being ushered in through the great doors soon fled. The captain led us towards the throne room, where the seneschal was to meet with the King and discuss plans for restoring the palace and dealing with the local famine. We passed through corridors scarred from the bite of duelling blades, and darkened by spatters of blood. Portraits of our ancestors had been cut from their frames and slashed; the golden frames had been stolen, the shreds of painted canvas left upon the floors. Statues, carpets, tapestries, sconces—all the things I had known since childhood, and thought permanent, as eternal as my family's right to the Crown, had been stolen. We walked on bare floors, past bare walls.

'They have taken everything,' Giovanna said bitterly. 'Everything.'

Ferrandino's tone was surprisingly hard. 'It is the way of war. Nothing can be done; complaints serve no good.'

She fell silent, but the hatred in her eyes did not ease.

In the alcove where I had killed the traitorous guard, blood still stained the floor and walls; the signs of my murderous act had yet to be cleaned away.

Our arrival in the throne room only increased my resentment. The windows that looked out upon the harbour had been broken, leaving jagged shards; empty wine bottles had been smashed in every corner. Peasant women were frantically sweeping up the glass with brooms.

'His Majesty, King Ferrandino,' the captain announced. The women stopped their work, so overwhelmed to see the King with his courtiers that one crossed herself instead of genuflecting. Another maidservant knelt on the top step leading to the throne, and was scrubbing the bare seat vigorously with a rag; she turned from the waist and bowed as best she could. The great chair itself had been hacked at; deep nicks in the arms and legs marred the pattern carved in the wood.

The throne cushion lay to one side on the floor; it had been slashed and stained with a dark liquid I thought at first was blood. I moved over to it, peered down, and recoiled at the smell of urine.

'Your Majesty, Your Highnesses!' the maidservant cried. 'Forgive me. There were so many things to clean—the French committed unspeakable acts, everywhere in the palace, before they fled. They even befouled the throne.'

'The only way the French could befoul our throne,' I countered swiftly, 'would be to set King Charles' twisted little arse upon it.'

At this, everyone in our company laughed, though there was little humour in the sound.

The doors to the King's office lay open; inside, Ferrante's great desk had been chopped into a pile of kindling, the unused remainder stacked beside the fireplace. A few rustic chairs, confiscated from a commoner's house, replaced the finer pieces which had once graced the chamber. The seneschal stood waiting.

'I apologize for the conditions, Your Majesty,' he said. 'It will take some time for us to import proper furniture.'

'It matters not,' Ferrandino replied, and went inside for his meeting.

The rest of us returned to our old chambers to oversee the unpacking of our belongings. I had not expected any of my furnishings to remain, but I had not expected to see Donna Esmeralda—who had sailed upon the same ship with us, but ridden in a different carriage with the other attendants—sitting on the floor in my bedchamber, her skirts swirled about her, a look of hatred on her face.

'Your bed,' she said, seething. 'Your fine bed. The bastards set it afire; there is smoke all over the ceiling.'

I was taken aback; I had never heard her use such language. But her husband had been killed fighting the Angevins—men of French descent, and probably no different in her eyes from those who had marched with Charles.

'It matters not,' I echoed Ferrandino. 'It matters not, because the bastards are gone, and we are here.'

And in Naples I remained. The first few months were difficult. Food was scarce and given the expense of rebuilding, the seneschal would not permit us to import wine or rations; we depended greatly on the few local huntsmen and fishermen who had survived the war. We drank water, and made do without our customary retinue of servants; often, I helped Donna Esmeralda, now my only attendant, perform menial tasks.

Yet each day brought improvement, and we were filled with optimism, especially since Ferrandino had the support of his people.

Then, in a chance moment of frustration, Jofre, tired of all the deprivation, said that we would be better off in Squillace. I at once requested an audience with Ferrandino, and quickly received permission to see him.

By that time, he had a desk—though not as grand a one as its predecessor—and a proper chair. He was in an expansive mood; now that the kingdom had stabilized, and sporadic fighting ceased, he had set the date for an official coronation ceremony and his wedding to Giovanna. He sat and listened as I said:

'You once told me my presence brought you good luck. Do you believe that?'

He smiled, and with a hint of teasing in his voice, replied, 'I do.'

'Then let me and my husband remain in Naples. Make it an official decree, that I should not have to return to Squillace unless emergency requires it.'

His gaze became serious. 'I told you once, Donna Sancha, that you could request anything of me and you would have it. This is a small favour to ask, and one that I will grant without hesitation.'

'Thank you.' I kissed his hand. I believed then that I had finally undone my father's heartless trick, and that I was at last safely home to stay.

My husband was displeased by the promise I exacted from Ferrandino, but lacked the courage to protest. Autumn came—and with it, according to Jofre, a papal brief ordering the doomsayer Savonarola to cease preaching, a writ the wild-eyed preacher ignored. Winter followed. By Christmas, the Castel Nuovo had begun to resemble its former self. We did our best to aid the poor and the starving, made so by Charles' destruction of that year's harvest; as for us royalty, we enjoyed our first decent feast to celebrate the Nativity.

By then, Donna Esmeralda and I were sleeping on an actual bed, and the windows in the palace had been repaired or covered with heavy cloth to keep out the chill air. Drowsy after our Christmas feast, I had gone to lie down when Esmeralda called to me from the outer chamber.

'Donna Sancha! Madonna Trusia is here!'

'What?' I sat up, fogged by sleep. For a moment, the announcement seemed very natural; it was Christmas, and my mother had come to visit her children, just as she did every holiday. I had forgotten that she had gone to Sicily; I had even forgotten about the uprising, and the French.

'*What?*' I repeated, this time properly startled, as my waking memory returned. I pulled a wrapper around my shoulders and hurried into my antechamber.

In the instant before I laid eyes upon my mother, I hoped that she had come to her senses, had accepted my offer to come and live in Naples. My heart ached to think of her, cut off from the world, trapped with a man who might have loved her in his tortured way, but had never known how to demonstrate that love properly; now that he had gone mad, he could not even acknowledge her presence.

One glance at Madonna Trusia drew from me a horrified gasp. I expected a smiling, radiant beauty; instead, standing just inside the doorway next to Donna Esmeralda was a stricken old woman dressed in black. Even her golden hair was veiled, like the sun blotted out by storm clouds. She was frail, thin, with an ashen pallor and grey shadows beneath her eyes. It was as though all my father's misery and pain had been transferred to her, sapping the joy and comeliness that had been hers.

My mother sagged into the nearest chair and spoke to Esmeralda without looking at either of us. 'Fetch my son.'

Beyond that, she said no more; she did not need to, for I knew at once what had happened. I pulled a chair close to hers, and took her hand; she bowed her head, unwilling to meet my gaze. We sat in silence, waiting. I felt a constricting ache at the base of my throat, but did not permit myself to cry.

After a time, Alfonso appeared. He, too, took a single glance at our mother and knew at once what had transpired. 'He is dead?' he whispered.

Trusia nodded. My brother knelt before her and hugged her skirts, his head in her lap. She stroked his hair; I looked on, an outsider, for my greatest sorrow was not my father's death, but the suffering it provoked in the two I loved most.

At last Alfonso raised his head. 'Was he ill?'

My mother put a hand to her mouth and shook her head; for a long moment, she could not speak. When she at last had a measure of control, she lowered her hand, and in a tone that seemed rehearsed, began to tell the tale.

'It was three weeks ago . . . He had seemed to come to himself previously, to realize what had occurred—but then he stopped sleeping altogether, and the madness returned worse than ever. He was angry, restless, often pacing and shouting, even when he was alone in his favourite chamber. You remember the room—the one with the great chair, and the sconce above it.

'That night,' she continued, with increasing difficulty, 'I was awakened by a great groaning, scraping sound coming from Alfonso's chamber. I feared he might have hurt himself, so I hurried to see him at once . . . I took a taper since he always sat in darkness.

'I found him pushing his chair across the room, and when I asked him why he was doing so, he answered irritably, "I have grown weary of the view." What else could I do?' She paused, filled with sudden remorse. 'The attendants were all aslumber, so I set down the candle and helped him as best I could myself. When he was satisfied, I left him in the darkness.

'I went back to bed, strangely agitated. I could not sleep—and only a few moments later, I heard another noise—this one not as loud, but there was something about it . . . Something so that I *knew* . . . ' She put her hands to her face and bowed beneath the weight of the memory.

From thence, she was only able to speak haltingly, so I summarize here what she relayed:

My father had carried in a second chair, one much lighter than the one he had used as a delusional throne, and set it beneath the heavy wrought-iron sconce suspended from the ceiling, then stepped onto its seat. He had procured a length of rope; this he knotted to his royal sash, which bore upon it jewels and medals won for his victories at Otranto.

The rope he fastened securely to an arm of the sconce; the sash he wrapped snugly about his neck.

The sound my mother heard was that of the lighter chair being kicked over.

The heart ofttimes knows things before the mind deduces them; the impact of wood hitting marble evoked in Trusia such alarm that she rushed, without wrapper or candle, into my father's chamber.

There, in the faint light of the stars and the beacon of Messina's harbour, she saw the dark form of her lover's body, rotating slowly in the noose.

Expressionless, toneless, my mother proclaimed, 'I can never rest now, for I know he suffers in Hell. He is in the Forest of the Suicides, where the Harpies nest, for he hanged himself in his own house.'

Still kneeling before her, Alfonso gently caught her hands. 'Dante is pure allegory, Mother. At worst, Father is in purgatory, for he did not know what he was doing. He did not even know he was in Messina when I spoke to him. No man would condemn another for an unknowing act—and God is more compassionate and wiser than any man.'

My mother looked up at him with an expression of pathetic hope, then turned to me. 'Sancha, do you believe this is possible?'

'Of course,' I lied. But if one put any faith in Dante, King Alfonso II would right now be in the seventh circle of Hell, in the river of blood which boiled the souls of those 'tyrants who dealt in blood and plunder'. If there were any justice, he would be trapped next to his sire, Ferrante, torturer, creator of the museum of the dead.

There was one other place he belonged—in the farthest depths of Hell, in Satan's jaws, the place reserved for the greatest traitors. For he had betrayed not just his family, but his entire people. There was no brimstone there, no fire, no heat—only the worst cold of all, cruel and bitter.

As cold as my father's heart, as cold as the look I had so often seen in his eyes.

My mother remained in Naples and recovered slowly from her sorrow. For myself, I prayed out of desperation to a God I doubted: *Keep my heart from evil; let me not become as my father was.* After all, I had already killed a man. Often I woke, gasping, feeling a spray of warm blood upon my brow, my cheeks, imagining that I wiped my eyes and gazed at the amazement in my victim's dying eyes. *A noble act*, everyone said. I had saved the King. Perhaps I had saved Ferrandino, but there was still nothing noble in the taking of a life.

Despite the tragedy of my father's death—the circumstances of which were hidden from the public and the servants and never discussed again within our family—life in Naples grew happy once more. Ferrandino and Giovanna were married in a glorious royal ceremony, the palace was refurbished and became once more a luxurious dwelling, and the gardens began to grow back. Under Alfonso's influence, Jofre became a dutiful husband.

Five months passed. By May of the year 1496, I had just grown comfortable in my contentment, and no longer dreamed every night of cannon fire and warm blood, no longer closed my eyes and saw the silhouette of my father's body dangling in the darkness. I had Ferrandino's promise that my husband and I would remain in Naples; I had the company of my mother and brother, and wanted for nothing. For the first time, I entertained the idea of raising my sons and daughters in Naples, amongst family members who would show them only love.

Pope Alexander, however, had other plans.

I was sitting with my mother and brother at supper when Jofre appeared with a piece of parchment in his hand, and a look of dread on his face. I surmised at once that he was obliged to tell me the contents of the letter, and that he was terrified of my reaction.

He had good reason to be afraid. The letter was from his father. I guessed correctly that the scene between us was about to become unpleasant, so I excused myself from supper, and we two went to discuss the matter in private.

According to Alexander, 'the war in Naples has reminded us of our own mortality, and the fragility of all life. We wish to live out the rest of our years surrounded by our children.'

All of them—including Jofre, and especially his wife.

I thought of the Count of Marigliano, who had visited me in Squillace at Alexander's behest, when I had been accused of unfaithfulness to Jofre. He had warned me in a discreet manner that one day His Holiness would no longer be able to contain his curiosity: he would want to see with his own eyes the woman his youngest son had married, the woman everyone claimed was more beautiful than his mistress, *La Bella*.

I cursed, I waved my arms at poor cowed Jofre. I insisted that I would not go to Rome, even though I knew my refusal was doomed. I went to Ferrandino and begged him to convince His Holiness to let me remain in Naples—but we both knew that a king's word held less sway than a pope's. There was nothing that could be done. After waiting so long for Naples to be returned to me, she was taken from me again.

Late Spring 1496

X

Jofre and I rode into Rome on the twentieth of May, 1496, to the chiming of cathedral bells at ten o'clock in the morning on a brilliantly sunny day. For the entertainment of the assembled crowds of noblemen and commoners, we organized ourselves into a parade, which would be met by Lucrezia Borgia, the Pope's second eldest child and only daughter, and led to the Vatican.

Alexander VI had done what no pope before him had dared to: he openly acknowledged his children as his own, instead of referring to them as 'nieces' or 'nephews', as other pontiffs had done in the past. It was said he loved them dearly, and this must have been the case, for he brought them all to live with him in the papal palace immediately after his election. Even outside my marriage to Jofre, I had heard talk of Lucrezia: it was rumoured that she was exceptionally beautiful.

'What is your sister like?' I had asked Jofre, on our journey northward.

'Sweet,' he had said casually, after a moment's reflection. 'Modest, and very charming. You will like her.'

'Is she beautiful?'

He hesitated at that. 'She is . . . pretty. Not so pretty as you, of course.'

'And your brothers?'

'Cesare?' A shadow passed over my husband's face at the mention of the brother I might have married. 'He is very handsome.'

'I meant his personality.'

'Ah. He is ambitious. Very smart.' Again, I detected dislike, but Jofre was swift to avoid the truth when it involved unpleasant matters. Even so, when I pressed about his brother, Juan, he scowled openly and said, 'You need not worry yourself about *him*. He lives in Spain with his wife.'

Great beauty has its price. Glad though I was that fate had dealt me fine features, I also knew well the jealousy they provoked in other women. Therefore, I took care that day not to outshine my sister-in-law: I wore the simple black dress of a married noblewoman, with the huge sleeves fashionable in the south; my horse was draped in black, and I rode a respectful distance behind my husband.

Jofre, however, was eager to impress Rome and his family with the glories of princehood. He insisted I be accompanied by my full court of twenty women, and a large retinue that even included jesters clad in the brightest shades of yellow, red and purple.

We entered the city from the south. I had never before set foot in Rome; awe overtook me as we rode through the worn city gates and looked upon the rolling hills. 'Over there,' Jofre called back to me from his steed, and pointed to his right as we made our way upon the Via del Circo Massimo; there stood the Arch of Constantine, the ancient prototype of my own great-grandfather's triumphal arch. Further down to our east rested the great Colosseum, the many-tiered stone ellipse where so many Christians had met their end, and the Pantheon, that temple to all gods, with its countless white columns and massive dome, the largest in all Rome—ironically far larger than any Christian church.

The only cities I knew consisted of one or two royal palaces, several smaller palazzi, a few cathedrals, and numerous whitewashed buildings crowded together on slopes and coastlines, on narrow streets. Rome possessed a grandeur and a scope beyond my ken. Spread out on land that continued beyond the horizon, the buildings possessed a size, an elegance, an ornateness that left me breathless. The streets were wide, filled with carriages of the wealthy; the palaces of cardinals and noble families were massive, of classic rectangular design, covered with marble statuary and *bas relief* scenes from pagan mythology. Any one of them was finer by far than Naples' dull brown Castel Nuovo, with its awkward, irregular shape.

Only the broad Tiber was a disappointment. When we reached the Ponte Sant'Angelo, the bridge alongside the great fortress of the Castel Sant'Angelo, crowned by a statue of the Archangel Michael, I first saw Rome's famous river. Its stinking waters were filled with floating refuse and crowded with merchant ships. But I was soon distracted by the sight before me: the sprawling cobblestone Piazza of Saint Peter's, and beyond it, the great sanctuary itself, older than a millennium, where the first pontiff's bones rested. Directly adjacent, on its northern side, stood the Vatican.

Just before we arrived at the vast piazza, we were met by scarlet-clad cardinals on horseback, and the papal guards on foot; the Spanish ambassador rode up to Jofre and greeted him. As our procession made its way into the square, I saw her from a distance, and knew her at once: Lucrezia.

She drew closer upon a white horse, while all those in her large entourage were mounted upon steeds of black or brown. Her attendants were clad in red-and-gold brocade, while she wore a gown of shining white satin and a gold brocade stomacher, trimmed with pearls. Upon her head was a golden net studded with diamonds, and round her throat a necklace fashioned of a great ruby surrounded by more diamonds.

She rode up to her brother. We three—I, Jofre, Lucrezia—dismounted, and she gave him a smile and welcoming kiss. Then she turned to me.

She had been chosen to greet us, Jofre had earlier explained, because she held a special place in the hearts of the people of Rome. To them, she was as the Virgin Mary: gentle and pure, imbued with a special love for her subjects. Even her name symbolized chastity and honour: she had been christened after that Lucrezia of ancient Rome who, having been raped by her husband's foe, chose suicide as the only noble option, for she would not live with shame as her companion.

Behind the pale, upward-curving lips, behind the gentleness emanating from this Lucrezia's gaze, I saw at once the jealousy hidden there—and the powerful intelligence. And at once I believed every story I had heard of Pope Alexander's deviousness and cunning, for here it was, reflected in his daughter.

Physically, she belied her reputation: she was no beauty—though her bearing held such pride and confidence as to make her seem attractive from a distance. Her face was as plain as Jofre's, weak-chinned, with a plump fold of neck beneath it; her eyes were large and a rather colourless shade of grey. Her hair, like her younger brother's, was pale coppery gold, and for the day's festivities it had been most carefully arranged into perfect, curling tendrils, which fell freely onto her shoulders and down her back, in the style of an unmarried woman.

She might as well have been. Jofre had shared with me the family gossip: that Lucrezia's husband, Count Giovanni Sforza of Milan, had taken every possible opportunity since their marriage to avoid his bride. At the moment, he was entrenched at his estate in Pesaro, refusing every summons from the Pope to return to his wife, much to Lucrezia's embarrassment. This astounded me; and when I asked Jofre, 'Why will he not come to her?' my husband—usually naively straightforward in other matters—would only answer, 'He is afraid.'

Afraid of Pope Alexander's wrath, I had assumed. Milan, which housed Sforza's duchy, had struck a deal with the French to protect itself; the region's rulers were no friends to Naples. Sforza's fear must have been that of political retribution.

Yet, when I considered it at length, I recalled that Sforza had absented himself from Lucrezia long before King Charles ever dreamed of setting foot in Italy. Did he so despise his wife?

In the piazza that morning, Lucrezia's expression, so cautious, so self-consciously pleasant and appropriate to the occasion, held no clue. 'Sister,' she said, just loudly enough to be heard by the crowds, just softly enough to be considered demure. 'Welcome to your home.'

We embraced solemnly, each kissing the other's cheeks. She grasped my arms in a manner that held me firmly in place, kept me from pressing too close against her; and in the instant that she pulled away, I caught the flicker of pure hatred in her eyes.

Lucrezia, beloved mistress of Rome, led us through the piazza and into the Vatican, and the magnificent chamber where Pope Alexander sat upon his golden throne, surrounded by the most powerful cardinals in Italy. The resemblance Lucrezia shared with him was striking: he had the weak chin, with many folds beneath it (for he had entered his sixth decade of life), and eyes of the same shape and size, though their colour was brown. His nose was more prominent, and his iron-grey hair was shaved in the monk's tonsure; the bald area of his scalp was covered with a white skull-cap. A great gold cross, glittering with diamonds, hung from his neck and rested just above his belly; on his finger he wore the ruby ring of Peter. He projected an aura of physical strength, for his chest and shoulders were broad and muscular, his face bright with life.

As we entered, he beamed like a lovesick bridegroom. 'Jofre, my son! And Sancha, my daughter! So it is true—you are every bit the beauty Jofre's letters claimed! Indeed, you are more magnificent than poor words could ever convey! Look!' He gestured to the assembly. 'Her eyes are green as emeralds!'

I did not hesitate. I was used to heads of state, uncowed by protocol. I strode forward without waiting for my husband and ascended the stairs to the throne, where I knelt and kissed the pontiff's satin-slippered foot, as ritual demanded. Some seconds later, I was aware of Jofre kneeling beside me.

Alexander was pleased by my forthright show of reverence, my lack of timidity. He placed a large, cool hand upon my head in blessing, then pointed to a red velvet cushion placed on the marble step just to the left of his throne. 'Here, my dear!' Take your seat beside me. I have reserved a special place for you.'

Jofre embraced his father, then went to stand with the cardinals, while I sat on the velvet pillow, keenly aware that, on the opposite side of the throne, rested another matching cushion.

My ladies-in-waiting filed through, each paying their respects to the Pope as I had. When all formalities were done, Lucrezia ascended the steps to the throne and took her place upon the red cushion opposite mine.

I did my best to catch her gaze, and was rewarded again with the most subtle and fleeting look of sheer loathing. A daughter's jealousy, I decided then; only later would I learn the true depth and cause of it.

'God is truly good to me,' Alexander exclaimed heartily, lifting his arms to gesture at me and Lucrezia, flanking him, 'to surround me with such beautiful women!'

The gathered company laughed. Smiling with feigned shyness at the compliment, I looked to my husband to ensure that he was pleased with my performance.

He was. But beside him stood another who was equally pleased—if not more. One of the cardinals, a man my own age, lean and bearded, dark-eyed, with hair blue-black as my own, met my gaze boldly. I felt my cheeks flush hot; I looked away, my smile grown tremulous.

But I could not help stealing another glance at the handsome young cardinal—only to see him still regarding me with unapologetic interest. *How dare he?* I told myself, trying to summon a sense of outrage, of disgust. *Here in front of my husband and His Holiness, and he a priest, a cardinal . . .*

Earlier, when I was fifteen, I had thought myself in love with

Onorato Caetani. But that affection had been nurtured by Onorato's kindness to me, and his skill at lovemaking.

The sensation that seized me that morning—the twentieth of May—as I sat on my velvet cushion beside the Pope and stared down at the man standing beside my husband, was swift, irrevocable, and violent, like a dagger plunged into the heart. I trembled. I did not want it; I did not seek it; yet there it was, and I was at the mercy of it. And I knew nothing of the man who had just stolen my soul.

I had come into Pope Alexander's household wishing to make a favourable impression, to be a good wife to his son, Jofre, and now I was utterly lost.

XI

After our official greeting, Jofre and I, along with our attendants and belongings, were led into the Palace of Santa Maria in Portico, next to the Vatican. It was a graceful structure with large arched windows to let in the Roman sun, and had been built for the purely carnal purpose of housing Pope Alexander's feminine entourage. The main floor contained a loggia which overlooked the vast gardens; Alexander had spared no expense for his women. Lucrezia lived here, as did Alexander's young mistress, Giulia Orsini, and his middle-aged niece, Adriana, procurer of his lovers. Other beauties who caught His Holiness' eye were housed here from time to time, and it gave my heart no ease to be led into this building, knowing its reputation—even though Jofre accompanied me.

I was even less encouraged to discover my husband's bedchamber was located in a different wing of the palace from mine, which was close to both Lucrezia and Giulia's suites. Under normal circumstances, a wife would not find it so troubling to be housed near others of her sex—except for the fact that Alexander seemed to have a peculiar penchant for married women. Even the extravagantly lovely Giulia Farnese did not arouse his passion sufficiently for him to bring her to the Vatican—until he married her off to his niece Adriana's son, the unfortunate, redundantly-named Orsino Orsini. His Holiness took special pleasure in violating the sanctity of other men's marriages.

Thus, when Jofre and I turned away from each other to go to our separate suites, I stopped, turned back, and put a hand to his still-smooth, boyish cheek. He faced me, smiling brightly, still flushed with the exhilaration of his grand return to his native city. He was fifteen years of age, and finally my height, with his hair still long and curling; as I held my hand to his warm cheek, I swore I would never let his own father make him a cuckold.

At the same time, I prayed I would never again set eyes on the striking young cardinal whose glance had aroused such a tide of passion in me.

It was a prayer like all the others: one that God would not answer.

We rested for a time after our journey. I tried but could not sleep, though the bed, with its pillows of brocade and velvet, its fine linens and fur throws was sumptuous, finer than any I had lain on in the Castel Nuovo. The Borgias were not timid about showing their wealth. As my ladies were unpacking and placing my belongings about the room, I spied a small, worn leather book in Donna Esmeralda's hand. Before she could put it down, I snatched it from her, settled upon a cushion, and began to read.

It was Petrarch's *Canzionere*, his love poetry dedicated to the mysterious Laura; the hand-sized tome had been a gift from Onorato. I had always been of two minds about Petrarch: on one hand, I found it achingly amusing that he should make such proclamations of maudlin sentiment, describing love as an arrow that had pierced him through the heart, yet blessing the day that such emotional injury had occurred. He always spoke of pain, burning, and chills. At times, I would read his poetry aloud to my ladies, in exaggerated tones and with such great sarcasm that eventually, I could read no more, and all of us would be overcome by laughter. 'Poor Petrarch!' I would sigh. 'I think he suffers not so much from love as the ague.'

Some, however, would not laugh quite as loudly, and said timidly, 'There is such a thing. One day, Madonna Sancha, it might happen to you.'

How I mocked them! Yet privately, I wondered whether they were right, and yearned secretly to experience such magic; was Petrarch serious when he spoke of being riveted by a single gaze from his Laura, and from that moment forever bound? Eyes it was with Petrarch, always the eyes.

Yet at midday on the twentieth of May, I sat and began reading with my customary mocking tone to my ladies as they bustled about the room. When I came to the line:

I fear, yet hope; I burn, and am ice.

My voice failed. Abruptly overwhelmed by emotion, I turned my face away; I closed the little book and set it down beside me on the cushion. The words described precisely what I had felt when I had locked gazes with the handsome cardinal; once again I experienced a helpless rush of feeling. Memory summoned the image of my mother's face, the sound of her voice, for once defiant: *You speak as though I had a choice.* At last, I understood what she meant.

The women slowed their movements, each in turn looking away from their work towards me; their smiles changed into expressions of concern.

'She is homesick,' Esmeralda said knowingly. 'Donna Sancha, don't be sad. Jofre is with you, and all of us, too; your heart will soon be here, as well.'

How could I tell her that my heart already *was* here—but not at all in the way that I wished?

Angry at permitting myself to be so easily smitten by a stranger, I rose, and stalked out onto the balcony, where I stared fiercely out at the gardens.

. . .

In the late afternoon, Jofre and I attended a feast thrown by His Holiness in our honour. The affair took place in the papal apartments. Flanked by guards and my ladies-in-waiting, we strolled together like young lovers, arm in arm, from the palazzo; the spring weather was beautiful, and the sun, now lower in the sky, cast a golden glow upon the great piazza and the shining white marble buildings that encircled it. Jofre smiled at me with pride. I clung to him—out of affection, the dear lad thought, and returned my tight grasp with a squeeze and a gaze—but it was out of trepidation. Only part of my concern was how I should handle any amorous advances from the Pope; my greatest worry was my attraction to the mysterious cardinal.

We made our way to the Borgia apartments. From the entry, I could look behind me and see, beyond the imposing Castel Sant'Angelo, greenery—carefully tended gardens and vineyards—stretching unbroken to distant mountains, and rows of orange trees dotted with evergreens. Flowers scented the cooling air.

We were announced, and entered, followed by our attendants.

The apartments were not vast, but the adornments were splendid; the ceilings were gold, the walls freshly painted with the enamel and gilt frescoes of Pinturicchio, with scenes both pagan and Christian. Beneath the frescoes hung tapestries of silk, and the floors were covered with carpets from the Orient. Everywhere were places to sit: plump cushions of velvet and brocade, stools and chairs.

The Pope, his broad shoulders covered with a robe of pure white, stood smiling at the entry to the dining chamber. Unlike Jofre, he was a large man, and filled the doorway, his arms spread wide in greeting; his broad shoulders, neck and chest made me think of a powerful bull. 'My children!' he cried, smiling, without a trace of pomp. 'Jofre, Sancha, come!'

He embraced first his son, then me, kissing me on the lips with troubling enthusiasm. 'Jofre, take your seat for supper. As for you, Your Highness,' he said to me, 'let me give you a tour of our apartments.'

I dared not protest; Alexander encircled my waist with an arm, then led me into a separate room where we were alone.

'This is the Sala dei Santi,' he announced, 'where our Lucrezia was married.' He did not bother to mention the groom.

I stared at my surroundings and did my best to suppress a gasp; I felt as overwhelmed as a simple commoner, for the first time glimpsing the interior of a palace.

The Castel Nuovo, which until that time had represented my idea of royal luxury, was furnished after the Spanish style, with whitewashed walls, arched windows and ceilings decorated with mouldings of dark wood. Adornments consisted of carpets, dull paintings, statuary. I had thought the furnishings ornate.

But as I entered the Hall of the Saints, my eyes were as dazzled as if I had stared directly into the sun. Never had I seen such intense colour, such profusion of decoration. The vaulted ceiling was covered with countless paintings, each separated by gilded mouldings, some contained within lunettes; the background colour was the deepest blue I had ever seen, from pure crushed lapis lazuli, against which were rich reds, yellows, greens, and more pure gold. Each wall bore a different fresco, representing a different saint: I noted Saint Susanna, haloed in a draping blue gown, accosted in front of a fountain by two lecherous old men; in the foreground were rabbits, symbols of lust.

'We paid Pinturicchio a pretty sum for the work. Beautiful, is it not?' my host asked quietly; then, with a leer, added, 'Though not so beautiful as you, my darling.'

I pulled away from him, and walked across flecked pastel marble toward a rendering of Catherine, disputing with pagan philosophers before the Emperor Maximilian; in the background, the Arch of Constantine was visible. The young saint, dressed like a Roman noblewoman in red and black, her golden hair flowing down to her waist, was unmistakably familiar.

'Why, it is Lucrezia,' I remarked.

The Pope chuckled, pleased. 'It is indeed.' There was naught of piety to him, only an earthy love of life. Appropriate, that he had taken the papal name of Alexander—not the name of a Christian, but of the Macedonian conqueror.

I gazed up at the ceiling. There were other tableaux—the martyred Saint Sebastian, Saint Anthony visiting the hermit, Paul—but the dominant painting was that of a pagan man and woman gesturing at a great bull. I noticed then that smaller pictures of the bull were repeated everywhere, interspersed with the symbol of the papacy, the tiara atop the crossed Keys to the Kingdom of Heaven.

'The Apis bull,' Alexander explained. 'In ancient Egypt, it was worshipped as an incarnation of the god Osiris. The bull appears on our family crest.' Before I could react, he once again moved close to me and wrapped an arm about my waist. 'It is a symbol of masculine strength and virility, you know.' Abruptly, he pressed a hand to my breast and attempted to kiss me; I slipped from his grasp and once again, walked quickly away. I understood why the pious Savonarola had called Alexander the Antichrist . . . for in the Pope's apartments, pagan symbolism took precedence over Christian.

The Pope let me go with a little laugh. 'You are a coy one, my dear. No matter; I enjoy the chase.'

'Your Holiness, please,' I said candidly. 'I wish only to be a faithful wife to your son. I do not desire to be a favourite; and you have your choice of so many women . . . '

'Ah,' he said, 'but of none so lovely.'

'I am flattered,' I countered. 'But please, let me remain simply your loyal daughter-in-law.'

He smiled smugly and nodded, but did not appear to change his plans for me. He gestured broadly. 'As you wish. Let us continue with the tour.'

We walked through different chambers, each as glorious as the first, each with a different theme: the Room of the Creed, the Room of the Faith, with a large mural showing the Adoration of the Magi, the Hall of the Sibyls, with paintings of Old Testament prophets announcing God's wrath, accompanied by stern-faced sibyls, pagan seeresses. I had never seen such a display of magnificence and wealth; I was in fact glad that I had visited the other chambers before we went to dine, so that I could avoid gaping at my surroundings like an awestruck peasant.

His Holiness made no further attempt to seduce me, and we at last joined the others for dinner in the Room of the Liberal Arts. Beneath a painting of The Arithmetic—a blond woman draped in green velvet, holding a golden tome—the Pope gestured to me. 'You will sit beside me.'

As he led me to the long dining table, covered with sconces and a great feast—roast fowl, venison, and lamb, wine and grapes, cheeses and breads—I passed by several cardinals, all of them Borgias, all of them clad in the traditional scarlet robes. I scanned their faces and failed to find my handsome man among them.

At the head of the table was the Pope's chair, taller and more ornate than the others; to his right sat Lucrezia. I curtsied; she gave me a prim little nod, her fine, small lips pressed tightly together, her eyes narrowed and managing, cleverly, to convey only to me the intensity of her contempt. Jofre noticed none of this subtlety, but kissed his sister and sat beside her.

My empty chair waited directly to the Pope's left; once again, I had been cast as Lucrezia's direct opposition. I moved to take it—and was stopped at once by the Pope's hand, firm yet affectionate, upon my shoulder.

'But wait! Our darling Donna Sancha has not yet met her new brother!'

My gaze followed the Pope's gesture to the chair beside mine. The young man sitting in it had already risen: a man my age. A strikingly handsome man, with a fine, straight nose and a strong chin, covered by a full beard.

'Cesare! Cesare, kiss your new sister, Sancha!'

He had his mother's features, and hair dark as jet, so I had not recognized him as a Borgia. Unlike the other cardinals, he had changed into the black frock of a priest—one of plain but elegant design. The gaze we exchanged was no less powerful than it had been earlier that morning, when I had looked down at him from my seat beside the papal throne.

I had known that Jofre had an older brother, Cesare, the Cardinal of Valencia, called by some Valentino. Yet I had not made the connection that morning at the papal audience, when Jofre had gone to stand beside him.

We turned to each other and performed a courteous but familial embrace, each clasping the other's arms above the elbows. I turned my cheek upwards towards him, and was startled when he bent down to plant a firm, single kiss upon my brow. His beard was full, thick, a man's, and I trembled as it brushed against my skin.

'You must hear my confession, Holiness,' he said, without taking his gaze from me. 'I envy my brother; he has captured a truly beautiful woman.' Everyone laughed politely.

'You are too kind,' I murmured.

Alexander took his seat—which allowed everyone to resume theirs—and smiling, gestured at Cesare. 'Is he not witty?' he said, with honest love and pride. 'I am blessed with the most beautiful and intelligent children in all Christendom; I thank God each one of you is now here with me, and safe.'

I had been repelled by the Pope's inability to control his lust—but now I noticed how his sons and his daughter bloomed beneath his heartfelt praise. Obviously, Alexander was a man of generous emotion, despite his flaws, and I wondered wistfully what it must be like to have a father so affectionate and kind.

I said and ate little during dinner, though the others laughed and spoke freely; I spent the time listening to Cesare. I remember little that he said, but his voice, his manner, were like velvet.

The feast was limited to family—an extended one, with many names to be committed to memory. I already knew Cardinal Borgia of Monreale, who had witnessed the consummation of my marriage to Jofre.

Long after the moon had risen, the Pope set his massive hands upon the table, and pushed himself up—which prompted everyone else at the table to stand.

'On to the reception,' he announced, his voice thick with wine.

Out we went, into the largest room in the apartments, where a small crowd waited. At the sight of us, musicians began to play their lutes and reeds. Though I had not been introduced, I recognized at once she whom Rome called *La Bella*—the infamous Giulia, with features as fine and fair as an ancient marble statue, and light brown hair braided, coiled, and covered by a net of gold, save for the fine, serpentine tendrils that framed her face. She wore a pale rose silk gown, with folds so numerous and of material so sheer that they rippled with her every movement. Her eyes were large and heavy-lidded, filled with an odd shyness and timidity for one who held the heart of such a powerful man. I sensed no malice in her, no pretence. His Holiness' favour had apparently been bestowed upon her without any effort or manipulation on her part; she gave the impression of a child overwhelmed by a too-magnificent toy.

With her was her husband, Orsino Orsini—he with a distracting monocular gaze, for he had lost an eye some years ago. Orsino was short, stocky of build, morose of expression and resigned in manner. He and his wife were closely watched by his mother, the Pope's niece, Adriana Mila, a stout matron with a shrewd, assessing glance and constant furrows of worry upon her brow. Adriana was a skilled tactician; she had earned a great deal of the Pope's favour not only by procuring Giulia for him, but also by raising Lucrezia in the Pope's household. Surely, no one brought up in this woman's care could learn the art of trust.

There were others there as well—nobles and their wives, attendants of the papal court, more cardinals, and suspiciously unattended women to whom I was not introduced. The event was supremely informal, not at all what I was accustomed to in Naples or Squillace, where Jofre and I took our thrones and nobles and family were carefully placed and served according to rank. A throne was carried in for His Holiness and placed where he might best watch the proceedings, but otherwise, everyone moved about freely, from time to time taking cushions or chairs whenever they wished, and vacating them just as easily, to be filled by another.

This did not trouble me; custom varies in all royal house-holds. But then a chair was brought for Giulia, that she might sit directly next to the Pope; and when he first caught sight of her, he went to her, and in front of the entire company, kissed her without modesty, then bade her sit beside him.

I was mildly scandalized. My mother was a prince's mistress, but my father would never have sat beside her or kissed her at a public affair; and this was, after all, the Vatican. I found it repugnant, too, that only a few hours before, the hands that now caressed Giulia had reached so easily for me. Still, I permitted myself no reaction; Jofre was my guide. He accepted his father's behaviour as quite natural, so I tried to, as well.

In the interim, wine flowed. I took mine mixed with water, and only a couple of glasses of that.

'I have been to Naples, and know something of it,' Lucrezia addressed me conversationally, 'but never to Squillace. Tell me of it.' Like me, she had taken care not to be affected by the wine; she was too busy judging me, assessing the potential for rivalry between us.

'Squillace is quite beautiful in its own way. It lies upon the coast of the Ionian Sea, and though the shoreline is not as scenic as Naples'—it has no Vesuvio, after all—the harbour is lovely. The city has many artists, many craftsmen known for their pottery and ceramics.'

'It is not as large as Naples?'

'No, indeed.' Jofre snickered a bit.

Cesare, up to this point silent, offered graciously, 'But nonetheless charming, I have heard. Size and beauty are not related.'

Lucrezia tilted her head; her eyes narrowed slightly. 'Ah. There are times I yearn for the simplicity of the provinces; Rome being so vast, and the demands on our time so great, it can be overwhelming. Still, we have the responsibility to impress the populace at all the social functions. Here, I am afraid, the people are far more jaded than those in Squillace, and expect more.'

I lifted my chin at the subtle insult: did she refer to my attire, deliberately matronly and sedate, that she might better shine at our first meeting? If so, I would not make the same mistake again.

'Lucrezia!' the Pope called, obviously quite tipsy from the wine. 'Dance for us! Dance with Sancha!' He had an arm around Giulia; she giggled as he drew her to him, nose to nose, and kissed her.

Lucrezia gave me another of her sidewise, faintly mocking glances. 'You of course know the Spanish fashion . . . or do they not teach that in the south?'

'I am a princess of the House of Aragon,' I answered, not kindly.

We joined hands. And as the Pope clapped from time to time with delight, and the musicians played, we performed the steps of an old-fashioned Castilian dance.

At that moment, I was glad to have been raised by my father, to have learned that men and women could behave with apparent courtesy, yet retain a talent for duplicity; I sensed Lucrezia was one such person. And so, as we made polite conversation during our little dance, I kept my wits sharp. Indeed, the instant came when Lucrezia intentionally skipped a step in the dance, and held her foot out precisely so that I would trip and embarrass myself.

I was ready. Perhaps I should have been kind, and simply avoided stumbling, pretending she had made an unintended move; but my father's ire and haughtiness rose in me. I deliberately brought my foot down upon hers.

She let go a little cry and turned to me sharply; though we continued through our movements, we shared the candid look of two opponents in a duel.

'How shall we play this, Madonna?' I asked mildly, though my gaze was hard. 'I did not come to Rome willingly; certainly I did not come to make an enemy. I have no wish to be anything other than a good sister to you.'

Mindful of those watching, she smiled prettily; it was the coldest, most terrifying expression I had ever seen. 'You are not my sister. And you will never be my equal, Your Highness. Mark that.'

I fell silent, not knowing how to ease her jealousy.

During our dance, servants appeared with trays of dainty chocolates. Alexander made a great show of feeding one to Giulia, then she fed one to him. Just as our dance was ending, and our audience applauded politely, Alexander—with a great boyish grin—hurled one of the chocolates some distance, hitting Cesare.

The dark-frocked young cardinal reacted with consummate grace; he smiled without surprise, retrieved the chocolate, and ate it with a relish that pleased his laughing father.

Then Alexander, with an exaggerated gesture, dropped a chocolate down Giulia's bodice.

For an instant, a look of consternation crossed the girl's face. She did not want her expensive gown ruined.

I caught the sharp gaze Adriana Mila shot her: it was a warning, a threat.

At once Giulia smiled, then giggled with a degree of sincerity only a man smitten by love could have believed. The Pope giggled too, like a naughty schoolboy, and fished his hand deep into her bodice between her snowy breasts, taking an inordinate amount of time and waggling his eyebrows with an expression of prurient delight calculated to entertain the crowd.

Those gathered roared with laughter.

Abruptly, Adriana went to Alexander's side, and whispered something in his ear; he nodded, then turned to Giulia and, taking her lovely face in his great hands, kissed her on the lips and murmured a promise to her. I suspected a tryst was arranged, and wondered whether a rumour I had heard was true: that the Pope had ordered a passageway constructed between the Palazzo Santa Maria and the Vatican, so that he could secretly visit his women whenever he wished.

Giulia nodded, her face bright, and left along with the unhappy Orsino, the two of them led by Adriana.

This was a signal to the guests that I did not understand: at once, a line of cardinals formed at His Holiness' throne, bowing and bidding him farewell; most of the nobles followed after.

The night was still early, but the celebration was now reduced to close family—and the unknown, unattended, extravagantly-dressed women.

Whores, I realized with sudden discomfort, even before His Holiness hurled yet another chocolate, which buried itself in the décolletage of the most buxom female present. The harlot laughed. She was an attractive young girl, golden-haired, but there was a hardness in her eyes despite her drunkenness. She leaned forward, the better to reveal her bosom, and half-ran, unsteady on her feet, toward Alexander.

He sat, ready for her. And the moment her brocade-covered breasts appeared before him, he thrust his face heartily between them and began searching for the hidden sweet like a dog hunting a morsel dropped from the master's table.

She laughed shrilly, pressing him hard against her with a hand at the back of his head. At last he withdrew, triumphant, his face smeared with chocolate, the candy between his lips.

Cesare's expression was reserved, noncommittal, as he stared down into his goblet. Obviously, this was something he was accustomed to, if not approving of.

I looked at once to Jofre; my little husband was laughing, himself quite intoxicated, and waved to one of the servants to bring a tray of sweets. I forgot myself: I failed to entirely hide my disgust.

Lucrezia caught this at once. 'Ah, Madonna Sancha, you *are* provincial.' And to prove that she was not, when the tray of chocolates arrived, she dropped one between her own breasts.

Cesare, with a deftness that lacked any hint of impropriety, caught the sweet at once between two fingers, and replaced it on the tray. 'You must give our new sister time,' he said smoothly, without reproach, 'to come to know us, that she might not be so shocked by our Roman ways.'

In response, Lucrezia flushed brightly. She set down her goblet on the tray, took the half-melted sweet, and settled it once more firmly in her bosom.

Without a word, she went over to her father's throne and gestured for the giggling harlot—who now was sitting on the pontiff's lap, moving her hips in a most lascivious fashion—to leave.

The woman did so, bowing sweetly, though it was clear she resented the intrusion. And Lucrezia took her place.

She sat upon her father's lap, and pressed his face to her small breasts; by then, Alexander was obviously drunk—but not too drunk to notice that the woman had changed.

As he searched, with lips and tongue, for the candy, Lucrezia turned her face towards mine, her eyes narrowed, filled with both challenge and triumph.

I turned about, skirts swirling, and left.

XII

Esmeralda and a trio of guards followed me as far as the door, but I whirled on them. 'I will be alone!' I demanded, in a voice that silenced even the formidable Donna Esmeralda. Normally, she would have refused to allow me to walk unaccompanied at night, but she was shrewd enough to know that I had reached a level of determination which allowed no argument. Besides, I had no fear; I always carried Alfonso's stiletto.

I stepped alone into the Roman night. The air was slightly chill, the piazza before me dark; the only light came from the moon, gleaming off the marble rooftops, and the flickering golden windows of the Borgia apartments behind me. I lifted my skirts and, as carefully as I could, made my way down the high stairs to the level of the street, and from there, turned and used the dull glow coming from the ground floor of the Palazzo Santa Maria to guide me to my new home.

I was hardly a prude. I had been witness to a certain amount of debauchery at the court of my father—and at that of my own husband. Party games with courtesans were not unheard of. But they were conducted discreetly, in the presence of only a trusted few.

Apparently, this Pope trusted many. Or perhaps no one dared speak. Either way, it was clear that the man who had so scandalized Italian society by accosting several married women in a cathedral garden had not changed a whit since ascending to the papacy.

I could overlook such a thing, though I had expected more discretion. And I had convinced myself, after His Holiness so easily gave up his attempts to pursue me that afternoon, that all I had to do was refuse him a few times and I would be left alone.

I had even been warmed by how Alexander doted on his children; I had longed for such paternal affection, and imagined how my life might have been had my own father been kindly disposed towards me.

But the oddly triumphant look in Lucrezia's eyes, as she pressed the Pope's face to her bosom, made me yearn instead for the home I had known. I could not hide my revulsion toward such a scene between parent and child—for an instant, in my imagination, my own father took Alexander's place, and I Lucrezia's. I could only shudder at the thought of pressing my own breasts to Alfonso II's lips, of my father groping me drunkenly. So repellent was the notion that I suppressed it immediately.

I now understood, too well, the cause of Lucrezia's jealousy . . . and it had nothing to do with my outshining her at social functions.

Her love for Alexander went beyond that of a daughter for her father. The gaze she had directed at me was that of a woman possessive of a lover, and challenging a rival: *Leave him; he is mine.*

The image of her, her young, white flesh unclothed, pressed against the aged, sagging body of the pontiff, made me ill; I stumbled along the edge of the piazza, drawing in the night air, laden with the marshy smell of the nearby Tiber, as if I could somehow cleanse myself of the memory of what I had just seen.

My instincts said that Lucrezia was a depraved, despicable creature. Her brazen behaviour with the chocolates hinted at a monstrous notion: that she granted her own father—the Pope—sexual favours.

I took a breath and steadied myself. I was a cynic, swift to judge. Away from my brother only a short while, I was already thinking the worst of everyone. How could I be more like Alfonso? I wondered. How would my brother react?

Surely I was wrong, I told myself. The two could not be physically involved; such an idea was too horrible to entertain. Lucrezia had a crush on her father, as some young girls do—and a fierce temper. She was jealous of sharing his affection, and was already forced to do so with Giulia; here was I, another woman who diverted Alexander's attentions from her. And Lucrezia had been so angered by my harsh response to her during our dance that she had lost control of her temper and wanted badly to shock me.

That is it, I told myself. *And perhaps she had drunk more wine than I realized. Perhaps she was not as sober as she seemed.*

This thought calmed me to a degree; by the time I arrived at the Palazzo Santa Maria, I was convinced that Lucrezia had resorted to outlandish behaviour out of childishness, and that Alexander had certainly been too intoxicated to realize he nuzzled at his own daughter's bosom.

The guards recognized me at once and permitted me entry. The ground floor loggia was well-lit, but the upstairs corridors were another matter, and I wandered in confusion until at last I found the entry to my suite.

I extended my hand to open the antechamber door. At once, my wrist was seized with brutal force.

I whirled. Beside me in the shadows loomed Rodrigo Borgia. Even the dim light could not hide the crudeness of his features—the receding chin that disappeared into folds of aging flesh, the prominent, slightly bulbous, irregular nose, the thick lips stretched now in a leer. His eyes were heavy-lidded with drink. The golden mantle was gone; he wore only his red satin robes and a velvet skullcap.

It is true, then, I thought with an odd detachment. *A secret passage between Santa Maria and the Vatican exists.* How else could His Holiness have left the celebration so quickly and be waiting here for me?

Standing next to him, I could not deny his physical advantage: I was not a large woman, and unlike his son Jofre, Rodrigo was a tall man, still powerful at sixty. My head did not come as high as his broad shoulders. His bones were large and thick, mine fine: his great hands together could encircle my waist, and he could easily snap my neck if he chose.

'Sancha, my darling, my dream,' he whispered, dragging me to him; the pressure on my wrist increased to the point of great pain, but I did not cry out. His words were slurred. 'I have waited all day for this encounter, all evening—nay, for years, since the first instant you were described to me. But the war kept us apart . . . until now.'

I opened my mouth to rebuke him. Yet before I could utter a word, he encircled me with an arm, placed a palm against the back of my skull, and forced my face to his. I struggled, but to no use. He kissed me, lips pressed to my teeth; the smell of foetid meat, mixed with wine, made me gag.

He let go my wrist and drew back, his expression that of the young lover hopeful for a reaction. I gave him one: with all my strength, I landed a blow on his cheek.

He took a staggering step back before regaining his uncertain balance. His eyes narrowed with surprise and rage; he touched the offended area, then dropped his hand and laughed derisively. 'You are too confident of your own worth, darling Sancha. You may be a princess—but do not forget, I am the Pope.'

'I will call for my servants!' I hissed. 'They are just beyond the door.'

'Call for them.' He smiled. 'And I will dismiss them. Do you truly think they will refuse to obey me?'

'They are loyal to me.'

'If they are, they will suffer for it.' He said this with surprising pleasantness and ease.

'How can you not be ashamed?' I demanded. 'I am the wife of your son!'

'You are a woman.' On his face, in his voice, was a sudden hardness, a meanness I had seen before only in his daughter's eyes. 'And I rule here. So long as you live in my household, you are my property, to do with as I please.'

To prove his words, he moved with surprising swiftness for one so full of wine, slipped a hand inside my bodice, and took my breast in his palm.

'Sancha, my darling,' he said, with pure petulance, 'am I so old, so hideous, that you cannot imagine loving me? I would adore you beyond words; there is nothing I would deny you. Only name what you would have. Only name it! I am forever good to those who love me.'

Before he could finish his utterance, I seized his hand and pulled it from my bosom. He, in turn, grasped both my arms and, with a movement so powerful the wind was knocked from my lungs, shoved me backwards against the wall. His bulk pinned me; I flailed, I kicked, but his strength held me fast. In each fist, he held my wrists, forcing my arms out and against the wall at shoulder height—in a barbarous parody of the crucified Christ—then smothered my face with his.

I coughed, hurling spittle on him; I choked as he forced his tongue upon me, into me. And then he raised my wrists overhead, taking one of his great paws to pin them both against the wall. With his other hand, he reached to lift my skirts, bending down as he did. Given his intoxication, the movement made him dizzy, and he swayed.

I used the opportunity to tear one hand free. In a flash, I reached for my stiletto, hidden just beneath my stomacher. I was thinking to discourage him, not to wield it. But when he realized I had broken away and reached up to correct the matter, his hand found the tip of the blade.

He shrieked, and at once recoiled. My eyes had adjusted quite well to the dim light by then, and I could see the hand he held aloft, thick fingers fanned out tautly. We both stared up at it in amazement. The stiletto had nicked the palm, a perfect stigmata, and blood already trickled down to his wrist. The injury was minor, the effect dramatic.

He directed his gaze at me. I saw there, in full hellishness, the hatred that had only glinted in Lucrezia's eyes. He let go a long hiss. Yet despite his fury, a second emotion played upon his features: Fear.

He is a bully but also a coward, I thought swiftly, *just as Father was*. I took advantage of this knowledge and advanced toward him, holding the stiletto threateningly aloft.

Rodrigo suddenly smiled, the intoxicated diplomat; his tone turned wheedling as he clasped his wounded hand in the other. 'So. It is true what they say: you are fearless. I had heard that you saved the King of Naples by killing a man.'

'With this very weapon,' I averred flatly. 'I slit his throat.'

'All the more reason to love you,' he proclaimed, with false good humour. 'Surely, Sancha, you are not so foolish a woman as to turn down such an opportunity . . . '

'I am, Holiness. Each time you come to me, you will receive the same response.' I glared at him. 'You are a father who claims to love his children. How would Jofre feel, to see us like this?'

Rodrigo bowed his head at my words, and stood in silence a time, swaying slightly. To my astonishment, he burst into tears and knelt. 'I am an evil man,' he said, his tone maudlin. 'Old and drunk and foolish. I am helpless around women; it is the curse of my life. Donna Sancha, you do not understand—your great beauty has made me lose my senses. But now you have won my respect, for you are not only comely, but brave. Forgive me.' His weeping intensified. 'Forgive me for dishonouring you, and my poor son so . . . '

His remorse, though abrupt, seemed sincere. I lowered the stiletto and took a step towards him. 'I forgive you, Holiness. I will never speak of this incident. Only let it never happen again.'

He shook his great head. 'I swear it will not, Madonna. I swear . . .'

I drew closer, thinking to extend a hand, to lift him to his feet.

He reared upwards suddenly, his head and shoulders delivering a blow that knocked me to the cold tile floor and sent the weapon flying. Where it went, I could not see; tangled in my skirts, I struggled to rise, realizing my vulnerability.

Yet my heavy skirts and velvet slippers allowed me no purchase. Rodrigo's bullish figure loomed before me and reached out . . .

In the same instant, a second figure appeared, equally tall but leaner, more proportionately built, and caught one of the Pope's arms.

'Father,' Cesare said, his manner easy and calm, as if he were rousing the old man from sleep rather than interrupting a rape.

Disoriented, Rodrigo whirled on his son, still ready to fight. He struck out—but Cesare, with a strength much greater than his father's, caught Rodrigo's arm, then laughed, as if it were all a splendid joke. 'Father! You have had too much wine—you know that if you wished to beat me, you could do so handily when sober. Come, Giulia has been asking for you.'

'Giulia?' The Pope looked back at me uncertainly. He had been all too sure of himself when accosting me, but suddenly he seemed no more than a confused old man.

Cesare jerked his head cursorily in my direction. 'You have no need of this one. But Giulia will grow jealous if you do not go to see her soon.'

The Pope scowled at me, then turned and began ambling down the corridor. Cesare watched him for a heartbeat—then, certain his father was well on his way, hurried over and knelt by my side.

'Madonna Sancha, are you injured?' His concern was urgent.

I shook my head. My shoulder and ribs ached, and my wrists were bruised, but I had not been seriously damaged.

'I will go and make sure His Holiness arrives at the correct destination. I must apologize for him, Madonna; he is drunk.' He extended both his hands, and helped me to my feet. 'With your indulgence, I will call upon you shortly, to make a better apology. Now I must tend to him.'

And he was gone.

I found the stiletto on the marble floor and replaced it; once more, my brother's gift had proved its worth. When I arrived at my chambers, the maids met me, wide-eyed and silent; only when I glanced in my mirror did I realize that my breasts had almost fallen out of my bodice, my skirt was torn, and my hair had spilled halfway out of its gold netting onto my shoulders.

Cesare made good his promise. Within moments after disappearing after his father—not even time enough for my maids to remove the golden net and completely brush out my tousled hair—a discreet knock came at my antechamber door.

I righted my bodice, dismissed my maids to their rooms and went to the door myself. I was still shaking from the physical exertion of the struggle, a fact I found highly annoying.

Cesare, sober, yet troubled after a controlled, dignified fashion, stood waiting. I bade him enter, and he stood, refusing an offer to sit.

'Madonna Sancha, are you quite certain you are unhurt?'

'I am certain.' I did my best to reflect his own dignity back to him. In truth, I cared not so much about the violation his father had just committed against my person as I did about what Cesare thought of me.

'I implore your forgiveness,' Cesare said, with a hint of passion in his otherwise cautious tone. 'His Holiness too often tries to forget the enormous concerns of state by immersing himself in wine. He is already fast asleep. I suspect he will have forgotten this entire incident come morning.'

And you are suggesting that I forget it as well, I wanted to say, but such would be impolitic. I had no choice but to do so; the

Pope had full power over my destiny. He could banish me, if he wished, to the prison in the Castle Sant'Angelo, on a mythical charge of treason; he could even have me murdered by one of his henchmen. I was grateful for Cesare's concern, for it meant I had more than the ineffectual Jofre as an ally in the Borgia household.

Instead I replied, 'There is physical evidence of the event. I pierced him . . . with a stiletto. His hand is injured.'

'It must not be a serious wound,' Cesare replied. 'I failed to notice it, and he did not complain of it.'

'It is not. But it left a mark, nonetheless.'

Cesare considered this a time; his expression reminded me of the surface of a lake when the water is very, very still. At last he offered, 'Then if my father does not recall the event, you and I shall both agree here and now that the wound was the result of an encounter with one of the courtesans. I shall tell him I witnessed this myself, and that the woman was dealt with harshly.'

I nodded.

Cesare returned the gesture in acknowledgment of our complicity, then bowed. 'I take my leave, Madonna.'

He turned to go—then stopped, and regarded me over his shoulder, again with that intense, dark-eyed stare that left me uncomfortable and thrilled at the same time. 'You are the only woman I know of who has refused him, Madonna. That requires great courage and conviction.'

I lowered my gaze. 'I am married to his *son*.' I was not simply replying to Cesare; I was reminding myself of the fact as well.

He fell silent a time. And then: 'A pity, Madonna, that you met the youngest before the eldest.' He ventured another glance at me; this time, I returned it boldly.

'A pity,' I said.

He smiled very faintly, then left.

XIII

Donna Esmeralda and my other ladies waited an appropriate half-an-hour before returning from the festivities to my chamber, by which time the maids had undressed me to my shift and untangled the golden net from my hair. They undid the elaborate coils and had finished brushing them out by the time Esmeralda entered, but I think I was still shaking then—and my expression must have been haunted. Certainly, the maids knew from my disarray and torn gown that something alarming had happened, but they were also wise enough to see that I was of a mood, so they kept silent.

Likewise, I knew from the way old Esmeralda's eyes narrowed when she saw me that she knew, as well—but she, too, asked no questions. There was no point in confiding in her; it would only serve to underscore her disapproval of the Pope, and belief in Savonarola—dangerous opinions to hold in the Vatican. Besides, she would learn what happened soon enough, given her talent for gathering information.

So long as my home was the Palazzo Santa Maria in Portico, I was no longer Sancha of Aragon, princess and natural daughter of the King of Naples. My domain was no longer my own to rule, my words no longer things to be carelessly tossed about without fear of reprisal, my actions no longer unguarded and free. I was Donna Sancha, wife of the youngest, least gifted bastard of the Pope, and I lived and breathed at His Holiness' pleasure.

I said nothing to my women, but let myself be put into my sumptuous new bed, my head cradled by soft feather pillows.

It was a troubled head. If the Pope remembered our encounter, his rage might well be fathomless. Cesare had said no woman had ever denied him.

At the same time I reprimanded myself, *You need not fear for your life. Perhaps Rodrigo is capable of political assassination for gain; but I am his daughter-in-law, and he knows Jofre loves me. Besides, he would never harm a woman.*

My worries over the Pope's reaction were equally balanced by the memory, revisited a thousand times, of Cesare's last words to me; of the small curve of a smile that played on his lips.

A pity, Madonna, that you met the youngest before the eldest.

Ah, the thrill the image brought me, the joy, which made me quake; for I realized I was not alone in my feeling. He was as bewitched as I.

I rose early the following morning, Whitsunday.

Though I had taken care the day before to dress discreetly, even matronly, in deference to Lucrezia, that morning I was filled with a strange wildness. I ordered my ladies to fetch one of my finest gowns, a delectable creation of brilliant green satin, with a forest green velvet stomacher corseted with golden laces. The tied-on sleeves were of matching velvet—great wings with narrow undersleeves of lighter green satin.

I watched Donna Esmeralda's lips thin with suspicion as she watched all of this, but she said nothing. When she took my brush and began to plait my hair, preparing to put it up in a sedate coil, as she had done every morning since my wedding, I waved her away.

'Just brush it out. I shall wear it down.'

She tucked her chin and drew back her head in disapproval. 'Donna Sancha, you are a married woman.'

'So is Lucrezia. She wears her hair down.'

She glared; without comment, she began brushing my hair, not at all gently. She was closer to me than my own mother, so I did not complain, or permit myself to yelp when she found a stubborn snarl and tugged without pity.

Once the brushing was accomplished, I demanded gems. Around my neck I wore one of the wedding gifts Jofre had brought me: an emerald the size of my thumb, heavy against my throat; and around my forehead was tied a headpiece of gold, with a smaller emerald that came to rest just beneath my hairline. The combined effect made my eyes glow greener than the jewels.

I might well have been on my way to a ball, not Mass.

Thus adorned, I went to my husband's chamber—and in the corridor just outside his door, discovered one of the previous evening's courtesans leaving his room. She had obviously spent the night there, then been shooed away by a servant, for her exit was less than ceremonious: her hair was down, her slippers in one hand, her gown so rapidly donned that her chemise had not been pulled through the openings in her sleeves and properly puffed. Her small breasts were on the verge of slipping from her loosely-laced bodice.

She was crouching, stealing away in such exaggerated fashion I found the effect comical. Her hair, falling in random tendrils, was a dubious shade of red, her eyes cerulean; they glanced up at me in alarm as I halted, blocking her path. Playing the role of injured spouse, I drew myself up quite straight, and stared down at her with a withering gaze worthy of Lucrezia.

'Madonna!' she whispered, beside herself; wither she did, then bowed very low. In such position she backed away from me, then turned and ran down the corridor, her bare feet slapping against the marble floor.

After a discreet moment's wait, I entered the antechamber and was told by Jofre's manservant that his master was still sleeping very soundly due to the effects of much wine.

I breakfasted alone in my suite, then became quite bored. The palace was very quiet; no doubt, Jofre was not the only one still clinging to his bed.

Mass was still hours away. It would be an occasion with more than the usual amount of fanfare, given the ecclesiastical significance of the date: Whitsunday, marking Pentecost, that rare event which occurred fifteen hundred years before, when the fire of God had so filled the apostles that they preached in tongues they had never learned.

Such a miracle seemed quite distant and meaningless to me that morning: I was alternately elated and terrified by what had happened my first day among the Borgias. Restless, I went downstairs through the marble-floored loggia and out into the beautiful courtyard garden that I had viewed the day before from my balcony. The day was sunny and warm, the garden delightfully fragrant: miniature orange trees in terracotta pots lined one walkway; the perfectly trimmed globes of greenery were redolent with white blossoms. On the other side were well-tended rose bushes, pushing forth delicate buds.

I walked alone, until I was out of sight of my balcony, out of sight of anyone—or so I thought—and at last, because of the increasing warmth, sat upon a carved bench placed beneath the shade of an olive tree, to fan myself.

'Madonna,' a man whispered, and I started, filled with the sudden conviction that Rodrigo had sent an assassin to accomplish his revenge on me. I gasped and put a hand to my heart.

Beside me stood a man dressed entirely in black—in what might have been a priest's frock, save the collar and cuffs were fine velvet, and the body of the garment silk.

'Forgive me; I have startled you,' Cesare said. The austerity of his dress served to underscore the severe handsomeness of his features. He scarcely resembled his two siblings at all; his hair was black, straight, cut in a simple style that fell halfway between his chin and shoulders; a dark fringe partially hid a high forehead. His beard and moustache were carefully trimmed, his lips and hands fine, quite unlike his father's; he had Rodrigo's dark colouring but his mother Vannozza's beauty. There was an elegance to him, a sense of presence and dignity that, despite all their jewels and finery, none in his family could match. In Lucrezia and Pope Alexander, I sensed connivance; in Cesare, I sensed breathtaking intelligence.

'It is hardly your fault,' I replied. 'I am ill at ease after the events of last night.'

'With good reason, Madonna. I swear that I will do everything in my power to prevent such a dreadful violation of decency from occurring again.'

I lowered my eyes, like a foolish girl glad that I was wearing one of my finest gowns. 'I fear His Holiness—'

'His Holiness still sleeps. I assure you, I consider it my duty to repair relations between the two of you. Now that he is older, too much drink makes him forgetful. But whatever he remembers of last night, I will lead him down the path that is to your best advantage.'

'I am in your debt,' I told him, then realized that courtesy had required him to stand in the bright sun, while I sat comfortably in the cooler shade. 'Please . . . ' I motioned for him to sit beside me, then added, 'I have thus far impressed your family less than favourably.'

Before I could continue my thought, he countered swiftly, 'You have duly impressed at least one.'

I smiled at the compliment, but persisted, 'Your sister does not care for me. I do not understand it, and would like to remedy it.'

Cesare looked away for a moment, at distant green hills. 'She is jealous of anyone who directs my father's attentions away from her.' He turned to face me, his expression earnest. 'Understand, Donna Sancha, that her own husband, Giovanni, does not wish to reside with her. This is a source of great embarrassment, which my father has tried repeatedly to remedy by begging Giovanni to return to Rome. Besides, my father has always doted on her, and she on him; but when she sees you are no real rival for his affections, she will come to trust you.' He paused. 'She was the same way with Donna Giulia; it took her a long time to realize a father's love for another woman and that for his daughter are not one and the same. I do not mean to imply, of course, that you would ever become involved in such a way with His Holiness . . . '

'No,' I stated firmly. 'I would not. I appreciate your insight, Cardinal.'

'Please.' He flashed a smile; the teeth beneath his moustache were small and even. 'Cesare. I am a cardinal not by calling, but at my father's insistence.'

'Cesare,' I repeated.

'Lucrezia can be very affectionate,' he said fondly, 'and quite passionate in her loyalties. Most of all, she loves to have fun, to play like a child. She has had few opportunities to do so, given the responsibilities of her position. She has a man's intellect, you know. My father relies on her as an advisor, more so than he does on me.'

I listened, nodding, straining to keep my focus on his words and not on the movement of his lips, on the high, sculpted angle of his cheekbone, on the glints of red in his beard, caused by the play of dappled light. But sitting beside him, I felt my lap growing warmer, as though the very muscles and bones and organs of my lower-half were melting and spreading outward into a pool, like snow in bright sun.

He finished his statement; my internal sensations must have been revealed in my expression, for an odd look of vulnerability, of tenderness, came over him. He leaned toward me and rested his palm gently against my cheek.

'You look like a queen this morning,' he murmured. 'The world's most beautiful queen, with the world's most exquisite eyes. They make the emeralds look common.'

I thrilled to the words; I leaned closer into his hand, like a cat seeking a caress. What I felt for Cesare was so powerful that I easily forgot my marriage vows.

At once, he pulled his hand back as if scalded, and jumped to his feet. 'I am a dog!' he proclaimed. 'The son of a whore, the greatest scoundrel among men! You have relied on me for protection from my father's lewd behaviour—and now I am no better than he!'

'There is a difference,' I said, fighting to keep my voice from shaking.

He whirled back toward me, distraught. 'How so? You are my brother's wife!'

'I am your brother's wife,' I whispered.

'Then how is my behaviour different from my father's?'

'I am not in love with your father.' I flushed, startled by my own words, by their brazenness; I seemed to have no control over myself or my actions. I was, as my mother had been, quite helpless.

Yet I did not regret my words. When I saw longing and joy rise together in his eyes, I proffered my hand. He took it, and sat beside me.

'I dared not hope—' he stammered, then began again, 'Since first I saw you, Sancha—'

He fell silent. Which of us initiated the kiss, I cannot say. He was holding himself back; he pressed me against him, kissing me repeatedly, at times gently nipping my lips with his teeth. I caught hold of his hand and laid it upon one of my breasts.

'Not here,' he breathed, though he did not remove his hand. 'Not now. There is too great a risk of being seen.'

'Tonight, then,' I said, trembling at my own audacity. 'You know the safest hour and place.'

'Here. Two hours past midnight.'

Thus our complicity was effected. Those words sounded sweet as music to me then; I had entirely forgotten the prediction of the strega, years ago, that my heart could destroy all I loved. Even if I had remembered her prophecy at that sunny moment in the garden with Cesare, I would not have understood it, would not have had the prescience to see how our passion for each other could, over the years, so horribly, inexorably, unwind.

When at last Jofre rose and dressed, the time came for him to escort me to Saint Peter's for Whitsunday Mass. This he did, squinting painfully at the bright Roman light, as the two of us processed with our attendants to the venerable cathedral next to the Vatican.

Fortunately, an excess of drink and strange women had left Jofre dulled and silent; while he cast a single curious glance at the magnificence of my dress, he did not press me as to the cause of my sudden shift in sartorial tactic. Nor did he seem to notice my new ebullience.

I could not repress my smiles. I felt overwhelmed each time I recalled Cesare's kiss. I no longer felt concern over what either His Holiness or Lucrezia thought of me. I cared not whether the Pope remembered my refusing him or not, or whether he intended revenge: so long as I lived long enough to meet Cesare in the garden, my joy was complete. All my thoughts, my emotions, were focused blithely on that one moment to come, when my love and I would be alone.

We entered the cathedral. Saint Peter's had been constructed a dozen centuries before, and its interior reflected its age. I had expected grandeur and glory, but the stone walls within were cracked and crumbling, the floor so worn and uneven I had to take care lest I stumble. Neither the hundreds of candles which had been lit, nor the gilded purple vestments on the altar, could ease the gloom; the wafting incense intensified the sense of closeness, the lack of fresh air. It was like walking into an immense crypt. This was appropriate, I suppose, since Saint Peter was reportedly buried beneath the altar.

Yet none of it could dampen my cheer. I separated from my husband, and went to take my place with the women of the Borgia household. Lucrezia had not arrived, but the delicate, ethereal

Giulia was already there, beside the keen-eyed Adriana and their ladies-in-waiting. We women stood in the front centre of the church, facing the altar while off to one side, a great throne had been erected for His Holiness, and beside it seats for the high-ranking cardinals and Borgia men. Many cardinals had already taken their places, but I found myself searching anxiously for only one: Cesare.

He had yet to come. Some time passed before we heard the sound of fanfare; at last, His Holiness appeared, clad in white satin robes and matching cap, and his long gold mantle. He nodded to me with a beneficent smile; if he held any rancour toward me, he failed to show it—and as for myself, I bowed most respectfully. Behind him came Cesare, who took the seat flanking the throne; Jofre sat beside him, and the rest of the seats were quickly filled with cardinals.

Behind Cesare came Lucrezia, with a dozen attendants. She was dressed in a blue-grey silk gown that made the best of her eyes. So expansive was my mood, so glad my heart, that I smiled brightly in welcome as she came to stand beside me, and embraced her with such enthusiasm that she was taken aback.

It being Pentecost, a visiting Spanish prelate had been invited to give the sermon. He was desperate to impress his distinguished audience with his erudition, for he droned on for an intolerable time. I had never realized that the fire of God, which caused supernatural wisdom to flow from the tongues of men, could be a dry and utterly boring topic.

He spoke for more than an hour—an unforgivable length, during which time His Holiness suffered two coughing fits and numerous cardinals fidgeted openly in their seats. One old Borgia dropped his head back, and, mouth agape, began to snore quite loudly.

I could not help myself. I began to giggle. I was able to suppress the sound sufficiently so that I did not catch the Pope's attention, but my entire body shook with the effort. My encounter with Cesare had left me in a strange and childlike mood; normally, I would never have permitted myself to behave with such indignity.

Yet my giggles were so utterly helpless that Lucrezia, that cautious creature, became infected herself. I gasped in a breath, met her gaze . . . and the two of us had to grasp each other's arms for support, lest we collapse upon the worn stone.

At that instant, a wicked thought seized me. Here we poor women were forced to stand upon unforgiving rock, our feet tiring during the endless sermon, while the men had the comfort of their chairs. But to my left was a flight of narrow stairs leading up to the wooden stalls built for the canons who sang the gospel. On this particular Sunday, the benches were empty.

I gave Lucrezia's sleeve a gentle tug, and gestured with my eyes at the stalls above and behind us. Her own eyes widened—at first with mild horror at the thought of impropriety. Reverence required us to keep our places during the sermon, and remain utterly still; such was especially important for a relative of the Pope. But as she considered the misdeed, horror transformed to evil gaiety.

I moved past the other ladies, and, unable to mask my mirth, scurried up the stairs like a girl, then dropped down onto the bench with an utter lack of decorum.

Lucrezia followed—though she moved up the stairs with exaggerated noise and difficulty, drawing more attention to herself and increasing the outrageousness of the act. She sat, emitting such a large, gusting sigh that the prelate giving the sermon paused and frowned, scandalized at the disruption. My ladies and hers were obliged to follow us up, a production which caused no small amount of noise for the prelate, who lost his train of thought and repeated the same sentence three times before regaining his composure.

I glanced over at the Pope; he was grinning openly, delighted at the playfulness of his women. I glanced at Cesare; he did not smile, but his dark eyes shone with humour.

Without looking at her, I leaned sideways towards Lucrezia and whispered, 'Please believe me: I have no designs on your father. I wish to be nothing more than your brother's wife.'

She pretended not to hear. Yet after a few moments had passed, I glanced over at her to find her gazing back at me, merry with approval. I had won another friend in the Vatican.

XIV

That night, I sent my closest ladies away from my bedchamber, saying I wished to sleep alone. They were used to my whims and did not question me, resigning themselves to sleeping in a nearby room. Before they left, I insisted my youngest maid, Felicia, set out a black silk gown and veil for me, saying that I missed Naples greatly and wished to wear nothing but mourning for the rest of the week.

I knew I should have consulted Donna Esmeralda—who had no doubt already found sources and gleaned as much information as possible about the members of the Borgia household. But so strong was my infatuation that I asked no questions; if Cesare was a rake, as lascivious and fickle as his father, I did not want to know. Even had I been told, I would have rejected such news.

I scarcely had time to blow out the oil lamp on my table when a swift knock came at the chamber door—one that made my heart sink, for I recognized it as Jofre's. Without waiting for a reply, he entered; in the yellowish light, I saw the sheepish leer on his face.

'Sancha, my darling,' he said. 'Is there a place in your bed for me tonight?' He shut the door behind him. He was slightly unsteady on his feet, and his eyes half-lidded; he was drunk, a condition I found him in often since we had come to live with his family.

I paled. 'I . . . I am feeling unwell,' I stammered, and as though I were a virgin, I clutched my chemise round my neck, lest he see too much flesh.

Jofre seemed not to hear the words. Fuelled by wine, he stumbled over to where I sat upon the bed, and laid his hands upon my breasts. 'I have the most beautiful wife in the world,' he slurred, 'and I shall take her now.'

I felt two things: pity for him, that I did not return his feelings, and fear, that the wine would cause him to fall asleep in my bed on the very night I had planned my first act of infidelity.

Had he been any drunker, he would have been incapable of the deed. I lay obediently on the bed and parted my legs for him. He, in turn, pulled down his leggings and hiked my underskirts up to my waist, crawled on top of me, and inserted himself.

What followed would not have inspired even the over-wrought Petrarch. Jofre lay atop me, unable to support himself with his arms, his face buried in my breasts. For a moment, he thrust madly, clumsily—then, having worn himself out, stopped and gasped for air.

'Can you ever love me?' he asked, his voice pregnant with tears. 'My Sancha, will you ever come to love me?'

'You are my prince,' I told him. I might deceive him with Cesare, but I could not lie to his face. 'I grow fonder of you with every passing day.'

His head lolled; sleep threatened.

I used a womanly trick explained to me before my wedding: I used the muscles that surrounded Jofre's organ to squeeze tightly, thus arousing him enough to continue his thrusting, and, at last, yield to pleasure and collapse.

He sighed and rolled over onto his back; I sensed that he was again on the verge of slumber, so I pulled up his leggings, then pushed him upright.

'You must hurry to your chamber,' I said, with no other explanation. 'Here. Let me help you.'

Weary with wine and sexual release, Jofre was too confused to argue. I half-supported him as he staggered back to the door.

As was our custom, I gave him a little kiss. 'Good night, my sweet.'

I returned to my bed. If all I had learned of God was true, then I was damned, and rightly so; guilt overwhelmed me. I did not want to betray my husband, yet my heart would let me do no else. *You are evil*, I told myself. *Wicked. How can you be so cruel to one who loves you?* But even as my legs were sticky with my husband's seed, I dreamt of his brother, and the encounter to come. The strength of my feeling for Cesare left me no choice. It seemed ironic that such a dazzling, magnificent thing as love had struck too late, after both parties had taken vows prohibiting its celebration.

I cleansed myself with a cloth. At last the time came; I rose, and struggled in the darkness to dress myself.

The other ladies were all sleeping, and undisturbed—but Donna Esmeralda had not been fooled. As I fought to lace my bodice with unskilled fingers, the stout old matron, dressed only in her white linen nightgown, came into my chamber.

She said nothing. Given the lack of light, I could not see her expression, but I could sense her disapproval, imagine her baleful stare.

'I could not sleep,' I said haughtily. At Esmeralda's continued silence, I demanded, 'At least help me with my bodice.'

Esmeralda obeyed, tugging on the gown not at all gently. 'This will only lead to more trouble, Madonna.'

I was too impetuous, too giddy with love to tolerate the truth. 'I told you, I cannot sleep! I will take some fresh air.'

'It is not seemly for a young woman to go out alone at this hour. Let me go with you, or call one of the guards.' Her tone was insistent.

'Lace my bodice, then leave me! I left the party last night alone, and arrived in my chamber safely, did I not? I can protect myself.'

For a time, she did not reply, merely finished her work, then stepped back. At last, she drew a breath; she knew me too well not to speak her mind.

'That is not quite the case, is it, Madonna? You required a good deal of help last night.'

I was too astounded to answer. How could anyone, besides myself and Cesare, know of His Holiness' indiscretion? If Donna Esmeralda was already party to the secret, then I had no hope of hiding an affair with Cesare from anyone at the papal court.

I told myself I did not care.

'I shall not speak of this to you again,' Esmeralda said finally. 'I know you are wilful and impervious to reason. But hear, if you can: this will only lead to greater danger than you faced last night, my Sancha. Not less. You are Eve in the Garden—and the serpent himself confronts you.'

'Leave me,' I commanded, and drew the veil over my face.

The night air had cooled only slightly after the summer-warm day; I was accustomed to the mists and fog of a coastal clime, but Rome afforded no such cloak. I relied on the darkness and my veil for disguise on this, my first sally into deception.

Overhead, clouds half-hid a waxing moon. In such feeble light, my vision obstructed by a film of dark silk gauze, I moved haltingly, like one near blind. The garden seemed totally unfamiliar, the bright colours of the foliage reduced to shades of grey, the roses and orange trees sudden strangers. I hesitated along the path, fighting panic. Had I taken this turn, or the next? If I became lost, would Cesare think I had played him for a fool, and leave the garden in disgust?

Or had he played me for one?

I chided myself for entertaining such fears; I hated the intensity of my love for Cesare, because it made me weak.

I drew in a steadying breath, made my decision, and took the nearest turn. As I did, I caught sight of the stone bench beneath the shade tree, and something dark moving against the pale stone: the outline of a man.

Cesare. I wanted to cry out like a girl and run to him, but forced myself to walk slowly, regally: he would have wanted no less.

He, too, was dressed in black, all but face and hands blending into the background of night.

He waited, tall and dignified, till I arrived beside him—then both of us dropped all restraint. I cannot say who moved first; perhaps we moved together, but I sensed no passage of time between the moment I stepped up to him and the moment my veil was thrown back and we were locked fast in an embrace, lips against lips, body against body, so intensely, so strongly I felt as though the edges of my flesh were dissolving into his. So great was the heat generated that, without our arms gripping each other, I would have fallen back, senseless.

To my dismay, he tore himself from me. 'Not here,' he said, in a voice hoarse and desperate. 'You are not some kitchen maid to be taken casually upon the dirt. Trust me; I have made arrangements. We will be safe.'

I replaced my veil; he took my hand. His step was certain; he knew his way well. He led me along the back of the palace, to an unguarded entrance leading to an unfamiliar corridor. This led to a heavy wooden door, which opened to another corridor . . . one long and of recent construction, crudely finished and unappointed. Its existence was clearly to provide private access, and nothing more. Wall torches lit our way.

After a moment, we arrived again at a door, which Cesare opened with a flourish. I frowned in puzzlement. Before us lay a great chapel, ancient and ornate; votive lamps flickered on the altar, and a great papal throne sat to one side, with stalls nearby for cardinals.

Cesare's lips curved. 'The Sistine Chapel,' he said, as he helped me through the doorway. 'We are in Saint Peter's.'

My veil brushed softly against my lips as they parted in astonishment. So *this* was the same passageway His Holiness used to travel swiftly to the Palazzo Santa Maria.

'Come,' Cesare said. We moved swiftly through the chapel, through the cathedral, and into the adjoining halls of the Vatican. Never did we encounter a guard; Cesare had taken pains to ensure our privacy.

He led me into the Borgia apartments, which I recognized from the previous night's gala; it gave me little comfort to think I would be so close to the Pope. Happily, Cesare led me in a different direction, and upstairs; at last we arrived at an unguarded suite, and he flung open the doors with a flourish.

'I have brought you to my own bed, and dismissed all the servants until morning,' he said, closing the doors behind us. 'How long you wish to stay is your own choice, Madonna.'

'Forever,' I murmured.

At once, he fell to his knees before me and embraced my skirts, his arms wrapped round my legs, his face tilted upwards. Utterly earnest, he proclaimed, 'Only say you wish it, Sancha, and I will give up the priesthood. My father wants me Pope, and so I must be a cardinal—but I am not suited by nature for such a calling. His Holiness will do whatever I ask of him; he would annul your marriage to Jofre. Surely you know your husband is not truly his son . . . '

Jofre not the Pope's son? The revelation startled some distant part of me, that small, detached and silent part not overwhelmed by Cesare's proposal and desperate to accept it. 'Then whose is he?' I whispered.

'The very legitimate offspring of my mother Vannozza and her husband.' Cesare smiled.

I wavered, thinking of myself and Cesare, free to love as we willed, free to bear children together. But Jofre and I were married; my own father and a Borgia cardinal had witnessed the physical consummation. There could be no grounds for annulment.

I pressed my fingers firmly against Cesare's lips to staunch the flow of his words. 'The marriage act was witnessed and cannot be undone,' I said. 'But now is not the time to speak of the future: now is the time for you to take me to your bed.'

He accepted this. He rose and, facing me, his fingertips beneath mine, led me back into his bedchamber.

The shutters were closed, but the room glowed with the light of twenty candles, placed about the room on gold sconces. There was a half-finished mural on the wall, of a pagan theme, and on the bed, a coverlet of crimson velvet. Fur throws covered the floor, and on a beautifully carved bedside table rested a flagon of wine, and two golden goblets, inlaid with rubies. This was the bed-chamber of a prince, not a priest.

I was prepared to throw myself down and hike up my skirts for a fleeting event, as I was accustomed to with Jofre. Yet as I neared the bed, Cesare arrested me with his voice.

'May I see you, Sancha, as God made you?'

I removed my veil and turned to face him, surprised by this request. I was near trembling with desperation to consummate the affair; I saw the quiver in Cesare's parted lips. The intensity in his eyes approached madness, yet in his tone, his manner, was delicate.

I lifted my chin, determined. 'Only if you return the favour.'

In reply, he unfastened his priest's robe and slipped it off, to reveal beneath a black tunic of alternating bands of black satin and velvet, and a sheathed dagger at his hip, and black leggings—the costume of a Roman gentleman. With swiftness and grace, he removed first slippers, then the tunic, revealing a high, well-muscled chest, with sparse, dark hairs at the hollow; he was lean, and his collarbone, hips and ribs showed prominently as he carefully pulled the leggings down over his sculpted thighs. When he finished, he rose and stood, humbly available for my scrutiny.

I stared in awe. I had never seen a fully naked man before. Even the pleasure-giving Onorato had never removed his tunic, and had only lowered his leggings as far as necessary during our dalliances. Jofre never removed his tunic, save for our wedding night, when custom required us to be naked, and I believe he removed his leggings completely only once. The closest I came to being unclad with Jofre were times such as this evening, when I had already removed my gown and wore only my shift. Even then, our relations took place under cover of clothing.

But here was Cesare, entirely revealed and glorious. I could not avoid staring at the place between his legs, where, emerging from a profusion of jet-black hair, his erect male organ pointed at me with a decidedly upward slant. It was larger than Jofre's, and I began to move my hand toward it, wanting to touch it.

'Not yet,' Cesare whispered. Like a lady-in-waiting, he moved behind me, and with surprising skill, began untying my sleeves. I pulled them off, laughing at the sudden sense of freedom, then waited while he unlaced my bodice.

That done, I pulled my gown down and stepped out of it. Such a heavy weight to bear, clothes. I was in a hurry to pull my chemise over my head, but Cesare spoke again.

'Stand in front of the candlelight—there.' He tilted his head, dark eyes shining with admiration. 'The effect is gossamer; like looking at an angel, through wisps of cloud.'

'Bah!' I pulled off the undergarment and flung it to the floor. 'To the bed!'

'*No,*' he countered, as emphatically as an artist demanding a masterpiece be admired. 'Look at you,' he breathed. 'One cannot question God's wisdom.'

I smiled at that—in part, at his adoration, in part, out of my own vanity. I was still young then, and had never suckled a child; my breasts had been called perfect by Onorato, neither too large nor too small, with a firm, pleasing shape. I knew, too, that the curve of my hips was womanly, and that I was not too thin.

He stepped up behind me and began to unfasten my hair, done up in a single fat braid to keep it out of my way while sleeping. When it was free, I shook my head and let it fall unhindered to my waist; he drew his fingers through it once, twice, sighing, then moved again to stand in front of me and study me as a painter might assess his own work.

Once again, he surprised me. As I stood there for his regard, he walked up to me, knelt again with the reverence of a pilgrim at a shrine, and kissed the dark mound of Venus between my legs. I started slightly—then started even more when he parted my nether lips with his thumbs and began to massage the region with his tongue.

Embarrassment warred with delight. I twitched, I shifted my weight from leg to leg, I tried, overwhelmed by the sensation at one point, to pull away from him, but he cupped his hands round my backside and held me fast.

'Stop,' I begged him, for I was swaying backward, near falling. In response, he half-lifted me and pressed me hard against the nearest wall. 'Stop,' I begged again, for the feeling was too intense to bear . . .

Only when I ceased begging and began moaning did he at last lift his face, wearing a self-satisfied, wicked little smile, and say, 'Now to the bed.'

He did not, as I had hoped, continue licking; instead, he kissed me full on the lips, his beard and tongue covered with my scent. For the first time, I experienced the warmth of flesh pressed against flesh, from head to breast to sex to legs to toe, and shivered: how could this be sinful, and not divine?

We wrestled. I could not, as I had with Onorato, lie back and let myself be the object of attention, a passive creature to be won: I fought, in the midst of Cesare's pleasuring me, to do the same for him. I *craved* to do the same for him. Some never-before tapped force within me rose, something at once bestial and holy. I felt consumed by flame—not bestowed by an external God, but arising from within, internal and intense, filling me and then bursting forth from the crown of my head, like an apostle at Pentecost, like one of the tapers flickering in the wall sconce near Cesare's bed.

He would not enter me: he made me wait, made me demand, made me plead. Only when I had crossed over into madness did he at last oblige me, and I clung fast to him, legs and arms grasping him so tightly they ached, but I did not care; I had him now, and would permit no escape. He laughed slightly, softly, at the ferocity with which I held him, but there was no detachment in it. I could see reflected in his dark eyes the wildness in my own: we were lost to each other. I was no more an ordinary lover to him than he to me. We were possessed of a passion that not all men and women have the grace to experience in their lifetimes.

He rode me—or I him, I cannot tell, for we moved of a singular accord—with alternating savagery and delicacy. During the latter times, as he moved inside me slowly, his eyes narrowed, his breathing slow and tortured, I tried to thrash, to force him back to more brutal love-making, but he held me fast, pinning my arms above my head, whispering, 'Patience, Princess . . . '

Once again, he drove me to begging—something I would do for no other man. I ached to be spent, to be done away with; but Cesare was determined to take me to the precipice of the greatest desperation I had ever known.

How much time passed since I had entered his chamber, I could not say. It might have been hours.

When I could bear no more, he tore himself away. This provoked the worst horror in me—such a thing could not be allowed. Yet he was stronger than I, and with that strength, gently applied, and calm words one might use to soothe an anxious beast, he coaxed me to lie back, and applied tongue and fingers to the delta between my legs.

I thought I had experienced pleasure before; I thought I had experienced passionate heat. But the sensation Cesare induced in me that night began slowly, building like an ember coaxed into raging flames. It seemed to begin outside myself, somewhere in the heavens above my head, and I felt it descend on me, an unspeakable, sacred force, inescapable, all-consuming. The room before me: the bed, my own naked skin, the walls and ceiling, the flickering light—even Cesare's face over mine, his eyes wide, burning with anticipation—disappeared.

I shall certainly go to Hell for saying it, but there seemed nothing in all the world but God, but bliss, whatever one must call the extreme sensation where all boundaries between self and the world disappear. Even I was gone . . .

Yet despite my absence from reality, I sensed union with Cesare again. He had mounted me in the midst of my ecstasy, merging with it, riding it until our voices joined.

I was quite used to repressing my moans of delight in the past, to reducing them to whispers, lest others hear. This experience tore from me a scream, one I was quite helpless to control. But it was not only my voice; Cesare joined in. Yet I could not have differentiated one of us from the other; the two of us made one sound—which surely was heard in every corner of the papal apartments.

We lay for a time on the bed. Neither of us spoke; I certainly could not, for my throat was rendered quite hoarse, and I was exhausted, my long hair stuck to my arms, my back, my breasts, with perspiration. At long last, Cesare turned to me and smoothed tendrils back from my forehead and cheek.

'I have never had such an incredible experience with a woman. I think I have never known love before now, Sancha.'

I coughed, then managed to whisper, 'My heart is yours, Cesare. And we are both damned for it.'

He rose to fetch me wine. A sudden playfulness overtook me—the same sort of silliness that had come over me in Saint Peter's—perhaps because of the sense of freedom provoked by ecstatic release. I would not, I told myself merrily, be deprived of the finest lover I had ever known, at least not so soon after being conquered by him. As he attempted to rise from the bed, I wrapped both my arms about his thigh.

He laughed—dignified Cesare, always in control, snickered in helpless surprise at the unexpectedness of the act. Nonetheless, he continued onward, struggling toward the carafe of wine, certainly thinking that I would not persist in such childlike behaviour.

Chuckling, I strengthened my grasp; he, in turn, would not be dissuaded from his task.

I held on even as he rose, clinging to his leg despite the fact that doing so pulled me from the bed onto the fur-carpeted floor. He gasped with hilarity and astonishment at the fact, and took one step, two; all the while, I held on firmly, forcing him to drag me along.

At last, he yielded, collapsing on top of me, and the two of us giggled on the floor like children.

When I returned to my own bed, I lay for a time listening to Esmeralda's soft wheezing breath, and stared up at the darkness. At first I dwelled in drowsy euphoria, reliving the moments of bliss with Cesare . . . and then guilt returned once more, bringing me to full, agitated consciousness.

I was, like my forebears, far too capable of cruelty and deception—especially when away from my brother's good and gentle influence. Only two days among the Borgias, and I was already an adulteress. What was to become of me, if I spent the rest of my life in Rome?

Summer 1496

XV

As pleasant as the month of May was in Rome, June turned warm, and July even warmer; August was intolerably hot compared to the temperate coastal cities I had lived in. It was the custom for His Holiness and his family, as well as everyone else of wealth, to retreat to cooler climes for the month. But this particular August marked the return of the Pope's son, Juan, from the court of Spain—and so, despite the heat, the occasion was marked grandly, with feasting and parties.

Despite my fears, I suffered no further advances from Alexander; I could not help thinking that Cesare had somehow convinced his father to let me be. But Cesare would say nothing to me of the situation; he only advised that I avoid, whenever possible, sitting next to His Holiness at festive occasions when there was much wine, that I behave and dress modestly around him, that when I sensed Alexander was becoming drunk, I distance myself from him.

All these things I did. However, I still sat across from Lucrezia, each of us on our velvet cushions on either side of the papal throne, at many of His Holiness' audiences. I believe Alexander liked the pair of us, one dark, one golden, as fitting feminine adornments to his throne.

Lucrezia was, as Cesare had said, her father's most respected advisor; often, she would interrupt a petitioner to whisper advice in Alexander's ear. She had her own little throne where she heard petitions as well. I listened to her a few times, and was impressed by her intelligence. Both she and her father were skilled diplomats; regardless of how Rodrigo Borgia had come to the papacy, he fulfilled its duties admirably.

My affair with Cesare continued, always with our passion consummated in his private chambers. I brimmed with happiness; it was difficult to hide such joy from others, to keep from showing Cesare affection in public. He, meanwhile, kept speaking of how he intended to leave the priesthood.

One night, after we had collapsed, exhausted after lovemaking, he turned towards me and gently brushed a stray tendril of hair behind my ear. 'I want to marry you, Sancha.'

Such words thrilled me; yet I could not deny the facts. 'You are a cardinal,' I said. 'And I am already married.'

He touched my cheek. 'I want to give you children. I would let you go to Naples—I know how you miss it. We could live there, if it would make you happy. I would only need to return to Rome a few times a year.'

I was near weeping; Cesare had read my heart and mind. He was right—nothing would make me happier. But such a thing seemed, at the time, quite impossible. And so I silenced him each time he broached the subject, for I did not want to nurse false hopes; nor did I want rumours to hurt Jofre. Cesare soon learned not to press. But it was clear that his frustration with his role as a cardinal was growing.

On the tenth of August, Juan, the Pope's second eldest son, at last arrived in Rome, leaving behind a pregnant wife and small son in Spain. After the French invasion, Alexander had often spoken of his longing to have all his children live with him, since he claimed to have become increasingly aware of his own mortality, and the fragility of life. It was for this ostensible reason Jofre and I had been summoned to Rome—and now, with Juan's appearance, Alexander's wish was finally accomplished. All four of his children were home. It struck me as odd that Juan did not bring his family with him, though none of the Borgias seemed to think this remarkable.

There was another reason for his arrival: Juan, Duke of Gandia, was also Captain-General of the Church, commander of the papal army, and his father had called him home to punish the House of Orsini, who had supported the French during the war. Juan's army was to attack and subdue every rebellious noble house in Rome, to make of each an example of Borgia vengeance. So long as Alexander was Pope, there would be peace in the Papal States.

Every cardinal in the city came out to greet the young Duke of Gandia as he arrived on horseback—on a steed bedecked with gold and silver bells. Yet Juan was not to be outdone by his mount: his red velvet cap and brown velvet tunic were heavy with gems and pearls; no doubt, beneath all the finery, he was melting in the August sun. I watched from a window in the Palazzo Santa Maria as Cesare met his brother and led him to his new home, the Apostolic Palace.

That night was cause for a great celebration—which required my attendance, along with the rest of the family. I dressed demurely, in black; Esmeralda was quick to mention all the rumours she had heard, that Juan was a scoundrel of the worst sort. Perhaps she feared I would ignore her warning concerning him, just as I had refused to listen to any of her unkind remarks about Cesare.

The feast came first at a private supper, with the papal family and related cardinals. I had learned to seat myself discreetly farther away from the Pope, that I might not summon unwanted attention; that night, he was flanked by Juan and, as always, Lucrezia. As for myself, I sat between Jofre and Cesare.

How shall I best describe Juan? A shooting star with a charm that dazzled, then faded as the man's true personality revealed itself. He entered the room late—thinking nothing of making His Holiness wait, and Alexander said not a word about the inconvenience, whereas anyone else's tardiness would be cause for insult.

Juan entered blazing: eyes bright with mirth (yet sly), smile wide (yet arrogant), laughter ringing through the halls. His lips were thick and crude, like his father's, his hair neither light nor truly dark; he was clean-shaven, and neither as handsome as Cesare nor as plain as Lucrezia. He had with him a friend—a tall, dark-skinned Moor (I later learned this was Djem, the Turk, a royal hostage in the papal court)—and the two of them were similarly dressed in silk turbans, and bright red-and-yellow striped satin robes. Around his neck he wore gold necklaces, so many of such weight that I did not see how he held himself upright.

In the centre of Juan's turban was a ruby twice the size of an eye, from which sprang a peacock feather.

Alexander trembled with delight, as though he had just been given a new virgin to deflower. 'My child!' he sighed. 'My dearest, dearest son! Oh, how dark the days have been without you!' And he clasped Juan to him, overwhelmed by happiness.

Juan pressed his cheek to the old man's—eclipsing the Pope's face, but allowing himself to study the reaction of his siblings from beneath half-lowered lids. All of us had risen when Juan entered, and I could not help noting the sudden tautness in Lucrezia's expression, the fact that her smile was small and insincere.

I caught, too, the glance that passed between Juan and Cesare—saw the gloating look of triumph on Juan's face, the look of calculated indifference on Cesare's. But beside me, my lover closed one hand into a fist.

We sat. Dinner passed with His Holiness speaking not a single word to any person other than Juan, and Juan was quick to regale us all with humorous tales of life in Spain, and why he was glad to be back in Rome. Questions about his wife, Maria Henriques, cousin to the King of Spain, were answered with a shrug and the bored reply, 'Pregnant. Always sick, that woman.'

'I hope you are treating her well,' Alexander said, in a tone of reproach mixed with indulgence. Juan's escapades with courtesans were legend—and twice he had kidnapped and violated two young virgins of noble birth shortly before their weddings. Only the Borgia coffers saved him from death at the hands of the women's male relatives.

'*Very* well, Father. You know I always take your words to heart.'

If any sarcasm dwelled in those words, His Holiness chose not to hear them. He smiled, the indulgent father.

Throughout dinner, Juan held court; he addressed himself to each of us, in turn, inquiring as to the state of our lives. Of Jofre, he asked, 'What now, brother? What did you do to win yourself such a magnificent bride?'

Before Jofre, blushing, could seize on a witty reply, Juan answered his own question.

'Of course. It is because you are a Borgia, and therefore fortunate; just as all we Borgia children are fortunate.'

Jofre fell silent, and his expression darkened slightly; I remembered how Cesare had once let slip that my husband was not considered the Pope's true son, which made Juan's comment a veiled barb.

Juan laughed heartily at it—he was already quite drunk, being even more predisposed to wine than his father. Alexander chuckled, taking the comment as a compliment to himself, but Lucrezia, Cesare and I did not so much as smile. Beneath the table, I put my hand upon my husband's thigh in support.

Lucrezia's conversation with Juan was more pleasant and animated; Cesare's discussion with his brother was curt but civil. Then the Duke of Gandia turned his attention to me.

'How do you find Rome?' he asked, eyes gleaming, his expression warm and enthusiastic. It was easy, at that moment, to see his father's outgoing nature in him.

I answered honestly. 'I miss the sea. But Rome has an allure of its own. The buildings are magnificent, the gardens beautiful, and the sun . . . ' I hesitated, searching for the right words to capture the essence of the light, which painted everything golden so that it seemed to glow from within.

'. . . is beastly hot in August,' Juan finished, with a short laugh.

I gave a small smile. 'It *is* beastly hot in August. I am used to the coast, where the weather is more temperate in summer. But the light here is beautiful. I am not surprised it has inspired so much art.'

This pleased everyone at the table, especially Alexander.

'Are you homesick?' Juan asked pointedly.

I wound my arm around Jofre's. 'Where my husband dwells, that is my home: and he is here, so how can I be homesick?'

This drew even more approval. My gesture was partly born of defiance: I disliked this man for insulting Jofre in front of his family. My love for Cesare filled me with guilt; I knew my words were pure hypocrisy. But though I did not love my husband, I still felt allegiance toward him.

The ever-present smirk of arrogance left Juan's lips: a surprisingly sincere wistfulness overtook his expression. 'God has smiled on you, brother,' he told Jofre quietly, 'to have given you such a wife. I can see that she is a great source of happiness to you.'

The Pope beamed, pleased with everyone's response. The conversation moved on to other topics, and at last, when we were all sated, Alexander called for the dishes to be removed. We moved out into the Hall of Faith, where more wine was served. On the wall was an almost-completed mural by Pinturicchio and his students, of the Pope himself kneeling in prayer, worshipping the risen Christ.

Alexander sat on the throne provided and gestured for the musicians to begin playing. That evening, it pleased him to see Juan and Lucrezia dance. As the tune was sprightly, Juan led Lucrezia onto the floor, she on his right, and the two began a fast *piva*: a short step to the left, one half-hop to the right, another left, then a pause. Both were exceptionally graceful, and Juan soon grew bored with simple movements. After the third step, he whirled about to face his partner, and, placing his palm against hers, led her in a *voltatonda*, a counter-clockwise circle consisting of the same basic *piva*. Alexander clapped in approval.

By the time the two dancers returned, both were flushed and perspiring.

'And now,' Juan told me, 'it is your turn to be my partner.' He bowed low, sweeping off his turban in a grand gesture, then tossing it aside as if it were made of rags, not silk and gems. His short, dark hair was plastered to his forehead and scalp with sweat.

The musicians played a languid, almost mournful melody; Juan chose a slower *bassadanza*, and we moved deliberately about the hall in a solemn four-step processional. For a time, we did not speak, merely performed as prettily as we could for the amusement of His Holiness.

After a pause, Juan remarked, 'I was most sincere when I said my little brother was lucky enough to have such a wife.'

I averted my eyes demurely. 'You are kind.'

He laughed. 'That accusation is rarely brought against me. I am far from kind; but I *am* honest, when it suits me. And you, Donna Sancha, are the loveliest woman I have ever seen.'

I said nothing.

'You are also bold enough to defend your husband in public—when he is too weak to do so himself. You are aware that His Holiness does not believe Jofre to be his son, but has accepted the word of his mistress out of kindness?'

I was too angry to meet Juan's insolent gaze. 'I have heard as much. It matters not.'

'Ah, but it does. Jofre, you see, will have his little principality in Squillace, and that will be the end of it. He has been accorded as many honours as he can ever hope to achieve in this life—and as I am sure a lady with your keen insight has guessed, he does not possess the intelligence of a true Borgia.'

Our hands were pressed together tightly as we danced; I wanted nothing better than to pull away from him, to upbraid him for his slurs. But the Pope was watching and nodding in time to the music.

'You, sir,' I replied, my voice trembling with anger, 'have just shown by your arrogant comments that you possess little of that intelligence yourself. If you had any sense at all, you would appreciate your brother, as I do, for his sincerity and his good heart.'

He laughed as if I had just said something remarkably charming. 'I cannot help but adore you, Sancha. You say what you mean and care not whom you offend. Honesty and beauty are an irresistible combination.' He paused. 'Come, come. I can understand why you pity Jofre and don't wish to hurt him. But there *is* such a thing as discretion.

'I am not one to hold back my words either, Sancha. I want you. You would be wise to ally yourself with me—for I am the favourite of all the Pope's children. I am the captain of his army—and some day I shall be secular ruler of all the Papal States.'

I could restrain my temper no longer, but lowered my hand and ceased dancing. 'I could never love someone so contemptible as you.'

The sarcastic smirk returned; his upward-slanting eyes narrowed as he replied, 'Do not play at self-righteousness with me, Madonna. You have already slept with two brothers.' Jealousy flickered across his features; I realized this had less to do with me and more to do with his rivalry with Cesare. 'What does it matter if you sleep with the third?'

I drew back my arm and slapped his cheek so hard my palm stung.

Alexander half-rose from his chair in alarm; Lucrezia put a hand to her mouth—whether in amusement or surprise, I could not tell.

Juan drew a dagger from his belt; the homicidal rage in his eyes made me certain this was to be the last instant of my life. His fury was wild and unrestrained, far from the cool, calculating hatred I had first encountered in his sister's eyes.

But Cesare rushed from his father's side and stepped between the two of us. Swiftly, he seized Juan's wrist and twisted it so that the latter cried out; the dagger fell to the stone floor.

'I will kill the bitch!' Juan whispered hoarsely. 'How dare she—'

It was Cesare's turn to strike his brother across the face. As the encounter between them turned into a full-fledged brawl, I hurriedly made my exit, ladies in tow.

XVI

By the time I arrived back in my chambers at the Palace of Santa Maria, I had grown even more agitated. The fact that I had slapped the Pope's favourite son in public took full hold of me, as did the knowledge that Juan would not rest until he had his revenge.

Worse, Cesare had stepped forward as my outraged protector—Cesare, and not my own husband. The former's passionate response would set tongues wagging in the court . . . and such rumours would hurt Jofre deeply. Not only would they damage my marriage, they would outrage Alexander, and destroy my friendship with Lucrezia.

Worst of all, I feared the news might reach Naples, and Alfonso . . . and I would not be able to lie to him, even in a letter. Having to admit my adultery to my dear brother would shame me most of all.

Fortunately, I was set to rendezvous later that night with Cesare in the garden, and I focused on the fact as a way to calm myself. Cesare's unparalleled skill at diplomacy would save me from Juan's wrath, just as it had saved me from Alexander's unwanted attentions; I waited restlessly until I could discuss the matter with him.

At last, the time came for me to set out. Instead of struggling with a full gown with bodice and sleeves that required lacing, I had taken to wearing a black silk chemise and an overgown that I could slip on easily. Again, there was always the veil, to protect me from recognition—and the stiletto in case I was accosted.

Thus disguised, I stepped silently out into the corridor. The hour was so late that few sconces were lit, but I made my way through the dimness with ease, as I knew my way well. Cesare had, as always, bribed the guards to keep them out of my path, and so I encountered no one.

But as I passed by the corridor that led to Giulia's and Lucrezia's apartments, I heard a woman cry out, as if in pain.

In retrospect, I should have been wise; I should have hardened my heart and continued onward—after all, my affair with Cesare was at stake. But the sound evoked in me concern and curiosity. Thus I took that irrevocable turn down the wrong corridor.

The moment I did so, intuition froze me to the spot, even though I at first could not identify what I saw. Soon enough, however, I distinguished Lucrezia's moon-coloured face in the dimness. She was still fully dressed in the gown she had worn to Juan's reception, and apparently just returning from it; her eyes were closed, her lips half-parted, and soft, regular moans escaped from her.

She was leaning forward, swaying, decidedly intoxicated, and perhaps about to be ill. I decided to help her, saying that I had been unable to sleep; perhaps she would remember little or nothing of my intervention the following day.

Luckily, common sense kept me rooted where I was—for in the next instant, I realized that I looked upon not just Lucrezia, but Lucrezia merged with another. Great male hands clasped her breasts, which had fallen forward out of her bodice, and her swaying was the result of a large, dark figure behind her, thrusting violently where her skirts had been lifted out of the way.

A lover, I realized, and was on the verge of scurrying away. I could scarcely blame Lucrezia for doing what I myself did—especially since her own husband had quite publicly deserted her.

Then she cried out, with drunken, lustful abandon, 'Oh, Papa . . . !'

A chill overtook me. I recognized the hulking figure at once—the white robe, the skullcap, and the face so similar to Lucrezia's own.

This is rape, I tried to convince myself. *Rape. I should sneak behind him with the stiletto . . . The poor girl must be too drunk to know what she is doing . . .*

'Papa!' she cried again, with the rapture of a lover, and I remembered the night when she had attempted to shock me by forcing her breasts to her father's lips.

I lifted a hand to my veiled lips and nearly retched. Fortunately, no sound came with the reflex, and the motion of my arm was undetected by the lovers, who were distracted by their own moaning. *Lovers*, I say, but the term here is profane; I thought of the passage in the Book of Revelation: of the painted whore, Babylon, astride the great horned Beast. The tangle of flesh and fabric that pulsed together here in the darkness was indeed something as monstrous.

'My darling,' I heard the Beast whisper. 'My Lucrezia, my own. You belong to no other as you do to me.'

His words were clear, unslurred. This was no drunken accident, but a consciously chosen embrace.

Bile stung my throat; my eyes watered. I turned and, as silently as I had come, hurried away from the sight.

I half-wanted to return to my chambers, to tremble in quiet revulsion at what I had seen. But this secret was too hideous to bear alone; I wanted the comfort of Cesare. And were I a member of Lucrezia's family, I would want to know the truth. I wanted to believe, as Alfonso would have, that she was young and confused—and that Rodrigo was taking advantage of that. As her older brother, Cesare needed to intervene, to protect her. Of all the Borgias, he seemed the most responsible, the most in control of his emotions; he would know best how to handle this dreadful situation.

I hurried from the corridor and left the palazzo through an unguarded back entrance. My steps along the garden path were swift and haunted: I understood far better, now, why Lucrezia had been jealous of my appearance in Rome. It had not been the girlish crush I had tried so hard to convince myself it had been, or simple envy over the fact I was shown more attention; I was in fact seen as a true rival for Rodrigo's sexual favours. Cesare had made a comment, too, that troubled me now: *She was the same way with Donna Giulia; it took her some time to realize that a man's love for a woman and for his daughter are not one and the same.*

Ah, but she had never come to realize it—nor had her father.

I could only pray that neither the Pope nor Lucrezia had seen me, or recognized me beneath my veil.

At last I arrived at the garden bench and the tree, and was relieved to see Cesare there, waiting for me as always. Normally, we embraced with a passionate kiss, but that night, I caught hold of his hands between mine.

A crease appeared between his dark eyebrows. 'Madonna. What has happened?'

I could not hide my agitation. 'First, I must know—are you all right? When I left, you and Juan—'

'Juan is an idiot,' Cesare said, his tone flinty. 'He has been put in his place. If he ever annoys you again, come to me at once. Fortunately, he is not here for long; he will be leading Father's army into battle shortly.' He tilted his head, studying me intently. 'But this has to do with far more than a buffoon such as Juan.' He drew back my veil, and put a gentle hand to my cheek. 'Look at you, Sancha. You are trembling.'

'I saw . . . ' I began, and could say no more.

'Sit. Sit before you fall.' He drew me down beside him on the garden bench.

'Your father and your sister . . . ' I began again, then stopped.

I needed say no more.

He dropped my hands as if they had become stinging nettles, and turned his face away quickly, but not before I saw the look of pain and humiliation there. 'You saw them,' he whispered, then let out a sound very like a groan. After a pause, he added, 'I had prayed—I had hoped—that it had stopped.'

'You knew.' There was no recrimination in my tone, only wonder.

He stared down at his lap, so that I could see his profile in the dim light; his expression hardened, and a muscle in his jaw twitched as he spoke. 'There is no reasoning with my father, Madonna. I have tried. I have tried . . . ' His voice broke on the final word. Then he gathered himself, and glanced up at me with abrupt dismay. 'Tell me they did not see you!' He caught my hands, his eyes wide with concern.

'No.'

'Thank God.' He sagged and let go a sigh of deep relief, which was short-lived. 'You did not speak of this to anyone? Not even to Donna Esmeralda, certainly?'

'To no one but you.'

Cesare relaxed once more. 'Good. Good.' He drew a finger tenderly along my temple, down the curve of my jaw. 'I am sorry. Sorry you had to witness such a thing . . . '

'Can you not force your father to stop this?' I asked. 'Say that you will tell the College of Cardinals, will make this knowledge public?'

His unguarded expression revealed his inner turmoil; at last, he said, 'All that I am to tell you must swear to keep secret.

'You can trust me with your life,' I replied.

He smiled humourlessly. 'That is precisely what I am about to do.' After a long moment of contemplation, he began. 'My father . . . is a good man. He loves his children more than life. You have seen how generous he is with his affections.' He paused. 'His love is genuine, and runs deep . . . and likewise, his hatred. He is exceptionally dangerous when provoked. Even . . . when his children are the ones who provoke him.' As I tensed beside him, he put a hand upon my arm to comfort me and said, 'Yes, he remembered—vaguely—the encounter with you. But you need have no fear. He found it amusing, considering it a diverting game of love. He prefers his women to be more yielding—not so "hot-tempered", as he put it. In other words, you were a bit too much trouble for him, and not admiring enough to suit his pride. I doubt he will trouble you again.' His expression darkened. 'But when it comes to politics, to true gain or loss—he can be deadly. And while there have been rumours, to actually expose his relationship with Lucrezia would jeopardize his political standing. Do you understand what I am saying, Sancha?'

'Did he threaten your life when you confronted him about your sister?' A sickening hatred overwhelmed me. What kind of man would use his daughter in such a manner, then speak of murdering his own son? I jumped to my feet. 'I am sorry I did not kill him with the stiletto!'

'Hold your tongue,' Cesare warned, and drew me back to stand before him; he touched his fingers to my lips. 'Such is the price of living with an exceedingly ambitious man. I do not know how to further impress upon you the need for silence, except to say: People have died for less. This secret is yours to keep for the rest of your life. And mine.' He studied me intently. 'You feel emotions very deeply, Sancha, and react swiftly, with passion. You must learn to temper that impulse if you are to survive here.'

'I heard a rumour,' I said, more quietly. 'About the death of Rodrigo's brother, who surely would have been elected pope . . . '

He held my gaze as he answered slowly, 'It is no rumour.'

'How can you bear it?' I whispered. My own father had been a tyrant—but even he would never have considered assassinating a member of his own family. Surely he never would have laid his hands on me, then threatened Alfonso with death if my brother tried to intervene.

Cesare shrugged; hardness crept into his eyes. 'Such is the price of being a Borgia.'

. . .

I was not of a mood to make love to Cesare that night; he understood, and we parted with grim reluctance. I could not help wondering how my brother would react to such shocking decadence—but I dared not relay this information to him, as it would upset him too greatly to know the truth about my life in Rome.

Afterwards, in my bed, I dreamed of the card the strega had drawn for me: The heart pierced by two swords—by evil, and by good. Rodrigo Borgia stood before me, smiling, and opened the breast of his white satin robe to reveal a red heart beating therein, skewered by two swords in the shape of a silver X.

One of the swords was much larger than its mate; I stepped forward and pulled it out. It came forth bloodied, but beneath the crimson stain I could easily read the legend inscribed on the blade.

EVIL.

Autumn 1496 – Early Spring 1497

XVII

My trysts with Cesare continued uninterrupted for the next few months. Save for that troubling night in the garden when I spoke of Lucrezia and Alexander, Cesare behaved as he always had—speaking more and more of how he could no longer bear life as a cardinal. He dreamed of marriage to me, he said, and a house full of our children. I listened with unbearable yearning—and at the same time, enormous guilt. My husband apparently knew nothing of my affair with his brother, and his happy innocence tugged at my dishonest heart.

I could only assume that Cesare's fight with his brother Juan had discouraged the latter, for Juan did not trouble me again during the hot months of August and September.

And then, as the heat broke with the month of October, I received a letter from my brother which bore on its pages much grief.

My dearest sister,

It is with the most unspeakable sorrow that I must announce the passing of our half-brother, His Majesty, King Ferrante II. He died of a severe infection of the bowels—

and his wife, Queen Giovanna, is prostrate with grief, as are we all. He has already been laid to rest in a temporary tomb in Santa Chiara, while construction begins on his permanent crypt.

It is a difficult thing for me to have to write you with such sad news. Even so, both Mother and I have great hope that we might see you again in the coming months, at the coronation of His Majesty, our beloved uncle, Federico.

I could bear to read no more, but let the pages drop to the floor. Fate seemed capricious and brutal to let young Ferrandino fight so long and hard to claim his throne, only to steal it from him so quickly. Even worse, he and Giovanna had produced no heirs, so the crown was forced to revert a generation backwards, to Federico.

I now had an excuse to return to Naples, my home. Normally, I would have seized the chance—but I could not bear the thought of returning under the pall of Ferrandino's death; nor was I eager to leave Cesare, even for an instant. So I remained in Rome, and sent my condolences to the family from afar.

The same month I learned of Ferrandino's death, Juan Borgia was sent to war. With his jewel-encrusted sword and the title of Captain-General of the Church, he rode out of Rome accompanied by the papal army and a goodly dose of fanfare.

Success came early to him—much to Cesare's bitter annoyance. ('God mocks me, letting my witless brother win through accident, not skill!') In rapid succession, the papal army seized ten rebel castles, all of them flying French colours. The Pope was giddy with delight; at dinner, he read Juan's dispatches—all of them brimming with self-congratulatory details. Lucrezia gave her demure little smile, and nodded encouragement to her father when he grew most excited; Cesare's lips grew tauter, thinner, until they entirely disappeared.

And then God delivered to Juan justice, in the form of a stout and fearless noblewoman named Bartolommea Orsini. She commanded the allegiance of a most powerful army, which defended her imposing fortress a hard day's ride northeast of Rome, at Bracciano, overlooking the great lake for which the city was named. The papal army had a special interest in defeating the Orsinis: their treacherous allegiance with the French and their kidnapping of Giulia had allowed Charles to invade Rome, and prompted Alexander to order Ferrandino's retreat to Naples. It was time, His Holiness had decided, to teach the Francophile Orsinis a lesson. There were other rebellious noble families who held lands within the Papal States—and the Orsinis were intended to be a lesson to them all, of what would happen to those who did not pay homage to the Pope as both their sacred and secular ruler.

Cesare relayed the entire incident to me with great detail and relish. Juan's initial success at war filled the Duke of Gandia, Captain-General of the Church, with an even more boundless hubris. He wrote a threatening letter to Bartolommea; she laughed aloud and spat on it. He wrote imperious missives to her army, demanding their surrender, promising them safety if they deserted their posts and came to fight on the side of the Papal States.

Bartolommea's men roared at the notion.

'Come,' they said. 'Come and fight. Come and taste real war, Captain-General.'

Juan studied the massive parapets of the Bracciano castle; he even drew up simplistic battle plans for storming the walls. But in the end, according to Cesare, who had read the letter the great Captain-General sent to His Holiness, Juan realized that the situation here was quite different: there was a chance his army might lose.

And so, entirely without pomp, his army left Bracciano in the night, and instead headed north, to a less imposing castle defended by a less imposing army at Trevignano. Bartolommea, victorious, left the French flag flying.

At Trevignano, Juan's men waged a fierce battle while he sent directives from the sidelines. It was not easy, but Alexander's army took the castle and sacked the town.

No time was permitted for rest, for in the meantime, more members of the Orsini clan, led by the patriarch Carlo, had raised money from the French and recruited an army composed of Tuscans and Umbrians. They moved south towards the fortress at Soriano, held by an Orsini cardinal who felt the Pope should limit his powers to the Church, and keep his nose out of the earthly affairs of the nobles in the Papal States.

Juan's army was obliged to meet their enemies there, several days' ride due north of Rome. The Orsinis were clever strategists; they quickly lured part of the Captain-General's troops away from the others, overwhelmed them, and launched a counterattack. This time, Juan was caught in the midst of the fighting and unable to flee to the safety of the sidelines. He took a slight wound to his shoulder, and lost five hundred men.

This was apparently an outcome he had never considered. He retreated at once, and his army had surrendered.

Now, at the dinner table, Alexander fumed; he rose from his chair, paced, and shouted—at Juan for his idiocy, at himself for not having invested in more men, more horses, more swords. He would empty every coffer in Rome, he swore, he would even sell his tiara . . .

But in the end, His Holiness was a practical man. He struck a deal with the Orsinis, accepting fifty thousand gold ducats and two more fortresses in exchange for the Pope's promise to make no further war. Alexander also agreed to ask my uncle, King Federico, to release Orsini prisoners who were being held in Naples.

In the meantime, he called Juan home.

In Rome, the autumn days are cool, a promise of the chill winter to come. Many in Italy would call such weather temperate, for snow has only rarely limned the ancient buildings and piazzas. But I was accustomed to winters that varied little from summers, and so I looked ahead to the approaching season with mild dread.

I spent as much time away from my ladies and to myself as possible: I have never been talented at dissimulation, and my discovery of the true nature of the relationship between Lucrezia and her father left me troubled. I secretly grew angry at Cesare: were I male, I told myself, I would have slain Alexander long ago to protect Lucrezia, and damn the consequences.

In reality I too shared complicity—for I kept the terrible secret in order to save my own skin. I was no better; I was an adulteress, betraying her own husband. So I was as good a friend to Lucrezia as I could be; she came to trust me after a fashion, although I understood now why she could completely trust no one. We danced together at parties, laughed, played chess (Lucrezia was brutally adept and always won) and at times went riding together in the Roman pine forests, attended by guards and our ladies.

Yet our companionship gnawed at me; I could not forget the jealousy she had shown me concerning her father's affections—nor could I forget the apparently genuine rapture in her voice when I witnessed her coupling with Alexander.

I tried to justify it in my mind, as Alfonso might: Perhaps, after living so many years in a corrupt household, she had found the boundaries between good and evil blurred. Or perhaps her ecstatic moans had been contrived, an effort to protect herself from Alexander's wrath.

I ate little, lost weight, and wandered the vast, labyrinthine gardens behind the Palazzo Santa Maria like a wraith during the day—and a black ghost on the appointed nights I met Cesare there.

On the 24th January 1497, Juan, glorious Duke of Gandia, celebrated Captain-General of the Church, came riding back into Rome—this time, with even more fanfare and celebration, as if he had come bringing victory and not defeat.

His Holiness had only words of praise for his inept son; all the curses Alexander had hurled at him during the war were now forgotten. At dinner, we listened to the Pope tell Juan how he was the papacy's great hope: how he would bring glory to the House of Borgia when he was well enough to return to battle. Juan, in turn, answered with his insolent little smile. (When, precisely, Juan might 'recover' was never mentioned; and I never saw evidence of the wound that had sent him running from the enemy.)

I knew Cesare to be a man of fierce will—yet his jealousy towards his brother so vexed him, he could not entirely hide it. In his bedchamber one night, after we had made love, Cesare explained in great detail how Bartolommea could easily have been defeated; he went on to describe how the territory of the Papal States could be expanded, as we lay on our backs and stared up at the gilded, domed ceiling.

'If we could get the backing of a much stronger army,' Cesare proclaimed, 'the Romagna could be ours. Here.' With his forefinger, he traced the outline of a crooked boot—Italy—upon the ceiling, then pointed to its uppermost left corner. 'There is the western border with France,' he said, 'and just to the right, Milan. Almost due east lies Venice'—he lowered his finger diagonally—'then down to Florence. North of her is the area called the Romagna, far-northwest of Rome, in the very centre.

'It is a simple matter of forcing loyalty from the barons in the Papal States—but Juan hasn't the hardness, the cunning, to do it—I do.' He sat up suddenly, enthused, eyes still focused overhead on imaginary lands to conquer. 'Once the Papal States are firmly united—and if we got support from Spain, and perhaps'—he shot me a sly sidewise glance—'Naples, we could take the entire Romagna.' He spread out his hand, gesturing at the broad area stretching northwest from Rome to the coast. 'Imola, Faenza, Forli, Cesena . . . The strongholds would fall before us, all in a row.'

'What of the D'Estes?' I interrupted casually. They were an extremely powerful family who had held a duchy in the Romagna for generations. The scion, Ercole, was a pious man, strongly loyal to the Church.

Cesare pondered this. 'The D'Estes' army is too powerful to

conquer; I would far prefer to ally myself with them, and have them fight on our side.'

I gave a small nod, satisfied. The D'Estes were my cousins on Madonna Trusia's side.

Cesare continued. 'Then we take Florence. It has never recovered from the loss of Lorenzo Medici; politically, they are still in chaos. So long as our army is strong enough to defeat the French . . . '

'And Venice?' I asked, amused and curious. I had never seen such fire in him outside of lovemaking, and was surprised by the depth of his ambition. 'There, you have no family to defeat, no barons. The citizens are used to a great deal of freedom; they will not easily surrender their appointed Council and accept a single ruler.'

'It will be difficult,' he admitted, his manner quite serious, 'but possible, with enough men. Once they see our other successes, they might as well open their gates to us.'

I laughed, not to mock him, but in amazement at his determination. He had clearly given these things much thought; he spoke as if they were already accomplished. 'I suppose you intend to walk up to France's back gate and snatch Milan away from the Sforzas,' I said. 'You are a supremely confident man.'

He looked down at me and smiled broadly. 'Madonna, you have no idea.'

'If you are busy fighting wars,' I asked—only half in jest, for I had never forgotten Cesare's words that had so touched my heart, 'when shall you find the time to take me to Naples, and give me children?'

The fierceness in his eyes and expression softened; his tone grew tender. 'For you, Sancha, I would find the time.'

But Alexander had decided: Cesare was to succeed him as pope, while Juan would ensure the House of Borgia's secular might. No matter that the former had no taste for his father's choices, and the latter had no aptitude. Alexander's decision was final.

. . .

On a chilly afternoon, I had wandered far into the garden, and found myself in a maze of boxwood hedges and rose thickets.

That day, my mind was once again on children—or rather, my lack of them. When I had first arrived in Rome, Alexander had constantly teased Jofre and me about when we would have children—but, after a time, when none appeared, his comments ceased. It did not seem to trouble Jofre overmuch, but I think we each secretly eyed the other, wondering: Was I barren? Or was the cause Jofre's left testicle, which had never fully descended?

The truth of the matter was that, for our first two years of marriage, I had not wanted children and so had made constant use of water and lemon juice. Over the past several months, however, it occurred to me that a child would bring me not only status in the eyes of His Holiness, but perhaps also some degree of physical security.

While it was common knowledge amongst those in the House of Borgia that Jofre was not Alexander's get, he had been acknowledged as an heir in a papal bull—and so his children would be regarded as Rodrigo's grandchildren, and accorded all rights. Besides, to the Borgias, appearance was more highly regarded than fact.

And I adored Cesare so desperately that the thought of bearing his child was magical; love transformed the notion of motherhood from duty to privilege.

I turned a corner of the maze and found myself in a *cul de sac*, where a bronze cherub poured water from a great jar into a marble fountain.

I found also that I was not alone. There stood Juan, dressed in a scarlet satin tunic and saffron leggings; for once he was without a cap or turban. He had begun to grow a moustache since the beginning of his dismal campaign but, like Jofre, his facial hair grew in scantily.

He regarded me, arms akimbo, legs spread and planted firmly, wearing his customary smirk. 'So,' he said, his tone faintly gloating. 'A lovely, sunny day. A bit cool . . . All the better for romance.'

'Then you had best go elsewhere,' I answered. My right hand moved instinctively to my hidden stiletto. 'You won't find it with me.'

Something in his expression shifted, hardened. 'I am a determined man,' he said, in a tone that made me glance about to see whether help was within earshot. 'Tell me, Donna Sancha'—he took a step closer, which caused me to retreat a step—'how is it that you are so attracted to Cesare, yet have nothing but disdain for me?'

'Cesare is a man.' I put special emphasis on the last word.

'And I am not?' He spread his hands, questioning. 'Cesare is nothing but a bookworm. He dreams of battle, but all he knows is canon law. Let him speak of strategy all he wants—but he is good for nothing but spouting Latin. He has never been tested in battle as I have.'

'True,' I replied. 'You have been tested, and found wanting. The instant a sword bit into your flesh, you ran squalling like an infant.'

The corners of his mouth turned downward; he moved more swiftly than I expected, and hit my jaw full force with his fist, knocking me backwards into the thicket. 'Bitch,' he said. 'I'll teach you respect for your betters. What I want, I shall have—and neither you nor Cesare can keep it from me.'

I flailed; the woody thorns cut into my flesh and tore my gown. Before I could regain my balance, Juan was upon me; he seized me by both arms, pulled me from the thicket, and hurled me down onto the gravel path.

In the instant before he could throw himself atop me, I grasped my stiletto, and slashed out in a broad swath, from his left breast upward to his right shoulder. It ripped through the fine satin easily, and I sensed that it caught flesh; a yelp from Juan and a darkening stain on the front of his tunic confirmed it.

I expected him to flee, as he had in war; indeed, he backed

away for an instant, wearing an expression of dismay and tender self-concern as he touched fingers to the wound, then examined them for blood. The sight of it—though there was little—ignited a bright hatred in his eyes, and he called a name hoarsely.

'Giuseppe!'

The boxwood rustled, and a servant emerged. Giuseppe was twice the width and half again the height of Juan. I panicked truly then. I pushed myself to sitting and swung wildly with my dagger. Giuseppe laughed, but his eyes were troubled.

Deftly, he pushed me down and clutched my wrists so hard the bones felt crushed to powder; I was forced to drop my weapon. I filled my lungs with air, and screamed pure fury into his face, praying that someone might be near the garden, staring out from the loggia—but the only response was the gurgling play of water from the cherub fountain.

Giuseppe crouched at my head and held my hands pinned fast as I kicked and thrashed with my legs; all the while, Juan loomed over me, triumphant, and unlaced his codpiece.

'So,' he joked with his henchman, 'the mare is still unbroken? We shall ride her all the same.'

I did not make the act either easy or pleasant for him; he had to use his full weight to pin me down, and he was smaller in build than Cesare, so the task took a great deal of effort for him. But in the end, he was the stronger; I the weaker, and so he succeeded in violating me. He forced my legs apart, digging his fingers deep into the flesh of my thighs, bruising me. Then he thrust himself inside me with a brutality that made me bite my lip lest I give him the satisfaction of crying out in pain.

As Giuseppe gripped my arms, Juan pounded against me, grunting, swearing, calling me profane names no man would call the lowest whore, while the impact pressed the pebbles beneath me into my skin. The event seemed to last a mortifying eternity. During it, I forced myself to separate myself from the horror of what was happening, to distance myself from a rage that verged on madness: *I am not here*, I told myself. *I am not here, and this is not truly happening* . . . I fought not to shriek, and instead, tried to summon memories from childhood, of myself, safe and happy, playing with my brother, Alfonso.

The indignity Juan inflicted on me excited him overmuch; in reality, it was not long before he let go an explosive cry and reared against me, his eyelids fluttering.

With a deep sigh, he withdrew from me with intentional roughness; his warm fluid spilled out onto my legs. 'There, bitch. Now you can say you have had a man.' He pulled one of my hands from Giuseppe's grip, and stared at my smallest finger, where I wore a small circlet of gold given me by my mother.

'A keepsake,' he said, smiling. 'That it what I need from my new lover, so I shall always remember this moment.' He stole it from rose, then rose, triumphant, swaggering. 'Now, Donna Sancha, if you have any iota of sense in that feminine head of yours, you will leave Cesare and come begging to me for more.'

In answer, I spat at him. Unfortunately, Giuseppe still held me pinned, so my spittle never reached its target. Juan laughed as he refastened his leggings, then to his servant said, 'Take her if you want. It is of no matter to me. One cunt is the same as another.'

And he strutted away, a peacock.

As for the servant: I lolled my head back, the better to see his eyes, and whispered, 'Touch me, and I swear your life is forfeit.'

To my astonishment, he replied: 'Forgive me, Madonna. To save my own life, I have aided this act—but I shall harm you no further, and shall pray each day to God for forgiveness—though I do not expect it from you.'

Then he was gone.

I rolled onto my side and at once took hold of my stiletto: throughout the brutal act, I had not allowed myself to lose the knowledge of where it rested in the gravel. Trembling, I replaced it in my dust-covered bodice. Fury, shame, and pain so overwhelmed me I scarce could stand; somehow, I managed not only to rise and collect myself so that my face was not a mask of terror, but to direct my shaking legs to walk.

• • •

I returned to my chambers and dismissed all my ladies—all save Donna Esmeralda. I allowed her to bathe me and put salve on the worst bruises, then dress me in a clean nightgown.

Afterwards, I began to shake with a violence so intense I feared it would split my body in two; then came a torrent of gasping, like a storm. But I would not weep because a man had hurt me; I would not weep, though in the end, I told her everything. Through it all, Esmeralda held me fast, as a mother would a child.

Spring–Summer 1497

XVIII

That evening, I sent a cryptic message via Esmeralda that only Cesare would understand: the black lady was ill. I was not of a mood to explain the events of the day to anyone, so I spent the night alone, save for good Esmeralda, with whom I shared the bed and whose quiet, stolid presence proved a great comfort. Out of respect for my misery, Esmeralda spoke only once—softly, but with a ferocity no less chilling: 'Do not fear, my Sancha. God is witness to the crime against you, and in time, He will take His revenge.'

The following morning, I was not even sure that I should tell my lover of his brother's crime. I worried Cesare might lose his head and react with violence—even though I dreamt of murdering Juan myself. But the Duke of Gandia was Alexander's favourite—and I feared, after learning that Cesare's own father had threatened him, that His Holiness would avenge any harm done Juan.

For two days, I feigned illness—turning Jofre away with the same excuse—and then Cesare sent a message back through Esmeralda, begging to see me at our usual place, if I was well enough.

I responded that I would meet him—for I missed him, but I

had already concocted an excuse as to why we should not have sexual relations that night. The bruises left on my back—imprints of each accursed pebble on the path where Juan had taken me—had faded slightly, as had the marks on my thighs and wrists, but were visible enough to draw questions.

So, veiled in black, I went at the appointed hour to the appointed place and found myself, for the first time, alone there. Cesare did not await me, as he always had; Cesare, in fact, never appeared.

My first reaction, being of royal blood and by nature impatient, was one of anger. How dare he insult me so?

My second reaction was one of fear. What if he had learned of Juan's crime, and had been injured or killed in his efforts to seek justice?

I lingered in the darkness, hoping Cesare would arrive with an explanation that would put my doubts to rest; but he did not come, and I returned to my bedchamber, troubled.

The next day, Cesare was immersed in Vatican business, and failed to appear at the family supper. I sent an even-toned letter asking whether there had been a misunderstanding, but a day passed, then two, and I received no reply.

My confusion grew. Even had Cesare miraculously learned of Juan's crime against me, that would scarce be cause for his sudden silence. If anything, he would be rushing to comfort me, to vow revenge against Juan.

My opportunity finally came at one of the many parties Lucrezia had planned. The great loggia of the Palazzo Santa Maria was the chosen site, large enough to allow for a good deal of dancing. His Holiness sat on a throne and enjoyed dictating who should dance with whom.

At one point, he demanded that Cesare and I dance together.

Fortunately, the music was loud, and we were not the only dancers on the floor. This gave me the opportunity to address Cesare quite frankly.

Lucrezia had desired a masquerade; I wore a mask of dyed blue feathers, while Cesare wore one of gilded leather. With or without the disguise, his expression would have been equally unreadable.

He took my hand with a distant air, and limited our contact to only what was necessary to perform the dance. Framed by shining leather, his dark eyes were impenetrable.

'You have ignored my messages,' I said, as we began our steps. It was difficult to keep the anguish from my tone; I felt doubly wounded, doubly betrayed. 'Why have you not replied?'

'I do not understand,' said he, with a coolness that chilled my blood. 'Donna Sancha, you ask a question whose answer you already possess.'

'I know this alone,' I countered, my voice shaking with hurt. 'That you will not see me. That you have shamed me by making me wait for you when you had no intention of coming. What is the cause of this sudden cruelty?'

The loathing in Cesare's manner and tone was unbearable. 'Ask Juan.'

I froze in mid-step; Cesare had to prompt me to continue. 'He told you what he did to me?' I was disbelieving. 'Then, pray tell, Cardinal, why are you angry with *me*?'

He looked on me with unspeakable disgust, and for a time said nothing. Finally, he offered, 'I do not understand your point, Madonna. You engage in an affair with my brother, and you ask the cause of my anger?'

'An *affair*?' I recoiled as if struck. 'He *violated* me against my will!'

Cesare remained unmoved. 'There is a witness who says otherwise.'

'And you would take this person's word over mine?'

'Madonna, Juan sports your mother's gold ring on a small chain round his neck—a love token. He wears it privately so that it does not show, but I have seen it. He confessed his love for you and yours for him—without knowing we two were intimate.'

I let go a gasp. For a time, I was speechless—too outraged, too wounded to know how to deal with the revenge Juan had taken on me—a hard revenge, indeed, for a rebuff and single slap in public. With his false words, he had destroyed the one thing that had brought me happiness since coming to Rome.

'This is a hellish lie!' I exclaimed. 'What kind of man—' I broke off, fighting to gather control of myself, for I had altogether stopped dancing, and had raised my voice to a shout. Others dancing near us stared and murmured; such was my fury that I cared not, even though Alexander was watching us with a frown.

In a lower tone, I hissed, 'I know what kind of a man. Your brother is a snake, the vilest, lowest sort of creature . . . He has not only soiled my honour, he has perpetrated the most heinous falsehood to punish me for my striking him in public. He *stole* that ring from me. I did not go to you that night because I was tormented, grief-stricken . . . and afraid that you might do something rash. So rash that I feared for your sake. Now I see I was quite mistaken.'

Beneath the mask, his lips twitched slightly, but he answered nothing.

'Bring forth your "witness"—Giuseppe, is it not? Let him look me in the eye and see if he is capable of repeating the lie—for it was he who held me down. Press him, and the truth will come out.'

'Giuseppe has been my trusted servant for years,' Cesare said. 'He despises Juan. There is nothing that would convince him to help my brother accomplish such an act.'

'Something did, Cardinal.' I paused in word only, my body still going through the meaningless machinations of the dance, following the rhythm of music that seemed tuneless. 'And Juan lies when he pretends to know nothing of our affair. In truth, I slapped him that very first night because he said I might as well bed him—since I had bedded both of his other brothers.'

Cesare hesitated at that—but then injured pride overtook him, and he replied, 'I will not be cuckolded, Donna. There is no point in arguing further on this matter.'

'So,' I countered softly, with a dignity and composure I did not feel, 'you choose then to put your faith in Juan's word over mine.'

He answered nothing.

'It is your brother, Don Cesare, and not I, who has played you for the fool,' I told him.

We completed our dance without a further word to each other.

That night I did not even attempt to lie in my bed. Love stripped me of all self-respect; as much as I had chided my mother for her unreasoning devotion to my father, I now found myself in the same position. Humbled, I dressed in my black tabard and veil, and moved alone through the secret corridor leading from Santa Maria to Saint Peter's. The guards knew enough to let me pass; when the single soldier at Cesare's antechamber door saw me, he discreetly moved down the corridor while I knocked upon the heavy wood.

The hour was late. Cesare answered the door himself, still dressed, and I found relief in the realization that sleep had not come easily to him, either. I was even more relieved to find him alone.

At the sight of me, veiled and speechless, he said nothing, merely scowled at me a time—then motioned curtly for me to enter.

At once I drew back my veil. 'Cesare,' I said, 'I cannot bear being separated from you. I am willing to debase myself in order to win back your trust.'

He stood waiting for further words, his handsome, bearded face tilted at a sceptic's angle, his arms folded across his chest; but I gave him action. I slipped out of my heavy tabard, then pulled my black chemise over my head; in an instant, I stood before him naked, and held forth my arms.

'Here are my wrists where Giuseppe held me,' I said, rotating them slowly to better show the yellowing bruises; then I turned and revealed my back, which Esmeralda said still bore numerous marks from the garden stones. I half-expected to hear Cesare gasp with sympathy, to curse his brother—but from behind me came only silence.

I faced him once again; there was doubt in his expression, and so I humiliated myself to the utmost degree, and parted my legs. 'Here.' I gestured at my thighs, at the dark bruises left by Juan's harsh hands upon the otherwise pale flesh there.

A long silence passed between us; heat rose to my cheeks, and I slowly gathered my clothing and slipped it back on. Yet I could not bring myself to leave him. I waited, desperate, heart pounding, eager for even the slightest sign that I had recaptured his trust.

At last he said, slowly, 'These could simply be the marks left by great passion.'

I gazed up at him, stricken to speechlessness. I left his chamber quickly, lest he see the depth of my hurt.

I did not return to my bed. Instead, I sought the dark privacy of the garden, and there sat, frozen by pain, until the night began to ease towards dawn.

XIX

Cesare and I were coolly civil on those occasions when we could not avoid each other. As for Juan, he made sure that rumours of our 'affair' spread throughout Rome. Otherwise, he let me be—other than occasionally inflicting a triumphant glance upon me, especially when he saw Cesare and I pass each other in silence. It was apparently enough for Juan that he had degraded me once—he did not need to repeat the offence.

Although Jofre had heard the rumours, he persisted in showing me kindness—which only served to deepen my melancholy. I slept poorly, ate poorly; my husband sent doctors to examine me and give me tonics, but they had no cure for the ailment from which I suffered.

Cesare's image was always before me; I could not rid myself of constant thoughts of him. Yet what more could I do to win him back? I had humiliated myself for him as I had for no other man; and I could not understand how he doubted my love or loyalty. How could he not believe me, when he had seen the bruises himself? How could he think me so duplicitous?

The answer came to me often, but each time I tried to stifle it:

Only a man capable of great treachery would suspect others of the same.

So distraught was I that I altogether gave up seeking the company of others. At every opportunity, I took to my bed. Letters from my mother and Alfonso, unread and unanswered, collected in a pile upon my bedside table.

Lucrezia noticed my sadness—and to my surprise, did her best to relieve it. She invited me to luncheons, with dishes designed to tempt my faltering appetite; she invited me for rides and picnics in the countryside. I was touched by her efforts. When we two were alone, she attempted to be my confidante, to learn the source of my sorrow.

But my silence was steadfast; Cesare had impressed well upon me the connection between survival and holding one's tongue when it came to the Borgias. So I smiled and accepted Lucrezia's friendship, but explained nothing.

One day, Lucrezia and a pair of her ladies came to my chambers. 'Come!' she announced. 'We are going to give alms to the poor!'

I had been ensconced in my bed, listless and bored. 'It is too cold,' I complained. In fact, the sky was cloudless, brilliant with sun.

'Bah!' Lucrezia said. She walked over to my bed, took the book from my hands, and pulled me up. 'It is glorious outside! Let us find you a proper gown!'

We went to my armoire, and just as if she were Donna Esmeralda preparing me for a ball, she chose one of my finest gowns, a creation of forest green velvet and gossamer sea-green silk; the sleeves were laced with gilt ribbon. When we both were properly bedecked—she in sapphire blue—she said:

'Ah, Sancha! You are far too beautiful to be so sad! Look at you—the loveliest woman in Rome. When the people see you, they will think themselves in the company of a goddess!'

I could only smile at her kindness. It was difficult to believe that this was the same woman who had eyed me with such suspicion and hatred when I first came to Rome—but her concern for me seemed genuine. Perhaps, once her trust was gained, it was whole-hearted; perhaps I had misjudged her, and she secretly yearned for a life that was good and simple.

So we rode into the city, in a fine open carriage, its lacquered door emblazoned with the Borgia crest: a fiery red bull.

We had not gone far when the people spotted us, and began to run toward the carriage, shouting blessings. Lucrezia leaned towards me and, from a velvet bag, poured into my lap the 'alms' I was to throw.

I stared down at the glistening heap. 'Lucrezia—these are gold ducats!' A single ducat could purchase a peasant a farm, a house . . . This was unthinkable generosity.

She grinned extravagantly. 'All the more reason for them to love us.' She stood, and hurled a palmful of coins into the waiting crowds.

Vigorous cheers soon followed.

I looked at her, her face flushed pink from the sun, her eyes bright with the joy of making others happy.

How could I deny her? I smiled, took a handful of ducats, and pelted them into the midst of the throng.

Giovanni Sforza, Lucrezia's long-absent husband, arrived that previous January. Apparently he could no longer ignore the Pope's increasingly insistent messages that he return and be a proper husband to Lucrezia.

And so Sforza was welcomed back to Rome—without the fanfare reserved for the Pope's children, and certainly without the celebration. Giovanni, Count of Pesaro, cut an altogether unimpressive figure. He was lanky and graceless, with an oversized Adam's apple and large eyes that bulged, so that he appeared perpetually startled. His personality was likewise grating: he was effusive at the wrong moments, cowering at others; I suspected Alexander had chosen him for his malleability. Lucrezia should have been able to handle him easily.

But no one had counted on the depth of Giovanni's fear: and he wisely feared the Borgias—especially since his native state of Milan, which his powerful family ruled, had been unwise enough to support the French King, Charles, during the invasion. At least, his unease was officially attributed to this.

For three months, Sforza played the role of Lucrezia's husband—rather skittishly, for, according to his servants, His Holiness had given him the choice between coming to his bride . . . or an uncertain and unspecified fate. The married couple were polite to each other in public, and were seen together only as often as circumstance demanded. But if any affection existed between them, I did not see it. Lucrezia played her role as wife with great dignity, though Giovanni's obvious desire to be elsewhere must have shamed her greatly. I did my best to distract Lucrezia from this pain with small adventures, just as she had done for me.

But no harm ever came to Giovanni. If anything, the Pope and his children did everything to make Sforza feel welcome and honoured; in all ceremonies, his rank was just below that of Juan and Cesare. In fact, on Palm Sunday, Giovanni was one of those very few allowed to receive the sacred palm blessed by His Holiness.

But on the morning of Good Friday, Sforza set out at dawn on horseback, and fled back to his native Pesaro, from whence he could not be coaxed.

Rumours abounded. One said that Sforza's servant had overheard Lucrezia and Cesare plotting his murder by poison; this was the most persistent.

But the cruellest words came not from the whispers of talebearers, but from Giovanni himself—charges he dared make only from the safety of his fortress in Pesaro. His wife had been 'immodest', he said, in rambling public letters explaining his situation. There were hints that this lack of modesty was barbarous in the extreme, something that no normal husband could ever be persuaded to tolerate.

I understood at once: Sforza had seen what I had seen between the Pope and Lucrezia. He knew what I knew—apparently *had* known about their illicit affair very soon after his marriage to the Pope's daughter. And his nerves had never permitted him to live under such a strain.

I could not fault the man. But my heart ached for Lucrezia. She had seemed relieved to have him back—and now, the act of his fleeing caused a swirl of gossip to envelop her. No one dared speak ill of His Holiness, or accuse him of initiating incest; but Lucrezia was not spared. *Whore*, they called her, *the Pope's wife and daughter*.

In Florence, Savonarola railed with uncommon fervour against the sins of Rome, going so far as to call for violence against the Pope and his Church. The reformer-priest wrote to the rulers of nations, urging them to seize Alexander's tiara; he called on the French King, Charles, to swoop down upon Italy and once again 'render judgment'.

The Pope immediately set to work on an annulment for Lucrezia . . . and excommunicated Savonarola in May.

Lucrezia bore it all as long as she could; and then, in June, without the knowledge or consent of His Holiness, she gathered up a select few ladies and retreated to the nearby Dominican convent of San Sisto. She would, she told her father, become a nun. She had finished with marriage, and men.

Alexander was furious. A marriageable daughter was a useful political tool, one he would not surrender. Days after Lucrezia's arrival at the convent, he sent an armed contingent of men, demanding that the nuns turn Lucrezia over, 'as it was best she be in the care of her father'.

This set Roman tongues wagging even faster. *See? He cannot bear to be without her for a day.*

The prioress of the convent, one Sister Girolama, confronted the men alone. No doubt, she was a brave and consummately eloquent woman, for the soldiers left San Sisto without their prize, much to Alexander's outrage.

Lucrezia would not return. I began to believe that she had been coerced into the incestuous relationship with her father. I felt deep, honest pity for the woman.

In time, Alexander cooled, and let Lucrezia remain at San Sisto. He thought that she would grow bored with monastic life, and yearn for her parties once more.

But there was one thing he did not know, which I was soon to learn.

I went *incognita* to visit Lucrezia at San Sisto, and was escorted silently to her suite by one of the white-robed sisters. Lucrezia's quarters were hardly spartan; they were lavishly-appointed, large chambers which had been constructed especially for visiting nobility, and Lucrezia had arranged for much of her own furniture to be brought, that she might be less homesick.

But she was not in; I was greeted by Pantsilea, who was scarcely older than Lucrezia herself, but had the air of a much more mature woman. Pantsilea was pretty, a warm, indulgent creature, slender and beautiful. Her black hair was smoothed back from her face revealing a severe, attractive widow's peak; and on this day, her normally-unlined brow was furrowed with worry over her charge.

'How is she?' I asked, with some alarm at Donna Pantsilea's expression.

'Madonna Sancha,' she said unhappily, and kissed the back of my hand. She spoke frankly, as we two were alone; Lucrezia's other two attendants had gone with her to chapel, and Perotto had been dismissed to the kitchen. 'I am so glad you have come. I have never seen her this distraught over anything. She does not eat, she does not sleep. I fear . . . Madonna, I truly fear that she will do something drastic.'

'What do you mean?' I asked sharply.

'I mean that she . . . ' Pantsilea's voice dropped to a whisper ' . . . she may try to end her own life.'

The statement so shocked me that I found no words for a reply—which was as well, since at that moment, we heard footsteps approaching. The chamber door soon opened, and Lucrezia appeared, flanked by her other ladies.

Dressed entirely in black, she was paler than I had ever seen her, with shadows beneath her eyes; any hint of her former gaiety had completely disappeared, replaced now with a sombreness that was heartbreaking to see.

'Donna Sancha!' she said, and gave me a ghostly smile. We embraced, and I felt her bones easily through the flesh; she had lost a great deal of weight. 'How good to see you!'

'I have missed you,' I said honestly. 'I wanted to see how you were.'

Lucrezia gave a wave of her hand, dismissing her ladies into the other chamber, so that we could converse in private. 'Well,' she said, still smiling her unhappy little smile, 'so you can see.'

She sat down upon a large floor pillow; I settled beside her and took her hand earnestly. 'Lucrezia, please. I am worried for your sake. Even Pantsilea is terribly concerned. You have shown me such kindness, and I cannot bear to see the vicious words of others harm you so.'

She startled me completely by erupting into tears. I held her for a time and let her sob into my shoulder, trying to imagine myself in her position—what a strange and horrible place, indeed!

And then she startled me even more thoroughly, when she raised her face and said, 'It is even worse than you think, Sancha. I think I am pregnant.'

I could not find my tongue.

'Giovanni is not the father,' she continued, in a wavering voice. 'If I were to tell you—'

I held up my hand. 'I know who the father is.'

She stared at me in amazement.

'But we shall not speak his name,' I said. 'For to do so might cost me my life. So let us agree that I can sympathize with your situation—but let us also agree that I have never uttered the father's name aloud. So it cannot be said for certain that I know the truth.'

'Sancha, how do you—?'

'I blame you for nothing, Lucrezia. My heart grieves to see you in such difficult circumstances. I can only offer my friendship and help.'

I watched her expression as curiosity melted away to sorrow again. I held her, thankful my own life was not so filled with misery.

At last she managed to contain herself, and drew back to study my face. 'Will you do one favour for me?' she asked, in a manner that sounded disturbingly akin to a request for a deathbed promise. 'Will you forgive Cesare for how he has wronged you?'

I stiffened. I was at once hurt and angered by the thought that Cesare had confided in anyone about our affair, and certainly about my horrific encounter with Juan—even if that person was his own sister.

'You must understand that Cesare has been miserable without you,' she persisted. 'He was a fool, because he has been betrayed by women many times . . . and your beauty makes him impossibly jealous. But I have never seen him so in love as he is with you. Have pity on him, Sancha.'

'Let Cesare speak for himself,' I responded coldly. 'Only then will I answer him.'

I returned that evening to the palace of Santa Maria. I did not for an instant believe that Cesare had experienced a change of heart; I felt Lucrezia was only being kind, trying out of a sense of loyalty to smooth things between us.

But before the sun was gone an hour from the sky, a knock

came at my chamber door, and a young servant girl left a sealed letter with Donna Esmeralda.

I took it from her greedily, and read it alone on the balcony overlooking the garden. It was written in Cesare's precise, measured script:

> *My dearest Sancha*
>
> *I have been the world's greatest fool to doubt you, and am deserving of no less than the punishments of the innermost circle of Hell. These I shall certainly suffer in this life if you do not have mercy and come to meet me tonight . . . But they are no more than I deserve. I shall await you, with my heart in my hands as a gift. Yet should you decide not to come, I shall understand entirely, and remain yours, forever.*
>
> *Cesare*

I did not want to go. I wanted to punish him, to make him wait as I had, my hope slowly dying, then turning to pain.

I wanted to go: to make his heart light up with joy at the sight of me, only to be wrenched in two when I spat in his face.

I wanted to go: to throw my arms about him, to rejoice that he was once again mine, to whisper vows of undying love.

In the end, I went.

Cesare knew what to do to win someone to his side. At the sight of me, he dropped to his knees, then pressed his forehead to the gravel. 'I shall not rise until you give me leave, Madonna.'

I studied him for a moment, thinking of Juan, thinking of the imprints such pebbles had left on my own skin, thinking of the indignity and hurt I had experienced since that day. At last I said, 'Rise.'

And drew back my veil.

XX

That night, my affair with Cesare resumed with all its former passion. He swore vengeance against Juan—but 'at a time and place where it will be appropriate.' I hushed him. What possible action could we take against Juan, the apple of the Pope's eye, without ourselves being endangered? All I wanted from Cesare was reassurance that I was forever protected from Juan's touch, and this he swore with a vehemence that was frightening.

The following morning, I rode back to San Sisto to visit Lucrezia. This time, I was armed with pastries and delicacies calculated to tempt her squeamish palate. It was early June, and the weather was extravagantly lovely; every fragrant flower was in bloom. I was ecstatic after the previous night's encounter with Cesare—so much so that I felt guilt at going to see Lucrezia, whose own life was profoundly unhappy.

I arrived at Lucrezia's convent chambers only to discover she was again in chapel: Pantsilea greeted me, this time even more distraught. She dismissed the other servants so that we two were alone, and only then did she show me the official document resting on a table.

I had a fair acquaintance with Latin, and read the document silently, with growing amazement. It stated that Lucrezia had been in Sforza's family

> *triennium et ultra translata absque alia exus permixtione steterat nulla nuptiali commixtione, nullave copula carnali conjuxione subsecuta, et quod erat parata jurara et indicio ostreticum se subiicere.*

Lucrezia's timid signature followed.

It was an appeal for a divorce, allowable under papal law, if, as the document stated, the marriage had not been consummated in three years. In addition, Lucrezia agreed to submit herself to a physical examination by midwives, to prove her virginity.

Pantsilea's great dark eyes were haunted. 'His Holiness is already accepting bids from suitors. He is thinking of this only politically, without any concern for Lucrezia's feelings. She has told me she will die before she marries again. She has been speaking strangely, Madonna, as if she is trying to say goodbye . . . '

She drew closer and, in a low voice, said, 'I could be killed for telling you this, Donna Sancha, but I accept such risk if it saves Lucrezia's life. She possesses a store of the canterella, some of which she has brought with her—'

I frowned, unfamiliar with the term. 'Canterella?'

She was surprised by my ignorance. 'The poison for which the Borgias are famous. Very lethal. I fear Lucrezia intends to take it herself—very soon. She was weeping as she signed the document, Donna Sancha. I think she has gone now to make her peace with God.'

I was aghast. 'Why do you tell me such secrets? What can I do?'

'I have been searching as quickly as I can for the canterella, to keep it from her, but I have been unable to find where she has hidden it. Can you help?'

I stared at her. She was asking me to endanger my life—but, I reminded myself, it was for Lucrezia's sake, Lucrezia who had been so kind when despair had overtaken me. I nodded assent.

'It is in a small, stoppered vial of green Venetian glass,' Pantsilea continued urgently. 'I have been going through her trunk, her jewels—but there is also a chance she has put it in one of her gowns.' She gestured at the great armoire.

I went to it and opened its doors as Pantsilea re-opened a trunk and set to work. Lucrezia had brought only four drab gowns with her; she had not come to socialize or tarry long. I understood the noblewoman's need for deception and protection: all my gowns had a small sheath in the bodice. Perhaps Lucrezia had designed something similar . . .

In order to examine the gowns properly, I had to step up into the armoire itself. The sleeves were the most obvious place, and it was there I began my search.

I had scarce started smoothing my hands over the fabric when I heard a man's voice in the corridor—a very familiar one, calling for Lucrezia. Before I could react, Donna Pantsilea closed the armoire doors over me, hissing, 'Do not move, do not say a word.'

This seemed ridiculous. All I needed to do was step from the armoire, close the doors, and behave innocently—hiding in the closet would provoke enormous suspicion should I be discovered. Why would Pantsilea want to keep my presence secret?

But the deed was done; I held still, staring through the small slit in the armoire doors as Cesare entered the chamber, then gave a cursory glance down at the divorce document.

'Call for Lucrezia,' he told Pantsilea curtly, 'then see that we are left alone.'

She nodded. Once she had left to obey, I almost emerged, thinking to tell Cesare that I had hidden as a joke to surprise him, since I had heard his voice in the corridor. But the more time that passed, the less like a joke my appearance would seem; and after all, we had been reconciled only recently. Both Cesare and Lucrezia would look askance at such a silly antic, so I stayed in my awkward position.

Cesare paced the room, intense and humourless. Apparently, he was attending to his father's business, but took no pleasure in the fact.

Lucrezia and her ladies then appeared. At the sight of Cesare, her heretofore glum expression brightened; she dismissed her attendants at once, and clasped her brother's hands.

They both looked down at the divorce decree.

'So, it is done,' Cesare said.

Lucrezia sighed unhappily—but certainly not fatally so, as Donna Pantsilea feared. Her tone was one of simple resignation. 'It is done.'

Comfortingly, Cesare stroked her cheek. 'I will make sure you have an agreeable husband. Someone of higher rank than Sforza. Someone young this time; someone handsome and charming.'

'There can be no one more charming than you.' She put her hands upon his shoulders, and he caught her by the waist; they kissed.

It was not an embrace between brother and sister.

Motionless in the armoire, I took in a long, silent breath along with a realization that pierced like a sword. I swayed beneath a wave of unspeakable revulsion; dizzied, I reached out a hand cautiously, soundlessly, pressing against polished wood to keep from staggering.

When they drew apart, Lucrezia said, 'I want the child to stay within the family.'

'The old bastard is convinced it's his,' Cesare replied. 'I've already talked him into signing a secret bull. The child will be a Borgia, with full rights. You know I will make sure it's always well cared for.'

She smiled and took his hand; he kissed her open palm.

'Poor Lucrezia,' he said. 'This isn't easy for you.'

She gave a sad little shrug. 'You have your own difficulties.'

'Juan is a buffoon. It's only a matter of time before he creates an opportunity for us to be rid of him.'

'You are too hard on him,' she chided gently.

'I am too honest,' he replied. 'And the only Borgia intelligent enough to be Captain-General.'

'The only *male* Borgia,' Lucrezia corrected him, and he smiled.

'That is true. Were you male, I would have no chance at the position; you would outwit me before I dared try.' He let go her hand, rolled the document into a scroll, then tied it carefully with a ribbon. 'I will take this to His Holiness. Will I see you tomorrow?'

His tone left no doubt that the purpose of the visit would be more than brotherly.

'Please.' Lucrezia dimpled. Then she paused, and added, in an odd little tone, 'Be kind to Sancha.'

He frowned, confused. 'Of course, I am kind to Sancha. Why should I not be?'

'She has been good to me.'

'I will be kind,' Cesare said, then in a lighter tone added, 'But when I am King of all Italy, we know who will truly be my queen.'

'I know,' Lucrezia replied. They had apparently discussed this topic before; yet she felt compelled to repeat, as Cesare made his way out the door, 'But be kind to Sancha.'

It did not take Pantsilea long to return and to think of an excuse to get Lucrezia to leave her chambers, so that I could escape.

I said nothing to Pantsilea about what I had seen and heard. I had no doubt that she had pushed me into the closet precisely so that I would discover truths even more dangerous than the revelation about the canterella.

In the moments before I left without seeing Lucrezia, I located a small glass vial inserted in a pocket sewn into the sleeve of one of Lucrezia's gowns. I hid it in my bodice without saying anything to anyone; and I was of such a mind that, when I took it back to my chambers at Santa Maria, I spent a great deal of time thinking about whether and how to put it to use.

XXI

That night I sent Cesare a note saying I was ill. I was indeed sick of spirit; my instinct, that Cesare had disbelieved me because he was capable of treachery, had been correct. But I had never imagined the depth of his duplicity: he had spoken with such hurt, such outrage, of his father's incest with Lucrezia, even while he was guilty of the same. Nothing Cesare had ever said could be believed.

Now, Alexander had been duped into believing Lucrezia's child was his—when in fact, it was her brother's. One thought repeated itself endlessly in my mind, as I stared from my balcony at the dark gardens:

What sort of monstrous family is this?

I could trust none of them; even my feelings toward Lucrezia became guarded. While she might have honestly liked me, and begged her brother to show me kindness, her notion of love and loyalty was twisted beyond comprehension. She had urged me to reconcile with Cesare even though she intended to remain his paramour.

I was so filled with grief that night, so near madness, that I clutched the vial of canterella in my hand and considered whether

I should swallow its contents. I hated Cesare with my entire soul . . . and at the same time, I remained fearfully, violently in love with him. The realization filled me with hopelessness. How had I failed to detect his treacherous nature? Surely there must have been signs—a faint coldness in the eyes, perhaps, a fleeting cruelty in the lips . . . Of all people, I should have seen them, for I had found them before, in my own father's eyes and lips; and though they were not outwardly visible in Ferrante, I had sensed them in his evil heart.

I left the balcony and stole silently through the bedchamber, where Esmeralda slept, out into the antechamber. There, carefully making my way in the darkness, I poured myself a goblet of wine, and with trembling fingers, struggled to open the glass vial.

An image, as if from a dream, coalesced before me in the shadows: my father's body, hanging from a great wrought iron sconce, with Messina's harbour as its backdrop.

My lips tightened; I straightened, and looked down at the vial with disgust. I swore to myself at that moment that nothing, no one—certainly not Cesare Borgia—would ever provoke me to take my own life. I would never become the coward my father had been.

For the rest of the night, I sat on the balcony, and cursed myself for not being able to control my feelings for Cesare. I knew not how long they would persist—but I was determined, for however long I lived, never again to indulge them.

In the morning, at first light, I wrote him a letter stating that, given the rumours surrounding 'family members' at the Vatican, it was best that we halt our trysts—at least for the time being, in order not to add to talk of scandal. I had Donna Esmeralda deliver it to one of his attendants.

He did not respond, in person or by letter; if he was wounded by my request, he did not show it in public, but treated me civilly.

For the next two days, I did not appear at the family suppers, and turned down Lucrezia's invitations to visit her. I could not bear to see her after learning what she knew. I lay abed during the days, though I did not sleep. Nor did I find rest at night; instead, I sat outside in the darkness, staring out at the starlit sky, wishing for an end to my pain.

I continued such self-indulgent behaviour until, in the late hours, Donna Esmeralda emerged onto the balcony in her nightgown.

'Donna Sancha, you must stop this. You will make yourself ill.'

'Perhaps I am already ill,' I said carelessly.

She frowned, but her expression remained one of maternal concern. 'You worry me,' she said. 'You act like your father did, when the times of blackness came over him.'

And she disappeared back into the bedchamber.

I stared after her, thunderstruck. Then I looked back at the sky, as if searching for an answer there. I thought of Jofre, my husband, a person to whom I owed amends. Perhaps he was weak in character, but he remained sweet-natured in the midst of wickedness, and unlike his so-called brothers, wished no one harm. He deserved a good wife.

I thought also of Naples, and of those I loved there.

At last I rose. I did not go to the bed with hopes of sleep, but instead went out to the antechamber and lit a taper, then found quill and parchment.

> *Dear Brother,*
>
> *It has been far too long since I have heard from you about life in Naples. Tell me, please, how you and mother are faring. Spare me no detail . . .*

With regard to Juan, Cesare had been right in saying that it would not take long before he created an opportunity for the family to be rid of him.

Only a few days after I sent Cesare the letter saying we should no longer meet, Cardinal Ascanio Sforza—brother of Ludovico Sforza, ruler of Milan, of relation to the maligned Giovanni Sforza—gave a great reception at the Vice-Chancellor's Palace in

Rome. Many distinguished guests were invited. Lucrezia was still closeted at San Sisto, but Jofre begged me to attend with him. Wanting to be an obedient wife, I agreed—even though the guest list included two men I wanted to avoid—the Duke of Gandia and his brother, the Cardinal of Valencia.

The Vice-Chancellor's Palace was undeniably grand: the estates were so large that we were obliged to ride up to the entry in carriages, and we entered the Great Hall—larger by thrice than the Castel Nuovo's—announced in turn. We Borgias arrived together, and were presented in order of our importance to the Pope: Juan first, removing his feathered cap and waving it at the crowd to the sound of cheers for the Captain-General; then Cesare, silent in black; and at last Jofre and me, the Prince and Princess of Squillace.

The surroundings were breath-taking; a large, three-tiered indoor fountain had been created. It was bordered by hundreds of flickering candles, whose light painted each drop of water golden. The floors were festooned with rose petals, perfuming the air; this effect was outdone only by the aroma of the food, borne on golden trays by servants. So vast was the room that even the large white marble statuary—of glorious naked men and women, apparently ancient Romans—seemed small in scale.

I summoned unfelt smiles and greeted those dignitaries I already knew, and let myself be introduced to those I did not. Mainly, I did my best to avoid Juan and Cesare.

As I strolled arm-in-arm with my husband through the assembly, we were met by Giovanni Borgia, the Cardinal of Monreale, who had witnessed our wedding night. The cardinal had grown even portlier, and the fringe of hair beneath his red skullcap had turned almost completely to grey, but his fingers sparkled as always with diamonds.

'Your Highnesses!' he cried, with an enthusiasm that reminded me of his cousin Rodrigo. 'How good to see you both!' He slyly scanned my bosom, then winked at Jofre and nudged him with an elbow. 'I see the roses are still blooming.'

Jofre laughed, a bit embarrassed by the reference, but replied, 'She has become even more beautiful, has she not, Your Holiness?'

The cardinal grinned. 'She has. And you, Don Jofre, have become a real man . . . no doubt because you have a real woman for a wife.'

I smiled politely; Jofre chuckled again. We were on the verge of moving on through the group to acknowledge the others when Cesare—much to my dismay—joined us.

'Don Giovanni,' he said warmly. 'You are looking as hale and hearty as ever.'

The Pope's nephew smiled. 'Life agrees with me . . . as I can see it does with both of you brothers. But Jofre'—his tone lowered and grew conspiratorial—'feed your wife some delicacies. She has grown a bit thin. Are you riding her too hard, my boy?'

Taken aback, Jofre opened his lips to reply; fortunately, the cardinal was at that moment distracted as our host, Ascanio Sforza, called to him.

My husband looked at me; he had been concerned for my health of late, kind and solicitous. 'I shall do that,' he declared. 'Let me find a servant to fetch you some food.' And he was off, leaving me alone with Cesare.

I tried to wander towards another group, but Cesare blocked my path, forcing me to stand alone with him.

'Now it is you who are unkind to me, Madonna,' Cesare said, his tone that of the pining lover. 'I understood your letter, and appreciate your desire for discretion, given the circumstances with my sister, but—'

I interrupted him. 'It is more than that. Juan spread rumours about us; we must do what we can to dispel them.' I tried to keep my expression controlled; I fought to pretend that I was doing this for our good, and not because I despised him.

Yet at the same time, another part of me yearned for him—a fact that filled me with shame and self-loathing. I looked upon him, so handsome, so self-possessed, so elegant and so evil.

He took a step closer; instinctively, I moved back, thinking of him winding his arms about Lucrezia's waist and proclaiming, *And you shall be my queen . . .*

'If there are already rumours, why should we suffer? Why not go on as we had before? We have had only one night together since our reunion . . . ' He paused to lower his face, then let go a sigh and lifted it again. 'I know you are right, Sancha, but it is so difficult. Give me hope, at least. Tell me when I can see you again.'

Blessedly, Jofre was returning; I turned eagerly towards my husband as he proffered me a plate of sugared almonds and sweetbreads. I addressed myself to the food and did my best to avoid Cesare's gaze.

As I ate, our attention was drawn by a loud, drunken shout from another corner; I recognized the voice as we all turned towards the source of the disturbance.

'Behold the lounging gluttons!' Juan slurred. Accompanied by one of his captains—who at the moment, was trying to quiet him—he gestured extravagantly at one of the guests: the corpulent Antonio Orsini, a relative of Giulia's husband and also of Cardinal Sforza. Orsini sat at a table beside his plump wife and two sons—both bishops—and was, at that instant, stuffing as much as he could of a roast duckling into his mouth. He was exceedingly rotund—so much so his hands could scarce clasp each other atop his huge belly; his face, puffed and fleshy, possessed no fewer than three folds beneath his chin, which even his dark beard could not hide.

'Perhaps, Don Antonio,' Juan called, in a voice loud enough to be heard by the entire assembly, 'if you did not linger over-long at the tables of your wealthier relatives, you would not be so fat!'

Some snickered.

Don Antonio set down the remaining piece of cooked flesh and waved his thick, grease-coated fingers dismissively. 'Perhaps, Don Juan, if you did not run so swiftly from your enemies, you would not be so lean.'

Many in the crowd *oohed*.

Juan drew his sword and staggered towards his mocker. 'You shall pay dearly for your insult, sir. I would challenge you to a duel—but, being a gentleman, I cannot take advantage of one so grotesquely incapable of physical exertion.'

Don Antonio rose and stepped forward; even this slight effort left him short of breath. 'I am perfectly capable of responding to your challenge, sir—but you are no gentleman. You are nothing more than a coward and a common bastard.'

Juan's eyes narrowed with rage—the same uncontrolled fury that had once been directed at me. I expected him to lash out; instead, white-faced and speechless, he whirled on his heel and strode from the palace.

Orsini laughed loudly. 'As always, a coward. See? He runs again.'

Ascanio Sforza, eager as a host to ease any unpleasantness, signalled for the musicians to play. Dancing commenced; I received several invitations, but refused them all. Soon I whispered to Jofre that I was tired and wished to return home. He sought Cardinal Sforza, that we might make our farewells.

But we were interrupted by a loud commotion at the chamber entrance: to the assembly's amazement, a contingent of a dozen armed papal guards marched inside, swords drawn, their expressions menacing.

'We seek Don Antonio Orsini,' the commander announced.

Cardinal Sforza rushed forward. 'Please, please,' he told the commander. 'This is a private residence, and a private dispute between two guests—and a minor one at that, provoked by wine. There is no call for such an extreme response.'

'I am here at the pleasure of His Holiness, Pope Alexander,' the officer replied. 'Both the Captain-General and His Holiness have been slandered. Such a crime cannot be overlooked.'

He led his troops past the astonished cardinal; as the rest of us watched, they seized the hapless Don Antonio. 'This is an outrage!' he cried, as his wife wailed and wrung her hands. 'An outrage! I have done nothing for which I can be imprisoned.'

But taking a prisoner was not the soldiers' intent. Instead, they dragged their victim outside onto the estate grounds, where a pair of their fellows had already secured a length of rope to an ancient olive tree. Two large torches burned on either side: this event was intended to be witnessed. We guests followed, stunned.

At the sight of the noose that awaited him, Don Antonio fell to his knees and let go a shriek. 'I apologize! Please, enough! Tell the Captain-General I beg his forgiveness, that I shall make whatever public apology he wishes!'

This will certainly stop this foolishness, I thought. But the commander said nothing, merely nodded to his troops. Don Antonio was prodded, moaning and trembling, to his doom. With difficulty, the soldiers helped him up onto a footstool beneath the tree.

Even to the last instant, I did not believe it would happen; I think none of us did. I clutched Jofre's arm, Cesare at my other side. We three stared, transfixed.

The noose had to be loosened to slip around Don Antonio's thick neck; he sobbed shamelessly as it was retightened.

Abruptly, the commander gave the signal for the stool to be kicked aside.

The crowd gasped, disbelieving. Only Cesare made no sound.

Don Antonio swung before us in the cool night air, his eyes wide, bulging, lifeless. So silent did our gathering become that for a time, the only sound was the creaking of the branch as the heavy body swayed back and forth.

I looked away—at Jofre first, whose gentle features were frozen in an expression of pure horror. And then I glanced at Cesare.

The cardinal's gaze was intent, pensive, that of an ambitious mind at work. He was staring directly at Don Antonio's body—yet he saw right through it, at an opportunity that lay beyond.

A week after, in mid-June, when Lucrezia had been at San Sisto scarcely a fortnight, Vannozza Cattanei threw a family party in honour of her sons. Jofre and I attended, along with Cesare and Juan in all his arrogant glory, as well as Cardinal Borgia of Monreale.

The setting was outdoors, to take advantage of the lovely weather, in a vineyard Vannozza owned. A great table had been set up to accommodate us and our courtiers; it was adorned with flowers and golden candelabra, flanked by many torches—though the celebration began in the afternoon, it was intended to continue past nightfall.

I held Jofre's arm as we were escorted onto the property. While he still indulged in courtesans and much wine, I turned a blind eye to such behaviour; instead, I focused on his goodness, and had decided to devote myself to pleasing him as best I could, for I knew not how else to give life meaning.

Once we had arrived at the party site, I was introduced to his mother for the first time. Vannozza was a handsome woman, auburn-haired and serenely confident; child-bearing had left her a bit thick-waisted, but she still possessed an attractive shape, with a full bosom and long, delicate arms and hands; her eyes were as pale as Lucrezia's. Her face was Cesare's—strong-jawed, with sculpted cheeks and a straight, prominent nose. On this day, she was dressed in dove grey silk, which accentuated her eyes and fiery hair.

I let go of Jofre's arm and took Vannozza's proffered hands; she studied me with a manner that was both calculating and warm. 'Your Highness. Donna Sancha.' We embraced, then she drew back to study me and waited until Jofre had moved out of earshot to say, 'My son loves you very dearly. I trust you are being a good wife to him.'

I returned her gaze openly, sincerely. 'I am doing my best, Donna Vannozza.'

She smiled with proud satisfaction at her three sons, as Jofre met Juan and Cesare and received a goblet of wine from a servant. 'They have done well for themselves, have they not?'

'They have, Donna.'

'Let us join them.'

We did so. I noticed at once that Cesare was dressed, not in his habitual black priest's frock, but in a magnificent scarlet tunic embroidered with gold thread; Juan was, as usual, dressed gaudily, in rubies, gold brocade and bright blue velvet, yet the Cardinal of Valencia looked far more striking.

I moved next to Jofre, and directed the requisite smile and nod at his two older brothers. 'Your Holiness,' I said to Cesare, averting my eyes as he kissed me on each cheek, as familial relations required. 'Captain-General,' I said to Juan. To my surprise, there was no gloating in the Duke of Gandia's eyes, no challenge, no guarded anger; his kiss was polite, distant. He behaved as one who had been chastened.

I greeted the other guests. When the time arrived to make our way to the table, Vannozza took my arm and said firmly, 'Here, Sancha. I have chosen the places for everyone.'

To my dread, she sat me directly between Juan and Cesare.

Fortunately, at the beginning of the dinner, we were all distracted by toasts, led by the matriarch, Vannozza. Juan was saluted first. 'To the Captain-General,' Donna Vannozza proclaimed, with gusto, 'who shall bring us all peace and prosperity.'

This brought cheers from Juan's grooms; he bowed grandly, like a gracious sovereign.

'To the wise and scholarly Cardinal of Valencia,' Vannozza proclaimed next. There were some polite murmurs, and then came the final toast.

'To the Prince and Princess of Squillace.' This was greeted with silent smiles.

Dinner, though interminable, did not go as badly as I had feared. Juan said not a word to me: he addressed himself to Cardinal Giovanni Borgia, who sat on his right. As for Cesare, he occasionally caught my gaze, his own dolorous, pleading. Once he tried to speak in my ear while the others were distracted, but I gently pushed him away, saying, 'The time is not right, Cardinal. Let us not cause ourselves further pain by speaking of our situation.'

He pressed back, and whispered, 'Look at you, Sancha—your

face is drawn, you have grown thin. Admit it: you are as miserable as I. But I see how you cling now to Jofre; do not tell me you would let something as ridiculous as guilt destroy our love.'

I looked at him, stricken. I could not deny my sorrow—but its cause went far deeper than Cesare suspected. I turned from him.

We said nothing more to each other. At last the sun set, and the tapers and torches were lit.

It was at this time that a stranger joined our group, a tall, lean man, his face entirely covered by a ceramic mask painted brightly in the Venetian style. With holes for the eyes and a slit mouth, it displayed a solemn expression; its forehead was inscribed with the symbol of the scales. His hair and body were draped in a full hooded cloak, further hiding his appearance. Our visitor knew everyone in our group, and greeted them by name, but he disguised his voice by deepening it; intrigued, we tried to guess his identity. It was the time of Carnival, with many masquerade parties being thrown in the city; we all assumed our guest had come from such a function.

Vannozza welcomed him to the table, and the servants brought a chair for him; I was delighted when it was placed between me and Juan, further separating us.

Juan was quite taken by our surprise visitor, and spent a great deal of time questioning him in an effort to guess his identity. The stranger completely charmed him, for as the night wore on, the two put their heads together and I overheard them making plans for further adventure after the party. At one point, Juan left to relieve himself of an overabundance of wine, and Jofre and I chose to make our farewells and return home.

But before I stood, I turned to the unknown man beside me and asked, *sotto voce*, 'I am leaving, sir. I am curious: will you confide in me your name? I promise, I will tell not a soul.'

He glanced over at me, and I saw an odd light flicker in the dark eyes behind the mask. 'Call me Justice, Madonna,' he replied in a soft voice. 'For I am here to put things aright.'

His answer evoked an odd chill in me. I regarded him in silence, then rose and hurried to my husband's side. As we embraced and kissed Vannozza during our leave-taking, Juan returned to the table and decided it was time for him and his mysterious friend to go in search of amorous women.

As the two left abruptly, without saying farewell to their hostess, I turned and glanced at Cesare.

The cardinal was just lifting his goblet to his lips, but I could see his eyes. They were focused on Juan and the stranger, with the same detached intensity they had directed at the corpulent body of Antonio Orsini, swinging from the olive tree.

None of us—His Holiness included—noticed Juan's failure to return the following morning. It was his habit, when he woke in a strange woman's bed, to wait until cover of evening to return to the Vatican.

But evening turned to night. Jofre and I had been invited to sup with the Pope, and listened to Alexander's worries. While we were at table, Juan's captain appeared, and announced that the Captain-General had failed to attend to pressing business that day.

Alexander wrung his hands. 'Where can he be? Why would he want to cause his poor father such worry? If something has happened . . .'

Jofre rose from his place and put a hand upon Alexander's shoulder. 'Nothing has happened, Father. You know how Juan is when he has found a new woman. He simply cannot deny himself another night of love . . . but I am sure he will return come morning.'

'Yes, yes . . . ' Alexander murmured, eager to seize upon such comfort.

I said nothing, but could not erase from my thoughts the image of the masked stranger called Justice.

With His Holiness sufficiently calmed, we retired and went to our separate beds. Some hours later, I was summoned from sleep by an armed soldier and led to the Vatican. The Pope was not sitting on his throne waiting for the traditional greeting of a kiss on his slipper; he was pacing, glancing out the window at the torches in the piazza below. I did not know it then, but these were the Spanish guards, patrolling the streets in search of their missing commander. Jofre stood beside Alexander, trying to keep an arm on his restless father's shoulder by way of comfort.

Only later did it occur to me that Alexander had not called on Cesare to console him.

'What is it, Holiness?' I asked; the situation did not lend itself to formality. 'What has happened?'

Alexander turned his face toward me, his great, broad brow deeply furrowed. Unshed tears shone in his eyes. 'Juan has disappeared. I fear the worst.'

'Father,' Jofre soothed, 'you have made yourself sick with worry. Juan has simply forgotten himself with a woman—as I said, he will certainly be home by morning.'

'No.' Alexander shook his head. 'I am the architect of this. I struck out foolishly at Ascanio Sforza's guest—I should never have had him hanged. God is punishing me by taking my favourite son.'

To his credit, Jofre did not even wince at his father's last two words.

A cold certainty settled over me. Juan was indeed dead, but not for the reason Alexander believed.

I struggled to find compassion in myself: Alexander had summoned me here for comfort. Lucrezia was no longer here to provide the soft, feminine presence that soothed his soul; and Jofre was gentle, unlike Cesare. How could I do what I had been called to do?

Following my husband's lead, I set a hand softly on Alexander's other shoulder. 'Your Holiness, this is now in the hands of God. Worry is fruitless; we will know Juan's fate when the time is right. Jofre is right: we must not be concerned until morning.'

He turned toward me. 'Ah, Sancha. I am glad I called for you;

you are most wise.' He clasped both my hands inside his great ones. Tears spilled from his eyes onto my skin.

'Perhaps we should pray the rosary for Juan's sake,' Jofre suggested quite seriously. 'Whether harm has come to him or not, it can only do his soul good.'

Both the Pope and I regarded him with scepticism; I realized, studying Alexander, that he believed no more than I in the efficacy of prayer. Yet such was his desperation that he hugged his son. 'You pray on my behalf, Jofre. My heart is too troubled, but it will do me good to hear you.'

Jofre gave me a questioning glance. I gave him a look that made it clear I did not wish to join him. Even if I had been a good Christian, I could not have engaged in the hypocrisy of praying for the likes of Juan; a part of me still desired revenge against the man.

Upon realizing that no one wished to join him, Jofre produced a rosary from his tunic—a fact that surprised me—and began to pray in all earnestness:

O Vergin benedetta, sempre tu
Ora per noi a Dio, che ci perdoni
E diaci grazia a viver si quaggiu
Che'l paradiso al nostro fin ci doni.

'O blessed Virgin, always pray for us, that God might forgive us and give us grace to live so that we might be rewarded with heaven upon our death.'

The situation was too grim for me to show any astonishment, but I was surprised to hear my husband repeat the *Vergin Benedetta* preferred by the common people, rather than the Latin version, *Ave Maria, gratia plenia*, which had been approved by his own father as the 'correct' version. Unlike the Pope, Jofre apparently believed in God; the prayer had obviously been taught him by a pious servant, and he had chosen it over the one he had been required to learn during his study of Latin.

If Alexander noticed the difference, he did not show it; he walked back over to the windows and continued to pace.

Over and over, Jofre repeated the prayer; it has been said that Saint Dominic recommended one hundred fifty repetitions a day, and certainly, Jofre must have come close to it before he was interrupted. The soothing, monotonous sound of his chanting brought me and Alexander a measure of calm, for at last His Holiness came back to his throne and sat quietly.

Sadly, it was shattered by the appearance of one of the guards, his uniform smeared with blood. We turned to regard him with horror.

'Your Holiness,' he uttered breathlessly, and knelt to kiss the pontiff's foot. Unable to speak, Alexander frantically gestured for the man to rise and give his report.

'We have found the Duke of Gandia's groom,' the guard said, 'in an alley near the Tiber. He has been pierced several times with a sword; he is dying, unable to give witness.'

Alexander put his head in his hands and slid from the throne to his knees.

'Leave us now,' Jofre commanded. 'Come back when you have news of the Duke.'

The soldier bowed and left, while we two went to the weeping Alexander and tried to wrap our arms about him as he swayed in misery on the steps. I did what was expected of me, as a good daughter-in-law—yet I was surprised to discover that, at the same moment I despised him, I could not help feeling pity for the old man's genuine suffering.

'This is my doing, O God,' he cried, in a voice so wrenching, so heartfelt I had no doubt it ascended straight to Heaven. 'I have killed my son, my beloved son! Let me die now—let me die in his stead!'

His wailing continued onwards for an hour, until another papal guard entered the room, accompanied by a peasant.

'Your Holiness,' the guard called out. 'I have here a witness who says he has seen suspicious activity relating to the Duke's disappearance.'

Alexander seized control of himself with a will admirable to behold. He rose—refusing Jofre's and my assistance—and with consummate dignity, went up to his throne and settled there.

The witness—a middle-aged man with a dark matted beard and hair, dressed in a torn, dirty tunic whose vile smell marked his profession as a fisherman—removed his cap and, trembling, ascended the steps to kiss the proffered papal slipper. He then descended and, twisting his cap in his hands, jumped when the Pope commanded, 'Tell me what you have seen and heard.'

His story was simple. On the night Juan went missing, the fisherman had been in his boat on the Tiber, close to the shore. Half-hidden by fog, he watched as a man riding a white horse approached the river from an alleyway. This was not in itself cause for interest, but what caught the fisherman's eye was the body thrown across the horse, carefully held in place by two servants. As the rider reached the river and manoeuvred the horse sideways, the two servants took the body and slid it into the river.

'Is it under?' the man on horseback asked.

'Yes, my Lord,' one of the servants replied.

But the body failed to cooperate; the servant had scarcely answered before the corpse's cloak ballooned with air, and pulled the body back up to the surface.

'Do what must be done,' the lord commanded. His servants pelted rocks at the body until it at last disappeared beneath the Tiber's black surface.

I kept my arms wrapped tightly around Jofre as he listened, horrified. As for His Holiness, he heard all of it with a hardened expression.

When the tale was done, he demanded of the fisherman: 'Why did you not report this at once?'

The man's voice trembled. 'Your Holiness, I have seen more than a hundred dead men thrown into the Tiber. Never has anyone shown any concern over one of them.'

As astonishing as this statement seemed, I did not doubt its veracity. At least two or three murders were committed each night in Rome, and the Tiber was the favourite repository for the victims.

'Take him away,' Alexander ordered heavily. The guard complied, escorting the fisherman off. When they were gone, the Pope again buried his face in his hands.

Jofre traversed the steps up to the throne. 'Papa,' he said, encircling his father with an arm. 'We have heard of a murder. We still do not know if it involved Juan.'

None of us dared mention that Cesare's favourite horse was a white stallion.

'Perhaps not,' Alexander muttered. He looked up at his youngest son with a flicker of hope. 'Perhaps all our grieving is for naught.' He gave a tremulous laugh. 'If it is, we must think of a terrible punishment for Juan, for troubling us so!'

He vacillated between hope and despair. So we remained with him another hour, until a third papal guard appeared.

At the sight of this soldier's expression, Alexander let go a howl. Jofre burst into tears; for the dread in the young soldier's eyes revealed what he had come to announce. He waited until the sounds of grief subsided enough for him to be heard.

'Your Holiness . . . The Duke of Gandia's body has been found. They have taken it to the Castel Sant'Angelo, where it will be washed for burial.'

Alexander would not be restrained, would not listen to reason: he insisted on going to see Juan's body, even though it had not been prepared for viewing, because he would not believe his son dead otherwise.

Jofre and I accompanied him. We flanked him as we entered the room where the women were gathering to wash the corpse; they bowed, astonished at the sight of His Holiness, and quickly left us alone.

Juan's body had been draped with a cloth; Jofre drew it back reverently.

The stench assaulted us at once. The body had been in the river a night and a day, at the height of summer.

Juan was grotesquely recognizable. The water had bloated his body to twice its size; his clothes were torn, his belly bulged out from beneath his tunic. His fingers were thick as sausages. It was hard to see him thus: swollen tongue protruding from between his teeth, eyes open, covered with a milky film, hair plastered to his face with mud. He had been stabbed repeatedly, drained of blood, his skin the colour of marble. Worst of all, his throat had been slit from ear to ear, and the gaping wound had filled with mud, leaves, and bits of wood.

Alexander screamed and collapsed. The combined efforts of Jofre and myself could not restore him to his feet.

Because of the heat, Juan was buried as soon as he was washed and redressed. The coffin was carried by members of the Duke's household and his closest men, followed by a contingent of priests. Jofre and I watched from the papal apartments as the torch lit procession headed for the cathedral at Santa Maria del Popolo, where Juan was interred beside the crypt of his long-dead brother, Pedro Luis.

The Pope did not attend—but he cried out so loudly that Jofre and I could not hear the other mourners. We stayed with him that night—unable to convince him to eat, drink, or sleep—and we never made any comment, then or later, about the conspicuous absence of Cesare.

Autumn 1497

XXII

Juan's death prompted an investigation directed by Alexander's most prominent cardinals, including Cesare, who made a great show of verbally attacking those suspected. The first investigated was Ascanio Sforza, the cardinal whose party guest had insulted Juan and been hanged for the crime. Cesare vilified Sforza, but the cardinal was wise: he did not bristle at the accusations, but cooperated utterly, insisting he had nothing to hide—a fact soon confirmed. Cesare grudgingly apologized.

Other enemies—Juan had earned many—were investigated, but time and persistence revealed no clues.

Or perhaps they revealed too much; less than three weeks after the crime, Alexander halted the search for the murderer. I believe he knew the identity of the culprit in his heart, and had finally given up trying to convince himself otherwise.

Wisely, Cesare had left Rome by that time on official business, presiding as cardinal legate at the coronation of my Uncle Federico as the new King of Naples. Under different circumstances, I would have seized the opportunity to visit Alfonso and Madonna Trusia; but Pope Alexander was not the only one immersed in mourning. Jofre was deeply saddened by Juan's murder, despite any jealousy he felt over his father's favouritism. I felt obliged to remain with him.

Jofre did not consider only his own sorrow; he asked me to visit Lucrezia. 'Please,' he begged. 'She is all alone at San Sisto, and I am too stricken to comfort her. She needs the sympathy of another woman.'

I did not trust Lucrezia; her kindly disposition towards me had not stopped her affair with Cesare, though she knew I loved him. She knew, too, of his ambition to become Captain-General, and may have approved of Juan's death—or had a hand in it.

Nevertheless, I went to the convent out of respect for my husband's wishes. Once again, I greeted young Pantsilea at the door to Lucrezia's suite; once again, the maidservant's beautiful olive-skinned features were taut with despair. 'Taking the canterella away has done no good, Madonna,' she whispered. 'Do not look so surprised—I know you took it, for Lucrezia has been near madness searching for it, and cannot find it. So now she is starving herself. She has taken no food for a week, no water for two days.'

Pantsilea led me back to the inner room, where, dressed only in a chemise although it was midday, Lucrezia sat propped up on the bed, her legs and stomach draped with fine linens. She was paler than I had ever seen her, her eyes and cheeks sunken, her expression one of complete listlessness. She looked over at me with disinterest, then turned her face towards the wall.

I went to her and sat at her side. 'Lucrezia! Pantsilea says you will take no food or drink—but you must! I know you are sad over the loss of your brother—but he would not want you to hurt yourself or your child.'

'To Hell with me,' Lucrezia murmured. 'And to Hell with the child. It's already cursed.' She directed a sharp glance at Pantsilea. 'Leave—and do not skulk at the door listening. You already know far too much: I'm surprised you've lived this long.'

Pantsilea listened, her hand over her mouth—not in shock at her mistress' words, but in sorrow over Lucrezia's air of hopelessness. She turned, shoulders slumped with the weight of her concern, and left, closing the door quietly behind her.

When she had gone, Lucrezia turned and spoke to me with deathbed candour. 'You say you know who the child's father is. I assure you, Sancha, you do not. You do not know how you have been cruelly deceived . . . '

I did not hesitate. If she was willing to be dangerously honest, then I would be, too. 'It is Cesare's.'

She looked at me a long moment, during which time her eyes grew wide, then stricken; her face crumpled into a mask of grief, rage, and terror combined. She seized my hands with the sudden ferocity of a woman in childbirth, then released wrenching, guttural sounds that I at first did not recognize as sobs.

'My life . . . is all lies,' she gasped, when she could draw a breath. 'At first I lived in fear of Rodrigo'—she did not say, *my father*—'and now we all live in terror of Cesare.' She nodded down at her unborn child. 'Do not think I did this for love.'

'He forced you?' I asked. Her misery was too abject to be feigned.

Lucrezia looked beyond me at a distant wall. 'My father had a daughter before me,' she said absently. 'She died many, many years ago, because she did not accept his advances with good grace.' She released an abrupt, bitter laugh. 'I have pretended for so long now, I no longer know the truth of my own feelings. I was jealous of you as a rival when you first came to Rome.'

'But *I* rejected your father, yet I am alive,' I blurted, then paused, realizing my admission would add to her pain.

Lucrezia's expression grew composed, her eyes cold at this revelation. 'You are alive because, had Alexander tried to seduce you again or harm you, Cesare would have killed him. If not immediately, then at some point, when it was to Cesare's advantage. You live because my brother loves you.' Her face contorted briefly again. 'But he wanted Juan's position . . . and Juan harmed you, so Juan is dead. Even Father will never dare accuse Cesare, though he knows the truth.

'And I am safe because I can always make a politically advantageous marriage. I have no cause to live.' Her expression grew piteous; she closed her eyes. 'Just let me die, Sancha. It would be a great kindness. Let me die, and flee to Squillace with Jofre, if you can.'

I studied her for an instant. I had never forgotten her unprompted remark to Cesare to be kind to me.

My worst fears about Cesare had just been confirmed. My life was in jeopardy; one false step, and the man who loved me might just as easily grow displeased and kill me. I lived or died at Cesare's whim, and I would not be able to keep him at arm's length forever.

But I was not the only one to be pitied; Lucrezia's burden was far greater than mine. She had been manipulated by two unspeakably wicked men since her childhood, with no chance of escape. She was truly the unhappiest woman on earth, in sore need of a friend.

I held her tightly. As desperate as our different situations were, we could comfort one another. 'I will neither let you die, nor will I leave you,' I vowed. 'In fact, I will not depart this room until you have had something to eat and drink.'

Slowly, with my repeated visits and encouragement, Lucrezia regained her appetite and improved in outlook and health. I promised repeatedly not to leave her, and she in turn swore to me that I would always have her friendship.

During my trips to San Sisto, Alexander received an epistle from the outspoken Savonarola, who still preached in defiance of the papal brief. The letter relayed sorrow over the loss of His Holiness' son, while also castigating the Pope for the sinfulness of his lifestyle. If Alexander repented, the priest urged, the Apocalypse could be averted. Otherwise, God would visit more sorrows on him and his family.

For the first time, His Holiness took Savonarola's words to

heart. He sent away his women—and his children. Cesare and Lucrezia were already gone, so Jofre received the imperious decree that he and I were to return to Squillace, until it pleased Alexander for us to return.

Jofre was crushed by what he considered a punishment; I was sorry to leave Lucrezia during her most desperate hour, but felt guilty relief at the news. We packed and made the trip southward to the coast, where we spent two months—August and September—free from Rome's crushing heat and scandals. Squillace was just as rocky, barren and provincial as I remembered; now that I had seen the glories of Rome, our palace seemed a pathetically rustic hovel, the food and wine atrocious. Nevertheless, I revelled in the absence of splendour; the bare whitewashed walls were refreshing, the lack of gilt soothing. I wandered the scraggly little gardens under the harsh sun, unafraid that an attacker might be hidden in the bushes; I roamed the corridors without concern that I might witness a horrific scene. I looked out upon the blue ocean—not caring that I had only a partial view from my balcony—and found it good, even if it was less beautiful than Naples' Bay. I ate fish cooked simply, with local olives and lemons, and found it as delicious as any feast in the papal palace.

Best of all, Alfonso came to visit.

'How you have changed!' I laughed, holding him tightly at first, then drawing back, our hands clasped, to admire him. He had grown into a tall, handsome man of eighteen, with a neatly trimmed blond beard that glinted in the sun. 'How is it possible that you have not married? You must be driving all the women in Naples mad!'

'As best I can,' he said, smiling. 'But look at you, Sancha—you have changed so! So grand you look! Such a lady of wealth and stature!'

I looked down at myself. I had forgotten the southern custom of dressing starkly; here I was, weighed down with diamonds and rubies round my neck and in my hair, dressed in a silver velvet gown with burgundy trim—in Squillace, of all places. This unnatural splendour seemed a reflection of the degree I had been corrupted by the Borgias; I yearned for Alfonso's presence to purify me, to bring out the goodness that had become hidden. I forced a smile. 'In Rome, we do not wear much black.'

'Because of the heat, no doubt,' he countered playfully, and I realized how terribly I had missed him. It was divine to be in the presence of a loving, guileless soul once more, and I enjoyed his company each day for as long as he was able to grant it. I knew we would not be allowed to remain in Squillace forever; this was a temporary respite. I lived as though these were my last days, for my final encounter with Cesare could not be delayed forever.

Yet in the presence of Alfonso's kindness, my heart, so scarred by Juan's brutality and Cesare's duplicity, began to heal; I thought often of Lucrezia, and wrote her many letters of encouragement.

Sadly, Alexander grew bored with his newfound love of piety, and soon called for us to rejoin him in Rome.

We returned to Rome in the late autumn, just before winter settled in. Cesare had already come home—still a cardinal, though he had convinced Alexander to begin the manipulations of Church law necessary to free him of his scarlet robes. Fortunately, he was distracted by the legal arrangements and dispensed with appearing at family suppers. I saw little of him during those weeks.

Lucrezia, meanwhile, remained at San Sisto until the days before Christmas, when she was commanded to appear at the Vatican by the cardinals who were to grant her divorce.

I visited Lucrezia in her chambers as Pantsilea tried to dress her—but she was several months gone with child, and even the fullest ermine-trimmed tabard worn over her gown could not hide the fact. We embraced and I kissed her; she smiled, but her lips trembled slightly.

'They will do whatever your father tells them,' I reminded her, but her voice wavered nonetheless.

'I know.' Her tone was uncertain.

'Things will improve,' I continued. 'Soon your confinement will be over, and we will be able to go out together. You have been very brave, Lucrezia. Your courage will be rewarded.'

She steadied herself and put a hand on my cheek. 'I was right to trust you, Sancha. You have been a good friend.'

I was told she conducted herself admirably in front of the consistory, and did not flinch when it was announced that the midwives had found her to be *virgo intacta*. Not one of the cardinals dared to mention the fact that, for the second time in history, God had seen fit to make a virgin pregnant.

From that moment on, Lucrezia remained at home in the Palazzo Santa Maria as a recluse. It was inappropriate for her to sit, heavy with child, beside her father's throne while he held audience, so she remained in her chambers.

In his daughter's absence, Alexander requested that I occasionally sit, not on Lucrezia's velvet cushion, but on the one he had once reserved for me; I could not refuse what was in essence a command.

One February morning I sat dutifully, listening to the plea a particular noble brought before His Holiness concerning an annulment he wished for his eldest daughter. I was quite bored and so was Alexander, who yawned several times, and kept adjusting his ermine wrap about his shoulders for warmth against the winter cold. Ancient cardinals stood in the room, shivering despite the fire blazing in the hearth.

Suddenly, shouts came from several rooms away.

'Bastard! Son of a whore! How dare you touch her!'

The tone was one of raw, unrestrained fury; the voice was Cesare's.

The nobleman who had been droning away stopped; all of us in the throne room stared, wide-eyed, in the direction of the commotion.

Rapid footsteps approached; Cesare was giving chase to someone headed directly towards us.

'I will kill you, you bastard! Who do you think you are, to have touched her?'

A young man came running at full speed into the throne room; I recognized him as Perotto, the servant who had accompanied me to and from San Sisto, when Lucrezia was confined there.

Cesare followed, red-faced and waving a sword, displaying an utterly uncharacteristic rage.

'Cesare . . . ?' the Pope asked, so startled his voice came out barely above a whisper. He cleared his throat and with greater authority, demanded, 'What is this about?'

'Help me, Your Holiness!' the distraught Perotto cried. 'He has gone mad, he is raving, spouting foolishness—and he will not be content until he has killed me!' He ascended the steps to the throne, threw himself at Alexander's feet, and grasped the hem of his white wool garment. I was so astonished that I rose without permission and scrambled down the steps, out of the way.

Cesare dashed at him with the sword.

'Stop!' the Pope commanded. 'Cesare, explain yourself!'

Such explanation was required, as was the cessation of hostilities, since grasping the hem of the Pope's garment was a sacred act, one that conferred greater protection than taking refuge inside a church.

In reply, Cesare lunged forward, turned the cringing, moaning Perotto over, and slashed his neck with the sword.

I recoiled and instinctively raised an arm to protect myself. Alexander gasped as blood sprayed up onto his white robes and ermine cape, spattering his face.

Perotto gurgled, spasmed violently for a long, terrible moment, then lay still, sprawled across the entire span of the steps to the throne.

Cesare watched, jaw twitching, with grim pleasure. When Perotto fell eternally silent, Cesare said at last, 'Lucrezia. *He* is the father. As her brother, I could not permit him to live. I was morally bound to seek vengeance.'

Alexander seemed less concerned with explanations than he

did with the blood dripping from his cheeks. 'Bring a cloth at once,' he ordered, to no one in particular, and then he looked down in disgust at Perotto's corpse. 'And take this mess away.'

The following morning, Perotto's body was found in the Tiber, with hand and feet bound. Custom demanded a symbolic display showing what would become of those who violated the Pope's daughter.

Floating nearby was the body of Pantsilea. Her limbs were unbound; she had been strangled, and a gag stuffed into her now-silent mouth, a clear sign to other Borgia servants of what became of those who knew and told too much.

Early Spring 1498

XXIII

Lucrezia gave birth in early spring. Before her delivery, she was spirited away from Santa Maria, lest her screams during labour reveal to Rome the 'secret' it already knew. Fuelled by the rumours, Savonarola's attacks on the papacy grew vicious: he called for an international council to be formed to depose Alexander.

The child was a boy—named Giovanni, at Lucrezia's insistence. I could not help wondering what Giovanni Sforza, now a disgraced, divorced man held in fatal contempt by the Borgias, thought of the infant being named for him, as if it were his own get.

The child was returned to the palazzo in the care of a wet nurse. It was kept in a distant wing, that its cries might not disturb the adult occupants. Lucrezia visited the infant as frequently as she was permitted, which was not often enough to suit her. When we were alone, she often confided in me about her heartbreak that she was not allowed to act as the boy's mother. At times, she wept, inconsolable with grief.

Once she was delivered suitors lined up for her hand, either disbelieving the charges brought by Sforza, or totally unconcerned by them. The political advantage was, after all, great.

The Pope and Cesare conferred at length about these men; some names they shared with Lucrezia, and she in turn shared them with me. There was Francesco Orsini, the Duke of Gravina, and a count, Ottaviano Riario. The most favoured one was Antonello Sanseverino, a Neapolitan—but an Angevin, a supporter of France. Such a match would put me at a grave political disadvantage within the family.

I was troubled as well by my role as Lucrezia's friend and confidante. I had seen the innocent Perotto's fate, and Pantsilea's, and knew the Borgias would not let years of loyalty interfere with their plans. If someone needed to be silenced—no matter how beloved, how trusted—then they were silenced.

Pantsilea's death left me with nightmares. I had never seen the corpse, only heard it described in great detail by Esmeralda, who by then had assembled a most impressive network of informants and spies. I often woke gasping to the image of Pantsilea's body rising like a cork from the depths of the dark Tiber, and her dead eyes slowly opening to regard me. Her bloated arm rose to point an accusatory finger: *You. You are the cause of my death . . .*

For I had taken the canterella, the poison, hidden in Lucrezia's gown. And I could not help thinking that the poor maidservant had been murdered because the poison had been missed. I assumed that Cesare had forced the poison on Lucrezia, with instructions. And when Cesare asked for it, Lucrezia would have been forced to explain that it was missing.

Pantsilea, of course, would have been first to be blamed.

In my less guilty moments, I convinced myself the young lady-in-waiting had died for the very reason symbolized by the gag found in her mouth: she had known too much, and needed to be silenced. Had she not, after all, pushed me into the armoire as a way of sharing what she could not say: the truth of the relationship between Lucrezia and Cesare?

. . .

Lucrezia was not the only one, that spring and summer, whose thoughts turned to marriage.

One day, I was summoned to the Vatican—to Cesare's office. The notice was signed 'Cesare Borgia, Cardinal of Valencia'.

I sat on my bed with the parchment in my hand. The moment I most dreaded had come. Cesare would demand to know the extent of my love and loyalty; he would accept no further excuses.

In the vain hope of preventing a private confrontation, I took Esmeralda and two of my younger ladies with me; we made our way on foot through the piazza to the Vatican. There we were escorted by two guards to the cardinal's office; at the entry, a single soldier waved my ladies away. 'His Holiness has requested that he meet with the Princess of Squillace alone.'

Esmeralda frowned at the impropriety, but my ladies were led to a waiting area, and I entered the cardinal's office unattended.

Cesare sat at a grand, gilded desk of inlaid ebony wood. Leather-bound tomes of canon law filled the shelves behind him; an oil lamp flickered on the desk. When the soldier escorted me in, Cesare rose, and gestured for me to take the padded velvet chair across from him.

I sat. The soldier was dismissed, and Cesare promptly vacated his desk and went down on one knee in front of me. He was wearing his official skullcap and scarlet robes; the silk hem rustled against the marble floor.

'Donna Sancha,' he said. Months had passed since he had bedded me, yet despite the formality of the situation, he spoke with the familiar affection of a lover. 'I have received official word from my father that I am soon to be relieved of the burden of monastic life.'

I was not fool enough to show my trepidation; instead, I kept my tone cordial. 'I am happy for you. This must certainly be a great relief.'

'It is more than that,' he said. 'It is a great opportunity . . . for us.' He took my hand gently, and held it in one of his; before I could react, he swiftly slipped a small gold ring onto my smallest finger.

The ring that had been my mother's; the ring that Juan had stolen from me the day he raped me. I managed, through an act of supreme self-control, not to wince. 'Where did you get this?' I whispered.

'Does it matter?' he asked, smiling. 'Donna Sancha, you know that you are, and have always been, the one great love of my life. Make my happiness complete. Say that you will marry me when I am free.'

I looked away, overwhelmed by disgust, but forced to convey a much different emotion. I remained silent a time, carefully searching for the proper words—but none existed that could save my life. 'I am not myself free,' I said at last. 'I am bound to Jofre.'

He shrugged, as if this were something easily cast off. 'We can offer Jofre the cardinalship; I have no doubt he would take it. It is easy enough to have the marriage annulled.'

'Not so,' I replied, my tone neutral. 'Cardinal Borgia of Monreale himself witnessed our first marital act. There is no doubt the marriage was consummated.'

The first traces of irritation crept into his voice as he began to realize that his case was lost, and he had no real idea why, which annoyed him even more. 'Cardinal Borgia is in our hands. He will say whatever we want. Do you not love me? Do you not wish to be my wife?'

'It is not that,' I said earnestly. 'I do not wish to shame Jofre. Such an act would surely crush him.'

He stared at me as if I were a madwoman. 'Jofre will recover. Again, there is the cardinalship, a position which will bring him power and riches to generously soothe his pain. We would send him to Valencia, to make the situation less awkward; you two would never need set eyes on each other again.' He paused. 'Madonna, you are not a fool. Quite the opposite: you are supremely intelligent. You realize I am to be Captain-General of my father's army.'

'I do,' I answered softly.

'I am not the ineffectual dolt Juan was. I see the opportunities such a position presents. I intend to extend the realm of the Papal States.'

'I have always known you were a man of great ambition,' I said, in the same uncritical tone.

'I intend,' he said, his voice hard, his expression intent as he leaned closer, 'to unite Italy. I intend to be its ruler. And I am asking you to be my queen.'

I was obliged to feign an expression of surprise, to pretend I had not already heard similar words while hiding in Lucrezia's closet.

'Do you not love me?' he demanded in frustration, letting the force of his emotions through. 'Sancha, I had thought that—surely I was not mistaken as to the depth of the feelings we shared for each other.'

His words pierced my defences. I lowered my face. 'I have never loved any man more,' I confessed, with regret. I knew my own heart: I could easily be corrupted, and play the malevolent queen to Cesare's king.

That gave him hope; he stroked my cheek with the back of his finger. 'It is settled, then. We will be wed. You are too tender-hearted toward Jofre; trust me, he is a man. He will recover.'

I pulled my face away from his outstretched hand and said firmly, 'You have not heard me, Cardinal. My answer is no. I am impressed and moved. But I am not the woman you seek for such a role.'

Red-faced, he dropped his hand and rose, his movements taut with repressed fury. 'Clearly you are not, Madonna. You are dismissed.'

He spent no further time trying to convince me; his wounded sense of dignity would not permit it. Yet I could tell, as I rose and left to join my ladies, that he was utterly confused, even hurt, by my rejection. He could not believe my given reason—concern for Jofre—as the truth.

I was relieved he appeared unable to divine the real cause—that I knew him to be a murderer.

I expected retaliation for my refusal. I kept my stiletto beneath my pillow, close at hand; even so, I slept fitfully that night. Every rustling breeze at the window, every creak in the corridor beyond seemed to me the sounds of an approaching assassin. I had rejected Cesare, and thought my life forfeit. I did not expect to live more than a matter of days afterward; I judged each morning I rose to be my last.

I told Lucrezia that I had turned down her brother's proposal. I was not entirely comfortable confiding in her, given her apparent talent for duplicity—indeed, I had consulted Donna Esmeralda regarding her trustworthiness, but even Esmeralda's gossips could not agree about Lucrezia's true character. Even so, I had to try to learn the degree of retribution I should expect from Cesare.

She listened to my news solemnly. She was honest—she did not say that I would never receive retribution. But she reassured me on one account. 'You must understand,' she said. 'I have spoken with my brother since. He nurses hope that you will come to your senses. I do not believe him capable of physically harming you; his heart is still hopelessly yours.'

This was of some comfort—yet I was troubled as I contemplated what retaliation Cesare *would* take, once he realized that I would never yield.

Lucrezia and I continued our friendship, and met almost daily. One morning in late spring, she came to my chambers with a request that I accompany her on a walk in the gardens, and I happily obliged.

When we were out of earshot of our ladies, who were walking several steps behind us, holding their own conversations, Lucrezia said coyly, 'So. You have spoken of your brother, Alfonso, and you claim that he is one of the most handsome men in all Italy.'

'It is no claim,' I replied, with easy good humour. 'It is God's own truth. He is a golden god, Madonna. I saw him last summer in Squillace, and he has only grown more handsome.'

'And he is kind?'

'No sweeter man was ever born.' I stopped in mid-stride and stared over at her, seized by a sudden wonderful conviction. 'You know all this; I have spoken of him many times. Lucrezia—tell me—is he coming to visit us at Rome?'

'Yes!' she said, and clapped her hands like a gleeful child; I grabbed those hands, smiling with joy. 'But Sancha, it is even better than that!'

'What can be better than a visit from Alfonso?' I demanded. What a fool I was; how ignorant!

'He and I are to be married.' She waited, smiling, for my exuberant reaction.

I gasped. I felt pulled down into a horrible black vortex, a suffocating Charybdis from which I could not extricate myself.

Yet extricate myself I did, through some involuntary grace. I did not—could not—smile, but managed to save the situation by pulling her to me solemnly in a tight embrace.

'Sancha,' she said, her voice muffled by my shoulder, 'Sancha, you are so sweet. I have never seen you so emotional.'

Once I had control of myself, I drew back with a forced smile. 'Have you kept this secret from me long?'

Silently, I damned Alfonso. He had said nothing to me of the marriage proposal. If he had, I might have had the chance to warn him, to explain the peculiar circle of Hell he was about to enter. But writing to him was out of the question; my letters would surely be taken aside and examined by Alexander and Cesare, given the political importance of this union. I was bound to wait until he arrived in Rome—as a bridegroom.

But had he not heard of Giovanni Sforza's charges? Had he been fool enough to disbelieve them? And all of Italy knew Lucrezia had just given birth. No doubt Alfonso accepted the lie that Perotto had been the father, and was willing to overlook Lucrezia's youthful indiscretion.

This was all my fault, I told myself, for sparing Alfonso the miserable truth of life in Rome.

I had wanted to protect him. And, like a good Borgia, I had learned to keep my mouth shut.

'Not so long,' Lucrezia replied in answer to my question. 'Father and Cesare did not tell me until this morning. I am so happy! At last, I will have a husband my own age—one who is handsome and kind. I am the luckiest woman in Rome! And your brother has agreed to take up residence here. We will all live together in Santa Maria.' She clasped my hand. 'I was so full of despair only a few months ago that I wanted to take my own life. But you saved me, and for that I shall always be grateful. Now I have hope again.'

Cesare could have chosen no more perfect way to make me hold my tongue, to mind my manners, to behave in whatever way he wished. He knew of my love for Alfonso—I spoke often of him at family dinners, and at our private trysts. Cesare knew that I would do anything to protect my little brother.

'I am glad for you,' I managed.

'I know how terribly you have missed him. Perhaps Father and Cesare were thinking of that, too, when they chose him.' The naiveté in her statement astounded me.

'I have no doubt they were,' I said, knowing that Lucrezia would never hear the irony in it.

I arrived in my bedchamber that night to find Donna Esmeralda weeping as she knelt at her shrine to San Gennaro.

'The end of the world is coming at last,' she moaned, clasping the small gold crucifix about her neck. 'They have killed him. They have killed him, and we will all pay.'

I pulled her to her feet and forced her to sit on the edge of the bed. 'Who, Esmeralda? Who do you mean?'

'Savonarola,' she said. 'Alexander's delegates. He would not stop preaching, so they hanged him, then burned his body.' She shook her head, whispering, 'God will strike Alexander down, Madonna. Mark my words: even a pope cannot continue in such wickedness.'

I put my hands upon her shoulders. 'Do not fear for yourself, Esmeralda: if it is true that God sees all hearts, then he sees yours, and knows you are a good woman. He would never have cause to punish you.'

I could scarcely say the same for myself.

When Esmeralda at last fell asleep, I pondered my brother's situation for hours. I remembered my grandfather Ferrante's words: *If you love him, look out for him. We strong have to take care of the weak, you know. They haven't the heart to do what's necessary to survive.*

I would do anything to save my brother's life—and Cesare was all too aware of the fact. I assumed that his choice of Lucrezia's groom was part of a plot intended to coerce me into marrying him.

The notion that once would have filled me with delight now made me shudder . . . for I knew that, to protect Alfonso, I would desert poor Jofre and marry a murderer.

Summer 1498

XXIV

Alfonso rode into Rome in the midst of summer; and I, in my desperation to speak to him privately, played the overeager sister and rode out alone to meet his entourage before it even crossed the Ponte Sant'Angelo, the bridge that led to Vatican Hill.

He rode on horseback at the front of his company, accompanied by several grooms, while wagons piled with his belongings and bridal gifts followed; I easily spotted the golden hair in the bright sun. I spurred my horse on, and when he recognized me, he gave a shout, and galloped forth to meet me.

We dismounted and embraced; despite my worry over his impending marriage, I could not help smiling with joy at the sight of him. He was as glorious-looking as ever, clad in pale blue satin. 'Alfonso, my darling.'

'I am here, Sancha! Here at last! I never need leave you again.'

His grooms trotted up to join us. 'May I have a moment with my brother?' I asked sweetly.

They acquiesced and rode back to join the slow wagons.

I put my cheek against his. 'Alfonso,' I whispered in his ear, 'as happy as I am to see you, you must not go through with this marriage.'

He released a disbelieving little laugh. 'Sancha,' he said aloud, 'now is hardly the time and place.'

'Now is the *only* time and place. Once we arrive at the Vatican, it will no longer be safe to talk freely.'

My tone was so fierce, so urgent, he grew sombre. 'I am already committed. To break the contract now would be unconscionable, cowardly . . . '

I drew a breath. I had little time to make my case, and my brother was a very trusting soul. How was I to relay quickly the degree of treachery I had witnessed? 'Ethics are of no use here. You know the lines written by the Aragonese poets concerning Lucrezia,' I said. I felt guilt, imagining what she would feel if she knew what I was telling her intended bridegroom.

'Please.' He blushed; he knew precisely to what I alluded.

I quoted Sannazaro. *'Hic jacet in tumulo Lucretia nomine, sed re Thais: Alexandri filia, sponsa, nurus.'* It was an epitaph suggested for Lucrezia: 'Here in her tomb lies Lucrezia in name, but Thais in fact: Alexander's daughter, spouse, daughter-in-law.' Pantsilea or some other soul must have shared Cesare's incest with Lucrezia with others, for even the poets in Naples and Spain had begun to write scathing couplets about her (in this case comparing her to the ancient Egyptian sinner-cum-saint, Thais, who had repented of her incestuous ways).

I did not need to say that the rumours were fact; Alfonso was quick enough to realize why I recited the verse.

'Sancha,' he said, his voice low and tense, his words swift. 'Even if every charge against her is true, I am not free. I have vowed to do this for the sake of Naples. Other men, with ties to France, have proposed—and we cannot permit any French influence on His Holiness. Without full papal support, the House of Aragon is doomed. The new French King has already proclaimed himself ruler of our territory; we must have the Pope on our side in case of another invasion.'

I fought to keep the anguish from my expression; Alfonso's entourage could not see me show anything but happiness. 'You do not understand—you will have to watch your every move. They are murderers,' I whispered, my expression as pleasant as if we were discussing the glorious weather.

'As are most rulers, among them our own relatives,' he countered. 'Am I not charming, Sancha?'

'The most charming man I have ever met—almost.' He tried to make me smile again, but I was too full of despair.

'I will charm even the Borgias. I will win their trust. I am not a fool; I will give them no cause to rid themselves of me. And the marriage has brought our family a great boon: the Duchy of Bisciglie.' He paused; his tone turned playful as he tried to turn my dismay back to joy. 'Is Lucrezia entirely cruel? Will she treat me badly? Is she a hideous hag?'

'No, no, and no.' I released a sigh of pure misery, realizing I had been defeated. Nothing would stop the marriage.

'You said in your letters that you and she are friends. You seem to have survived thus far.'

'After a fashion, yes.' I paused. 'Lucrezia has actually been quite kind to me.'

'Then she is not a heartless monster. And I am not here to judge her. I will treat her well and be a good husband, Sancha. I can think of no better way to win over her father and Cesare.'

I put my hand on his bearded cheek. 'You could not be any other kind of husband, little brother. I pray God you take care.'

I rode into the city with him. Cesare was waiting to receive him in front of the Vatican. The Cardinal of Valencia's manner was at once cordial and cool; he was sizing up this man who might exert untoward influence over his sister, and I believe he was justifiably concerned. I did my best not to reveal my inner turmoil.

At last we dismounted, and I followed as my brother was led up the Vatican steps into the building itself and the throne room, where Alexander sat waiting, bedecked entirely in white satin, with his heavy gold-and-diamond cross upon his breast.

Lucrezia sat on the velvet cushion beside him. Like her groom-to-be, she had dressed in palest blue—in her case, a gown of silk, with silver trim and seed pearls covering the bodice, and a matching cap; her cheeks were flushed, and she looked almost pretty, with her golden ringlets spilling past her shoulders. At the sight of Alfonso, her face lit up like a beacon; she was unquestionably besotted with him from the first instant.

Alexander seemed besotted himself. He broke into a broad grin, and said, 'The bridegroom, and new Duke of Bisciglie! Welcome, Alfonso! Welcome, dear son, to our family! So, Lucrezia, the rumours are true—your husband-to-be is an exceedingly handsome man!'

Alfonso dutifully knelt to kiss the Pope's slipper; once that formality was dispensed with, Alexander rose and stepped down to put his arm around his future son-in-law's shoulders. 'Come. Come. We have prepared a fine dinner—though I think we should not eat too much, for tomorrow there is the wedding-feast!'

He laughed, and Alfonso smiled. In the interim, Lucrezia rose from her little cushion and descended the stairs. When Alfonso encountered her, he bowed and kissed her hand.

'Madonna Lucrezia,' he said—and only my brother could speak with the sincerity to make the following words convincing, 'you shine like a star at night. Compared to your beauty, everything that surrounds you is darkness.'

She giggled like a child; Alexander beamed in approval of such pretty words. He replaced his arm around Alfonso's shoulders, and the two of them headed for the papal apartments and the waiting banquet, while Lucrezia followed with a dreamy expression. Cesare went next, his features arranged pleasantly, but his gaze piercing; I brought up the rear, wearing a frozen smile.

. . .

The wedding was held in the Hall of the Saints, where the ill-fated marriage to Giovanni Sforza had taken place. The guests were few, mostly the Vatican household and some cardinals.

Lucrezia looked lovely in a gown of black satin, with a gold stomacher seeded with diamonds. She and Alfonso might have been mistaken for brother and sister, with their golden curls and pale eyes—just as, ironically, I might have been mistaken for the sister of the dark-haired Cesare, who was dressed in black velvet for the occasion. Out of deference for the bride, I dressed in sombre Neapolitan garb.

During the wedding, I stood next to Jofre—with Cesare uncomfortably close, just on my husband's other side. As Cardinal Giovanni Borgia asked the bride and groom to utter their vows, the acting Captain-General of the papal forces, Juan de Cervillon, unsheathed a handsome jewelled sword and held it over the heads of the new Duke and Duchess of Bisciglie. It symbolized that these two should never be parted by any cause; as I stared at the shining blade, I thought of the strega's card—the heart pierced by two swords. I had blotted much of the incident from my memory, but now more of it returned at the sight of de Cervillon's weapon, with haunting force.

I will never resort to evil! I had proclaimed haughtily. Certainly, I could think of no worse evil at the moment than being forced to wed Cesare.

Then you condemn to death those whom you most love, the strega had said.

I watched the proceedings with no emotion other than fear.

But Alfonso and Lucrezia were all smiles. The two could not have seemed happier; I held onto the fact desperately, hoping it would spare my brother the pain I had encountered at the Borgias' hands.

Alfonso gave his answer in a sure, strong voice; Lucrezia's reply was soft and shy as she gazed upon him with honest devotion. One look at her eyes, and at Alfonso's, and I knew: they had been

struck by the same thunderbolt that wounded me the day I met the Cardinal of Valencia.

Soon the presiding legate pronounced the pair man and wife. Radiant, Alfonso and Lucrezia processed arm in arm from the Hall, followed by Captain de Cervillon and Cardinal Borgia.

Unfortunately, as the rest of us began to leave from the private chapel to the reception area, an argument began. 'The Princess of Squillace is sister to the groom, and her party will proceed next,' Donna Esmeralda insisted in a strident voice. Soon she was shoving one of Cesare's grooms aside; his servants were demanding precedence over mine. It is impossible to completely hide one's personal feelings from one's servants, and Cesare's people and mine were, in a matter of seconds, at each other's throats. One of Jofre's grooms stepped forward and demanded, 'Let the Prince and Princess of Squillace pass!'

In reply, he received a swift blow to the jaw, and fell back into the arms of his fellows. Donna Esmeralda and my ladies began shrieking; it did not help that His Holiness' entourage became caught up in the mêlée as well.

More punches were thrown, and swords drawn; the Pope's attendants became so terrified, they ran up the steps behind the altar and fled the chapel, leaving Alexander unprotected in the middle of a brawl. 'Enough!' he shouted, flailing his arms, his golden mantle very nearly pierced by a blade, and in danger of slipping from his shoulders. 'Enough! This is a happy occasion!'

His pleas were drowned out by shouts. Jofre's groom recovered enough to wrestle his attacker to the floor; the pair blocked any progress in or out of the chapel.

'Stop!' Jofre called, his voice adding to the cacophony. 'Stop this idiocy at once!'

The task fell to Cesare. Without a word, he drew a dagger and in a swift, single movement was leaning over the two fighting men, the tip of the blade in reach of either's throat. The ferocity in his gaze convinced the two wrestling that he would not hesitate to spill blood, even here, even now, on his sister's wedding-day.

The room fell silent. 'Disengage,' Cesare said, in a deadly low voice, yet all heard it.

The grooms rolled aside, and stood, wide-eyed and complacent.

'Where is His Holiness' entourage?' Cesare asked, in the same calm, low—yet altogether terrifying—tone.

His groom pointed to the altar, and the steps that led back toward the private papal chambers. 'Hiding, Your Holiness.'

'Fetch them. He is to process next, and must be attended.'

The groom sped to the altar, and up the stairs. Cesare, his dagger still drawn, but lowered, glanced at Jofre's groom, the other participant in the altercation. 'He will no doubt need help,' the cardinal said.

With exaggerated eagerness, Jofre's groom followed. It took some minutes before the full entourage appeared, but at last, the Pope was able to leave the chapel. Graciously—or rather, with the appearance of graciousness, Cesare insisted on my entourage departing next.

The ceremony was followed by a protracted supper, then dancing. Alfonso was, as always, filled with such charm and good cheer that even the Borgias were infected. For the first time since I had come to Rome, the Pope danced—first with Lucrezia, then with me. Despite his great size, he was possessed of the same athletic grace as his son Cesare.

I was especially happy to see that no courtesans were present—not even the Pope's mistress Giulia. He seemed to be trying to convince Alfonso that the rumours surrounding the Sforza scandal and the birth of Lucrezia's child were untrue; regardless, I was relieved that the celebration did not spiral downwards into the Borgias' customary lewdness. The Pope drank far less wine than his custom, for once considerate of Lucrezia's happiness. Even Cesare was pleasant.

Alfonso and I performed a Neapolitan dance for His Holiness, and my brother's eyes were bright, his smile genuine. I knew that part of his joy came from knowing we two would be together again—but I could also see that his delight with Lucrezia was sincere. They had, as Alexander put it jocularly over supper, 'taken to each other. Look at those two! It is as though the rest of us do not exist. Shall we all retreat quietly, lest we disturb them?'

I could not understand why my little brother, who had his choice of more beautiful and honourable women, should fall in love with Lucrezia; I only hoped for his happiness.

After much dancing, theatricals were presented on a small stage that had been erected in the reception area. One presentation involved a beautifully dressed maid who coaxed a unicorn to lay its head upon her lap. The maid was played by none other than Giulia, the Pope's mistress, but this was not the greatest irony, for I at last recognized, from his body and movements, the man beneath the heavy unicorn's mask, a full headpiece with a gilded horn, and holes for the eyes and mouth.

It was Cesare Borgia, portraying the very symbol of chasteness and loyalty.

As dawn approached, Lucrezia and Alfonso retired together, with a smugly smiling Giovanni Borgia following them. My poor brother was about to be subjected to the same indignity I had—that of having the leering cardinal witness his first sexual union with his spouse. At least, I reflected, Alfonso did not have the added embarrassment of having his own father watch the proceedings; I wondered whether the cardinal would comment about roses.

A few weeks after the marriage, Cesare was granted what he had dreamt of for years: the chance to present his case before the consistory of cardinals, asking them to free him from a vocation for which he had never been suited. In exchange, he swore that he would surrender himself to the service of the Church and go at once to France, where he would do everything necessary to save Italy from another invasion by another French king.

There was no more doubt that Cesare would be granted his petition than there had been doubt that Lucrezia would be declared *virgo intacta*.

Cesare got his wish. No sooner had it been granted than he began looking about for a suitable mate. I steeled myself for the worst, expecting to receive another summons to his office: to my astonishment, Lucrezia revealed that he had chosen Carlotta of Aragon—my cousin, the legitimate daughter of Uncle Federico, the King of Naples.

I was ecstatic; I thought I had underestimated Cesare. Lucrezia had said that he truly cared for me—and perhaps that was why he wished neither to coerce me, nor cause me harm. Even better, his choice of bride made Alfonso's position, as a Prince of Naples, more secure in the House of Borgia.

Carlotta was at the time in France, being educated at the court of the piously Catholic, pro-Borgia Queen Anne of Brittany, widow of *Re Petito*, Charles VIII, who had died that spring. Cesare dressed himself in his best finery, and, astride his white horse shod with silver, headed north. He was confident he would win Carlotta's hand, for the new King, Louis XII, greatly desired a divorce from his crippled, barren wife, Queen Jeanne, so that he could marry Anne, whom he loved.

And Cesare was just the person who, as the Pope's son, could deliver a writ of divorce directly into Louis' hands—for a price.

With a sigh of relief, I watched him ride away, believing my country's troubles had at last ended.

Autumn–Winter 1498

XXV

A hot, brutal summer finally gave way to autumn, then a mild winter. My life in Rome had never been more pleasant; Juan was dead, Cesare was busy with politics and courtship in France, leaving me in the company of my husband, my brother, Lucrezia, and Alexander.

Away from Cesare's and Juan's demeaning barbs, Jofre was more at ease and kinder. Alfonso was by nature in good spirits, and his love for Lucrezia made him even more jovial and charming; he brought out a sweetness in Lucrezia that I had only glimpsed earlier, but which now became a constant of her nature. And because his family was happy, Alexander was happy. His daughter had made a good match, and was now a duchess instead of a mere countess; his eldest son was about to make an even better match, and there was now the prospect of legitimate grandchildren.

Because of our shared love for Alfonso, Lucrezia and I became closer than ever before. I tattled on Alfonso for all his little idiosyncrasies, and Lucrezia loved to listen to stories of his childhood—how he had once tried to set fire to the tail of the Queen's lapdog, to see whether it would burn like a candle, how he had almost been swept out to sea as a child of four, and nearly drowned. And she confessed to me how he snored, drawing in great puffs of air—*ah, ah, ah*—then at last letting them go with one great, sonorous gust.

I forgot the canterella I had hidden with the jewels in my bedchamber. I forgot its source; I even forgot the sight of Lucrezia in her father's carnal embrace, the passionate kiss she had shared with her own brother. (Lucrezia reported with great relief that the Pope had left her alone ever since her pregnancy, either because old age had taken the fire out of him, or because he no longer wished to fan the rumours provoked by the birth of the illegitimate child he had supposedly got on her.) She also confessed that she and Alfonso spent every night together in her bedchamber, and he always woke there, rarely spending time in his own chambers in the men's wing of the palazzo. 'I had never dared hope,' she confided, quite wistfully, 'that my own husband should also be my ardent lover.'

One winter morning, when the bright sun had taken all the chill from the air, we women decided to go on a picnic in Cardinal Lopez's vineyard. It was too lovely to stay inside, and Lucrezia seemed restless with an anticipation I did not understand, until she settled beside me in the carriage and confessed, 'I have a secret. I have not told anyone, not even Alfonso—but I must tell you.'

I was lazily enjoying the sun on my face. 'Secret?' From Lucrezia's smug smile, it was obviously a happy one. I suspected a party, or a gift she had obtained for her new husband.

'I am pregnant. Two months now without my monthly courses.'

'Lucrezia!' Genuinely pleased, I grabbed her shoulders. 'You are sure then? There is no other cause?'

She laughed, delighted with my response. 'I am sure. My breasts are so tender, I can scarcely bear for Alfonso to touch them. And I must eat, eat all the time—or else I become too ill to tolerate the smell of food. You must play the fool, and tell no one—I intend to surprise him with the news at supper tonight.'

'He will be so excited. And your father, too.' I smiled at the thought of playing aunt to my brother's child.

Once we arrived at the vineyard, we found the perfect pastoral setting: a copse of tall pines perpendicular to a clearing of grass and wildflowers, then rows of grape arbours, their gnarled vines bare of leaf or fruit. The land sloped gradually downward, providing a pleasant vista. A table had been brought, and as the servant girls busied themselves with unloading the food and wine, Lucrezia looked the setting up and down, dropped her ermine cape casually on the grass, and said: 'It's a perfect day for a race.'

I laughed. It was an entirely girlish suggestion—yet, when I met Lucrezia's mischievous gaze, I saw that she was serious. 'Your condition, Madonna,' I said, under my breath.

'Don't be ridiculous!' she countered. 'I couldn't be healthier! And I am so excited about telling Alfonso—if I don't do something, I'll go mad from the energy.'

Grinning, I studied her: she had put on a bit of weight since marrying my brother, and brimmed with vigour. She was used to a great deal of walking and riding; a short run would not tax her in the least, pregnant or not. 'Race, then, Duchess,' I said. I eyed the perfectly straight rows of grapevines, and said, 'It *is* an ideal setting.'

'Then let's run.' Lucrezia pointed to the first break in the arbour. 'That's our end-point; first one to reach it wins.'

I slipped off my cape and tabard; both hems were long and would trip me. Lucrezia removed her own tabard as I asked, 'And what are the stakes?'

She frowned, thinking, then one corner of her lip curled upward. 'A diamond. Either you take one from me, or I take one from you.'

'But whose choice?' I persisted.

'The loser's,' she said, suddenly timid.

I folded my arms and shook my head, and she laughed.

'All right, all right, victor's choice. I suppose I shall have to win, then.'

We held our skirts high, called for Donna Esmeralda to give the signal—and then were off.

It was scarcely a fair contest. I was taller and longer of limb and won handily, kicking up a great deal of dust. 'So,' I gloated, 'I will have to pick out your finest diamond.' Lucrezia rolled her eyes and made a fine show of being worried, when we both knew that I had no intention of claiming my prize.

Lucrezia demanded a rematch; when I refused (for I did not want her to tire herself), she insisted on racing the younger ladies-in-waiting. At one point, there were four ladies taking the runner's stance, waiting for Donna Esmeralda to give the signal—two in each wide row.

I grew mildly concerned, for Lucrezia's face was quite flushed, and she had begun to perspire, despite the coolness of the day. I decided to insist that lunch be served and all exertion end by the time Donna Esmeralda called for the runners to start.

As the last race began, I moved away from the arbours, toward Donna Esmeralda and the table, laden now with a tempting array of foods; Lucrezia would no doubt be hungry after all her activity.

I was looking away when I heard the subtle, troubling sound of flesh and bone colliding with earth. A shout followed. I turned to see Donna Esmeralda running as fast as her stout form would allow, towards two women in the arbour path. At the same instant, I spotted the second woman in mid-fall, her green brocade skirts ballooning above her in the air. I, too, ran until, like Esmeralda, I stood beside Lucrezia and the young lady-in-waiting who had fallen atop her, and now pushed herself slowly up and away from her mistress.

'Lucrezia!' I cried, kneeling down beside her. She was unconscious and frighteningly pale. I looked accusingly up at the poor lady-in-waiting, who stood trembling, knuckles to her mouth. 'What happened?'

'I don't know, Madonna,' she said, her voice tearful. 'She was running and, I think, tripped on her slipper. She fell, and I could not stop in time . . . ' She gazed at us, her young face terrified of rebuke or punishment, but we had no interest in her, as she was unharmed. Lucrezia had taken the brunt of her fall.

I patted Lucrezia's cheeks; they were cool, but she remained in a faint. I glanced up at Donna Esmeralda, all business.

'The Duchess of Bisciglie is pregnant,' I said. 'We must get her back to the palazzo at once, and call for a doctor and midwife.'

Donna Esmeralda gasped at this news, then ran to fetch the young male drivers of our carriage, who had been off hunting. Within half-an-hour, we were back in the carriage. Esmeralda and I spread Lucrezia out across our laps, and I kept my hand pressed to her forehead, worrying about the potential for fever, and cursing myself for ever allowing the first race to be run.

By the time we arrived back at the palazzo, Lucrezia had come to herself—though she was somewhat shaken and had to be reminded of the fall.

'That damned slipper!' she cursed—trying to fend off the carriage driver—who insisted on carrying her into the palazzo—but in the end yielding. When he, for modesty's sake, left her at the door of her bedchamber, we women surrounded her, propping her up as she staggered to her bed.

Each step caused her pain. 'It is only my back,' she said nonchalantly, 'and a headache. I will be better by the morrow.'

The midwife awaited her, and Lucrezia submitted meekly to an examination. When the older woman at last emerged from the bedchamber, Donna Esmeralda and I leapt up from our seats to hear the news.

'The duchess has taken serious blows to the head and back,' the old woman reported. 'She shows no fever, no bleeding or other signs of losing the child—but it is too early to know.'

Donna Esmeralda and I consulted with Lucrezia's head lady-in-waiting, and I decided that we would tell the doctor not to come. His arrival might be noted by others, as his appearance always indicated a serious malady, whereas the midwife was often consulted for minor female complaints. There was no point in alarming the Pope and Alfonso. We would retain the midwife, and watch Lucrezia over the next several hours to see how she fared.

By that time, it was afternoon. Fortunately, no family supper was planned for that evening, since we women were expected to return late from our picnic.

At Lucrezia's request, I went in and sat beside her. She was nauseated and refused offers of food or drink; her head pained her greatly, and she could barely open her eyes. Still, she insisted on remaining cheerful and conversing with me, her forehead covered with cool, damp cloths.

'All this trouble over a stupid slipper,' she told me. 'The left one was too loose; I was of a mind to pull it off and run barefoot. I should have. We could have avoided all this foolishness.'

'Donna Esmeralda would never have permitted it in cold weather,' I retorted lightly, with the same good humour, though I was racked with guilt and concern. 'She would have worried you would catch the grippe. So you would have had to wear the accursed slipper regardless.'

'Alfonso will be so worried,' she whispered. 'Have you told him?'

'Not yet.'

'Good.' She closed her eyes. 'The surprise will have to wait, then, until I am better.' She sighed. 'He is going to find out soon enough about my fall. He will come here sometime after nightfall.'

'He is a strong young man,' I said. 'He will recover from the shock.'

She smiled weakly, then grew silent. After a time, she fell into a light sleep. I felt relief, thinking her discomfort had eased, and she would now improve. But the midwife insisted on remaining nearby.

Lucrezia woke a few hours after sunset, with a great, terrifying moan. I leaned forward and clasped her hand. Her teeth were chattering; she was suffering too greatly even to speak.

The midwife lifted the covers and examined her, then—with a sombre glance that broke my heart—shook her head.

'She is bleeding,' she reported. 'We can expect the worst.' She turned to Donna Esmeralda and ordered several towels, a sheet, and a basin of water, then looked at me again, with a grim expression born of years of sad experience. 'It would be best, Madonna Sancha, if you left.'

'No!' Lucrezia cried, in the midst of her groaning. Her flesh was white, beaded with sweat. 'Sancha, do not leave me!'

I strengthened my grip on her hand. 'I will not leave,' I said, my voice steady, full of a strength I did not feel. 'I will stay here with you until you tell me to go.'

She relaxed only for an instant; another wave of agony soon gripped her, and she squeezed my hand with crushing force.

Esmeralda returned to the room, having ordered the servant girls to fetch the required objects. 'Summon His Holiness and the Duke of Bisciglie to the antechamber,' I told her. 'It is time they were notified.'

'Sancha!' Lucrezia gasped. 'They will be so worried . . . Will you be the one to tell them?'

'I will tell them,' I soothed, and picked up the cloth that rested on her forehead. The side resting against her skin had grown warm, so I turned it over to the cooler side, and gently smoothed her brow with it. 'I will be gentle, and make sure they do not worry overmuch.'

'Yes. Yes. They both worry so . . . ' Lucrezia whispered, then gritted her teeth as another spasm overtook her.

Since Alfonso resided in the palazzo, he arrived first; I sent Donna Esmeralda out into the antechamber to tell him that Lucrezia had fallen in the vineyard, and that I would be out with more news as soon as His Holiness appeared. Esmeralda was a skilled dissembler, and played her part admirably; I could just make out her calm, even tone as she spoke to Alfonso. She stepped back inside the chamber with a confident nod; no doubt my brother thought his wife had merely turned her ankle.

But soon Lucrezia's cries grew so loud that Alfonso, out in the antechamber, surely heard them. They must have stricken him to the core, so I extricated myself from Lucrezia in order to explain the situation. Fortunately, the Pope arrived just as I was embracing my brother.

At the sight of our agitated expressions, Alexander reacted with his overly emotional nature; his eyes welled up at once.

'Dear God! It sounds as though she is dying! I could not imagine this was so serious . . . Sancha, what has become of our daughter?'

I pulled away from Alfonso. 'Lucrezia is young and strong; she will no doubt survive this. It seems she was with child, but that child is surely lost now. She was racing her ladies in the vineyard . . . '

'Racing in the vineyard! Who allowed this?' Alexander demanded, with a fury born by grief. 'Did she know she was pregnant?'

'I think she knew. It was a simple accident, Your Holiness. The exercise should not have hurt her. Her slipper was loose, and she tripped over it, and another girl fell on top of her.'

'Who?' Alexander's tone grew vengeful.

Alfonso in the meantime was ignoring his father-in-law's rantings; he listened to the information, then buried his face in his hands and whispered, 'Pregnant . . . ' At the same instant Alexander demanded the name of the culprit, Alfonso lifted his face and asked, 'You are sure Lucrezia will be all right?' He turned his worried gaze towards the moans coming from his wife's bedchamber.

I put a hand on my brother's shoulder. 'It is hard now, but the midwife says she is young, she will survive this, God willing.' To Alexander, I lied. 'I do not even remember which girl fell, Your Holiness. It was an act of God, and not the girl's fault that Lucrezia's slipper was loose.'

The Pope covered his face and moaned with a misery to rival his daughter's. 'Ah, my poor daughter! My poor Lucrezia!'

'Be strong,' I told them both. 'Lucrezia has asked me to stay with her. But I will come and tell you news as soon as I can.'

I left them to comfort each other, and returned to Lucrezia's side.

Lucrezia's suffering continued for two more hours, after which she was delivered of a small, bloody child; I saw the poor, barely-formed creature myself as the midwife caught it on a towel and examined it. It was too soon to tell whether a son or daughter had been lost.

Blessedly, Lucrezia's moans ceased at once, but she wept at the realization that she no longer carried the child. The bleeding that followed was scarce, a good sign, and she finally fell into a sleep that the midwife pronounced healing.

The duty fell to me to inform father and husband of the bad and good news: that Lucrezia had miscarried, that no permanent damage had been done, and she was expected to recover quickly.

I kept my promise to Lucrezia: I went back into her room, where I dozed on a great velvet pillow while she slept through the night. I did not leave until the next morning, until convinced all was well.

Spring 1499–Winter 1499

XXVI

Fortunately, the midwife's prediction was correct: Lucrezia made a full recovery, and in time became annoyed with the over-attentiveness and coddling that her father, Alfonso, and I shamelessly heaped on her. Although there had been some jealousy between Donna Esmeralda and Lucrezia's new head lady-in-waiting, Donna Maria, they now became united in their goal of ensuring that the Duchess of Bisciglie was always warm, pampered, and overfed.

In only a few months' time, our solicitousness was repaid. Lucrezia walked with me out of earshot of our entourages one April evening, after supper, as we strolled from the Vatican back to the palace, and whispered, 'I am pregnant again. But we must tell no one for some time, until I am sure the child is safe.'

'No races,' I hissed back at her, and she had enough of a sense of humour to smile wryly back at me.

'No races,' she agreed.

We smiled and linked arms, warmed by our shared secret. Rome seemed to me a safe haven that night, with the lanterns of boats twinkling below us on the Tiber, and the golden glow emanating from the graceful arched windows of the palace we approached.

. . .

Meanwhile, events in France were not proceeding precisely according to Cesare Borgia's plan. The writ was to be delivered by Cesare, and presented to the King only in exchange for Carlotta of Aragon's hand.

Thus armed, Cesare had left for France. I put the matter out of my mind, confident that Alfonso's and my political status in the House of Borgia was now secure.

Upon Cesare's arrival in France, he was directed by Carlotta and her father, King Federico, to entreat Louis for his permission to wed her; the King, however, while receiving Cesare politely, refused to discuss the subject. In the interim, Louis insisted on having the writ of divorce turned over to him—so fiercely that Cesare began to doubt for his safety. He stalled for as long as he could, but in the end, he yielded to Louis' demand, and turned over the writ.

The instant Louis had what he desired, Cesare lost all advantage, and the French King would hear no more about Carlotta.

In frustration, Cesare turned again to Carlotta's father, Federico of Naples—who, after being evasive for a great deal of time, finally flatly rejected Cesare's offer. Typically outspoken, Uncle Federico commented disgustedly that he would not have his daughter wed to a man with a reputation as an 'adventurer'. In other words, he was saving his daughter for a legitimate suitor, not a pope's bastard who had so lightly freed himself of priestly vows, and certainly not a man with a rumoured penchant for murder.

Cesare's appeals to Louis were ignored. By this time, months had passed. Cesare threatened to return to Italy, and the Pope made noises about finding him an Italian wife—but the Duke of Valencia was not given leave to depart France, or even the King's court.

Instead, he was offered the hand of one French princess, then another; in time, a whole procession of French beauties was offered to him, and he must have finally realized the truth. While he was being treated well, he was the King's prisoner until he relented to Louis's plan: a French wife for Pope Alexander's son.

In late spring Don Garcia, Cesare's personal messenger, arrived in Rome from France. The news was of such import that His Holiness invited Garcia to join us at the family table at supper—although Garcia stood to recite his piece.

Cesare was betrothed, and the King of France had given his approval. The bride was Charlotte d'Albret, the King of Navarre's daughter, and Louis' cousin.

Beside me, Alfonso listened carefully, his expression revealing no sign of his inner distress; on my other flank, Jofre let go a cheer on behalf of his brother. It did not occur to him that his bride and brother-in-law were now in grave political danger.

With Juan dead, Lucrezia was Alexander's favourite child; but a son always takes precedence over a daughter, so the Pope's first loyalty—and his fear—was owed to Cesare. And Cesare had chosen to ally himself with France—out of spite and a desire for revenge on me, and perhaps the entire House of Aragon, after the all-too public sting of Carlotta's refusal.

As for His Holiness, he showed a maudlin pleasure. 'At last, all my children shall be wed,' he sighed, 'and perhaps I shall soon be a grandfather.'

Lucrezia directed at me a complicitous little smile, one I could barely return, for I was heartsick.

After supper, I contrived a moment alone with Alfonso in his chambers, before he went to Lucrezia for the night. Such was my level of unease and suspicion that I demanded Alfonso dismiss all his servants—including the most trusted men who had served him for years in Naples. I insisted we retire into his bedchamber after locking the door to the outer suite, for I worried that someone might press an ear there and listen to any conversation held in the antechamber.

I spoke first, before Alfonso had the opportunity.

'If Cesare goes through with this, a French invasion is inevitable—and we are doomed. You know how easily Lucrezia rid herself of her first husband.' I sat on a tufted ottoman and shivered, drawing my fur wrap tightly about me.

Alfonso stood with his back to me in front of his balcony. He had thrown open the shutters, and took in the warm spring air as he stared out at the night. The darkness framed his golden head and his square, muscular shoulders, clad in the palest green brocade. He appeared strong and resolute, invincible, but as I studied his pose, I read the concern in his posture, saw a tension not there before supper.

Alfonso most deliberately closed the shutters, and turned away from the balcony—movements that revealed a rare anger rising in him. His face showed strain; I knew my comment had provoked him, but I also knew I was not the sole source of his ire.

'That was *not* her doing. She fought the divorce as best she could, and is still deeply shamed by it. Her father coerced her.'

'Nevertheless, she does as she is told.'

His manner turned uncharacteristically cool. 'Do not be so certain. We love each other, Sancha. Lucrezia has been misused by her father for far too many years, and her loyalty to him is strained. But she knows *I* would never hurt her, never betray her.'

'I can only hope you are right. But there are others whose fates I dare not speak of—' I was thinking of Perotto, of Pantsilea . . . and mostly of Juan, whose relation by blood could not save him.

Alfonso flared. 'I will not hear such talk. Lucrezia is my wife. And she is incapable of even the mildest cruelty.'

I turned conciliatory. 'I love Lucrezia as a sister and friend. I am not accusing her of anything. But Cesare . . . ' I lowered my voice at once. 'If he decides to ally the papal army with France . . . '

Alfonso's anger fled, replaced by sombreness. 'I know. We must take great care from now on. There will be spies; we dare not take the chance of speaking freely, even in front of our own servants, and we must watch everything we put into writing.' He paused. 'I will meet privately with the Spanish and Neapolitan ambassadors. There are cardinals with strong ties to Spain and Naples who can be trusted, and have the Pope's ear.' He forced an encouraging smile. 'Do not fret, Sancha. The deed is not yet accomplished; I will do everything in my power to stop this marriage. And I will have Lucrezia speak to her father as well; she has more influence over him than anyone.'

'Lucrezia!' I exclaimed. 'Alfonso, you dare not speak to her about any of this.'

He looked at me, his hurt tempered by indignation. 'I speak to Lucrezia about everything,' he stated simply. 'She is my life, my soul. I could hide nothing from her.'

Despair settled over me like instant nightfall. 'You must understand, little brother. Lucrezia's first loyalty will always be to her family.' And as he opened his mouth to protest, I raised a hand for silence. 'That shows no weakness in her character, but rather a strength. Confess, Alfonso: to whom are you more loyal? The House of Borgia, or the House of Aragon?'

He sighed. 'You have a point, my sister. I will be discreet in what I discuss with my wife. In the meantime, have faith: I will lobby with all my ability against this French marriage.'

I tried to have faith. Alfonso performed as promised, and the representatives of both the Spanish and Neapolitan Kings warned the Pope of dire consequences should Cesare's marriage to Louis' kinswoman be allowed. Alexander seemed to listen.

But one morning in mid-May, as Lucrezia and I sat on our velvet cushions, flanking Alexander's throne as he heard petitioners, the arrival of a visitor was announced. Cesare's messenger, Don Garcia, had just dismounted his horse after a hard four-day ride from Blois in France.

He had news for His Holiness, happy news, the page reported, but he begged Alexander's forbearance: he had scarcely slept and could not stand. He wished to make his report after some hours of rest.

Alexander, in his excitement, would not hear of it. He dismissed the petitioners, summoned Jofre, Alfonso, and the exhausted rider to his throne. The family arrived, followed by Don Garcia—leaning heavily on a servant, for he could not walk unaided.

'Your Holiness, forgive me,' Garcia begged. 'I will tell you this: that your son, Cesare Borgia, the Duke of Valentinois, is now four days' happily wed to Charlotte d'Albret, Princess of Navarre, and the marriage was consummated before King Louis himself.'

I listened woodenly. Alexander clasped his hands, ecstatic. Later, I learned he had helped seal the marriage months before, by granting Charlotte's brother a cardinal's hat—even as he had pretended to listen to the Spanish and Neapolitans.

'So it is done!' He studied the swaying, worn messenger and demanded, 'Someone bring a chair! I give you leave, Don Garcia, to sit in my presence—so long as you give a complete, full account of the wedding. Leave no detail out.'

A chair was brought; reluctantly, Garcia dropped into it, and—prodded by the Pope's questions—droned on for a full seven hours. Food and drink was brought after a few hours for the speaker and his audience. I sat and listened, growing ever more horrified as Alexander grew ever more delighted.

I heard how Cesare and his bride—'quite beautiful, with pale, delicate skin and fair hair,' according to Garcia—exchanged rings in a solemn ceremony. Cesare had, in a manly display, consummated the marriage physically six times in front of King Louis, who applauded and called him 'a better man than me.' So many distinguished guests, including the King and his entourage, attended the reception afterwards that there was no room for them all, and they were forced to hold the celebration outdoors in a meadow.

. . .

The Pope revelled in Cesare's union. Each visitor to the Vatican was regaled with the story of Cesare's wedding, complete with His Holiness bringing out mounds of jewels he intended to send his new daughter-in-law, and holding each gem up to the light for the visitor to admire.

Alfonso and I could only attempt to control the damage. One cardinal whose help Alfonso had solicited, Ascanio Sforza, gently tested the waters in the midst of a conversation with the Pope concerning Church business. He did not believe, Cardinal Sforza told His Holiness, that Louis really intended to invade Naples, since Queen Anne and her people were against it. Besides, the French had already learned their lesson, when King Charles was forced to retreat in humiliation.

The Pope laughed derisively in Sforza's face. King Federico should take care, Alexander remarked, grinning, lest he find himself in the same position as my father had—believing all the while that the French would never come, then fleeing when Charles' army neared Naples' gate.

Upon hearing this, I lost hope—even though Alfonso continued his political lobbying in secret. I took wicked pleasure in one thing: the news that university students in Paris were performing comic parodies of Cesare's wedding; the Roman sense of grandeur was considered vulgar and extreme by French standards. Cesare's silver-shod horses had made him a laughing-stock.

Jofre finally realized that I was no longer in His Holiness' good graces, and decided the best course of action was to prove himself a true Borgia, like his brothers. In the company of Spanish soldiers, he roamed the streets at night, drunk and wielding his sword in a pale imitation of Juan, but Jofre's gentle nature had never equipped him for fighting.

He continued this behaviour even though I pleaded with him to stop. I think my concern made him feel more manly. I cannot blame him: he wished to help me; and perhaps, if he had the standing of his siblings, he might have had his father's ear. But he did not—and there was nothing he could do to sway His Holiness in my favour.

But he could at least begin to act like a Borgia. No doubt this is what he supposed he was doing the night I was awakened by a shout outside my bedchamber.

'Donna Sancha! Donna Sancha!'

I sat up in bed, hand to my pounding heart, wakened after hours of deep slumber by a male voice in my antechamber. Beside me, Donna Esmeralda woke at once; my other ladies stirred with startled cries.

'Who is it?' I demanded, in my most authoritative voice. I struggled from my covers as one of the ladies hurriedly lit a lamp.

'It is Federico, a sergeant in the Spanish Guard, one of your husband's men. Don Jofre is seriously injured. We have taken him up to his bed and called for the doctor; we thought you should be notified.'

'Seriously? How seriously?' I demanded, my tone rising with panic. By this time, I had clasped my velvet wrap about me and run out into the antechamber, where Federico stood holding a lantern. Dressed in civilian clothing, he was perhaps eighteen, dark as a Moor, his hair plastered to his brow with sweat. The lower-half of his tunic hung low, neatly slit by a swiping blade that had failed to penetrate the skin; the gaping hole revealed part of his bare abdomen and the top of his breeches. His black eyes glittered from too much wine.

But his voice and stance were steady; he had been frightened into sobriety. 'He has taken an arrow in the thigh, Madonna.'

Such a wound was easily fatal. Without calling for attendants, I ran barefoot into the corridor. I do not remember crossing the building or ascending the stairs to Jofre's suite; I only remember men bowing, doors opening, until I was at my husband's side.

He lay pale and sweating on the bed, his brown eyes wide with pain. His men had cut away his leggings and breeches, exposing the wound, and the arrow, half-broken, its point firmly lodged in my husband's thigh. The flesh around the arrow was purplish-red and swollen, bleeding copiously, rivulets running down either side of the leg. A sheet had been folded several times and placed beneath the wound; it was soaked through.

Jofre was alert, and I took his hand; his grip was limp but grateful, and he tried to smile up at me, but could produce no more than a sickly grimace. 'My darling,' I said; they seemed the only words I could utter.

'Do not be angry, Sancha,' he whispered. The smell of alcohol emanated from his breath and clothes—I realized that his men had probably poured wine on the wound to cleanse it. Even so, he and his entourage had been quite drunk, a fact that had no doubt facilitated the current crisis.

'Never,' I told him. 'Never.' There was no guile in Jofre. If he had done anything amiss, it was only out of the hope of eventually helping me. 'Who did this to you?'

Jofre was too weak to answer; instead, I heard Federico's voice behind me; the young soldier had kept pace with me and followed me into his master's chamber, but I had been too distraught to notice. 'One of the sheriff's soldiers, Madonna Sancha. We were crossing the bridge by the Castel Sant'Angelo when the sheriff demanded we halt and be inspected. Don Jofre identified himself as the prince of Squillace, but the sheriff chose not to believe him, Madonna, and . . . ' He paused, editing the story for my sake. 'Words were exchanged. Apparently, one of the soldiers felt that the Prince insulted the sheriff, for he fired an arrow, and you can see the result.'

I was aghast. 'Has the sheriff been arrested? And the soldier who fired the arrow?'

'No, Madonna. We were too concerned for the prince's sake. We brought him here immediately.'

'Something must be done. The men responsible must be punished.'

'Yes, Madonna. Unfortunately, we do not have the authority.'

'Who does?'

Federico considered this. 'Most certainly, His Holiness.'

The Pope's doctor appeared, an elderly heavy-set man in dress as fine as any Borgia's, obviously put out at being roused in the hours before dawn. He scowled mightily, his thick black eyebrows rushing together, at the sight of me.

'No women. I must remove the arrow, and will have no fainting here.'

I scowled even more fiercely back at him. I would not be treated in such a dismissive manner—but more importantly, I would not allow myself to be forced from Jofre's side.

'I am no delicate maiden,' I insisted. 'Do your work, and leave me to comfort him.'

This time, Jofre succeeded in producing a pale smile.

I held his hand and wiped the sweat from his clammy brow as the doctor proceeded to examine, to prod, then to cut about the wound. Fortified wine was brought, and I held the silver goblet to Jofre's trembling lips and urged him to drink.

When he had taken an amount sufficient to please the doctor, the worst of the surgery commenced. The doctor gripped the shaft with both his hands and pulled. Jofre gritted his teeth and moaned, but at last was reduced to keening aloud and bearing down like a woman in childbirth.

After several tries, the arrow came free, and Jofre fell back, limp, though still in pain. Much blood came with it—a fact the doctor pronounced good, as it would help to cleanse away the dangerous rust and lessen the chance of infection. The wound was washed once more with fortified wine, then bandaged.

I stayed with Jofre that night, not daring to sleep even when he at last dozed, despite his misery.

Spring–Summer 1499

XXVII

In the morning, I left my slumbering husband, put on proper dress and went to His Holiness' apartments quite early, before he left for the day's official business.

He received me in his office, seated behind a grand, gilded desk. I curtsied, then said urgently, 'Your Holiness. Your son Jofre was wounded last night in an altercation with the sheriff.'

'Wounded?' He rose, instantly concerned. 'Is it grave?'

'It was last night, Holiness. Jofre's thigh was pierced by a rusty arrow; he survived the night through the grace of God. There is no fever yet; the doctor is hopeful he will recover. But his condition is still serious.'

I watched as he relaxed slightly. 'How did this happen?'

'Jofre was with some of his men last night, quite late; they were crossing the bridge at Sant'Angelo when the sheriff stopped them and demanded to know their business.'

'As well he should,' Alexander said. 'I have spoken to Jofre about his late-night escapades. He has been going about with his Spaniards, looking for fights. And it seems he finally managed to find one.'

His tone was dismissive; I stared at him and gasped aloud.

'Your Holiness, the men responsible for wounding Jofre must be brought to justice!'

Alexander sat, clearly no longer concerned by the matter; he beheld me with his great brown eyes—eyes that appeared benevolent on the surface, yet hid such a conniving soul. 'It sounds as though they were doing their duty. I cannot "punish" them, as you ask, for it. Jofre received what he deserved.' He looked down at a paper on his desk, ignoring me.

'He is your *son!*' I exclaimed, no longer trying to hide my anger.

He glanced up at me coldly. 'Of that, you were misinformed, Madonna.'

My temper seized hold of my tongue before my intelligence could. 'You have told the world otherwise,' I countered sharply, 'which makes you both a liar *and* a cuckold.'

He rose again at that—swiftly, with an anger to match mine, but before he could respond, I turned my back on him, deliberately not requesting permission to take my leave, and stormed from the room, slamming the door in my wake.

Afterwards, I became convinced I had greatly worsened Alfonso's and my situation. By afternoon, I had grown so agitated over my misdeed that I went searching for my brother, and was forced to wait several hours until his return from a hunt.

We met in our typical clandestine fashion—in Alfonso's inner sanctum, with the door to the outer chamber locked. As my brother listened, resting in a chair after a hard day of riding—too worn even to remove his cape before sitting—I paced before him and confessed my idiocy and sense of guilt.

He shook his head indulgently and sighed. 'Sancha, you must realize: your displays of temper might greatly annoy Alexander, but in the end, he understands that you were defending your husband. No ill will come of your encounter.' There was no point in trying to convince him otherwise; he was too accustomed to seeing the good in people. No matter how long he remained in Rome, he would never understand the Borgia talent for treachery.

I let go a sigh; but then Alfonso added, 'You have not worsened our situation. Indeed, our situation can scarcely grow any worse.'

And he told me, at last, the fact he had kept hidden from me for some days: that the representatives of the Spanish King, Ferdinand, had grown increasingly outraged by Alexander's actions. In fact, they were setting sail in the morning for Spain, in order to meet with Ferdinand himself. Their departure was intended as a deliberate affront to the Pope, and before they took their leave, they relayed to His Holiness their belief that the papal army had been receiving munitions from France, smuggled in wine barrels.

Alfonso conveyed this with a heaviness that was born of far more than physical exhaustion. With one temple resting on his fist, he said wearily, 'And the Pope has managed to so thoroughly infuriate the Spanish with his constant flattery of King Louis that the ambassadors insulted Alexander outright. In fact, Garcillaso de Vega had the courage to tell His Holiness directly: "I hope you are forced to follow me to Spain—as a fugitive, on a barge, not on a fine ship such as mine.' "

I could not help emitting a gasp of delight at the thought of de Vega putting Alexander in his place; at the same time, I knew such frankness would only draw vengeance. 'What did the Pope say?'

'He sputtered,' Alfonso said. 'He said that Don de Vega dishonoured him, to accuse him of complicity with France. He said that his loyalty to Spain remains unchanged.'

I was silent; I studied my brother carefully. I feared that Lucrezia still influenced him so greatly that he might try to dismiss the Spanish ambassadors' retreat as an overreaction; but he did not. His expression remained grave, troubled.

After a pause, Alfonso spoke again, his tone one of frank defeat. 'I have been talking regularly with Ascanio Sforza,' he said. 'He points out that while Lucrezia may love me, her voice will go unheard in this matter as far as the Pope is concerned. She protested her divorce from Giovanni Sforza vigorously, but in the end, it made no difference.'

I held my tongue, gracious enough not to point out that I had said the same weeks ago and been dismissed. Instead, I said, 'Only one person has Alexander's ear, and that is Cesare. He is the greatest danger we face.'

Alfonso pondered this gravely, then continued. 'Sforza is thinking of leaving Rome. He is unsure how long it will be safe for supporters of the House of Aragon to remain here.'

I froze. I knew that Cesare's political manoeuvring with the French left my brother and me in a grave situation. But the actual physical danger—the fact that the Borgias might try to assassinate Alfonso—had never seemed entirely real until that moment, when I looked at my gentle brother and realized what Cesare had done: the House of Aragon was in dire peril. The French alliance had even given the Pope the audacity to deny Jofre's paternity to my face.

Had Cesare's claim that he wished to marry Carlotta of Aragon merely been a ruse? Had he always intended to wed a bride chosen by King Louis, and to ally himself with my country's worst enemy? If he desired revenge against me, he could do no better than to threaten Alfonso; I cared more for my brother's life than my own.

With the French army at the Pope's disposal, Cesare could take even more than Alfonso from me: he could take Naples.

At once I was transported into the long-ago past. I sat in the strega's dark cave near Monte Vesuvio, saw her handsome features soften behind a veil of black gauze, heard her melodious voice proclaim:

Take care, or your heart will destroy all that you love.

Cesare, I thought, in an instant of wild fear, and instinctively laid a hand upon the stiletto always hidden in my bodice. *Cesare, my heart . . . My black, evil heart. I cannot let you destroy my brother.*

. . .

Jofre made a complete recovery, and gave up his foolish night-time raids. Alfonso and I stayed in Rome even in July, after Ascanio Sforza left for Milan to support his brother, Duke Ludovico Sforza. The French army had already crossed the Alps and were massing for an attack on that northern city.

My concern was for Alfonso alone: he was male, considered capable of political influence. I was only a woman, and therefore seen as an inconvenient spouse, but not a direct threat. We both tried to reassure ourselves that we were safe, especially since Lucrezia was four months pregnant, and Alexander was excitedly awaiting the birth of his first legitimate grandchild—heir to the Houses of Aragon and Borgia.

The Pope constantly repeated the claim that King Louis would never invade Naples; the French King was interested only in the region of Milan, he insisted, and nothing more. Once Louis had Milan firmly in his grasp, he and his army would leave.

We were desperate to believe Alexander's tales.

But Alfonso was able to believe them only so long. He was hiding a secret from me, one I can still not forgive him for, even though I know he kept it only to protect me.

King Louis took control of Milan easily; the citizens, concerned for their necks, poured out into the streets to welcome him. As for Duke Ludovico and his cousin, Cardinal Sforza, they were unable to mass sufficient support to repel an invasion. Realizing this, they fled even before the city opened its gates to the French army.

Riding with the King was Cesare Borgia.

We were only two days into August, and the mornings were still pleasantly cool, when Lucrezia invited me to join her for a luncheon on the loggia of the palazzo. We were indulging in the happy talk of women when one of them is soon to deliver a child, when our conversation was interrupted by the appearance of papal attendants, then His Holiness.

He strode across the loggia with an uncharacteristic speed and intensity, his broad shoulders hunched forward. I was reminded of the Borgias' family crest, for Alexander resembled nothing so much as an angry, charging bull.

He neared; the whiteness of his satin robes accentuated the ruddiness of his round face, the darkness of his narrowed eyes. His gaze pierced like a blade, and it alternated between me and Lucrezia; clearly, we had both done something to foster his fury and contempt.

We rose to our feet, Lucrezia struggling because of the burden she carried; but Alexander signalled at once for us to retake our seats.

'No!' he called. 'Sit—you will need to.' His tone was harsh, his expression thunderous. He arrived at our table and hurled a missive down next to Lucrezia's plate. I sat, wooden, scarcely daring to draw a breath.

Lucrezia paled—perhaps she suspected what I was too startled to intuit—picked up the letter, and began to read. She let go a gasp, then a strange, nervous laugh of disbelief.

'What is it?' I asked, softly lest I further provoke His Holiness' rage.

She gazed up at me, dazed; I thought she might faint. But she composed herself and spoke; I heard the approach of tears in her tone. 'Alfonso. He says he is no longer safe in Rome. He has gone to Naples.'

'And he beseeches you to join him!' Alexander bellowed, sweeping a great hand toward the letter; Lucrezia cringed, as if fearing he might strike her. 'You had best swear, before God, that you knew nothing of this.'

Lucrezia blinking rapidly, whispered, 'I knew nothing. I swear.'

Alexander continued his ranting. 'What kind of traitorous man is this, who accuses his own family—accuses *me*—of disloyalty, then leaves his poor, expectant bride? Even worse, what kind of cur puts his wife in such a position, asking her to desert her own blood, knowing of her familial and political responsibilities?'

I wanted to strike him myself then. I was furious at him for insulting my brother, a man more decent than Alexander could possibly fathom; and I was likewise furious at Alfonso for fleeing Rome without telling me.

At the same time, I understood why he had remained silent; such a secret put my own neck at risk. By leaving me behind, obviously not privy to his plans, Alfonso had ensured that I would be regarded by the Borgias as harmless.

'You will of course not respond,' Alexander ordered his daughter harshly, entirely unmoved by the tears that spilled down her cheeks, onto the parchment that lay next to her half-eaten luncheon. 'Your movements in this house will be watched carefully from this moment forward, for you will be going nowhere without my permission, I assure you!'

He turned on me. 'As for you, Donna Sancha—you can begin packing your trunks this very instant. Clearly, King Federico does not wish to leave behind any of his belongings here, so you will be following your brother to Naples.'

My cheeks flushed hot. I rose, my voice cold but shaking with anger. 'I will do as my husband tells me to do.'

'Your husband'—Alexander loomed threateningly close—'has no say in this household, as you well know. I expect you to vacate the palazzo no later than tomorrow, and take your Aragonese temper and arrogance with you.' He wheeled about and stalked off with the vigour of a much younger man, his pages scrambling to follow.

Lucrezia was left to sit, stunned, staring down at the letter written by the man closest to her, who was by now so far away. I went to her, knelt, and threw my arms around her. I closed my eyes, for I could not bear to look on her face, where one could see her very heart breaking.

'Sancha,' she said, drawing in a breath. 'Why can I not simply have a happy life with my husband? Am I such a wretched, awful woman, such a horrible wife that men should flee me so?'

'No, my darling,' I told her truthfully. 'These are political matters that have everything to do with your father and Cesare, and nothing to do with you. I know how greatly Alfonso loves you. He has told me so many times.'

This only made her more sorrowful. 'Ah, my Sancha, do not tell me you are leaving me, too.'

'Dear Lucrezia,' I murmured into her shoulder. 'Sometimes, we are forced to do what we least desire.'

Jofre argued with his father, but we understood that it would do no good. Unlike Alfonso, I did not entreat my spouse to follow me: I do not believe Jofre felt confident enough to leave behind the only privilege he ever enjoyed—that of being a Borgia, if in name only.

That morning, I commanded all my servants to commence packing.

At nightfall, Jofre came to me in my chamber and sent Esmeralda and the servants away. 'Sancha,' he said, his voice trembling with emotion. 'This is a horrid thing Father has done to you. I can never forgive him. And I will never be happy without you. I have been a pitiful husband; I am not ambitious or handsome, or strong of will, like Cesare—but I love you with all my soul.'

I flushed at the mention of Cesare and wondered whether Jofre had known of our affair. It would have been impossible to have lived in Rome without hearing the rumours, but I had hoped my husband—always wanting to believe the best of people—had ignored them.

'Oh, Jofre,' I replied. 'How is it you have remained such a guileless soul in the midst of such deceit?' I took him in my arms, and that night, he bedded me, for what might well have been the last time.

Jofre left before dawn. By noon of the following day, my servants had stored in trunks all I wanted; most of my finery and elaborate gowns I abandoned.

As I left my chambers en route to the waiting carriage, Lucrezia appeared in the corridor, her eyes red-rimmed.

'Sister!' she called as she approached. She was already slow of step, being four months with child. 'Do not leave without allowing me to bid you goodbye!'

When she neared and threw her arms around me, I whispered, 'You must not do this. The servants will see, and report this to the Pope—he will be angry.'

'Damn Father,' she said vehemently, as we embraced.

'You are brave and kind to come,' I said. 'It breaks my heart to say farewell.'

'Not farewell. Only goodbye,' she countered. 'I swear to you, we shall meet again. Upon my life, I will see you and Alfonso restored to good graces within this family. I will not let either of you go.'

I held her tightly. 'My darling Lucrezia,' I murmured, 'you have my friendship and loyalty for life.'

'And you mine,' she proclaimed solemnly.

We drew apart to study each other, and she gave a forced little laugh. 'Here now. Enough of sadness. We will meet again, and you will be by my side when your brother's first child is born. Think on that happy time to come, and I shall do the same, each time sorrow threatens. Let us promise each other.'

I managed a smile. 'I promise.'

'Good,' she said. 'I will leave you now, with the knowledge that our separation will be a short one.' She turned, with such courage and determination that I straightened my shoulders.

It was the year 1499. It had been rumoured by the common folk and proclaimed passionately from pulpits that God would see fit to end the world in the coming Jubilee Year of 1500. Surely it felt to me, as I prepared to leave the Palazzo Santa Maria under a pall of shame, that my own world was already ending . . . but in truth, the rumours were right. The end of my world was coming, but not until the following year.

Late Summer 1499

XXVIII

As I rode away from Rome, I held my head high. I refused all sense of embarrassment at having been banished so rudely by Alexander from the place I had come to know as home. Any shame belonged not to me or my brother, who were innocent of any wrongdoing, but to Cesare and his inconstant father. Even so, my heart ached at the thought of leaving Lucrezia and Jofre behind; I found no small irony in the fact that I, who had been so unhappy at the thought of coming to Rome, was now so unhappy to leave it for the place I loved best.

On the second day of travel, we caught sight of the coast, and the sea; it was, as always, a tonic for me. By the time I arrived in Naples, my sorrow had eased somewhat, and I was glad to be home; but my joy was dimmed by Alfonso's honest sorrow. I had seen the stricken look on Lucrezia's face the day that her father told her Alfonso had gone. Yet as much as she loved my brother, Alfonso adored her even more—and each day in Naples, I was forced to gaze upon a face more troubled, more heartbroken than Lucrezia's.

They maintained a constant correspondence—read by both His Holiness' and our own King Federico's spies—in which they proclaimed their constant devotion to one another, and in which my brother constantly begged Lucrezia to join him; on that issue, she never replied.

We soon learned that Lucrezia had been 'honoured' by being appointed Governor of Spoleto—a town far north of Rome, and thus much, much farther from Naples. For a woman to be granted a governorship was an unheard-of thing, preposterous; it must have caused a stir within the Pope's consistory of cardinals. Yet, such was Alexander's faith in his daughter's intellect and judgment, and his utter lack of faith in Jofre's, that he never considered granting my husband the governorship. Or perhaps it was due to the fact that the Pope could not bear to overlook one of his own children to grant a boon to a child not truly his.

Yet this 'honour' was no prize at all, but a courteous way for Alexander to keep both his children prisoner, lest they flee to the arms of their departed spouses. Jofre wrote me a stilted letter explaining that he was attended by six pages 'sworn to keep me company and protect me night and day, never to leave my side'. In other words, he could not escape to join me even had he wished. I had no doubt Lucrezia was similarly accompanied.

I was not surprised to hear of Alexander's precautions; Alfonso told me how he had been forced to outride the Pope's police on the morning he had fled Rome. They had pursued him until nightfall, when he managed to make his way to Genazzano, an estate owned by friends of King Federico's; only then did the papal forces give up their pursuit, and, said Alfonso, 'had they captured me, I am not sure I would be alive to speak these words now.'

The revelation terrified me, and I began to feel uneasy at the thought of my brother and Lucrezia reuniting in Rome. I was torn: away from Lucrezia, I began to remember Cesare's deviousness. While she might do her very best to protect her husband, what was to stop Cesare from doing him harm?

And Cesare despised the entire House of Aragon for personal and now political reasons.

. . .

Only two weeks after our arrival in Naples, I enjoyed a morning of riding with my ladies in the countryside. The air was cool and damp from the ocean breeze, but the sun provided a perfect degree of warmth; I could not help thinking of the miserable heat being suffered by those in Rome.

I arrived back at our palazzo to discover Alfonso receiving a distinguished guest: the Spanish Captain Juan de Cervillon, who had been part of Lucrezia and Alfonso's wedding party. While Captain de Cervillon's position required him to live in Rome, his wife and children resided at their family estate in Naples. I presumed he had come south on personal business, and had stopped to visit us as a courtesy.

I encountered him and Alfonso greeting each other at the entry to the Great Hall; I stopped as I passed by, on my way to a change of clothing, and welcomed the captain.

He was in his fourth decade, with dark colouring, a well-groomed, handsome soldier. He cut a dashing figure in his dress uniform, decorated with a number of medals for his heroic service over many years to His Holiness as well as other popes and kings. As I arrived, he bowed low, the sheathed sword at his hip swinging behind him as he did so, and kissed my hand. 'Your Highness. It is always an honour and pleasure to see you again. You are looking well.'

'Naples agrees with me,' I said bluntly. 'It is always good to see you, too, Captain. What happy circumstance has prompted you to come?'

He stood facing away from Alfonso, and so missed my brother's warning glance at him; I was concerned and intrigued. So; I was not supposed to have known about de Cervillon's visit. This realization made me all the more determined to remain and be party to whatever conversation passed between my brother and the captain.

'I am here at the official request of King Federico,' de Cervillon answered honestly. 'His Majesty has been in communication with His Holiness, Pope Alexander, who is eager to negotiate the return of the Duke of Bisciglie to Rome. Of course,' he added, lest I be offended, 'this would include your return as well.'

'I see.' I forced the alarm I felt from my expression. I turned and gestured for my entourage of ladies to leave me and continue on to my chambers, then turned back towards my disapproving brother and Captain de Cervillon. 'Then I should most certainly be included in this conversation. Please, gentlemen.' I gestured at both my brother and the captain to enter the reception area. 'Let me not slow our progress.'

Alfonso shot me a look that was at once angry and indulgent; angry, because I was overstepping my bounds by intruding on what should have been a private conversation between the two men; and indulgent, because he knew that attempting to exclude me from the meeting would be useless. He sighed, called for a servant to bring drink and some food for Captain de Cervillon, then motioned us both into the reception area.

I was worried that the Pope was softening towards Naples—and, odd as it may sound, I did not want him to invite my brother and me back to Rome; as sad as Alfonso was, I knew he was physically safe at home. Alexander's recent change of heart had come in response to an angry letter from King Federico, who had become incensed when he heard of the Sforzas's flight and Louis' conquest of Milan. Our King had sent a message to Alexander: *If you will not defend Naples, I shall find an ally in the Turks.*

This was a startling and grave threat, for the Turks were Rome's most feared enemies. Federico's challenge had the desired effect: Alexander was swift to reassure him that Rome was, and would always remain, Naples' most loyal protector. Alfonso and I sat, as our station in life required, while de Cervillon stood with a soldier's stiff formality to give what turned out to be a report.

'Your Highnesses, King Federico has finally managed to negotiate an agreement with His Holiness which he feels is satisfactory.'

It was clear from Alfonso's expression that he had heard about these negotiations, and had been updated as to their content, but I had not.

'What sort of agreement?' I asked. It was inappropriate for me, a woman, to interject myself into the conversation, but both my brother and de Cervillon were quite used to my personality and thought nothing of it.

'His Holiness personally guarantees the safety of the Duke of Bisciglie—and your safety, too, Your Highness—if he will return to his wife, the Duchess, in Rome.'

'Spare me!' I could not hide my sarcasm. 'We all know that Alexander has invited King Louis to Saint Peter's for Christmas Mass. Are we expected to attend with him?'

'Sancha,' Alfonso countered sharply. 'You know that His Holiness has since changed his attitude after King Federico's response. He has made his apologies and pledged his support for Naples.'

'Still, I must insist on speaking frankly here,' I said. 'Who is the instigator of the negotiations? King Federico, His Holiness . . . or Cesare Borgia?'

De Cervillon regarded me blankly.

'Lucrezia,' Alfonso answered, an undercurrent of indignance in his tone. 'She has been lobbying her father steadily since her arrival at Spoleto; she has also been in touch with King Federico via the Neapolitan ambassador. She has never given up hope.'

'I see.' I lowered my face. I did not wish to seem ungrateful for Lucrezia's help; I longed to see her and Jofre again myself. Yet, for fear of Cesare, I could not believe for an instant that my brother and I could safely return to Rome.

Alfonso was surprisingly mistrustful. 'I will consider the Pope's offer only if he puts quill to parchment.'

De Cervillon reached into his jacket, and produced a scroll sealed with wax. 'Here is the writ, Duke.'

Alfonso broke the seal and unrolled the parchment; a look of surprise dawned over his features as he read to the end of the document. 'This is His Holiness' signature.'

'It is indeed,' de Cervillon verified.

I insisted on studying the writ myself, despite the fact that I knew any promises contained therein were worthless. It guaranteed my safety and Alfonso's, should we choose to rejoin our spouses in Rome. In addition, Alfonso was to be granted 'compensation' for any inconvenience in the form of five thousand gold ducats, and additional lands once belonging to the Church were to be added to his and Lucrezia's estate in Bisciglie.

I, being merely Jofre's wife, was offered nothing.

I handed the document back to Alfonso with a sense of dread. I knew, from the lovesick hope in his eyes, that he had already made up his mind to return. It had only been a matter of time.

My brother rolled the parchment back up. 'I appreciate your bringing this to our attention, Captain. Please thank the King for all his efforts on our behalf; but at this time, I require some time to consider His Holiness' offer.'

'Of course.' De Cervillon snapped his heels together smartly and again bowed. When he rose, he said, 'I wish to convey to both Your Highnesses the depth of loyalty and respect I possess for both of you. Please know that I would gladly surrender my life to protect you. I would not bring you such an offer were I myself not entirely convinced of its genuineness.' There was an integrity, a humble goodness in his eyes and tone, that convinced me that he meant from his heart every word he uttered. He was too kind, I thought, too excellent a human being to have to serve the likes of the Borgias.

'Thank you, Captain,' I replied.

'You are an uncommonly fine man,' Alfonso told him, 'and we have and will always hold you in the highest esteem.' He rose, indicating that the meeting was at an end. 'I will notify King Federico and His Holiness of my decision within a few days' time. And I will remark to them both, Captain, on the excellence of your attitude and your service.'

'Thank you.' De Cervillon bowed again. 'May God be with you.'

'And with you,' we echoed.

. . .

Alfonso could not bear to wait even the few days he had mentioned to de Cervillon. That night, he composed three letters—one to King Federico, one to His Holiness, and one to his wife—saying that he would rejoin Lucrezia as soon as the Pope gave him leave.

I went riding again the following morning—this time alone, intentionally slipping away from Donna Esmeralda and my servants and guards. I had a task to perform, and was in no mood for company.

I rode inland, away from the harbour and the smell of the sea, to where the land was dotted with foliage and orchards. I rode toward Vesuvio, the now-stilled volcano, dark and massive against the blue sky.

Twice, I took wrong turns; the landscape had changed over the years. But instinct eventually guided me back to the ramshackle cottage built into the hillside. There was no donkey braying now, but a silent mule, and even more chickens, wandering freely in and out of the open doorway.

I stood on the threshold and called: 'Strega! Strega!'

There was no answer. I stepped inside, ducking my head at the low ceiling; sun streamed in through the unshuttered windows. I tried to ignore the spider webs in every corner, and the chickens perched atop the crude dining-table; chicken dung covered everything, including the straw mattress in the corner.

'Strega!' I called again, but all was silence; disappointed, I decided that she had probably died years ago.

I turned to leave; but before I did, instinct bade me try one last time. 'Strega, please! A noblewoman has dire need of your services. I will pay handsomely!'

Someone stirred in the inner chamber built into the hillside. I drew my breath and waited until the strega appeared.

She stood in the dark portal leading back to the cavern, still dressed entirely in black and veiled. In the streaming sunshine of the outer room, I could see she had grown gaunt. Her hair had gone silver, and though one eye remained amber, the other was opaque, milky white.

The woman regarded me with her good eye. 'I have no need of your money, Madonna.' She held an oil lamp in her hand; without further comment, she turned and retreated back into the chamber hewn from the cavern. I followed. Once again, we passed a feather bed—still clean and grandly appointed—and a large shrine to the Virgin, the altar covered in thorny roses.

She motioned, and I sat at the table covered in black silk. The strega set the lamp down beside us.

'Madonna Sancha,' she said. 'Long ago, you were told your fate. Has it come to pass?'

'I do not know,' I replied. I was dumbfounded by the fact that she recognized me—but I decided that she had probably never entertained a royal of the realm until the day I came to her. Certainly she would have remembered a visit by a princess as easily as I had remembered her.

'And you have . . . concerns.'

'Yes,' I answered. I was terrified of returning to Rome, terrified of the fate that might await me and my brother there.

'I will not read your palm,' she said. 'I learned all I could from it when I last took your hand.'

Instead, she silently produced her cards and fanned them out face down upon the black silk. She spoke not a word, merely gazed at me with her one good eye from behind her veil of gauze, the other, clouded eye staring at a point far beyond, at the future.

Choose, Sancha. Choose your fate.

The cards had grown even more weathered and dirty. I took in a breath, held it, and tapped the back of the card farthest from me, as if by choosing it, I could somehow distance myself from what was to come.

The strega held my gaze fast and turned the card over without looking at it.

It was a heart, pierced by a single sword.

I cringed at the keenness, the deadly length, of the blade.

She smiled faintly. 'So. You have already fulfilled half your destiny. Only one weapon remains to be wielded now.'

'No,' I whispered, stricken. A vivid memory returned: the sensation of my hand upon the stiletto, as it tore into the throat of Ferrandino's would-be assassin. I recalled the shudder of the handle as the narrow blade bit into bone and gristle, the warmth of the blood that rained down upon my brow and cheeks. If that deed had been the first part of my fate, what second horrific act was required of me?

Kindly, she caught my hands in hers; her grip was strong and warm. 'Do not be afraid,' she said. 'You possess all that you need to accomplish your task. But you are torn. You must seek clarity of mind and heart.'

I pulled away from her. I rose and slapped a gold ducat on the table, which she stared at as though it were some odd curiosity; she made no move to touch it. Meantime, I swept out of the cottage without another word, and rode home at a furious gallop.

I was a fool that day; or perhaps my mind was simply overwhelmed by fear, but I remained outraged by the strega's suggestion that I was anything other than helpless in the hands of the Borgias. I retired to my bed early that night, but I spent hours staring up into the darkness, in the grip of a cold panic that would not ease.

I closed my eyes and saw the image of my own heart, red and beating, skewered now by a single sword. I saw myself stepping forward and hoisting the sword above my head, with a surge of pure hatred: hatred for Cesare Borgia.

'No . . . ' I whispered, too softly for the sleeping Esmeralda and my other ladies to hear. 'I cannot, must not, commit murder, or I will become as Ferrante, as my father . . . I will go mad. There must be another way.'

I had another reason to be reluctant to commit such a crime. What I had not wanted to admit to myself, even then, was that my heart still belonged to Cesare. I abhorred him fiercely . . . yet a part of me still cared for him and could do him no harm. Like my mother, I was cursed: I could not altogether stop loving the cruellest of men.

I lulled myself to sleep by telling myself lies: that Cesare had no cause to hurt me or my brother, that the Pope would abide by his agreement.

Autumn–Winter
1499

XXIX

In mid-September, I returned to Rome, and Alfonso rode on northward to Spoleto, where his now very-pregnant Lucrezia awaited him. They spent a full month there, and I cannot blame them; they had a freedom and safety that they could not enjoy in Rome.

As soon as I had freshened up from my long journey, Jofre arrived, beaming, at my chamber. 'Sancha! Each time I set eyes on you, I realize I have forgotten how beautiful you are!'

I smiled at him, grateful for his warm, loving welcome under such awkward circumstances, and embraced him. 'I have missed you, husband.'

'And I you—terribly. There is so much news to speak of, but we will save it for supper. Come, let me take you to Father and Cesare. I know they will be eager to see you.'

I smiled kindly and did not share with him my doubt.

He led me proudly on his arm, oblivious to the strained political situation my very person represented. As I walked with him from the Palazzo Santa Maria through Saint Peter's Square, I realized I had missed the scope and grandeur of Rome. It was dusk, and the fading sunlight painted the white marble of the papal palace and Saint Peter's a glowing pink; surrounding the great buildings were the glorious gardens, still in bloom. Even the broad curves of the winding Tiber, gleaming quicksilver, held a certain charm.

I clung tightly to Jofre's arm as we entered the papal palace and its profusion of gilt and eye-dazzling paintings. This time, when I entered Pope Alexander's throne room and bent to kiss his satin-slippered foot by way of greeting, I was received with far less enthusiasm than I had been upon my first arrival in Rome. Cesare, standing beside his father dressed in the uniform of the Captain-General, watched the gesture with hawk-like intensity. .

'Welcome, my dear,' Alexander said, with a forced little smile. 'I trust your journey was an uneventful one. Forgive us if we cannot sup with you tonight; Cesare and I have much strategy to discuss. Jofre can share with you all the affairs of the family.'

He dismissed me with a little flick of his fingers. As I turned from him, Cesare stepped forward, took my hands, and planted a formal kiss upon my cheek. As he did so, he breathed into my ear: 'You will learn from him that you made a mistake in rejecting my proposal, Madonna. Time will serve to underscore your foolishness.'

I showed no reaction, only smiled cursorily at him, and he back at me.

At supper, which I took with Jofre in his chambers, my husband was brimming with news, and spoke so excitedly and at such length that he scarcely touched his food.

'Father and Cesare are making plans,' he announced proudly. 'It is all secret, of course. Cesare will lead our army into the Romagna. It is a good move not only for the papacy, but for the House of Borgia . . . ' He leaned forward across the table and whispered conspiratorially, 'The entire Romagna is to be made a duchy for Cesare. Father has issued a bull to those rulers who have failed to tithe regularly—almost all of them. Either they surrender their lands to the Church . . . or face its army.'

I set down my goblet, suddenly unable to eat or drink. Memory transported me back to the moment I lay naked on Cesare's bed and watched him gesture sweepingly at an imaginary map on the ceiling, at the great area that lay northeast of Rome. 'Imola,' I said suddenly. 'Faenza, Forli, Cesena.'

Jofre shot me a curious little glance. 'Yes,' he affirmed. 'And Pesaro—especially since its lord, Giovanna Sforza, made such vile accusations against Lucrezia and Father during the divorce.'

'They will all fall easily to Cesare and his army, no doubt,' I said. My eyes narrowed slyly. 'Especially now that King Louis has supplied him with troops.'

My husband swallowed his wine too suddenly, which provoked a fit of coughing. I watched in silence. I had come to rely on Donna Esmeralda and her network of servant-spies for a great deal of information; from her, I had recently gleaned a most unpleasant truth: Cesare had been planning, ever since his marriage to Charlotte d'Albret, to trade his military services in Milan for French help in achieving his long-dreamed-of conquest of Italy. He had said, on the night he traced the map on the ceiling, that all he needed to fulfil his goal was an army strong enough to defeat France; perhaps he had realized that such an army would never materialize, for he had turned to the enemy itself for help.

'It is merely a trade,' Jofre said at last, wiping his eyes on his sleeve. 'Cesare helped them in Milan; now they are helping him in the Romagna. But they have made it clear they no longer have any designs on Naples. Even if they did, Cesare would never permit it.'

'Of course,' I replied, not even trying to sound as though I believed a single word.

This dampened Jofre's enthusiasm; our supper continued quietly, and we took care to speak of things other than politics.

. . .

By the time Alfonso and Lucrezia made their way back to Rome in mid-October, the bull had been promulgated—and Cesare moved into the Romagna with his army, which now included almost six thousand men given him by King Louis.

All of us in the household—Lucrezia and Alfonso, Jofre and I—were forced to listen every night at the supper table to Cesare's most recent exploits. Unlike his predecessor, Juan, Cesare had a keen mind for strategy and was a brilliant commander, and Alexander was unceasingly vocal in his praise of his eldest son. He could scarcely contain his joy on those days when the news from the front was good, and could not contain his irritability and temper on those days when it was bad.

In the beginning, the word was good. The first ruler to fall was Caterina Sforza, a Frenchwoman, regent of Imola and Forli, and niece of the vanquished Ludovico. The city of Imola surrendered immediately without a struggle, overwhelmed by the size of Cesare's army. Forli, where Caterina ensconced herself in the fortress, held out for three weeks. In the end, Cesare's soldiers stormed over the walls; Caterina's attempt at suicide failed, and she was taken prisoner.

His Holiness left out part of the tale of Caterina's capture, the part that I learned from the lips of Donna Esmeralda.

'She is a brave woman, the Countess of Forli, even though she is of French blood,' Esmeralda proclaimed later that evening, when we two were alone in my bedchamber. 'Braver by far than the bastard who captured her.' Her lips thinned briefly at the thought of Cesare, then she returned to her tale. 'Bravest in all the Romagna. When her husband was murdered by rebels, she led her own soldiers on horseback to the killers, and watched as every member of the group was slain.

'And she is beautiful, with hair of gold and hands they say are soft as ermine. So courageous was she that, when Cesare and the French came, she stood on the city walls of Forli, undaunted by the smoke and the flames, and directed the defence herself. She tried to take her life before she could be captured—but Cesare's men were too fast for her. She demanded to be turned over to King Louis . . . and the French soldiers so admired her, they wanted to set her free. But Don Cesare . . . ' She grimaced with disgust, and stared hard at me. 'Did I not try to warn you, Madonna, that he would bring only evil? He is possessed by the Devil, that man.'

'You did,' I replied softly. 'You were right, Esmeralda. Not a day passes that I do not wish I had heeded your words.'

Mollified, she continued her tale. 'The swine wanted her for himself. She travels with him everywhere, Madonna. During the day, she is held prisoner, then at night, he has her brought to his tent. He treats her like a common whore, coercing her into the most depraved acts, forcing himself upon her whenever it pleases him. And she a woman of noble blood . . . They say that even King Louis is upset, and personally scolded Cesare for such despicable behaviour towards a female captive.'

I turned my face away, trying to hide from Esmeralda my fury and pain. Cesare had proven himself to be as brutal a soul as the brother he had murdered. I closed my eyes and recalled that horrible moment of helpless rage when Juan thrust himself inside me, and wished suddenly to weep for Caterina. Towards Cesare, I felt unspeakable contempt, and anger towards myself, that I should also feel stirrings of jealousy.

'Pesaro is next,' Esmeralda continued. 'And there is no hope for its people, since that coward Giovanni Sforza abandoned them long ago. Cesare will take the city easily.' She shook her head. 'There is nothing to stop him, Donna. He and the French will march through all of Italy, until there is nothing left. I fear for the honour of every woman who lives in the Romagna.'

There was, however, one cause for happiness in our strained household: Lucrezia was due to give birth any moment, and both she and the child—who kicked vigorously in her belly—were robustly healthy. Alfonso and I clung to this solitary source of joy and hope, for a grandchild of both Borgia and Aragonese blood would predispose Alexander more kindly towards Naples.

The time came on the last night of October. I was preparing for bed. My ladies had already removed my gown and headdress, and were brushing out my hair when a call came at the antechamber door. I recognized the voice at once as that of Donna Maria, Lucrezia's head lady-in-waiting.

'Donna Sancha! My mistress's time has come, and she has asked for you!'

Esmeralda at once fetched a tabard for me; I fumbled into it and hurried off with Donna Maria.

In the Duchess of Bisciglie's bedchamber, an empty cradle had already been filled with a cushion, awaiting the arrival of a new young noble.

In one corner of the room, an old, ornately-carved birthing chair which had been used by Rodrigo Borgia's own mother had been brought in. There Lucrezia sat, her cheeks flushed, her brow glistening with sweat. A fire roared in the hearth, but she also wore a heavy robe to ward off the cold; it had been pulled up to the level of her hips, above the opening in the seat of the birthing chair, so that her femaleness was exposed for the midwife's examination. A fur throw rested near her bare legs, so that she could cover herself either for comfort or modesty's sake.

Beside her knelt the same midwife who had attended her a year earlier, during her miscarriage. The old woman was smiling; at the sight, I felt enormous relief.

As for Lucrezia, her eyes held some of the panic and fear experienced by all young mothers in labour; but there was a joy there, too—for this time, she knew, her suffering would bring about a happy ending.

'Sancha!' she gasped. 'Sancha, you are soon to be an aunt!'

'Lucrezia,' I countered gaily, 'you are soon to be a mother!'

'Here!' she called. She let go of her tenacious grip on the arms of the chair and held out her hands to me. Once again, I took them. This time, there was no guilt, no sorrow, only whispers of anticipation, of the wondrous end that was to come.

Her labour lasted well past midnight, into the hours before dawn. The labour pangs were intense, but not brutal; the midwife reported that the babe was well-placed, and that, since Lucrezia had had a successful delivery once before, its entry into this world would be easier.

Before the sun rose on the first day of November, Lucrezia let go a mighty shriek and bore down with all her might—and my brother's only child came forth squalling, caught by the strong, weathered arms of the grinning midwife.

'Lucrezia!' I cried, as she gasped and bore down again, for the afterbirth was coming. 'The child is here! It is *here!*'

Her head lolled back against the chair with exhaustion; she gave a deep sigh, then smiled, while Donna Maria sent for the wet nurse.

And then the midwife, who was already bathing the child, corrected me. '*He* is here,' the older woman announced proudly, as if she were somehow responsible for the fact herself. 'You have a son, Madonna.'

Lucrezia and I looked at each other and laughed aloud with delight.

'Alfonso will be so proud,' I said. In truth, I was as proud and filled with adoration for the child as if it had been my own, perhaps because I had long ago realized that I would never have one.

Once the infant was washed, the midwife swaddled it tightly in a soft woollen blanket. She lifted it, ready to present it to its mother, but I jealously intervened, snatching the child from her and cradling it in my arms.

Its features were still flattened from the trauma of birth, its little eyes squeezed tightly shut; on its scalp was a damp fringe of golden down. It certainly could have resembled no one so early in its life, but I looked down at its curled fists, laughed softly as it opened its tiny mouth in a yawn, and saw nothing but Alfonso. I had already convinced myself that the little heart beating within its chest would be just as kind and good.

A love washed over me, of an intensity I would have thought impossible—for at that instant, I realized I loved that infant more fiercely than my own life, more than even my own dear brother. For its sake, I would gladly have committed any act.

Alfonso, I thought fondly, *little Alfonso*. It was the custom to name sons after their fathers, and I carefully delivered the child into Lucrezia's arms and waited for the pronouncement that would bring me such pride and delight.

Lucrezia gazed down at her new son with beatific love and joy; there was no question that she would be the world's most affectionate mother. With infinite contentment, she looked up at those of us surrounding her expectantly, and stated: 'His name is Rodrigo, for his grandfather.'

And she immediately directed her full attention back to her child.

I was glad she did so, so that she could not see my indignant expression: she might as well have slapped my face. So it was that I learned my darling nephew's own mother considered him more a member of the House of Borgia than of Aragon.

My brother was overjoyed, and took the news of the child's name with a great deal more aplomb than I did. 'Sancha,' he told me privately, 'it is not the case for every child that his grandfather is the Pope.'

The child's birth seemed to restore Alfonso's and my status completely: baby Rodrigo's arrival was celebrated in a manner befitting a prince. Alexander doted on the infant completely, and described him to all visitors with the same enthusiasm and pride he had formerly reserved for Cesare's exploits; he visited the child often, and cuddled him in his arms like an experienced father. There could be no doubt his affection was utterly genuine, and so he, Alfonso and I suddenly enjoyed lengthy conversations about the wonders of little Rodrigo. I began to feel safe in Rome again.

Only ten days after the baby's birth the baptism was held, with great pomp and ceremony: Lucrezia was ensconced in the Palazzo Santa Maria, in a bed with red satin appointments, trimmed in gold, and greeted scores of prominent guests who filed past her bed to give their regards.

Afterwards, little Rodrigo—wrapped in gold brocade trimmed with ermine—was carried in the strong, dedicated arms of Captain Juan de Cervillon into the Sistine Chapel. I realized how deeply my brother had suffered in Naples: no doubt he had feared he would never be able to set his eyes upon his own child.

Now, thanks to de Cervillon, we were both able to witness the baptism, a beautiful and solemn ceremony. Following the captain in the procession were the Governor of Rome, the Imperial Governor, and the ambassadors from Spain and Naples; Alexander could have put on no greater show of support for the House of Aragon.

Baby Rodrigo behaved himself perfectly, remaining somnolent during the entire ceremony. The omens were all good: Alfonso and I were joyful, once again relaxed, and deeply relieved.

Relieved, that is, until the day Cesare Borgia left his army outside Pesaro's walls and chose to return to Rome incognito, with the Borgia men's favourite attendant, Don Morades, as his sole companion.

I did not set eyes on either him or his father for the space of two days after his arrival; they remained ensconced in a private chamber in the Vatican, discussing war strategy and politics. No one was trusted—even servants who had been with the Pope for years were dismissed from the room, lest they overhear a word of the discussion.

Lucrezia said nothing, but I know that Cesare's failure to make so much as a perfunctory visit to her chamber or to acknowledge the birth of her child pained her as much as it relieved her. Despite their cruel misuse of her, she still seemed to love her brother and father, and yearned to please them. I suppose I understood; after all, as much as I had despised my own father, I had always secretly desired his love.

Since little Rodrigo's birth, Alexander had seen the child daily, and invited us to family suppers where the child was the main topic of discussion. Now, we were shunned.

It was not until late on the third day of Cesare's visit that he appeared.

Lucrezia was a doting mother. Rather than consign the child to the nursery in the care of the wet nurse, as most noble mothers did, she insisted on keeping the child's crib in her bedchamber, where the nurse also slept. Perhaps she feared harm might come to the child if it remained out of her sight overlong—but at least part of the reason was pure affection. The child was, for her, like Alfonso: a creature that wanted nothing more than to love her, unlike the other men in her life.

I spent my days—and sometimes my nights—in Lucrezia's chamber, holding little Rodrigo and helping tend to him, even though such was the business of servants.

On the afternoon Cesare appeared, we women were, as happens when infants come, exhausted and resting. Lucrezia sat sleeping in her bed, propped up on pillows; I sat nearby in a cushioned chair, my chin dipped toward my chest, dozing. The wet nurse lay on the floor, snoring, and Rodrigo was silent in his cradle.

A very soft sound, that of cautious footfall, woke me—but even half-asleep, I recognized the owner of the step: Cesare. I did not lift my head or change the rhythm of my breathing, but instead peered through the veil of my eyelashes to study the man.

He still wore black—no longer a priest's frock, but a tailored velvet suit that showed off his muscular form. During his time in battle, he had grown leaner and tanned; his beard was fuller, his black hair longer, falling straight onto his shoulders.

Thinking himself unseen, he stole catlike into the chamber and did not dissemble, but let his expression be frank, natural. I was astonished at its hardness, at the coldness in his eyes.

Stealthily, he moved over to the cradle, where the baby slept. *Now*, I thought, *his face will soften; even a soldier, even a murderer, cannot look on that child and be unmoved.*

He tilted his head to one side and studied the infant.

I had thought, when I first met Lucrezia, that I could never have seen a gaze more filled with jealousy and hatred; I was wrong.

In Cesare's gaze was naught but pure murder. He leaned down, hands resting on his knees, over the little cradle, one lip twisted cruelly.

Fear seized me. I had no doubt that in the next instant, he would strangle the child, or press his hand tightly over its tiny nose and mouth. I bolted upright, hand upon my hidden stiletto, ready to draw it, and cried out:

'Cesare!'

His nerves were so steely, his manner so smooth, that he did not stir, did not flinch; instead, his expression transformed itself instantly into one of affection and kindliness. He smiled down at the infant, as if he had always been doing so, then calmly, slowly turned his head towards me, and straightened.

'Sancha! How good to see you! I was just admiring our new nephew. Amazing, how much he looks like Lucrezia when she was a baby.'

'Cesare?' Lucrezia stirred sleepily. At the sight of her brother, she came alive. 'Cesare!' she called out, with happy excitement. There was no reservation in her tone or expression, no sign of her hurt over Cesare's snub.

Cesare went over to his sister, motioning for her to remain in the bed. 'Rest, rest,' he said. 'You have earned it.' They embraced, both smiling, then Cesare retreated from her a bit and, turned to me to kiss my hand.

The touch of his lips against my skin both thrilled me and made my skin crawl. He was to all appearances the affectionate brother: there was no trace of the monster who had leaned over the baby's crib.

'You have a beautiful son, Lucrezia,' Cesare told her, which made her beam with pride. 'I was just telling Sancha, it is like looking at you when you were a baby, not so many years ago.'

'You were so protective of me, even then,' Lucrezia said happily. 'Tell me, will you be staying with us a while?'

'Sadly, no,' Cesare replied. 'I had only time enough to conduct some vital business with Father. I have to return to the field at once. Pesaro waits.'

She coloured slightly at the mention of her former husband's city, then said, 'Oh, but you must stay! You must spend some time with the baby!'

Cesare sighed, an impressive show of reluctance. 'It breaks my heart,' he said. 'But I have come to say both hello and farewell; I am on my way this instant back to my men. Of course,' he added solicitously, 'I could not leave without seeing you and little Rodrigo.' He gave me a cursory glance and added, as an afterthought, 'And Sancha, too.'

'Very well,' Lucrezia said sadly. 'Then give me a kiss, and the baby one too, before you go.' She paused. 'I will pray for your safety and your success.'

'I am glad for your prayers,' Cesare said. 'I will need them. God be with you, little sister.' He embraced her again, and kissed her solemnly on each cheek; she did the same to him, and so they took their leave.

Cesare turned to me, uncertain; I held back my hand and instead gave him a nod. 'I shall pray, too,' I said, though I did not say precisely what those supplications would contain.

'Thank you,' Cesare said, and then he moved toward the cradle.

I rushed to arrive there first, and held little Rodrigo tightly in my arms as his uncle bent down and gave the infant a kiss.

. . .

In the end, my prayers, and not Lucrezia's, were answered.

Cesare rode northward and returned safely to his camp; but before he could arrive at Pesaro's city gates, his French army was called away by King Louis. Duke Ludovico had rallied enough forces to make a formidable attempt to retake Milan (a fact which no doubt must have given Cesare's beautiful prisoner, Caterina Sforza, good cause for gloating).

Bereft of soldiers, silently cursing the French, Cesare was forced to abandon his efforts to take Pesaro.

At supper, His Holiness flushed red with rage as he recounted the tale, and railed about the fickleness of the French King.

It took all my self control to suppress a satisfied smile at the news.

Late Winter 1499

XXX

Word came from the battlefield that Cesare had reluctantly negotiated a truce with Giovanni Sforza in Pesaro, and was returning home, escorted by the papal army and accompanied by his lovely prisoner, Caterina Sforza, who would be relegated to the strong stone walls of the Castel Sant'Angelo. I dreaded his arrival.

Donna Esmeralda constantly bore fresh, troubling gossip. Around Rome, a new phrase had become the fashion: 'the Borgia terror'. This was used to describe the mental state of those unlucky enough to serve the Borgias and be privy to their secrets, for the price of such was becoming more and more obvious.

It was widely accepted as fact—though scrupulously ignored by the family—that Cesare had murdered his brother Juan out of an overwhelming desire to seize all of Italy for himself. It was fate, not coincidence, that he had been named for the imperial rulers of ancient Rome.

So it surprised no one when the Spanish Constable of the Guards—a man once trusted and honoured by Cesare, but who had lost his master's favour—was found floating in the Tiber. His hands had been tightly bound behind his back, and his body shoved inside a burlap sack.

I never spoke of such things to Lucrezia or Jofre, nor did His Holiness mention them during his audience or at our now occasional suppers, even to denounce the heinous charges against his favourite son. It was as though the incident with the poor constable had never occurred, as though the man had never existed.

There were other deaths Esmeralda spoke of: two occurred under curious circumstances in Cesare's camp.

The first was the mysterious passing of Bishop Ferdinando d'Almaida. D'Almaida, rumoured to be as wicked and ambitious as any Borgia, relentlessly shadowed Cesare from the instant he married Charlotte d'Albert all the way to the battlefield in Romagna. Many suspected him of being a spy for King Louis.

One day, Cesare declared to his men that d'Almaida had suffered a mortal blow 'during the course of battle'—but no one was permitted to view the corpse, and a hasty burial followed. Servants who bathed the body reported that the bishop had never received a single wound; the cause of death, instead, was 'Borgia fever'—a condition caused by a steel-blue powder.

Canterella: a second new term came into fashion, and was whispered throughout Rome.

Sometime after, another victim fell, Cardinal Giovanni Borgia, known as 'the Lesser'. This cardinal was a young cousin of the Borgias, of a different branch of the family from Cardinal Giovanni Borgia of Monreale, 'the Greater', who had presided at my nuptials.

Whatever this unfortunate young Giovanni knew that endangered him, I cannot say. I do know this much: the man was greatly in debt, and close to his more powerful kin. He had set out from Rome to meet with Cesare privately in the Romagna—ostensibly to congratulate him on his recent conquests at Imola and Forli.

But before Giovanni could reach Cesare's camp, he was consumed by a sudden ague—'Borgia fever', no doubt; the symptoms of the canterella were coming to be known as a high fever and a bloody flux. The cardinal died shortly thereafter.

His body was sent back to Rome, where it was swiftly interred at the cathedral at Santa Maria del Popolo. The grave was unmarked.

One night at supper, Jofre remarked that the cardinal's passing had been a shame.

His Holiness slammed his fork down on the table with such force that we all started; I looked up from my meal to see him red-faced, scowling.

'Do not mention that name to me ever again,' Alexander scolded his son, with a ferocity that left us all silent for some time after.

'Did I mention what Baby Rodrigo did today, at luncheon?' Lucrezia asked gaily, breaking the awkward pall.

This soothed His Holiness; he turned towards his daughter and smiled expectantly.

'He is so strong—always kicking his arms and legs—and I know he is far too young, but today, he pulled so hard upon my arm, I thought he would sit up on his own.'

Alexander's mood immediately became indulgent. 'You were a strong baby,' he said, with paternal pride. 'You and Cesare. Both of you sat up and started walking early; why, I had you upon a saddle with me by the time you were barely two years old.'

Lucrezia returned his smile, relieved that Alexander's ill humour had passed.

At supper's end, Lucrezia went over to her father and said softly, 'You must forgive Jofre. I know he did not mean to trouble you with sad thoughts.'

The Pope's expression once again grew forbidding; he narrowed his eyes at her. 'Talk of death over food,' he said shortly, 'is bad for the digestion.'

. . .

Not long after little Rodrigo's baptism, Alfonso and I received a formal request from Captain Juan de Cervillon for an audience. I was more than happy to grant it, for he had been so kind to us, and of such great service.

We received him in Alfonso's antechamber on a bright, sunny winter morning, and I could not help but think of the meeting we had had that past summer, in Naples. I hoped the news he brought was as good, for as long as Alfonso and I had de Cervillon for a friend, I knew he would always work ceaselessly on our behalf to maintain the best possible relations between Naples and the Pope.

He appeared before us, once again dressed smartly, his sabre sheathed at his hip, his dark hair streaked with silver, and bowed to us as we sat before him.

I smiled and proffered my hand for him to kiss. 'Captain, you are cheerful this morning. I hope you bring happy news.'

'Both happy and sad,' he said, but with a gaiety he could not entirely mask, despite his formal military manners.

'Speak, dear friend,' Alfonso said, curious.

'Your Highnesses, I wished to take my formal leave of you before I depart for Naples.'

'Ah!' Alfonso replied. 'Then you are visiting your family for Christmas?'

'It is not a visit,' de Cervillon said. 'His Holiness has given me permanent leave to return to my native city.'

I felt two separate emotions: an honest sorrow to see the good captain go, and a selfish fear. With de Cervillon gone, who would be our champion?

My brother's face showed only sadness over the loss of a friend. 'Dear Captain,' he said. 'I am sad for our sakes, as we will miss you; but I am happy for yours. You have spent too many years away from your wife and children in the service of His Holiness.'

De Cervillon acknowledged this with a nod. 'I have petitioned King Federico, that I might serve him.'

'Then Naples has a lucky king,' I said at last. 'And the Pope has lost one of his finest men.' Despite my best efforts, I could not entirely hide my disappointment. De Cervillon saw it and said:

'Ah, Your Highness, I am so sorry to make you sad.'

'I am both sad and happy, as you said,' I told him, forcing a feeble smile. 'I will miss you, but it is not good for any man to be away from his family. Besides, I am sure we will meet again; you will visit Rome, and I will some day visit Naples.'

'That is true,' de Cervillon acknowledged.

My brother rose; echoing our last meeting in Naples, he said, 'God be with you, Captain.'

'And with you both,' de Cervillon responded. He bowed once again, then left. We stared after him a time in silence.

'We will never see him again,' Alfonso said finally, giving voice to my thoughts.

My brother's words were prophetic, but not in the way I envisioned. Here is the tale as told by Esmeralda:

That very evening, before his scheduled departure the following morning, the captain attended a celebration thrown by his nephew. As he walked home through the streets, warmed by wine and thoughts of home, he was accosted.

If there were witnesses, none ever came forth: his bloodied body, pierced several times through by a blade, was found lying on the street. The attack had happened quickly; I am convinced that whoever attacked de Cervillon was known to him, and in fact considered a friend—for the captain's sabre had never even been withdrawn from its sheath.

Like other Borgia victims, Church officials seized control of the corpse. Once again, the customary viewing of the deceased was not permitted; in fact, de Cervillon was buried within an hour after his discovery.

For a full day, I grieved for him and would not eat or drink. Indeed, I grieved for all of us.

Winter–Early Summer 1500

XXXI

On the eve of the year 1500, a great feast was thrown in the Sala dei Santi, the Hall of the Saints; the family and many powerful cardinals and nobles were invited. A massive table had been brought in to accommodate the guests and a surfeit of delicacies; enough spiced wine was poured to fill the River Tiber. I had become inured to the excessive grandeur of the papal palace, but on this night, it seemed once again impressive, even magical. The mantel and table had been swathed in evergreen garlands, and decorated with orange pomanders, all of which gave off a sweet scent; the walls and lintels bore swags of gold brocade. The great fireplace had been lit, along with more than a hundred candles, filling the place with such a warm glow that our golden goblets, the gilded ceilings, and the polished marble floors danced with light; even Saint Catherine's blond hair sparkled.

His Holiness was in an exceedingly jovial mood, despite his frailty. He had aged noticeably of late: his eyes had yellowed with jaundice, his hair had turned from iron grey to white. The folds of skin beneath his weak chin had grown pendulous, and his cheeks and nose were ruddy with broken veins. Yet he was dressed resplendently in a mantle of gold-and-white brocade studded with diamonds, and a skullcap woven from pure gold thread, created especially for the event.

As he lifted his goblet, his hand shook slightly. 'To the year 1500!' he cried, to the large assembly gathered about him at the table. 'To the year of Jubilee!'

He smiled, the proud patriarch, as we echoed his words back to him. He then sat, and gestured for us all to do the same.

Since this was such a momentous occasion, Alexander felt compelled to deliver a small speech. 'The Christian Jubilee,' he announced, as if we were not already familiar with the term, 'was instituted two hundred years ago by Pope Boniface VIII. It is based on the ancient Israelite custom of observing one sacred year out of every fifty—a time when all sins were forgiven. It is not,' he added, with a waggish air of pedantry, 'from the Latin word *jubilo*, "to shout", as most Latin scholars assume, but rather from the Hebrew, *jobel*, the ram's horn used to mark the beginning of a celebration.' He spread his hands. 'Boniface extended the fifty years to one hundred . . . and here we are, only hours away from an event most never live long enough to experience.'

His tone grew prideful. 'All of the hard work we undertook last year—the widening of the roads, restoring gates and bridges, repairing damages to Peter's basilica—is now worthwhile.' Here, he paused as the cardinals, many of whom had been involved in overseeing the work, applauded. 'Rome is ready, as we all are, for a time of great joy and forgiveness. I have issued a bull proclaiming that those pilgrims who visit Rome and Saint Peter's during this Holy Year shall have all their sins forgiven. We expect more than two hundred thousand souls to make the journey.'

I listened, smiling, as I sat alongside my brother and Lucrezia, for it was difficult not to be swayed by the feeling of excitement and anticipation that filled the crowd; but my joy was tempered by worry, my desire to forgive thwarted by hurt. I knew not what the year might bring, because at that very moment, Cesare Borgia fought alongside the French in Milan. I glanced over at Alfonso beside me, and he took my hand and squeezed it by way of understanding and reassurance.

As for Lucrezia, she did not notice my or Alfonso's concern. She was listening to her father with an expression of rapt enthusiasm; now that she had both her husband and baby, she had immersed herself in happiness. I do not think she permitted herself to consider the possibility that her brother might interfere; she had so long been denied a normal life that I could not blame her for wanting to remain ignorant. Her contentment showed that night in her appearance: I had never seen her look so beautiful as she did during those days with Alfonso.

Fortunately, the Pope's lecture was short, and we soon commenced dining. After we ate and the plates were removed, I did not linger long at the festivities, but stayed only so long as courtesy demanded.

I returned to my bedchamber to find Donna Esmeralda huddled before her shrine to San Gennaro.

'Esmeralda! What has happened?'

She looked up at me, her olive-skinned face, framed by grey hair beneath a black veil, streaked with tears. 'I am begging God not to bring an end to the world.'

I released a long breath and calmed myself, mildly annoyed by her superstitious attitude. Many country priests had seized upon the notion that 1500—a date created by man—was of such importance to God that He had chosen it for the Apocalypse. I had heard other servants whispering to each other fearfully about the possibility. 'Why would God do such a thing?' I demanded. My tone was not sympathetic; I felt I did Esmeralda no kindness by encouraging her unwarranted terror.

'It is a special date. I feel it in my bones, Donna Sancha; God will no longer delay His judgment. Nearly two years ago, the Pope murdered Savonarola . . . and now the time has come for Alexander to be punished and all of Italy will suffer with him.'

'Italy already suffers,' I answered softly—but she suffered at Cesare's hands, not God's.

I let Esmeralda be. I undressed myself and went to bed, where I listened to her anguished prayers long into the night.

I woke on the first day of the new year to find that the world had not been consumed by brimstone, as the priests had predicted. Instead, it was a cool winter's day, and a sullen Donna Esmeralda dressed me in my best finery, as I was required to appear in public. Alfonso, Jofre, His Holiness and I travelled in a carriage at a respectful distance behind Lucrezia across the Sant'Angelo bridge into the city. She rode on horseback to the cathedral of Saint John Lateran, preceded by an entourage of four dozen riders, who cleared the streets for her.

Once on the steps of the cathedral, dazzlingly clad in pearl-studded white satin and a long ermine cape, her golden curls streaming down her back, Lucrezia released flocks of albino doves heavenwards. She was a lovely sight, her arms wide in a gesture of supplication, her face flushed from the cold, tilted up toward the clouded sky.

She prayed briefly, asking God to grant special favour to those pilgrims who made the pilgrimage to Rome.

Within weeks, footsore travellers began to arrive. The bridge of the Castel Sant'Angelo was filled with a solid mass of moving bodies on their way to and from Saint Peter's. Those who could not afford the comforts of an inn—or who could find no room, because of the growing crowds—brought their blankets and slept on the steps of Peter's basilica. Each time we moved through the piazza, or processed to Mass, we encountered them, and soon grew so used to the sight, we no longer noticed them.

This was but one sign of the Pope's care to show his daughter special favour—his method, I believe, of distracting Lucrezia so that she believed all was well with her little family. Alexander granted Lucrezia many new properties, including one estate belonging to the Caetani family of Naples—the same family to which my long-ago love, Onorato, belonged.

If she had any fears on Alfonso's behalf, she distracted herself from them by conducting a platonic, courtly love affair with the poet Bernardo Accolti of Arezzo, who arrogantly referred to himself as *'l'Unico',* the 'unique'.

There was little unique about Accolti's poetry, however. He sent reams of it to Lucrezia, in which he proclaimed his undying passion for her, casting Lucrezia as his Laura and himself as the suffering Petrarch.

Lucrezia showed me the poems herself, rather timidly. When she saw that I could not entirely hide my disdain of them, she laughed at them with me—but I could see she was flattered by them. The event inspired her to set her own hand to writing poetry, which she also shyly handed me.

I told her—and meant it—that she was a far better poet than Accolti. At least, she was far less given to swooning, tears and sighs in verse.

While Lucrezia was busy distracting herself, the second battle for Milan took place. Duke Ludovico launched a battle against the French forces and was captured, doomed to imprisonment for the rest of his life; nor did his brother, Cardinal Ascanio Sforza escape.

With the House of Sforza firmly defeated, the French looked southward to Naples, that glittering ocean gem they had so long coveted.

His Holiness' reassurances were drowned out by the voice of every other Italian, which echoed in my ears constantly, a silent shout: The French were going to take Naples. It was only a matter of time.

I did not doubt that Cesare Borgia would ride with them.

The following month, Cesare returned home, in a grand display viewed by all Rome. In a stroke of brilliance, he decided not to fuel rumours regarding his arrogance and ambition and took care to avoid staging a pompous, victorious entry.

I watched from the loggia of our palazzo as the parade passed through the streets. It began with no fewer than a hundred carriages rolling past, the horses and wagons caparisoned in black. It soon became clear that this was a funereal procession, indicative of mourning within the House of Borgia for its most recently lost member, Cardinal Giovanni the Lesser, who had died so swiftly and mysteriously on his way to 'congratulate' Cesare.

No herald announced the Captain-General's return: the trumpets remained silent. There was no colour, no pageantry; drums did not roll, nor fifes play. The soldiers—hundreds of them, also in black—marched in a stillness broken only by the rumble of wheels and the clatter of hooves.

Next in the procession came Jofre, on horseback, and after him, Alfonso, forced to take part in this solemn parody.

Last to come was Cesare—again, dressed simply but most elegantly in a well-cut suit of black velvet.

A space followed in the procession, then lesser members of the household and the nobility followed.

The parade ended at the fortress of Castel Sant'Angelo, where the prisoner Caterina Sforza was already ensconced. There, the muted tone of the parade was suddenly cast off when rockets were fired into the air from the top of the tower.

The resulting display, mirrored in the nearby River Tiber, was dazzling. The fireworks were so timed that the explosions—if one used one's imagination—formed the head, trunk, and limbs of a man. (Cesare had intended to represent a warrior, Jofre informed me later that evening.)

The fireworks continued for some time, with each fresh launch growing more ambitious than the last, and drawing even greater roars of appreciation from the crowd.

From her chamber in the Castel Sant'Angelo, Caterina must surely have been watching.

Then came the *coup de grace*. Some two dozen rockets were fired all at once. The resulting explosions were so loud, I covered my ears at the discomfort; the open shutters rattled so terribly, I feared they would fall to the ground.

Cesare Borgia was home, and he intended all of Rome to know it.

A party was thrown that night in the Captain-General's honour, in the Hall of the Liberal Arts. Family obligation forced me to attend; fortunately, the number of guests was staggering, and I successfully avoided Cesare for most of the evening. Out of apparent jealousy towards his brother, Jofre succeeded in becoming drunk early, and devoted his attention to one of the women hired to entertain the male revellers. It stung me; I had hoped that over time I would grow used to Jofre's dalliances—but I felt it unbecoming of a royal wife to show jealousy in such matters, and so I carefully avoided the two.

Instead, I paid my respects to His Holiness and most of the cardinals in the consistory, as well as all the nobles. Vannozza Cattanei was also there, to my surprise, for I had never before encountered her at any functions in the papal residence. We greeted each other warmly, as if we were old friends.

When the time was right, I took my leave of Alexander and hurried for the door, grateful that I had managed to make an escape without confronting the guest of honour. I signalled for Donna Esmeralda and my other ladies to attend me, and summon guards to escort us home through the crowded piazza.

But once I stepped out into the corridor, my wrist was grasped, gently but insistently. I glanced up to see Cesare, just as he gestured for Esmeralda and the others to give us a moment alone.

My heartbeat quickened. No longer did I thrill to the touch of his flesh against my own; now I felt only loathing—and concern that my overwhelmed emotions might cause me to lash out harshly, which would further imperil Alfonso and Naples.

Cesare led me further down the corridor, away from the noise and the guests. When he was certain we could not be heard, he said in his customary self-possessed tone, 'Perhaps you realize now the life you have rejected.' He eyed me carefully. 'It is not too late for that to be changed.'

I gasped aloud; the sound ended in a short laugh of disbelief. 'Are you propositioning me?'

Immediately, his voice and expression grew even more guarded. 'And if I am . . . ?'

I pulled my hand free from his grasp; my lips twisted so that I could give no reply. There might have been a time, before he murdered Juan, when I would have been overjoyed to know that he still possessed affection for me. Now I felt only disgust.

He made note of my reaction; when he spoke again, his tone was mocking. 'But of course, you are still loyal to Jofre. I see that, like a good wife, you have ignored the fact that he has already left in the arms of a courtesan.'

I smiled coldly, refusing to respond to his barbs. 'I hear you have come, more and more, to take after your brother Juan. No woman in the Romagna is safe from your unwanted affections—least of all Caterina Sforza.'

He gave a small, cruel grin. 'Are you jealous, Madonna?'

A part of me was, indeed—yet the greater part of me knew only revulsion. I could not hold my tongue. 'Jealous, Captain-General? Of the pox you have tried to hide beneath your beard? Of the souvenir the French whores have bestowed on you? I am sure your new wife will be delighted when she learns you have brought her a gift from your travels.'

For I was close enough to notice the scars and fresh red sores upon his cheeks. We Neapolitans called it 'the French curse'; the French tried, naturally, to blame it on the prostitutes they had encountered in Naples. I took small comfort in knowing the disease would shorten his life; in later years, it might well drive him to madness.

Anger sparked in his eyes; I had managed to land a successful blow. I turned away, satisfied, and headed back towards my ladies.

From behind me came soft, but in no way tender, words: 'I had to try one last time, Madonna. Now I know where I stand; now I know what course to take.'

I did not bother to respond.

Miraculously, we moved safely from spring into summer without incident; King Louis made no move towards Naples, and life within the Borgia household was uneventful.

Using the pressing concerns of the army and political affairs as his excuse, Cesare absented himself from all our suppers with the Pope. I did not speak to him again after that first evening he returned, and scarcely saw him, save in passing; the looks we exchanged were cold. Donna Esmeralda relayed that when he was not with his father or French representatives, hatching plots, Cesare spent his nights with courtesans or the much-abused Caterina Sforza, smuggling her from her cell at the Castel Sant'Angelo to his quarters. Her guards said that she was beautiful, Esmeralda whispered, with hair paler than straw, and skin so milky it glowed at night like opals. She had been plump before her capture, but Cesare's abuse had left her drawn and thin.

I never saw the woman myself, but there were times when I thought I sensed her sorrowful, outraged presence in the same corridors I had once wandered on my way to Cesare's private chambers. I felt some jealousy towards her, true; but my overriding emotion was one of kinship. I knew what it was to be violated, helpless, bitter.

Nor did Cesare make any pretence, in public or private, of showing Alfonso or the baby any regard. Yet for all of Cesare's contempt for the House of Aragon, His Holiness continued to show us great warmth personally, and took care to give Alfonso a prominent place in all ceremonies. I believed that Alexander, in his heart, truly supported Naples and Spain, and detested the French, despite his apparent joy at his eldest son's marriage to Charlotte d'Albret. But I remembered too, how Lucrezia, pregnant with her brother's child, had wept with horror as she confessed how even the Pope feared Cesare. The question was whether His Holiness had the strength of will to continue in his averred role as Naples' champion.

In early summer, Alexander fell victim to a mild attack of apoplexy, which left him weak and abed for several days.

For the first time, I considered the fates of those of us who remained after Rodrigo Borgia perished. All depended on whether Cesare had the chance to establish himself firmly as Italy's secular ruler first. If he did, then Alfonso and I would be banished at the least, murdered at worst; if not, then all depended on who emerged from the consistory of cardinals as the new pope. If he was sympathetic to Naples and Spain—and all indications were that he would be—then Alfonso could retire with Lucrezia to Naples without fear, while Jofre and I could return to the principality of Squillace. This latter scenario seemed far more desirable than our current circumstances.

And Cesare would find himself *persona non grata* in Italy. He would have to rely on King Louis' graciousness in allowing him to return to his long-suffering bride.

I confess, I found myself addressing God for the first time in years during the week of the Pope's illness; my prayers that week were dark and tainted.

Please, if this will save Alfonso and the baby, then take His Holiness now.

Alexander, of course, recovered quite handily.

God had disappointed me once again; but He soon spoke out vehemently, in an unexpected fashion.

On the next-to-last day of June—Saint Peter's day, commemorating the Church's first pope—Alexander invited all of us, including his little namesake Rodrigo, to visit him in his apartments.

It was an unusually warm day, and the sky had filled with fast-sailing black clouds that swiftly blotted out all trace of blue. The wind began to gust. As we—Lucrezia, Alfonso, Jofre and I—walked with our attendants from the palazzo toward the Vatican, a sudden cool rush of air caused the skin on my arms and neck to prick; with it came a loud clap of thunder.

Little Rodrigo—then eight months old, of good size and strength—wailed in terror at the sound, and struggled so vigorously in his nurse's arms that Alfonso took him. We hurried our pace, but did not manage to escape the downpour; a cold, sharp rain, complete with stinging hailstones, began to pelt us as we hastened up the Vatican steps. Alfonso tucked the baby's head beneath his arms and crouched, protecting his son as best he could.

Wet and dishevelled, we passed the guards and made it through the great doors into the shelter of the entrance hall. As Alfonso held his whimpering child, Lucrezia and I both fussed over the baby, using our sleeves and hems of our gowns to dry him.

As we stood near the entrance, a loud *boom* rattled the heavy doors and the very floor beneath our feet; all of us were startled, and the baby shrieked with abandon.

Alfonso and I looked at each other in alarm, remembering the horrors we had witnessed in Naples, and simultaneously whispered: 'Cannon.'

For an instant, I entertained the wild notion that the French were attacking the city; but that was madness. We would have had warning; there would have been reports of their army marching.

Then, from deeper inside the building, we heard the frenzied shouts of men. I could not make out their words, but their hysteria was clear enough.

Lucrezia turned towards the sound; her eyes widened suddenly. 'Father!' she screamed, then picked up her skirts and ran.

I followed, as did Jofre and Alfonso, who first handed his child to the nurse. We ran up the stairs full tilt—the men quickly passing us, as they were unencumbered by long gowns.

On the corridor leading to the Borgia apartments, we were

greeted by a dark haze that stung eyes and lungs; as I followed behind Alfonso and Jofre, I, too, stopped in horrified amazement at the archway that led into the Hall of the Faith, where His Holiness supposedly sat on his throne, expecting us.

The place where the throne had rested was now a great dust-clouded pile of wooden beams, shattered stone, and masonry: the ceiling above had collapsed, bringing down with it the carpeting and furniture housed on the floor above.

The carpeting and furniture I recognized, for I had seen them many a night in Cesare's chamber. I felt a pang of wicked hope: if both Cesare and the Pope were dead, my fears for my family and Naples could be laid to rest with them.

'Holy Father!' 'Your Holiness!' The Pope's two attendants, the chamberlain Gasparre and the Bishop of Cadua, cried out desperately for him as they bent over the rubble and tried to peer beneath it for signs of life. It had been their shouts we had heard—and now Lucrezia and Jofre added their voices as well.

'Father! Father, speak to us! Are you injured?'

No sound came from the daunting heap. Alfonso went in search of help, and soon returned with half-a-dozen workmen bearing shovels. I held Lucrezia as she stared aghast at the pile, certain that her father was dead; I, too, was certain of the same, and struggled between guilt and elation.

It soon became clear that Cesare had not been in his apartment, for there was no sign of him. But no fewer than three floors had collapsed upon the pontiff. The amount of rubble was formidable; we stood for the space of an hour while the men worked vigorously under Alfonso's direction.

At last, Jofre, who had been growing increasingly distraught, could no longer contain himself. 'He is dead!' he cried out. 'There can be no hope! Father is dead!'

The chamberlain, Gasparre, also a man of emotion, took up the phrase as he wrung his hands in despair. 'The Holy Father is dead! The Pope is dead!'

'Quiet!' Alfonso commanded, with a harshness I had never before seen in him. 'Quiet, both of you, or you will plunge all of Rome into chaos!'

Indeed, beneath us we could hear the sound of footfall as the papal guards rushed to surround the entrance to the Vatican; we could also hear the voices of servants and cardinals as they echoed the cry.

'The Pope is dead!' 'His Holiness is dead!'

'Come,' I coaxed Jofre, luring him away from the rubble to my side. 'Jofre, Lucrezia, you must be strong now and not add to each other's anguish.'

'That is true,' Jofre said, with a feeble attempt at courage; he took his sister's hand. 'We must trust in God and the workers now.'

The three of us linked arms and forced ourselves to wait calmly for the outcome, despite the frenzied sounds on the floor beneath us.

From time to time, the men would cease their digging, and call out to the Pope: no response ever came. He had certainly expired, I assured myself. In my own mind, I was already back in Squillace.

After an hour, they managed to work through the masonry deeply enough to discover an edge of Alexander's golden mantle.

'Holy Father! Your Holiness!'

Still no sound.

But God was merely playing a trick on us all. In the end, after they pulled away timbers and gilded tapestries, they discovered Alexander—covered in dust, terrified into muteness, sitting staff-straight upon his throne, his huge hands tightly gripping the carved armrests.

The cuts and bruises were so small, we could not even see them then.

Gasparre led him to his bed while Lucrezia summoned the doctor. Alexander was bled and developed a slight fever; he would see no one save his daughter and Cesare.

An investigation commenced. It was at first speculated that a rebellious noble had launched a cannonball—but in fact, a lightning strike, combined with a fierce gale, brought the roof down. It was mere chance that Cesare had left his chambers only moments before.

This was a divine warning, many whispered, that the Borgias should repent of their sins, lest God bring about their downfall. Savonarola had spoken from beyond the grave.

But for Cesare, it was a warning that he should commence sinning with a vengeance, to secure his place in history while his father still breathed.

Summer 1500

XXXII

Given his strong constitution, Alexander recovered quite swiftly. The thunderbolt from God gave His Holiness a sense of mortality and a renewed appreciation of life; he began to spend less time with Cesare contemplating strategies for conquest and more time in the company of his family—which consisted of the swiftly-growing baby Rodrigo, Lucrezia, Alfonso, Jofre, and me. Once more, we supped nightly at the Pope's table, where he discussed domestic matters instead of politics. A chasm was growing between Cesare and Alexander in terms of loyalty; I only hoped that the Pope was powerful enough to emerge the victor.

My private apocalypse began on the fifteenth day of July, barely two weeks after the ominous collapse of the ceiling upon the papal throne. We dined that night with His Holiness, and Lucrezia and I struck up a comfortable conversation with her father, one that we were reluctant to abandon when Alfonso stood up and announced:

'With your leave, Your Holiness, I am tired this evening and wish to retire early.'

'Of course, of course.' Caught up in the discussion, Alexander dismissed him cursorily but civilly, with a wave of his hand. 'May God grant you a good night's rest.'

'Thank you.' Alfonso bowed, kissed Lucrezia's hand and mine, then was off. I do not remember what we were chatting about, but I remember looking up at him, and being touched by the weariness in his face. Rome and its wicked intrigues had aged him; the sight prompted a distant memory: I was a mischievous eleven-year-old in Ferrante's palace, taunting my little brother about our grandfather's museum of the dead.

How can you stand *it, Alfonso? Don't you want to know if it is true?*

No. Because it might be.

There were many things I wished I had never discovered; many things I wished I had been able to protect my brother from in Rome, allowing him to live in ignorant bliss. But such had been impossible.

I felt an odd desire to leave my conversation with Lucrezia at that moment and see Alfonso home—but to do so would have been rude. In retrospect, I cannot help but wonder how our lives would have changed had I accompanied him. Instead, I smiled up at him as he planted a kiss upon my hand; when he was gone, I dismissed all previous thoughts as useless worry.

An hour or two later, Lucrezia, the Pope and I had moved our talk out into the Hall of the Saints; our voices echoed off the walls of the vast, near-empty chamber. I had grown tired and was thinking of departing when we heard thunderous footfall and the alarmed voices of men headed towards us. Before I had time to realize what was occurring, soldiers had entered the room.

I looked up swiftly.

A uniformed papal guard, accompanied by five from his battalion, walked up to Alexander. He was a youth, no more than eighteen, his expression dazed, his complexion ashen with fright.

Protocol demanded that he bow and ask permission to address His Holiness; the boy opened his mouth, but could not bring himself to speak.

In his arms, limp and pale as death, was my brother. I thought at once of the image of the Virgin, cradling the pierced and perished Christ.

Blood streamed from Alfonso's forehead, painting his golden curls crimson, obscuring half of his face. The mantle he had worn earlier that night was gone—torn away—and his shirt slit in those areas where it was not stuck to his flesh with blood. One leg of his breeches was likewise soaked scarlet.

His eyes were closed; his head lolled back in the soldier's arms. I thought that he was dead. I could not speak, could not breathe; my greatest fear had come true at last. My brother had perished before me; I no longer had reason to live, no longer had reason to abide by the morals of decent men.

At the same time, I saw the depth of my foolishness in a flash: I had always known, deep in my heart, that Cesare would try to kill my brother, had I not? It was the greatest possible revenge he could possibly take on me for rejecting him—greater, certainly, than taking my own life.

Had he not threatened as much at our last private encounter?

Now I know where I stand; now I know what course to take.

Lucrezia bolted to her feet, then fainted without a sound.

I left her on the floor and rushed to my brother. I put an ear to his gaping mouth, and nearly collapsed myself with tormented gratitude to hear the sound of his breath. *God,* I swore silently, *I will do whatever You require of me. I will run from my destiny no more.*

He was alive—alive, but terribly wounded, if not mortally so.

Behind me, Alexander had climbed down from his throne and was reviving his daughter.

I believe that determination and the realization that she was desperately needed returned Lucrezia almost at once to her senses. 'I am well!' she called, angry at herself for a show of weakness at such a time. 'Let me see my husband! Let me go!'

She pulled away from her father's embrace and stood beside me as both of us assessed Alfonso's wounds. I wanted to scream, to faint as Lucrezia had. Most of all, I wanted to strangle His Holiness as he stood there, feigning innocence, for I had no doubt he had full knowledge of the planned attack.

I stared at Alfonso's limp and beautiful form; like his wife, I forced myself into a state of preternatural calmness. In my mind, I heard my grandfather's voice. *We strong must take care of the weak.*

'We cannot move him,' Lucrezia said.

I nodded. 'We need a room here, in these apartments.'

Lucrezia glanced at her father—not with her usual adoration and solicitousness, but with an uncharacteristic strength. In her grey eyes lay a clear threat should her command not be carried out. Alexander buckled at once.

'This way,' he said, and gestured for the soldier carrying Alfonso to follow him.

He led us to the nearby Hall of the Sibyls, where the guard gently laid Alfonso down on a brocade-covered bench. Lucrezia and I followed so closely, we pressed against the soldier on either side.

'I will summon my doctor,' Alexander said, but his words were ignored as Alfonso suddenly coughed.

My brother's eyelids fluttered, then opened. Gazing up at Lucrezia and me, hovering tightly over him, he whispered: 'I saw my attackers. I saw who directed them.'

'Who?' Lucrezia urged. 'I will kill the bastard with my own hands!'

I knew my brother's next word even before he uttered it.

'Cesare,' he said, and fainted again.

I let go a curse.

Lucrezia winced, and clutched her midsection, buckling forward as though she herself felt the bite of a blade; I caught her elbow to steady her, thinking she might fall.

She did not. Instead, she gathered herself, and showing no surprise at this horrifying revelation, addressed her father in an even, businesslike tone, as if he were a servant.

'You may call for your doctor. But in the meantime, I shall send for the King of Naples' own doctor. And the Spanish and Neapolitan ambassadors must be summoned at once.'

'Send for water,' I added, 'and for bandages. We must do what we can before the doctor gets here.' As my brother was still bleeding, I unfastened my sleeves at the shoulders and removed them, then pressed the heavy velvet fabric to the gushing wound on his brow. I called upon my father's coldness, his lack of feeling, and for the first time, was grateful to find it in myself.

Lucrezia followed my example; she, too, removed one of her own sleeves and applied it to the wound on Alfonso's thigh.

'Send for Alfonso's grooms—and my ladies!' I demanded. Suddenly, I wanted nothing more than the comforting presence of Donna Esmeralda, and the company of our most trusted people from Naples.

In our desperation, Lucrezia and I failed to realize that the Pope himself took note of most of our requests, and ran to relay them to servants. One or two of the papal guards attempted to leave to follow our orders, but I looked up at them sharply. 'Stay here! We cannot be without your protection. This man's life is at stake, and he has enemies within his own household.'

Lucrezia did not contradict me. When her breathless father returned, she said, 'I must have a contingent of at least sixteen armed men at the entrance to these chambers at all times.'

'Surely you do not believe—' her father began.

She eyed him coldly, her expression showing she most surely *did* believe. 'I *will* have them!'

'Very well,' Alexander said, in a voice oddly quieted—by guilt, perhaps, at seeing the grief he had allowed Cesare to inflict on Lucrezia. For the first time, the Pope demonstrated publicly the coward that he was: his inconstancy was not so much the result of political scheming as it was the result of being pulled in opposite directions by his advisors and his children.

. . .

We were soon surrounded in our sanctuary by the Neapolitan and Spanish ambassadors, the Pope's doctor and surgeon, Alfonso's servants and mine, as well as a cadre of armed guards. I insisted that mattresses be brought in—I would not leave Alfonso's side for an instant, nor would Lucrezia. I also called for a cook stove for the hearth. Conscious of the canterella, I intended to prepare every meal for my brother with my own hands.

Several hours later, Alfonso came to himself long enough to reveal the names of the men who had accompanied him when the attack occurred: his squire, Miguelito, and a gentleman-in-waiting, Tomaso Albanese.

Lucrezia summoned both men at once.

Albanese was still being tended to by the surgeon and could not be moved, but Miguelito, the squire, came almost immediately.

Alfonso's favourite squire was still a youth, but tall and well-muscled. His shoulder was bandaged, and his right arm rested in a sling. He apologized for not having looked in after his master sooner, but his pallor and weakness made it clear his own wounds were serious. In fact, he was so unsteady on his feet that we insisted he sit, and he leaned back in the chair with a grateful sigh and rested his head against the wall.

Lucrezia had a glass of wine brought for him; he sipped it from time to time as he told the tale she and I insisted on hearing.

'We three—the duke, Don Tomaso and I—were headed from the Vatican towards the Palazzo Santa Maria. This naturally required us to pass by Saint Peter's—where many pilgrims were already sleeping on the steps.

'We thought nothing of them, Madonna; perhaps I should have been more alert for the duke's sake . . . ' Guilt crossed his plain, strong features. 'But we passed by what seemed nothing more than a group of common beggars—six, I believe, all dressed in rags. I thought they had taken vows of poverty.

'As I say, we gave them no notice; the duke and Don Tomaso

were immersed in conversation and, I admit, I was not on my guard.

'Suddenly, the beggars on the nearby steps leapt up—all of them brandishing swords. They had been lying in wait for the duke, for I heard one of them call out to the others just as we passed.

'They surrounded us at once. It was clear they were trained soldiers; fortunately—as you well know, Donna Sancha—we were trained, too, in the Naples style of swordsmanship. Your brother—your husband, Donna Lucrezia—was the most skilled and the bravest of us all. Despite the fact that we were outnumbered, Don Alfonso fought so well that he held off his enemies for some time.

'Don Tomaso, too, fought hard and well, and showed admirable courage in protecting the duke. As for me—I did my best, but it breaks my heart to see the noble duke lying there so pale and still.

'Despite our best efforts to protect him, the duke was wounded. Still he kept fighting, even after he was bleeding terribly from the leg and shoulder. It was not until he received the final blow to his head that he at last fell.

'At that time, his attackers converged on him. Other men—dark-clad, whose faces I did not recognize—had brought horses, and the attackers tried to pull Don Alfonso toward them.

'Don Tomaso and I renewed our efforts, for we realized that if our master was taken from us, it would surely mean his end.

'We began to shout for help, directing our cries first toward the Palazzo Santa Maria, and the guards stationed there. I gathered my master into my arms, and began to carry him in the direction of the palazzo, while Don Tomaso valiantly struck out with his sword against the attackers who remained standing—three by this time.

'It was then that I saw two other men waiting in front of the palazzo, blocking access to the guards at the gate. One was an assassin on foot, his blade drawn and waiting, and the other sat on horseback . . . '

Here, young Miguelito's voice dropped to a whisper, after which he fell silent. At first, I thought exhaustion and loss of blood had prompted a sudden weakness in him, especially after the effort of speech; I urged him to take more wine.

Then I caught the look in his eyes; it was not exhaustion, but fear that held his tongue.

I shot Lucrezia a glance, then turned back to the squire. 'This horse,' I said slowly. 'Was it white, shod with silver?'

He stared up at me, stricken, then looked over at Lucrezia.

'Your master has already named Cesare as his attacker,' she said, with an evenness I admired. 'You are among the friends of Naples here, and I am deeply indebted to you for saving my husband's life. I swear that no harm will come to you for repeating the truth.'

The young squire gave a reluctant nod, then admitted hoarsely, 'Yes. It was Don Cesare, the Duke of Valencia, on horseback. I feared for my master, so I went the opposite direction, back to the Vatican, while Don Tomaso kept the would-be assassins at bay. The two of us shouted until the papal guards opened the gates and admitted us; at that moment, our assailants fled.'

'Thank you,' Lucrezia told him, in a blunt, flat tone I had never heard before—the sound of her true voice, unaffected and unfrightened. 'Thank you, Miguelito, for telling the truth.'

For the next few days, the suite in the Borgia apartments—guarded constantly by soldiers and Alfonso's most trusted men—became a peculiar Hell. We set up screens, dividing the brilliantly frescoed Hall of the Sibyls into an inner and outer chamber, so that we might have more privacy. Furniture was brought in, and with our attendants, including Donna Esmeralda, we set up a primitive camp in our luxurious surroundings, as though we were at war.

Within an hour after being sent for, the Pope's physician arrived. He examined Alfonso, and, to Lucrezia's and my relief, proclaimed that, given my brother's youth and tenacious constitution, he would survive, 'so long as his wounds are tended conscientiously.'

That they would be so tended was without question, for there were no nurses in all the world more conscientious than Lucrezia and myself. We cleaned and dressed the wounds with our own hands; with Esmeralda's guidance, I cooked Alfonso's favourite childhood dishes myself, and Lucrezia held cup and spoon to his lips. In our devotion to him, we were united, so much so that we began to anticipate what the other required without the need for words.

Alfonso began to recover quickly, though his injuries were grave and would have killed a lesser man. He woke by nightfall of that first terrible day, and asked coherently after the health of his squire, Miguelito, and Tomaso Albanese. He sighed thankfully on hearing they had both survived.

'Lucrezia,' he said with sudden urgency (though he was too weak even to sit), 'Sancha—neither of you can stay here with me. It is not safe. I am a doomed man.'

Lucrezia's cheeks coloured brightly; with a vehemence that took us aback, she said, 'I swear before God, you are safe from Cesare here. If I must strangle my brother with my own hands, I will let no harm come to you.' And she struggled, for Alfonso's sake, to suppress an onrush of tears.

I held her; and as I did, swaying and patting her on the back as one would a child, I explained to Alfonso all the precautions his wife had taken: how the Spanish and Neapolitan ambassadors were, at this very instant, in the antechamber, and how the doors were guarded by more than two dozen soldiers.

In response, he took Lucrezia's hand, feeble as he was, and kissed it, then forced a smile. She in turn broke free from my arms and herself smiled wanly. It was painful to see them each trying to be brave for the other's sake.

Both were terrified; both knew that the makeshift bedchamber in the Hall of the Sibyls was the only bright spot in a dark and shadowy Rome, where Cesare Borgia lurked, waiting to strike again.

On the second day, Alfonso was well enough to eat a little; on the third day, he was well enough to sit up and speak at length. On the fourth day, the doctors from Naples arrived: Don Clemente Gactula, the King's physician, and Don Galeano da Anna, the King's surgeon. I greeted both men warmly, for I had known them when I was a girl, and they had tended my grandfather, Ferrante. Lucrezia consulted them on how soon Alfonso could be expected to walk, then be able to sit on a horse, then to ride: she did not say as much, but we all understood. The sooner Alfonso was able to travel and flee Rome for the safety of Naples, the better. And from Lucrezia's attitude toward her brother and father, I had no doubt that this time, she would not let her husband leave her behind.

Alfonso continued to improve, and developed no fever. Either Lucrezia or I remained in the room at all times, and most of the time, both of us were there; we slept on the floor only inches from Alfonso's bed, and the three of us took our meals together.

Every moment, I was wary, waiting for the next attempt on my brother's life.

One afternoon as I was bent over the hearth like a scullery maid, basting a trio of roasting pheasants, I heard the sharp voices of men out in the antechamber.

Lucrezia was seated beside the bed, reading poetry to her husband; we three glanced up at the commotion, just in time to see Cesare Borgia—flanked on either side by one of our trusted guards—enter the bedchamber.

Lucrezia hurled her little leather-bound volume to the floor and leapt up, her face contorted with rage. 'How could you!' she shouted. At first, I thought she addressed her brother, until she continued: 'How could you permit *him*, of all people, in here!'

'He requested it, Madonna,' one of the guards replied meekly. 'We searched him for weapons; he is carrying none.'

'It matters not!' Lucrezia's voice quavered with rage. 'You are never to let him in here again!'

Cesare listened to his sister's ranting with utter equanimity; even the look of hatred on Alfonso's face did not ruffle him. I rose and planted myself between Cesare and my brother.

'Lucrezia,' Cesare said soothingly, 'I understand your anger. Believe me when I say that I share it—and that I was most distraught, Don Alfonso, to hear of the attempt on your life. But I have been maliciously and wrongly accused by your squire—Miguelito Herrera, is that not the boy's name? I assure you, I am entirely innocent of any hand in this. I greatly resent the implication that I would harm a relative. I wish to conduct an investigation so that I can clear my name and regain your trust.'

When Cesare finished his smooth little speech, a pregnant silence ensued.

'You fool,' Alfonso whispered.

I turned. My brother's eyes blazed with hatred.

'You *fool*,' Alfonso repeated, his voice growing louder with each word. 'You thought, because I had fallen, that I did not recognize you there, on your fine white stallion with its fine silver hooves.'

Cesare's expression darkened dangerously.

'I saw you,' Alfonso stated heatedly, 'and so did Don Tomaso as well—and he is in a safe place under heavy guard. So you see, there would be no point in your murdering Miguelito. We all saw you—and everyone here knows.'

'I have tried to make peace,' Cesare said in a low voice, and turned to go. The guards escorted him out as Lucrezia called after him, in a tone filled with venom:

'Yes, go, murderer!'

But Alfonso had not finished addressing his brother-in-law, despite the fact that Cesare was already moving out into the antechamber. 'So now you must kill us!' Alfonso cried after him. 'The ambassadors, the doctors, the servants, the guards—all of us!'

I followed Cesare all the way to the outer doors, my hatred for him drawing me like a magnet.

Just before the guards parted to let him go, I called out his name.

He turned to face me, expectant, uncertain.

For a moment, I thought to seize my stiletto, and kill him on the spot—but I knew I had no chance. I would be stopped by him or one of his guards before I could do him any harm . . . and it could always be claimed that I acted at the behest of my brother. It would do Alfonso and Naples no good to act here, now.

Instead, I spat directly into his face. The spittle caught the edge of his beard and dripped down onto the fine black silk of his well-fitted tunic.

He loomed toward me, so abruptly two of our guards drew their swords. In his dark eyes was pure murder. Had we been alone, he would have struck me dead and taken pleasure in the act.

As it was, he simply leaned forward and, smoothing an errant lock of hair behind my ear, whispered into it:

'What failed at lunch will succeed by supper.'

He drew back and smiled—tenderly, evilly—at the response his words provoked in me.

Then he turned abruptly and left, moving confidently between the parted rows of guards.

XXXIII

After Cesare left, I stood in the antechamber, too stunned and outraged by his deadly promise to move. Although my body remained still, my mind was active as never before. I knew beyond doubt that unless severe measures were taken, Cesare would kill my brother. I could no longer close my eyes to the truth and hope blindly for a happy outcome.

His words had an electrifying effect on my senses as well: I saw my surroundings with exceptional clarity, and for the first time, understood their significance.

This was the Hall of the Sibyls. On the walls before me, rendered in vivid crimsons, lapis lazuli and gold were the Old Testament prophets, most bearded in white, faces lifted towards Heaven, hands gesturing up at the judgment coming to strike men down.

Beneath them were the fierce-eyed sibyls, staring out at the same gathering doom.

I thought of Savonarola railing from his pulpit, calling Pope Alexander the Antichrist. I thought of Donna Esmeralda on her knees before San Gennaro, weeping because this was the year of the Apocalypse.

The face of one particular sibyl—she golden-haired and fair, not dark and veiled—caught my eye. In that instant, every word of the strega's prophecy returned as if she had uttered it afresh, through the sibyl's lips:

For in your heart lies the fates of men and nations. These weapons within you—the good and the evil—must each be wielded wisely, and at the proper time, for they will change the course of events.

And I had cried, *I will never resort to evil!* I had tried to convince myself once that the worst evil I had to face—one I had rejected—was marriage to Cesare Borgia.

The strega had replied calmly, *Then you condemn to death those whom you most love.*

She had shown me my fate again so clearly, the second time I had gone to see her. I had already wielded one weapon, she said; I had only to wield one more. I had always understood the meaning. I had simply not wanted to admit it to myself.

Standing in the Hall of the Sibyls, I realized that I had a choice. I could rely upon diplomacy, upon the Pope's good graces, upon luck, upon the unlikely hope that Cesare's threat had been empty, that he would not strike again.

And Alfonso would die.

Or I could accept the fact that destiny had placed in my veins the cold, calculating blood of my father and old Ferrante. I could accept that I was strong, capable of doing tasks that those with gentler hearts could not.

I made my decision then: for love of my brother, I chose to murder Cesare Borgia.

I moved about the rest of the day in a state of cold detachment, performing my nursing duties, smiling and talking with my brother and Lucrezia while I secretly pondered how best to move against the Captain-General.

Obviously, any attempt that could be traced back to us

Neapolitans was out of the question, as was any that followed too soon on the heels of the attack on Alfonso; the Pope would be swift to blame my brother, and seize upon the excuse to have him executed. If my attempt failed, Cesare himself would do the honours. As much as I yearned to commit the deed with my own stiletto, as much as I yearned for vengeance to come quickly, subtlety was essential. We would have to wait. Best to strike when Alfonso was well enough to flee to safety.

The solution, I decided, was a hired assassin—one contacted through a series of channels, which would make it difficult for anyone to discover the source.

I did not even consider asking Jofre for help. As jealous as he might be of his older brother, he had neither the stomach nor the ability to hold his tongue. Nor did I ask Lucrezia, though she surely knew of such contacts; it was one thing for her to protect her husband, another to ask her to kill her brother. I did not want to test her loyalties too far.

There was one person who knew more people than any of us, who was tied to a network where she could obtain the most intimate knowledge of any event or person—and she was the only one whose integrity I trusted as much as Alfonso's. She, I decided, would be the first link in my chain.

That night as Alfonso and Lucrezia lay sleeping near each other, I rolled gently onto my side and rose, then took a few steps over to the small mattress where a supine Donna Esmeralda slumbered.

I knelt beside her and whispered her name into her ear; her eyes popped open as she gasped and gave a start. I put a hand over her mouth to quiet her.

'We must speak outside,' I said softly, and gestured towards the doors which opened onto the small balcony.

Sleepy and confused, she nonetheless obeyed, and went out onto the balcony, where she waited while I closed the French doors silently behind us.

'What is it, Madonna?' she hissed.

I moved next to her, so close that my mouth grazed her ear as I whispered, my voice so low I scarce could hear my own words. 'You were right that Cesare is evil, and the time has come for him to be stopped. Today, he told me outright that he intends to finish his crime—to kill Alfonso.'

She recoiled and made a soft sound of distress; I pressed a finger to my lips for silence.

'We must be utterly calm about this. I am sure you know of servants who can contact someone . . . a man whose services we can buy.'

Her eyes widened; she crossed herself. 'I cannot be a party to murder. It is a mortal sin.'

'The guilt is mine alone. I am ordering you to do this; God knows you bear no blame.' I paused. 'Don't you see, Esmeralda? At last, we are doing Savonarola's work. We are stopping evil. We are the avenging hand of God against the Borgias.'

She grew very still as she contemplated this.

I gave her a moment, then pressed my case again. 'I vow before God; I entreat Him. This blood is on my head alone, and no one else's. Think of the sins Cesare has committed—how he murdered his own brother, how he has raped Caterina Sforza and countless other women, how he has brutalized Italy and betrayed Naples . . . We are not the criminals here. We are the instruments of justice.'

Again she was silent. At last, her expression hardened; she had made her decision.

'How soon is this to be accomplished, Madonna?'

In the darkness, I smiled. 'When Alfonso is well enough to make an escape. Let us say one month from this very day—no later.' I knew that Cesare was bound by the same restrictions as I; if he attacked my brother again too soon, even if by surreptitious means, everyone would know him to be the guilty party. And Naples and Spain would raise an outcry so great that Alexander would not be able to ignore it.

'One month, then,' she affirmed. 'May God keep us all safe until then.'

Two weeks passed; July gave birth to August. During that time, Donna Esmeralda made the necessary arrangements, though she shared with me no details, for my protection. A trusted maidservant retrieved a jewel from my chambers; this was used to pay our unknown assassin.

Despite the steamy Roman heat, Alfonso developed no infections, no fevers—the result of the fastidious nursing he received from me and Lucrezia. In time, the deep slash in his thigh healed well enough for him to walk very short distances; he spent much of his time walking to and from the balcony, where he stared out at the lush Vatican gardens. Eventually, we pulled cushioned chairs out onto the balcony, with ottomans so that he could prop up his wounded leg; he sat there often and took the sun.

He and I were sitting there one afternoon conversing; Lucrezia had yielded to stress and exhaustion and lay fast asleep on her little mattress back in the bedchamber. The sun was setting, sinking down between columns of clouds that glowed deep coral-red. 'I was a fool ever to return to Rome,' Alfonso admitted bitterly. His natural cheerfulness was a thing of the past; these days, whenever he spoke, there was a hardness in his tone, a note of defeat. 'You were right, Sancha. I should have stayed in Naples and insisted Lucrezia join me there. Now we are all endangered on my account.'

'Not Lucrezia,' I countered wearily, 'or little Rodrigo. The Pope would never allow harm to come to one of his own blood.'

Alfonso regarded me, his eyes filled with a hollow matter-of-factness. 'The Pope no longer controls Cesare. You forget, he could not stop him from killing Juan.'

I fell silent. I had not shared with him the fact that I had set into motion a plot against Cesare's life; he would never have approved. Only Esmeralda and I shared the secret.

One of the guards—quietly, mindful of the fact that Lucrezia was sleeping—stepped out onto the balcony and bowed to us. 'Donna Sancha,' he said. 'Your husband, the Prince of Squillace, has asked permission to visit you. He waits now at the door to the apartment.'

I hesitated, uncertain, and glanced quickly over at Alfonso.

In all this time my husband had not communicated with me. I knew that he had not supported Cesare's action—he doubtless deplored it. But I also knew that he was by nature reluctant to anger his older brother.

'Search him,' Alfonso ordered.

'We have already taken the liberty, Duke,' the soldier offered. 'He carries no weapons. He says he merely wishes to be permitted inside to have a word with his wife.'

I rose, motioning for my brother to remain as he was. 'I will speak to him.'

I left Alfonso and the balcony and passed noiselessly through the bedchamber into the antechamber. The latter was not as full as it had been in the first days after the attempt on Alfonso's life. The Spanish and Neapolitan ambassadors had gone, leaving behind their representatives; but the Neapolitan doctors rested there, always on call.

As I approached the now-open doors, the guards blocking them parted so that I could see Jofre.

'Sancha, please,' he said, his expression forlorn. 'May I see you for just a little while?'

'Shall I come out?' I asked. Alfonso was the target; I was not afraid for myself.

My question made Jofre visibly nervous. 'No,' he said. 'It will be more comfortable for us in there.' He nodded at the antechamber.

I considered this. For the merest instant, I entertained the thought that Cesare had sent his little brother in the role of the world's unlikeliest assassin; then I dismissed it at once. I knew Jofre's heart; it might often grow faint, but it was incapable of malevolence.

'Let him pass,' I told the guards.

Jofre entered and embraced me at once. His grip contained true passion and sorrow as he whispered in my ear, 'Forgive me. Forgive me for not coming sooner. Cesare threatened to kill me if I came, and even Father forbade me to visit. I tried before, without success, but I was determined to see you.'

I drew back from him a bit and studied him. In his voice, his face, his every gesture, was nothing but sincerity, and I believed him.

Believed him, which was not the same as trusting him. He meant well, but was not strong enough to be allowed access to secrets. I resolved to say nothing of our plans to smuggle Alfonso to Naples as soon as possible, or of our secret correspondence with King Federico. Certainly I would never reveal to him my terrible plot against Cesare. But the concern in his eyes made me draw him further into the apartment, away from the eyes and ears of the guards and the ambassadors, past the sleeping Lucrezia, out onto the balcony where Alfonso sat.

'Don Alfonso,' Jofre said at the sight of him. 'Dear brother, forgive me for the sins of my kinsman. It has been whispered often enough that I am not a true Borgia—no, do not protest, Sancha, I have heard all the rumours. Neither of my brothers was ever known for their kindness; they have insulted me mercilessly on that account. Perhaps it is just as well, for I want no blood in my veins capable of such a foul crime.'

Alfonso had stared at him with mistrust before he began his speech; but once my brother heard Jofre's words, his expression softened, and he extended his hand. Jofre caught it and squeezed it firmly, then turned back to me.

'Sancha, I have missed you so. I do not like being apart from you. I cannot stand to see you or your brother prisoners within your own home.'

I shook my head sadly. 'What can we do?'

'Cesare listens to no one's counsel, of course. He continues to have nothing but contempt for me. I have tried speaking to Father, but it is of no use. In fact . . . ' He lowered his voice. 'I have come to warn you.'

Alfonso snickered sarcastically. 'We are quite aware of the danger that faces us.'

'Hold your laughter,' I said. 'Let us hear what my husband has come to say.'

'I wish to know nothing of your plans, to hear nothing of them,' Jofre told us. 'I have come only to tell my Sancha that I love her and will do anything for her; and I have come to tell you, Alfonso, what I heard my father say to the Venetian ambassador.'

Alfonso became immediately sombre. 'What did you hear?'

Venice was a friend of Naples and enemy of France. 'During an audience with His Holiness, the ambassador mentioned that he had heard rumours that Cesare was responsible for the attack on you,' Jofre answered. ' "Indeed," Father said. "Well, we are Borgias. People are always creating idle gossip about us."

'To which the Venetian ambassador replied, "That is true, Holiness. But I am curious to know whether *you* believe it is merely a rumour . . . or a fact."

'My father's face turned quite red at that point, and he demanded, "Are you accusing my son of attacking Alfonso?"

' "No," said the Venetian. "I am asking you whether the Captain-General *did* attack him or not."

'Finally,' Jofre reported, 'my father cried out in exasperation: "If Cesare attacked Alfonso, then certainly Alfonso deserved it!" '

We considered this for a long moment.

At last, my brother said softly, 'So. Now we know where His Holiness stands.'

I felt a thrill of fear. If the Pope secretly supported Cesare and was merely pretending to assist Lucrezia out of a desire to manipulate her, then perhaps we could not afford to wait to assassinate Cesare. Yet if he were killed now, the Pope might well retaliate against my brother . . . It seemed an impossible situation.

'I wanted you to know,' Jofre said.

Despite my fright, I was impressed by Jofre's loyalty. 'What you have done took a great deal of courage,' I told him. There, on the balcony, I kissed him out of gratitude.

He could not stay; I realized that his life might be at risk. I held his hand and escorted him back to the door, where we whispered our goodbyes.

'I want only to be with you again,' Jofre said. I did not hurt him by telling him the truth: that I yearned, not for him, but for Naples, and would never breathe easy again until Cesare was dead and Alfonso and I were home, truly home, by the sea.

Alfonso reluctantly told his wife what Jofre had relayed to us concerning her father. The news disturbed her greatly at first; but then, she admitted that she was not surprised by Alexander's inconstancy.

Soon our secret arrangements with King Federico of Naples were confirmed: in the hours before dawn, Alfonso and Lucrezia would both be led by a contingent of our soldiers down to a rarely-used side entrance which opened onto an alleyway. The papal guards at that entry—men in the employ of the Pope, who might sound an alarm—had already been smuggled into our apartments by Lucrezia, who had shown them the incredible jewels from her collection, jewels which would be theirs so long as they held their tongues and cooperated. The nurse who cared for little Rodrigo—who spent his nights in the nursery, away from his parents—was allowed to have her choice of Lucrezia's gems, and chose the most precious ruby. In return, she would bring the child to his parents on the appointed night.

Once Alfonso, Lucrezia and child were outside the Vatican, a group of two dozen armed Neapolitan men would be waiting with horses and a carriage, and escort them out of Rome before Cesare or the Pope discovered their disappearance.

I had already resolved to go with them and to take Donna Esmeralda with me, though I said nothing of this to Jofre.

The escape was planned to take place in a week—assuming Alfonso continued to improve.

As hopeless as I had felt, being confined to a single suite in the Vatican, surrounded by guards and constantly fearing for my brother's life, the realization that our imprisonment would soon end buoyed my spirits. Lucrezia's mood, too, began to lighten as the time approached, especially as it became clear that Alfonso would be well enough to travel.

I stared often at the portraits of the sibyls, especially the one with the hair of gleaming gilt. She scowled fiercely, her forbidding gaze focused on a distant, terrifying future.

In the interim, we were visited by the Venetian ambassador himself, who confirmed the story Jofre had told us. He kindly offered his assistance; we thanked him, and said we would call upon him when the need arose.

No doubt his presence in our chambers prompted concern in His Holiness, for Lucrezia was soon summoned to an audience with her father.

She returned from it shaken but resolute. Alfonso asked the question with a mere glance.

'My father told me himself of his conversation with the ambassador,' Lucrezia said. 'He claimed that he lost his temper because of the aggressive, heated tone of the man's questions, and misspoke himself.' This surprised me not at all, for the Pope was aware of the Venetian's visit. 'He regretted his statement that Alfonso deserved whatever blow Cesare dealt him. In fact, he asked me to relay his personal apology to you.'

'If His Holiness wishes to apologize to me,' Alfonso countered coldly, 'why does he not do so himself?'

Lucrezia looked to her husband, and I caught the flicker of anguish in her eyes. Despite her outrage at the murder attempt on her husband, a part of her—that part that craved normal paternal affection—wanted badly to believe her father. I felt a pang of despair. 'Perhaps he is ashamed of Cesare,' she offered. 'Perhaps he has not come because he is embarrassed.'

'Lucrezia . . . ' Alfonso began, but she interrupted him hurriedly.

'He pointed out as well that we are guarded by *his* soldiers, and no harm has come to us in all this time. He is hurt to think that we believe he supported any attack on you. He has offered us any assistance we desire.'

'You cannot trust him, Lucrezia,' Alfonso said tenderly.

She nodded, but her expression revealed inner torment.

The following day—as if he had heard Alfonso's words—the Pope appeared. The soldiers parted without questioning our visitor, or announcing him; they did, after all, serve him.

Surprisingly, Alexander arrived without a single attendant—and when Alfonso, Lucrezia and I looked up at him from our seats in the antechamber, in the company of the Neapolitan doctors Galeano and Clemente—he held up a large, gnarled hand and gestured for us all to remain seated. Out of respect, the doctors rose, bowed, and took their leave.

'I have not come as a pope,' Alexander said, once they had gone, 'but as a father.' And with a slight groan and a great sigh—for age was continuing to take its toll upon him—he sat across from us three and leaned forward, his palms resting upon white satin-covered knees.

'Alfonso, my son,' he said. 'I asked Lucrezia to offer my apologies, and to explain my hasty words to the Venetian ambassador. I realize in retrospect how they might be misconstrued. I wish to make it clear that, while Cesare is my son, and also the Captain-General of my army, we are often at odds with each other. I have reproached him severely for his involvement in the attack upon you—though he continues to deny any part in it. Cesare is a soldier, and cold-hearted, nothing like me.' He focused his yellowed eyes intently upon my brother and said, 'You must understand, *I* could never raise a hand against my own blood. It is not in me; nor would I ever support it. My heart was broken—once again—to hear what Cesare had wrought against you.'

With that last phrase, he was indirectly admitting to Cesare's guilt in Juan's death. I knew the old man had been truly grief-stricken by Juan's murder—and for the first time, it occurred to me that Alexander might be telling the truth. Perhaps he had no foreknowledge of the assassination attempt on my brother. He had, after all, done everything Lucrezia and I had requested. If he truly supported Cesare, all he needed do was refuse to call for his doctor, and refuse to grant Lucrezia soldiers to guard the doors to the apartment. He could have forced us all to watch Alfonso bleed to death.

No, I told myself, horrified that I was beginning to actually be swayed by Alexander's argument. *No, he is doing this because he realizes he is losing his daughter, and he will say anything to try to keep her in Rome.*

He paused; none of us spoke, for we were all startled into silence by his frank speech.

'I pray every night that God might pardon my son for his actions,' Alexander continued sadly. 'And I pray God might take pity on me for being such a foolish old man that I did not find a way to stop terrible things from happening. I hope, Alfonso, that someday you will be able to forgive me for my negligence. In the meantime, know that whatever protection, whatever assistance you require while under my roof, I will gladly grant.' He rose, again releasing a little groan. Alfonso stood as well—prompting His Holiness to gesture for him to retake his seat. 'No,' Alexander insisted. 'Sit. Rest.'

But Alfonso remained stalwartly on his feet. 'Thank you, Your Holiness, for your visit and your words. God be with you.' His tone was undeniably courteous, but I knew my brother. He had not believed a word of the Pope's speech.

'And with you.' Alexander blessed us all with the sign of the cross, then left.

After her father's visit, Lucrezia grew and remained visibly saddened. Perhaps she had finally realized that she would be breaking with her family forever by leaving for Naples, and would certainly never see her father alive again. I was sorry for her, but at the same time, I could not repress my growing joy at the thought of soon being free from the treachery of the Borgias; indeed, I looked forward to the moment I heard news of Cesare's death.

We were to leave in the pre-dawn hours of the twentieth of August.

Two days before, the eighteenth of August, began as a quiet morning—a content one for me. In my own mind, I had already left behind the possessions I had acquired in Rome. I dared not risk asking Jofre to bring me anything to take to Naples. He would be hurt by my abandonment—but if he truly loved me and wanted to follow, he could find a way.

In the meantime, I was content to travel to Naples with nothing more than the two gowns I had with me. I cared not if I ever saw my jewels again.

And so that morning I was cheerful, Alfonso restless, and Lucrezia sombre, for I think she had already begun to miss her family and Rome. We behaved as naturally as we could so that no visitor would guess our time in the Hall of the Sibyls was coming to an end. Lucrezia asked to have little Rodrigo brought to our apartment, and we played with him all morning: he proved a fine distraction for us, for he was crawling now, and we had to chase him all over the apartment to keep him out of mischief. At last, the little boy fell asleep in his father's arms, and Lucrezia stared for an hour at the two with a love so profound I was moved.

By lunchtime, however, she sent little Rodrigo back to the nursery to be fed, and we were left with nothing but our own thoughts to entertain us.

In the afternoon, drowsy after a sleepless night filled with thoughts of Naples, I went with Lucrezia to the bedchamber, where we both collapsed upon our mattresses. I fell asleep almost at once, though I doubt Lucrezia did; I remember, just before drifting towards slumber, hearing her toss restlessly.

I was wakened by the sound of footsteps, marching, and a man's voice, calling a command—then the sound of more footfall, of soldiers leaving. The sound provoked such anxiety in me, even before I was fully conscious, that my heart pounded fiercely. I scrambled from my bed and rushed into the antechamber.

The papal guards who had protected us were gone; in their place was a squad of unfamiliar soldiers, and a dark-haired, red-caped commander with a dignified military bearing that reminded me of the deceased Juan de Cervillon.

Most of the soldiers had drawn their blades. As I watched, a pair of them went over to Don Clemente and Don Galeano, and secured the doctors' hands behind their backs with chains.

'Madonna Sancha,' the commander said politely, and bowed low. 'May I inquire as to the location of your brother, the duke?'

'I am here,' Alfonso said.

I turned. My brother stood in the doorway, one hand upon the wall. In the other hand he held his dagger, and in his eyes was the look of a man ready to fight to the death.

Lucrezia rushed from the antechamber to stand in front of her husband. 'Don Micheletto,' she said, with unmasked contempt. 'You had no right to dismiss our guards—they were there on His Holiness' orders. Call them back at once, and take your men with you.'

I recognized the name, though not the face—Micheletto Corella was Cesare's second-in-command.

'Donna Lucrezia,' he said, again with the same mild courtesy, as though his men bore gifts of fruits and flowers rather than swords, 'I am afraid I cannot obey. I have orders from my master, the Captain-General, and I am bound to follow them. I am to arrest all the men here, including the duke, on charges of conspiracy against the House of Borgia.'

A sickening sensation, cold and burning, consumed my entire being. The plot against Cesare had apparently been discovered—and attributed to my brother.

'This is a lie,' Alfonso said, 'a fact of which you are well aware, Don Micheletto.'

Micheletto failed to react with defensiveness. 'I am merely doing my duty, Don Alfonso. I have been told that you, along with other conspirators, are planning to assassinate both Don Cesare and the Holy Father. I am to escort you to the prison at the Castel Sant'Angelo.'

'My father will never support this!' Lucrezia countered. 'He has guaranteed Don Alfonso his protection. Moreover, he has already stated his opposition to Cesare on this matter, and would be furious to know that you are here, attempting to arrest my husband. If you lay a hand on him, it will cost you your life! I will see to it myself!'

Micheletto considered this quite seriously; uncertainty crept into his expression. 'I have no desire to disobey His Holiness, for he is my ultimate commander. I would be happy to wait should you wish to consult him.' This was not unreasonable, as Alexander was at the moment only two doors away. 'If His Holiness dismisses us, I am willing to go without my prisoners.'

Lucrezia headed for the now-unguarded, flung-open doors. As she passed me, she caught the crook of my arm. 'Come,' she commanded. 'Between the two of us, we will convince my father. I am sure he will come and speak to Don Micheletto directly.'

I pulled free of her grasp, shocked by her naiveté: Did she, clever Lucrezia, really believe it safe to leave Alfonso unattended, with only a dagger and some unarmed servants to defend himself against a squad of Cesare's men?

'I will stay,' I insisted.

'No, *come*,' she said. 'The two of us together can persuade him.'

She tried again to catch my arm.

She is mad, I thought. *Mad, or more foolish than I ever knew.* I backed away from her and said, 'Lucrezia, if one of us does not remain with my brother, he is lost.'

'Come,' she repeated, and this time, her tone rang hollow. She reached for me again, and this time, understanding the game with a sense of unspeakable betrayal and fury, I felt for my stiletto.

Panic seized me then: The protection Alfonso had bestowed on me so long ago was missing. Someone—when I was asleep, or otherwise diverted—had stolen it from me, someone who knew that Corella was coming, and that this very scenario would unfold.

But only three people knew of the stiletto's existence: Alfonso, who had given it to me, Esmeralda, who dressed me . . . and Cesare, who had rescued me the night I used it against his drunken father.

I gazed upon Lucrezia with unspeakable fury at her betrayal; she looked away.

I lunged between Micheletto and my brother. I could do no more than try to shield Alfonso with my own body.

At once, a pair of soldiers was upon me. Together, they pushed me forward, past Don Micheletto and his men, out into the corridor. I went reeling and fell hard against cold marble.

Tangled in my skirts, I struggled to rise; I succeeded only after Lucrezia had stepped outside the apartment.

The doors closed behind her with a slam that echoed down the long Vatican corridor.

As they did, she sank slowly to her knees, to the sound of the bolt sliding into place on the other side of the thick wood.

I glared at her, unable to comprehend the monstrousness of her actions, but she would not meet my gaze. Her eyes, focused on some far-distant spot, were dead—devoid of any light or hope.

I screamed at her, with such volume, such force and fury that my lungs were left burning, my throat ragged, raw.

'*Why?*'

'*WHY?*'

I lurched forward and sank to her level; if I had still possessed my stiletto, I would have killed her. Instead, I pummelled her with my fists—feebly, for grief had devoured my strength, leaving my limbs heavy, numb.

She reacted limply, like a corpse, making no move to defend herself.

'Why?' I screamed again.

She returned to herself as though from a great distance, and whispered, 'Rodrigo.'

With the release of that single word, she began to weep—silently, without expression, like ice melting.

At first, I thought she meant the Pope, and recoiled in disgust: was this some conspiracy she and her lover-father had planned?

And then, seeing the purity of her grief, I understood with sudden horror that she meant her child.

The baby. Cesare must have threatened her with the only thing that could possibly make her betray her husband, for there was only one in all the world Lucrezia loved more than Alfonso.

At the moment that I hated her most, I understood her best.

Shrieking my brother's name, I raised my arms and beat vainly against the heavy doors until my hands were bruised and aching, while Lucrezia softly wept.

XXXIV

A long, dreadful silence ensued from within the closed apartment, broken only by my cries for Alfonso, and Lucrezia's gentle sobs.

At last, the doors opened, and Don Micheletto emerged.

I rose and tried to move past him, to see for my own eyes the inevitable result of my brother's return to Rome—but soldiers barred my entry and my view.

'Donna Lucrezia,' Micheletto said, his tone smooth and dolorous, 'an unfortunate accident has occurred. Your husband fell and reopened one of his wounds. I regret to be the bearer of such sad news, but the Duke of Bisciglie has died of a sudden haemorrhage.'

Behind him, from Pinturicchio's frescoes, the sibyls glared mutely down at the ghastliest of crimes.

'Liar!' I shrieked, beyond all self-control. 'Murderer! You are as evil as your master!'

Micheletto was also as self-possessed as Cesare; he ignored my words as if I had never said them, and instead directed his attention to Lucrezia.

She did not respond, did not stir at the commotion surrounding her. She remained dazed, seated on the floor with her back to Micheletto, silent tears still streaming down her face.

'How terrible!' the commander murmured. 'She is in shock.' He reached for her arm, to assist her to her feet; I leaned forward and slapped him on the cheek.

He drew back, startled, but was too cold-blooded to redden; he composed himself at once.

'Do not touch her!' I cried. 'You have no right—you filth, with your hands tainted by her husband's blood.'

He merely shrugged, and watched calmly as I helped Lucrezia rise. She did so like a puppet, with no will of her own; hers, after all, had been stripped away by her brother and father.

Meanwhile, soldiers led away the arrested doctors, Clemente and Galeano, as well as Alfonso's male attendants. The ambassadors' representatives were firmly dismissed, and when the Neapolitan at first refused to leave, a blade was held against his throat until he yielded.

A large group of papal guards then emerged, those on the outside trying to shield from view the burden their comrades in the centre bore: my brother's body.

Lucrezia turned away, but I pressed forward, trying to see Alfonso for the last time; I caught only a glimpse of golden curls, speckled with blood, of an arm swinging limply down. As the men passed, I tried to follow, but a pair of soldiers stepped forward, barring my way. They forced me back, and moved into position, flanking me and Lucrezia; they had clearly been assigned to guard us.

'The King of Naples shall hear of this,' I raged. 'There will be recompense.' I scarcely knew what I said; I only knew that no words would ever be strong enough to avenge the crime committed here. Don Micheletto did not even try to feign concern; one of the soldiers laughed aloud.

Donna Esmeralda and Donna Maria joined us; the guards waited until Alfonso's body had been far removed from our sight, then prodded us to move.

In those early moments, my mind refused to accept what had just happened. Numbed, I shed not a single tear as we were led away. Once we had left the Borgia apartments, and were in a corridor leading out of the Vatican, I spied on the floor a heart-wrenching sight: a dark blue velvet slipper, one Alfonso had worn during his month of convalescence in the Vatican; it had fallen from his body as the soldiers bore him away. I leaned down and picked it up, then clasped it to my bosom as though it were a holy relic—indeed, it was to me, for my brother had the heart of a saint.

The guards were wise enough not to take it from me.

Clutching Alfonso's slipper, I staggered outside into a landscape made meaningless and unfamiliar by grief. The voices of the pilgrims crowding Saint Peter's piazza were a harsh, incomprehensible babble, their moving bodies a vertiginous blur. The gardens, lush and verdant in the humid summer heat, seemed mocking, as did the breathtakingly lovely marble entrance to the waiting Palazzo Santa Maria. I was offended: how dared the world parade its beauty, when the worst possible event had just occurred?

I stumbled, and several times came close to falling: I believe Donna Esmeralda caught me. I was aware only of a rotund black-clad body next to mine, and a pair of familiar, soft arms.

The soldiers spoke: I did not understand them. I know only that at some point, I found myself sitting not in my own chambers, but in Lucrezia's more luxurious ones. She was there, weeping, along with Donna Maria; Donna Esmeralda sat next to me, and from time to time, asked questions which I did not answer.

Had I possessed my stiletto in those first dreadful hours, I would have slit my own throat. It mattered not to me that I would have yielded to cowardice, as my father had: nothing mattered at all. A blackness had settled over me, one far more profound than that of my father's chamber in Messina.

In my mind, I was a petulant eleven-year-old rebuking my father for punishing me by separating me from Alfonso. It was not fair, I had told him, for my brother to be hurt, too.

My father had smiled cruelly—as cruelly as Cesare Borgia—and taunted me. *How does it feel, Sancha? How does it feel to know you are responsible for hurting the one you love most?*

For my efforts to save Alfonso by assassinating Cesare had directly resulted in my brother's death.

I have killed him, I told myself bitterly. *I and Cesare.* If I had never allowed myself to fall in love with Cesare, had never come to reject his offer of marriage, would my brother still be alive?

'You lied,' I told the strega, whether aloud or silently, I do not know. 'You lied. . . . You said if I wielded the second sword, he would be safe. I was only trying to fulfil my destiny . . . '

In my imagination, the strega appeared before me—tall, proud of bearing, veiled. Like the sibyls in the glorious Borgia apartments, she remained maddeningly silent. 'Why?' I whispered, with the same raw fury I had shown Lucrezia. '*Why?* I was only trying to save the best and gentlest of souls . . . '

At last the initial shock of the event wore off and the brutal reality of my brother's death overtook me. Cesare and my father became intertwined in my thoughts, as the cruel, dark-haired man who had taken Alfonso away—a cruel man I had helplessly loved, and also been forced to hate.

As a child, I had cried when my father separated me from my brother; afterwards I had sworn that I would never again let a man bring me to tears. I had not cried when my father hanged himself, when Juan violated me, when Cesare rejected me. But the grief that welled within me at the knowledge that Alfonso and I were now forever parted was too vast, too deep, too violent to be denied. Involuntary sobs racked me, shook my body; I pressed my face to my knees and wept with a force that caused physical pain. For several hours I loosed the tears held in check for most of my life, until my skirts were soaked through; even then, I continued weeping, as Esmeralda gently lifted me and wiped my face with a cool cloth, then put a towel upon my knees to absorb the dampness.

Alfonso, only my darling Alfonso, would ever have my tears.

Eventually I grew exhausted and spent; only then did I become aware of Lucrezia's loud wailing. I looked on her with a mixture of pity and virulent hatred; she was like Jofre, weak. Weaker, certainly, than I had judged. In her shoes, I would have struggled to find a solution, to save both husband and child . . .

But perhaps she had never really wanted to. Perhaps her helpless love for Cesare had been even greater than mine.

Regardless of the truth, all that had given my life meaning had been taken from me. I no longer had the heart or strength to care about Lucrezia's difficulties. And when she approached me, with the most piteous tears, and tried to embrace me as she begged my forgiveness, I resolutely—but not harshly—pushed her away. I was done with the House of Borgia and its duplicity.

It was dusk when I finally noticed that Donna Esmeralda had gone to the antechamber door, and was entreating the guards. 'Please,' she said. 'Donna Sancha has just lost a brother, and Donna Lucrezia a husband. Do not deny them the opportunity to view the body and attend the funeral.'

The guards were young men, sworn to obey their masters, but not pleased by the injustice of our situation. One, especially, was manifestly distressed by our grieving.

'Forgive me,' he replied. 'It is out of the question. We have specific orders not to allow anyone to leave these chambers. No one in the household is allowed to see the body, or witness the burial.' And then he flushed slightly, realizing that he might have revealed more than his commander wished, and fell silent.

'Please,' Donna Esmeralda pleaded. She persisted until the guard relented.

'Have them come quickly, then, to the loggia. If they stand out on the balcony, they will be able to see the procession pass by.'

At that news, Lucrezia rose. Wearily, I did the same, and followed the soldiers to stand in the warm night air.

Shadows, that is all I remember of it. Perhaps twenty flickering torches surrounding a coffin borne on the shoulders of a few men, and the silhouettes of two priests. I knew my brother's body had been treated like those of other Borgia victims: washed hastily and stuffed into a wooden box.

Alfonso deserved a grand funeral, with hundreds of mourners; his goodness had earned him the most beautiful prayers and eulogies, with parades of popes and emperors and cardinals, but he was buried in haste in the dark by men who did not know him.

I decided then that God, if He existed, was the cruellest of them all—more treacherous than my father, than Pope Alexander, than Cesare—for He was capable of creating a man filled only with love and kindness, then cutting him down and disposing of him in the most heartless, meaningless fashion. One thing was true in life: there was no justice for the wicked or the good.

Lucrezia and I watched as the little procession headed not for Saint Peter's, as was my brother's due, but for a small, obscure chapel nearby, Santa Maria delle Febbri. There, I later learned, Alfonso was unceremoniously stuffed in the ground, with only a small stone to mark the site.

Donna Esmeralda brought me parchment and quill, and gently prompted me to write a letter to my Uncle Federico concerning Alfonso's murder; I paid no attention to what happened to it afterwards, for I permitted myself to descend into darkness again at once. I did not sleep, eat, or drink; spent by weeping, I merely sat, too overwhelmed to do anything but sit and stare out from the balcony at the gardens.

Lucrezia was likewise helpless. In the presence of my brother's love, she had blossomed; when he had been wounded, she had found in herself a will and strength none of us had known she possessed. Now, all of that had died within her, and she had no heart for revenge. She did nothing day and night but weep. She could not even care for little Rodrigo. Morning dawned, and the nursemaid appeared at the door, clasping the sturdy toddler's hand.

'He has been crying, Madonna, and asking for you,' she said to

Lucrezia—but the mother lay abed, her face turned to the wall, and would not even acknowledge the boy. 'He has not seen you or his father today, and he is worried.'

His soft sobbing wakened me from a condition deeper and darker than slumber. I blinked, and rose . . . then knelt, and opened my arms, for the first time letting go of Alfonso's slipper. 'Rodrigo, darling . . . Your mother is tired this morning, and needs a bit more rest. But *Tia* Sancha is here, and so happy to see you.' Some unexpected grace permitted me to smile; cheered, the boy ran to me, and I enfolded him in my arms. As I buried my face in his hair, I understood Lucrezia a bit better; at that moment, I would have sacrificed anything for that child.

But there had to have been a way to avoid sacrificing something equally as precious: Alfonso.

A wave of tears threatened: how like my brother he looked, with his curls and his blue eyes! But for Rodrigo's sake, I steadied myself, and kept the smile upon my face. 'Shall we go outside? Shall we play?' He was fond of races—like his aunt and his mother—and he especially liked me to run against him, since I always let him win.

The guards were kindly; they gave us leave, and one accompanied us at a distance. I led the boy out to the gardens, where we played hide and seek in the hedges; in my nephew's blessed presence, I found a temporary respite. But when the time came for the boy to return to the nursery, I returned to the palazzo and relentless grief. I found my brother's slipper where I had dropped it, and once again clutched it desperately to my breast.

For two days, I remained with Lucrezia in her quarters, both of us under constant surveillance. During that time, His Holiness did not come to comfort her, nor did he bother to send his condolences. I heard no word from Jofre.

On the second day after Alfonso's death, Lucrezia was summoned to meet her brother Cesare at the Vatican.

This was no casual summons, nor a simple family conference: Cesare sat at a table with his sister in a grand hall, the two of them surrounded by no fewer than a hundred of the Captain-General's armed guards.

That is all Lucrezia would tell me of the meeting—and that she only revealed gradually, over the course of several hours. She returned afterwards, so deeply shaken she dared not weep. But immediately on her return, she had little Rodrigo moved from the nursery permanently into her chambers. I have no doubt Cesare reiterated his threat on the child's life, lest Lucrezia publicize the murder or make any appeals to her father that would cause Alexander to sympathize with Naples instead of Cesare's choice, France.

Within a day after her harrowing encounter with Cesare, Lucrezia's tears returned. She refused her father's summons to supper, then to audiences, where he wanted her to sit on her little cushion on the step beneath his throne, as she had in the past.

Lucrezia would have none of it. She had cooperated to save her child, but her grief was too great, her rage too deep, to pretend that Alfonso's murder had not happened. She lay in bed and ignored all her father's appeals.

Alexander soon grew angry, to the point of sending Lucrezia a missive stating that he no longer loved her.

Lucrezia batted not an eye; her father's disapproval no longer evoked in her desperate attempts to please. In response, she announced that she would seclude herself, along with her child, at a pastoral estate she owned in Nepi, just north of Rome.

She spoke as though she intended to remain there forever. No one dared tell her what all of Rome knew: that the Pope and Cesare were already planning her next marriage. Seeking the alliance that would bring the best political advantage for the House of Borgia. Meanwhile, Donna Maria busied herself with packing most of Lucrezia's belongings—with the exception of the beautiful gilded and bejewelled gowns, worn in happier times. In Nepi, there would be no ceremonies, no celebrations, only the wearing of black.

Lucrezia desired to have me in her company at all times; I wondered why, since I could no longer show her the unrestrained warmth I had before her complicity in my brother's death. Nor could I provide comfort: I was lost in my own grief, unable to emerge from it for anyone save my nephew. Perhaps she wanted my presence out of a yearning to be close to whatever reminded her of Alfonso; perhaps she did so out of guilt.

Regardless of her reason, she invited me to accompany her to Nepi. I accepted only because little Rodrigo was going; Donna Esmeralda took charge of gathering the belongings I would need during my long absence from Rome.

While armed soldiers stood outside my open antechamber doors (since Alfonso's death, I was frankly guarded at all times, Lucrezia more subtly so), I sat in the bedchamber and supervised Esmeralda in her task. It had been more than a month since I had entered the rooms that had for so long been my home. In my absence, many things had been taken: the fine draperies, the silver sconces, the fur carpets and the gilded brocade coverlet from my bed.

Once again, I wanted little of Rome: no sumptuous gowns, only the plain black dresses I had brought with me as a new bride, which were better suited for mourning. I wanted my dog-eared copy of Petrarch, the slipper which had fallen from my dead brother's foot, and little else.

While Esmeralda worried with my clothing, I went to my cache of jewels, hidden carefully in a secret compartment in my armoire, thinking that perhaps I should take a few of the most valuable of them—not because I wished ever to adorn myself again, but because I was already thinking of a possible escape from Nepi, if I could convince Lucrezia to bring the boy with us to Naples. I would need bribes for the guards, and money to run the household.

With that in mind, I surreptitiously pored over my casket of jewels, and hid the largest and most valuable of them between my breasts.

It was then I caught sight of the innocuous-looking slender glass vial, small and green amidst the glittering gems.

The canterella.

My heart skipped a beat. I still lived beneath the shadow of the darkest grief, and I knew I remained with Lucrezia at present only because of His Holiness' tolerant attitude towards his daughter. Once Cesare persuaded Alexander, I would be either imprisoned or murdered. I had no desire to live as a prisoner of the Borgias—and I would not give Cesare the pleasure of being the one to take my life. I would far prefer eternity in Hell as a suicide.

I slid the little green glass vial beneath my bodice, into the special pocket for my now-confiscated stiletto. It fit neatly.

God Himself arranged the timing: no sooner had I hidden the vial than I heard marching in the corridor outside my door.

I rose, and was composed and calm when I faced Cesare's soldiers, led by none other than the apologetic Don Micheletto.

'Well,' I said. 'You have come for me at last.'

Late Summer 1500–Spring 1501

XXXV

I was escorted to the Castel Sant'Angelo. Don Micheletto walked alongside me, and soldiers kept their distance both ahead of us and behind us, as if they had come merely to provide for my safety.

The entire event possessed an air of unreality, as though it were a dream; everything seemed false, illusory, save one single fact: Alfonso was dead.

Nevertheless, I reminded myself that I was a royal of the House of Aragon, and moved with grace and pride though surrounded by my captors. The guards blocked the gaping pilgrims and shoved the more curious ones aside as we marched through Saint Peter's square, then onto the great bridge that led to the forbidding stone keep of Sant'Angelo.

I did not turn to look back at the Palazzo Santa Maria; my life there was slipping away from me, along with my sanity, like a hand being withdrawn from a glove. I was naked, bare. Alfonso was gone, little Rodrigo was gone, the trust I had put in Lucrezia was gone. Even my husband—who had impressed me earlier with his apparent loyalty—had abandoned me.

We walked along the bridge over the curving Tiber, leaden,

fouled by the unseen corpses of Borgia victims. I prayed that I would soon join them.

Beside me, Micheletto spoke, his tone gracious and deferential. 'His Holiness thought that a change of scenery might help ease your grief, Your Highness. We have arranged new quarters for you, which I hope you will find suitable.'

My face twitched with hatred. 'Tell me, sir, is that a spot of blood upon your hand?'

Unwittingly, he actually lifted his hands and spread the fingers out, examining them; only after a glance at my expression of grim gloating did he lower them and attempt to hide his embarrassment at taking my question literally.

'I thought so,' I said. 'Did Cesare have you kill my brother yourself, to make sure the deed was properly done?'

His smile faded; he made no further attempt at conversation until we arrived at our destination.

I had never before visited the Castel Sant'Angelo, and knew only of its infamy as a prison. I suspected I would be deposited in a filthy little cell with a bed of straw and chains upon the bare walls, and rusting iron bars in place of doors.

Don Micheletto and I strolled past well-tended gardens to a side entrance; there, he signalled for all but two of the guards to remain behind. I was led through corridors that reminded me of the palace where I had so long resided.

At last my guide opened the finely carved wooden doors to my 'cell'. Inside lay my new apartments; in the antechamber, I recognized a chair which had been taken from my suite in the Palazzo Santa Maria; the floors were covered with my fur carpets. In the inner chamber on the bed was my brocade coverlet, and my drapes, and the silver sconce upon the wall. Beyond was a small balcony, overlooking more gardens.

I observed this dully, without comment. I would have preferred more brutal surroundings to reflect my grief. I found no comfort in this luxury, this familiarity.

I turned to find Micheletto smiling at me.

'Donna Esmeralda will be joining you, of course,' he said. 'She is gathering a few more of your things. Please feel free to request whatever you wish. Given the recent terrible events, all we ask is that, if you wish to stroll the grounds, or visit your husband at Santa Maria, you request an escort.'

'Who arranged this?' I demanded.

A corner of Micheletto's mouth quirked even higher. 'In all confidence, Your Highness: Don Cesare. He regrets the demands of politics, and any sorrow they have caused you. He has no desire to cause you further despair.'

Be kind to Sancha, Lucrezia had said. Cesare, she claimed, still loved me.

But I did not want his kindness. I wanted but one thing: revenge—and barring that, oblivion, if I could find within myself the courage to seek it.

Donna Esmeralda and a group of servants arrived bearing more of my belongings, as promised; I endured the commotion in silence. Meanwhile, I determined to take my life with the canterella that very night, to protest my brother's death—though I knew it would separate me from him forever, if the stories about the afterlife were true. He was surely in the highest circle of Heaven, while I, a suicide, would be consigned to Hell.

I did not know what quantity of the poison would be needed, how many men my little vial was capable of putting to death; therefore, I decided to ingest the entire container. Perhaps that way I would go swiftly, without too much of the legendary suffering the powder produced. I would have to wait until Donna Esmeralda was distracted, and I could block my actions from both her and the guards' view by going out onto the balcony.

I spent the rest of the day sitting in the chair in the antechamber, stroking the soft blue velvet of my brother's slipper while the servants put my rooms in order. At dusk, a fine supper was delivered to my door. I could not eat, despite Esmeralda's coaxing; she had what she wanted of my portion and her own, then servants bore the platters away.

But I asked for wine, and kept a flagon and goblet beside me. As she had each night since Alfonso's death, Esmeralda beseeched me to come to bed; as always, I refused, saying I would come when I was tired. Fortunately, she was weary after all her work, and fell asleep early. When I heard her rhythmic breath, I knew my hour of opportunity had come.

I filled my goblet and rose casually, mindful of the guards outside my door, then slipped through the bedchamber where Esmeralda lay sleeping. She had left a candle burning for me; I took it out onto the balcony, and set it upon the ledge so that I could see in order to accomplish my final task.

I set my goblet down as well, then with trembling fingers found the vial of canterella hidden in my gown. I drew it forth, and held it up to the light.

The glass glinted brilliant and green as an emerald; I stared at it for a moment, transfixed, overcome by the gravity of what I was about to do.

And as I stared, an image formed within the glass, tiny but perfect and complete in detail.

It was my father's corpse, hanging from its medallion-laden noose.

I screamed. I cast the vial from me; it clattered to the ground without breaking, and rolled away. My surroundings whirled: arms flailing, I fell to the floor, in the process knocking the taper over the ledge, so that I was suddenly in total blackness.

And in that blackness, my father's corpse loomed larger than life. It swung before me, there on the balcony; its cold, stiff legs brushed against my shoulders, my face, and I scrabbled away on hands and knees, sobbing.

Once backed into a corner, I cringed and tried to shield myself with my hands. 'You must promise me, Alfonso!' I shrieked. 'We must take a solemn oath never to be apart again . . . for without you, I will go mad!'

Before me stood my brother, just as he had been the day he

came to Rome to marry Lucrezia, young and handsome and smiling, dressed in pale blue satin. 'But Sancha, your mind is perfectly sound.' His tone was matter-of-fact. 'With or without me, you need never fear madness. You have simply tried to kill the wrong man.'

I screamed again, and ran staggering back into the dark bedchamber; a stout figure caught me. I struggled to break free until I realized it was Donna Esmeralda, shouting:

'Sancha! Sancha!'

I sagged against her and sobbed; she clutched me with fierce tenderness. 'I tried to be a murderess,' I gasped into her soft, sturdy shoulder, 'and instead, killed my own brother.'

'Hush,' Esmeralda commanded. 'Hush. You committed no crime.'

'God is punishing me . . . '

'This is foolishness,' Esmeralda insisted. I could not see her face in the night, but my cheek lay against her collarbone, and I felt the vibration of her firm voice within her chest, the solidity of her conviction. 'God loved Alfonso. He knows it is not fair that your brother should die while Cesare lives. Judgment is coming for the Borgias, Donna. Do not weep.' I calmed at her words; she paused, then spoke her mind. 'Savonarola was right . . . this pope *is* the Antichrist. Alexander always intended to let Cesare kill Alfonso; he knew it even when he came to the Hall of the Sibyls and swore otherwise. He is as guilty as his son—perhaps more so, for he could have stopped all this evil at any time.'

She led me to the bed, and tucked me in, fully dressed as I was, then lay down beside me. 'Here. I shall not leave your side. If you grow frightened, simply reach for me. I will be here. God is with us, Donna. He has not forsaken us.'

After she fell asleep, I sat up in bed, terrified, convinced I was a girl back in Naples, and that the surrounding darkness held the mummies of my grandfather's museum. I shivered beneath the covers as an image formed before me: that of the leering, leather-faced Robert, his painted marble eyes gleaming, a thin hank of auburn hair hanging from his puckered skull, as he gestured sweepingly.

Welcome, Your Highness . . .

I wept. I wanted no welcome; I did not want to enter Ferrante's grisly kingdom of the mad and the dead.

As the sky lightened before dawn, I crept out to the balcony and recovered the vial of canterella, then hid it with my jewels before Esmeralda woke. Soon, I told myself. Soon, I would be strong enough to use it.

I remained in a state of perpetual twilight. During the days, followed at a courteous distance by a guard, I wandered through the labyrinthine gardens until I reached a state of exhaustion. At night, I sat in a chair out on the balcony and stared hard into the darkness, at times overcome by panic because I could not see Vesuvio. I told Esmeralda I dozed outside in my chair—but I slept not at all, and my mind took on the frightening clarity and swiftness of a madman's.

I was frantically pacing through the gardens one day when I heard the bells of Saint Peter's toll . . . and at once, Donna Esmeralda's words seized my fevered consciousness and would not let go. At that moment, I received a divine revelation, the knowledge of how to bring judgment down upon the Borgias. But subterfuge was called for. I stopped in mid-stride and waited for my panting guard to catch up to me.

'I shall go up to the loggia now,' I said sweetly. 'I should like to look out at the city.'

I made my way quickly back into the building and up the stairs, until I reached the great loggia that overlooked the Castel Sant'Angelo Bridge. The broad street was filled with pilgrims and merchants, all of them close enough so that I could easily toss something for them to catch; they were well within earshot.

'Citizens of Rome!' I cried, leaning over the balcony's edge. 'Pilgrims to the Holy City! Hear me! I am Sancha of Aragon, whose brother Alfonso was murdered by His Holiness, Alexander VI, at the hands of the Captain-General, Cesare Borgia! This pope is the Antichrist, just as Savonarola said: he is an adulterer and murderer many times over! He killed his own brother to obtain the tiara, permitted the murder of his own son, Juan, and now he has killed Alfonso, Duke of Bisciglie, husband of Lucrezia—'

A guard caught me by a wrist and attempted to drag me away; I laughed, and with a lunatic's strength, broke free.

'Pilgrims! Romans! God calls for you to bring Alexander down! Go now! How many must die? How many must be killed before he is punished for his crimes?'

Men and women on the street below gathered, and stared up in amazement at me. An old nun, veiled in summer white, crossed herself and uttered a prayer; a black-frocked young priest gestured to his companion and pointed up at me. Commoners stopped, some with brows furrowed, others laughing.

Why did they not take action? I wondered. Why did they not rush at once to the pontifical palace, and drag Alexander out into the streets? My message was so clear, so indisputable . . .

I continued my ranting for some time; at last, a pair of soldiers managed to restrain me. I looked into their eyes, hurt, bewildered. 'Have you not heard what I have been saying? Can you not see the evil? You have arms—use them!'

But they wielded no weapons against the Pope; instead, they dragged me, cursing and kicking, to my chamber. Afterwards, I vaguely remember Donna Esmeralda's troubled face, and a doctor's, and being forced to drink a draught that left me stuporous. At last I slept.

When I woke, Jofre appeared. From that day on, he visited me every evening—more often than he ever had when my presence at the Vatican was welcome. He brought me small gifts—jewels, keepsakes. One night, he smuggled me a miniature portrait of Alfonso that had belonged to Lucrezia, which she had not been permitted to take with her to Nepi.

Donna Esmeralda stayed by my side constantly. I was no longer allowed out on the balcony at night, but was compelled to lie in my bed beside her after drinking the bitter sleeping draught. I was compelled, too, to eat at least a bit of food each time it was brought, and so I regained partial composure. I learned to interact pleasantly with Esmeralda and Jofre when required, and to maintain while with them the appearance of sanity, even if I did not entirely possess it.

So I spent my days idly, roaming the gardens accompanied by a sentry. Only then, away from my husband and Esmeralda, did I allow full reign to my madness: I muttered under my breath with each step, holding long conversations with Alfonso, my father, and most of all, with the deceitful strega.

The heart pierced by one sword: this was what I possessed now, but my efforts to wield it against Cesare had failed. I felt that sword within me as one feels a thorn; it pricked and rankled me. 'Why was I not permitted to kill him?' I asked the strega, and the only answer I received, again and again, was:

At the proper time . . .

At night—despite the doctor's potion—I dreamed: nightmares of Alfonso's white, slashed body being carried away from me by laughing soldiers.

Months passed. The miserable summer turned from autumn to winter. Jofre sent over some of my finest gowns for me to choose from, and I attended Christmas Mass with him at Saint Peter's, as if I were not a prisoner of the House of Borgia. I passed both the Pope and Cesare, though neither met my challenging gaze or acknowledged my presence. After the Mass, I was not invited to the family dinner, which Jofre was obliged to attend, but banished back to my apartment at the Castel Sant'Angelo.

It was as though I were neither living nor dead, but in a sort of purgatory: as a member of the House of Aragon, I was considered too dangerous to live among the Borgias and be privy to their secrets; at the same time, being the wife of Jofre, who knew so few of those secrets, I was not deemed enough of a threat to kill.

Spring came. I lived numbly, without meaning, the boredom of my days broken only by my conversations with the dead and visits from my husband. Jofre tried his best to lift my spirits, but the moments without the distraction of his presence were dark indeed.

I continued to walk the gardens for hours at a time, trying to exhaust myself so that sleep would come more easily and with it, oblivion. One afternoon, walking along a gravel path flanked by a hedge of roses in full, fragrant bloom, I spied another noblewoman walking towards me, followed at a respectful distance by a guard.

I thought to turn and run. I was in no mood for company or light-hearted chatter; but before I could make my escape, the woman neared and greeted me with a nod and a beckoning smile. She turned to her guard and called, 'We will walk together a little way.'

Her young soldier nodded and mine seemed not to care; the two men apparently knew each other and were content to walk behind us, conversing quietly.

The woman bowed. She was perhaps twenty-five years of age, with lustrous black hair and the classic, handsome face of an ancient Roman statue. 'I am the Countess Dorotea de la Crema.'

'I am the madwoman Sancha of Aragon,' I said.

She was not at all shocked; her smile filled with irony. 'We are all Cesare's madwomen here. I, too, am one of his prisoners.' Her voice softened with sadness. 'When he marched his army between Cervia and Ravenna, he killed my husband and seized our estate.' She fixed her great dark eyes on me. 'It is said you were his lover.'

After living so many years in the Borgia household, I appreciated her bluntness. 'I was at one time,' I answered. 'But I could not love a man who proved to be a murderer. I despise him now with my entire soul.'

She nodded, approving. 'Then we have something in common. After he killed my husband, he took me as his prisoner. Like Caterina Sforza, who is also here, he treated me lavishly, but each night, he raped me. I think, had I been willing, it would not have pleased him as much.' She looked away, at the muddy Tiber. 'Now that I am here, he has grown bored with me and leaves me alone, for which I am grateful. But until he is defeated—or until the Pope dies—I am trapped here.'

'So it is for me,' I said gently. 'I am sorry for your husband.'

'And I for your brother,' she said. Apparently, Dorotea was privy to all the news concerning me.

We walked quite a distance that first day; over the weeks that passed, we began to confide more in each other. Like me, Donna Dorotea was outspoken, driven to the edge of sanity by the crimes committed against her, and no longer interested in her fate. We spoke openly about the Borgias' crimes, and our lives. It was a relief to unburden myself of terrible secrets—and amusing to discover Dorotea already knew almost everything that I revealed.

In her, I found a respite from my solitary madness during the days; but away from her company, especially at night, the spectres returned: the mummified Robert, Alfonso, my father, the enigmatic strega. Each day, I struggled to find the strength to face the canterella; each night, I found it lacking.

During this time I received a letter from Lucrezia at Nepi. The wax seal had been broken; I sat in my antechamber for a long time with the letter in my lap, trying to decide whether to feed it to the flame of a nearby taper.

At last I unfolded it and read:

Dearest Sancha,

First, I must beg forgiveness for being a dreadful correspondent and not writing to you earlier; I confess, in the first dark days here, I had not the heart to pick up a quill. But time has had a slight healing effect, and I wanted to tell you, as soon as I was able, how terribly I have missed your company. Without your loyal friendship and good heart, the days are long and lonely.

Little Rodrigo misses you, too; he asks constantly for his Tia Sancha. You would not recognize him: he has grown so! Each day he comes to resemble his father more and more.

There is little news to tell: the days are all the same, and blur together. But I must report that, not long after my arrival, Cesare and his army came and made camp here one night. I was obliged to entertain him, and the more outstanding members of his company.

He travels now with the artist and inventor, Leonardo da Vinci. Don Leonardo came to supper that night. He is a kindly old man, eccentric-looking, with a crooked nose, large, startling eyes, and long white hair and beard which are both unkempt. Despite his age, his mind is exceptionally keen. Cesare says he is an engineering genius, and has proven of great use in terms of using explosives for the demolition of bridges. I only know that he was very gentle and possessed of a fine sense of humour. While we sat at dinner, he called for parchment, and produced a quill and ink which he keeps on his person at all times; while Cesare spoke at length about the military campaign, Don Leonardo proceeded to draw. Rodrigo appeared, and showed quite an interest: I was about to take the child back to the nursery and chide him for bothering a guest, but Don Leonardo was very sweet, and let Rodrigo sit on his knee and watch while he made his sketch.

Back to Cesare, and his campaign. I must mention here another member of his company, a certain Niccolo Machiavelli—a tight-lipped, unpleasant man—who scarcely touched his supper because he was recording furiously in a diary while my brother spoke, as though Cesare's words were pearls.

My brother told me he took the properties surrounding Bologna and Florence easily; the great cities signed over fortresses and estates out of fear of his army, since it has been strengthened by a gift of ten thousand men from King Louis. Cesare now says he is invincible, and can march through Italy and seize whatever lands he wishes.

Once my brother was done speaking, at the end of the supper, Don Leonardo presented me with a completed sketch. I was very flattered, for it was a rendering of me as I had appeared at the table; yet I was surprised to see how very sad my own expression was, for I had been making an effort to seem bright and lively for my guests.

Beneath my portrait, Don Leonardo had written a line from the poet Sannazaro:

Per pianto la mia carne si distilla.

My flesh melts away with my tears.

He is very wise, Don Leonardo. He sees through outward appearances to the very soul of the person, and has the magical talent of conveying what is in a heart using mere parchment and ink. There are many other things I could tell you, but a letter is not the best means for conveying what I wish to say. I shall have to wait until I can see you again in person.

I pray for you each night, sister, and think of you with

great fondness. Never did I find a better or more trustworthy friend. May God keep you well.

Affectionately,

Lucrezia

I folded the letter back up and put it for safekeeping inside my little copy of Petrarch. I understood that Lucrezia could not fully share her thoughts with me; I understood her allusions to her great sorrow, her hints that she was overwhelmed by guilt, her statement that she was 'obliged' to entertain her brother—which meant she had done so quite unwillingly. She had hinted at her longing for forgiveness.

I could not, would not respond. What news had I to share? That I had gone mad with grief, due in part to her treachery? That the only thing that brought me joy was the thought of revenge against Cesare?

Later, I privately showed the letter to Dorotea de la Crema. Her lips thinned as she read; at last, she nodded. 'Cesare is seizing whatever lands he wishes,' she confirmed. 'And whatever women, too. I have heard the latest news; when he conquers a new town, he seizes all the noblewomen for his travelling harem. And every night, he chooses a new woman to humiliate.'

Such news fuelled my hatred, and made me dream at night: of seizing the sword that still impaled my heart, of using it to strike out, with a flash of steel, and sever Cesare's head from his body in a single, avenging blow. Of smiling as I watched the head topple and roll away from the falling corpse, of watching the most evil blood to fill any veins flow freely as the Tiber.

Oddly, in the dream, I heard my brother's voice cheerfully repeat: *You have simply tried to kill the wrong man.*

Summer 1501 – Early Winter 1503

XXXVI

The egg has cracked, Alfonso said. He was dressed, as always, in pale blue satin; his visage was uncharacteristically stern, a warning. *And this time it cannot be repaired . . .*

I woke with a gasp to a humid August morning, and the sound of Esmeralda's cries out in the antechamber. I ran out to find her huddled over, clutching her heart, as if she was in the grip of a fierce pain.

'Esmeralda!' I rushed to her side and caught her fleshy upper arms. She was older now, and quite plump; I thought at once of Ferrante's attack of apoplexy, and helped her to a chair. 'Sit, darling . . . ' I rose, found wine and poured a goblet, then raised the rim to her lips. 'Here, drink. Then the guard will fetch the doctor.'

She took a sip, coughed, then with a dismissive wave of her hand, wheezed, 'No doctor!' She looked up at me, her eyes full of grief, and said wretchedly, 'Oh, Donna Sancha! If only this were something a doctor could help . . . ' She drew a gasping breath, then added, 'Do not call the guard. I just spoke to him. He brought news . . . '

'What has happened?' I demanded.

'Our Naples,' she replied, wiping her eyes with a corner of her pendulous sleeve. 'Oh, Madonna, it breaks my heart . . . Your uncle, Federico, was forced from the throne into exile. King Ferdinand the Catholic and King Louis—they conspired and joined their armies; now they share rule of Naples. Today, the French and Spanish banners both fly over the Castel Nuovo. Ferdinand is now regent of the city proper.'

I released a long breath as I knelt slowly beside her. Even though Alfonso's death had stolen from me my reason and joy, there had always remained the faint but distant hope that someday, I might return home—to the royal palace, to Federico and the brothers, and the family I had known. Now that, too, had been taken from me.

The royal House of Aragon was no more.

I was too stunned for speech. Donna Esmeralda and I remained silent, grieving in silence for some moments until I said knowingly, a corner of my lip twitching with hatred: 'And Cesare Borgia . . . he rode with King Louis' army into the city.'

She looked at me, astonished. 'Why, yes, Madonna . . . How did you know?'

I did not answer.

I fell again into a numb despair, one that even Esmeralda and the doctor's draught could not pierce. My only respite came during my walks with Donna Dorotea—who now did almost all of the speaking while I listened, mute and uninterested.

One day she brought news of Lucrezia, who had returned to Rome that autumn in response to the adamant summons of her father. Dorotea relayed an encounter between the Pope and his daughter. In the papal throne room, in the presence of Lucrezia's ladies, the Pope's servants and the chamberlain, His Holiness told Lucrezia that he and Cesare had studied the suitors lined up for her hand. They had chosen one: Francesco Orsini, the Duke of

Gravina. Orsini had proposed marriage to Lucrezia a few years earlier, but had been rejected in favour of my brother.

Now, Alexander informed his daughter, she would become the Duchess of Gravina. Politically, this was the wisest course of action.

No, Lucrezia had told her father. She would have nothing to do with the man.

Startled, Alexander had asked her reason.

'Because all my husbands have been very unlucky!' Lucrezia announced angrily, and stormed from the chamber without asking His Holiness' leave.

Word of this spread quickly throughout Rome. When the Duke of Gravina heard of her refusal, he took great offence (or perhaps he considered the truth of Lucrezia's words), and withdrew his offer at once.

Shortly thereafter, I found myself restless one evening, and took to wandering the corridors. Winter was approaching, and I kept my cape wrapped tightly about me as I headed for the loggia, to take in the bracing night air.

Even before I stepped from the landing onto the floor, I could hear the bells of Saint Peter's, singing a funeral dirge.

Staring out over the balcony's edge, pale as the fur she was wrapped in, stood a small, slender woman wrapped in white ermine, accompanied by guards who waited at a respectful distance. I was so distracted by the bells, I was almost upon her before I noticed her.

She was one of the most beautiful creatures I had ever seen, more beautiful even than the Pope's former mistress, the delicate Giulia. This woman was alabaster-skinned, golden-haired, with blue eyes brighter than any gem; in her bearing was a rare dignity and grace, and in her gaze was a profound sadness. I understood at once why Cesare had wanted to possess her.

'Caterina Sforza,' I breathed.

She turned her striking features toward me and regarded me. There was no hostility in her gaze, no condescension, only a grief that verged on madness.

She moved slightly aside, making room at the balcony. It was a clear invitation and I took it, stepping up to stand beside her.

She was silent some time, gazing out again at the piazza in front of the great stone edifice of Saint Peter's, where a torch-lit funeral procession was slowly making its way out of the cathedral and into the street. From the number of mourners, I judged the deceased to be a person of some importance.

At last Donna Caterina sighed. 'Another cardinal, no doubt,' she said, in a voice stronger and more resonant than I would have expected, 'cut down in order to finance Cesare's wars.' She paused. 'Each time I hear the bells toll, I pray they are for the Holy Father.'

'I pray they are for Cesare,' I countered. 'He is a far worthier candidate for death.'

She looked at me, tilting her lovely head and appraising me frankly. 'It is better if Alexander dies first, you see,' she explained. 'For if his son predeceases him, he will simply find another Cesare to head his army, and continue the Borgia terror. It is a game they play together: the Pope merely pretends not to be able to control Cesare's cruelty, but believe me, each hand knows exactly what the other is doing at all times. Of course, if Alexander were to die . . . ' She leaned toward me and lowered her voice conspiratorially. 'Surely I told you what the Venetian ambassador said to me, long ago, about Cesare.'

I smiled politely. 'We have never spoken, Madonna.' I could not fault her for her confusion; I was not in full possession of my senses myself.

She seemed not to hear my words. 'It was some time ago, before he murdered Lucrezia's last husband. Cesare was busy testing the waters, playing Spain against France, and France against Spain, waiting to see which alliance would prove the most advantageous.' She laughed softly. 'He was so inconstant . . . He actually went to the Venetian ambassador at one point and swore allegiance to Venice. He said that he trusted neither France nor Spain to protect him should anything happen to the Holy Father. And the ambassador told him, most frankly, 'You would certainly need help, it is true; for if anything ever happened to His Holiness, your affairs would not last three days.' She laughed again, and directed her attention once more to the torches moving silently through the dark streets of Rome.

I followed her gaze and contemplated the tiny travelling flames, the small black shapes of the grieving that faded into the surrounding night. Born of madness or not, my brother's ghost had spoken the truth: I had tried to kill the wrong man.

For the first time since coming to the Castel Sant'Angelo, I considered the canterella in my possession not as a means of self-destruction, but as a solution to the problems facing all of Italy. I returned to my rooms and sat brooding for hours. I possessed the weapon, but not sufficient knowledge of its use; nor did I have the means to deliver it to its target. I was watched at all times: I could scarcely walk into the Vatican and offer His Holiness a cup of wine. Esmeralda, too, was closely guarded; she no longer possessed the freedom to contact an assassin.

'I am ready,' I whispered to the strega in the darkness. 'But if I am to fulfil my destiny, you must send help. I cannot accomplish this alone.'

The next day at dusk, as I sat in my antechamber with Donna Esmeralda waiting for supper to be delivered, the doors were thrown open without the usual courteous knock. We turned; the two guards flanking the entrance bowed low as first Donna Maria, then Lucrezia herself, entered.

Donna Esmeralda rose and stared balefully at the two women, her arms folded across her chest in silent disapproval of our visitors.

I said nothing, but stood and studied Lucrezia. She was clad in blue-green silk skirts, with a matching velvet bodice and sleeves; her neck sparkled with emeralds, and diamonds dotted the gold netting covering her hair. She was dressed grandly, in the Roman style, while I had gone back to wearing unadorned Neapolitan black.

But all her finery could not hide her pallor, or put the spark of life back into her haggard, hollow eyes. Sorrow had worn her; any prettiness she ever possessed had fled.

At the sight of me, she gave a small, tentative smile and spread her arms.

I offered no welcome. I stared steadily at her, my arms at my sides, and watched her smile fade to an expression of veiled hurt and guilt.

'Why have you come?' I asked. There was no rancour in my tone, only bluntness.

She motioned for Donna Esmeralda and Donna Maria to step outside into the corridor; after they complied, she ordered the guards to close the doors, giving us privacy.

Once assured our words had no witnesses, she answered, 'I was in Rome.' Her voice was soft, tinged with shame. 'But I shall not remain here long. I had to see for myself how you were faring. I have been worried; I heard you were unwell.'

'It is all true, what they have said,' I told her flatly. 'I quite lost my mind. But it returns to me now and again.'

'And it is all true, what they have said about me,' she replied, with a trace of irony. 'I am obliged to marry again.'

I had no reply for such a statement—not when Alfonso's ghost hovered between us, a silent rebuke.

Lucrezia's gaze was fixed not on me, but down and away, on a distant spot in the past, as though her explanation were an apology to my brother, not to me. Her face grew taut with loathing and self-disgust. 'I refused at first—but I am far too valuable a political commodity to have my own way. My father and Cesare . . . I need not tell you what pressure they brought to bear on me.' A slight flush coloured her cheeks, as an unspoken memory provoked her anger; she gathered herself, and finally looked directly at me.

'But I convinced them to let me make the choice, leaving them with final approval. They agreed. I have made it, and they have approved.' She drew a breath. 'I chose a D'Este of Ferrara.'

'A D'Este,' I whispered. My cousins in the Romagna. Cesare never dared attack them; their army was too strong. He had long ago told me that he would prefer to make them his allies.

'Cesare likes the arrangement, because he thinks it will bring him more soldiers,' Lucrezia confided. 'I was required to visit them, so the old duke, my potential father-in-law, could be assured I was a "Madonna of good character", as he put it.' She gave a wry, fleeting smile. 'I passed old Ercole's test. But what I did not tell Father or Cesare is that the D'Estes will never be convinced to fight for the papacy. They are good Catholics, but they are wise: they do not trust Pope Alexander or his Captain-General.

'Duke Ercole insists that I go to Ferrara to wed his son, and live there afterwards, which I have agreed to eagerly. I will never again return to Rome. I will stay with my new husband, surrounded by a strong family and a strong army which cannot be bent to the Borgias' will.' Her voice grew laden with emotion. 'His name is Alfonso.'

It took me a moment to realize that she had uttered the name of her intended groom: Alfonso d'Este, my brother's cousin.

'So you see,' she continued, 'this is to be our last meeting, Sancha.' She regarded me with sad affection. 'If there was only something I could do to help your circumstances . . . '

'There is,' I answered immediately. 'You can do me one final act of kindness.'

'Anything.' She waited, eager, expectant.

'You can tell me how much of the canterella it takes to kill a man.'

She was utterly startled at first, then composed herself and grew very still. Through the distant look in her eyes, her expression, I watched her travel back to the convent of San Sisto, where she had been pregnant with Cesare's child, and so filled with despair that she planned to end her life.

I watched her recall the missing vial of poison.

She studied me intently then; our gazes met, both steady. In that wordless exchange, we shared complicity in a plot as solid, as explicit in goal as any hatched by her brother and father. *To kill a man,* I had said. She knew, from the resolve in my shoulders, in the upward tilt of my jaw, that I had no intention of using the vial's contents on myself.

I was never so sure of her loyalty, or her gratitude.

'Only a few grains,' she replied at last. 'It is extremely potent. It is slightly bitter, so sprinkle it onto food—something sweet, like honey or jam, or directly into wine. That way, the victim cannot taste it.'

I gave a slow nod. 'Thank you.'

In the next instant, it was as though we had never spoken of such things; her expression changed abruptly. A look of yearning crept into her eyes, a plea. I countered quickly before she could ask the question:

'Do not ask me for forgiveness, Lucrezia, for I can never give it.'

The last flicker of hope in her eyes died, like a flame extinguished. 'Then I will pray to God for it,' she said solemnly. 'And I will ask only that you remember me.'

I yielded then. I stepped forward and embraced her tightly. 'That I can do.'

She wrapped her arms about me. 'Good-bye, Sancha.'

'No,' I responded sadly, my cheek against hers. 'This is farewell.'

Preceding Lucrezia's departure for Ferrara, there were numerous celebrations in the city. Dorotea and I watched from the loggia on clear nights as all manner of sumptuously-dressed nobles and dignitaries processed through the streets and piazzas to the Vatican, on their way to pay their respects to the bride-to-be. There were fireworks, and cannons; Dorotea enjoyed the distractions, but they only fuelled my hatred.

One morning, as I sat in my antechamber reading, the doors to my apartment opened. I looked up, annoyed at the unannounced intrusion.

Cesare Borgia stood in the entrance.

War had aged him, as had the pox; even his beard, which now bore traces of premature silver, could not hide the prominent scars on his cheeks. There were streaks of silver as well in his hair, which had begun to thin, and shadows beneath his jaded eyes.

'You are as beautiful as the day I first saw you, Sancha,' he said, his voice wistful, soft as velvet. His flattery was wasted. My lips twisted at the sight of him; surely he could only bear evil news.

Then I saw the solemn little boy holding his hand, and let go a sound that was both a laugh and a sob. 'Rodrigo!' I threw down my book and ran to the child at once.

I had not seen my nephew in more than a year, but recognized him immediately; his golden curls and blue eyes were unmistakably my brother's. He had been dressed in a princely little tunic of dark blue velvet.

I sank to my knees before him and spread my arms. 'Rodrigo, my darling! It is your *Tia* Sancha, do you remember me? Do you know how I love you?'

The little boy—almost two years of age, now—turned away at first, and rubbed his eyes with his fists, embarrassed.

'Go to her,' Cesare murmured encouragingly, and nudged the boy towards me. 'She is your aunt, your father's sister . . . She and your mother loved each other very dearly. She was present the day you were born.'

At last Rodrigo seized me with impetuous affection. I enfolded him in my arms, not understanding why Cesare was granting this precious visit, and for the moment not caring. It was pure bliss. I pressed my cheek against the child's down-soft hair as Cesare spoke, his tone uncharacteristically awkward.

'Lucrezia cannot take the child with her to Ferrara.' It was not the custom to permit a child from a previous marriage to be raised in another man's household. 'She has asked that you raise him as your own. I did not see the harm in it, and so I brought him.'

Despite my joy, I could not resist hurling a barb. 'A child ought not be raised in a prison!'

Cesare answered with astonishing mildness. 'It will not be a prison for him, but a home. All privileges will be accorded him; he will be free to come and go, to visit his grandfather and uncles whenever he wishes. Anything he needs will be provided at once, without question. I have already arranged for him to have the best tutors when the time comes.' He paused, then the cool, arrogant tone I knew so well resurfaced. 'He is, after all, a Borgia.'

'He is a prince of the House of Aragon,' I said heatedly, without easing my hold on the boy for an instant.

At that, Cesare graced me with a thin smile, but there was only humour, no malevolence, in it. 'Servants will be arriving soon with his things,' he added, then left me to ponder how such a monster could at times be so human.

I called for Donna Esmeralda, to show off my newest, most precious jewel; the two of us covered the bewildered child with kisses.

Lucrezia had betrayed me and Alfonso had died, but they had left me the greatest of all gifts: their son.

From that moment, all traces of my madness disappeared. Little Rodrigo restored my hope and purpose. I realized that I had not destroyed all that I loved; and I began to entertain the idea of escaping with the child to Naples, ruled now by King Ferdinand of Spain. I could never return to the Castel Nuovo, but I would not be unwelcome in the city I so adored. My mother, my aunts, and even Queen Juana still lived there. I would be among family there. The women who had known my brother could now know his son.

I had the weapon to achieve my goal; thanks to Lucrezia, I had the knowledge to use it. Only one thing remained: the means to deliver it. Now that sanity had returned, I remained patient, willing to bide my time, to consider carefully how to fulfil the destiny the strega had foreseen.

I spent my days caring for Rodrigo. It took him time to accept that he would not see his mother again; most of all, he missed his nurse, who had gone as part of Lucrezia's entourage to Ferrara. Many nights he kept Donna Esmeralda and me up with his crying—but in truth, I slept better than I ever had before the child's arrival. Happily, Jofre enjoyed his nephew's company as well; he was fond of playing with the child, and on those evenings my husband came to dine, he carried Rodrigo to bed.

A docile year passed; summer went swiftly, and winter came again, too soon. The boy thrived and grew. Cesare, fortunately, spent all of his time with his army; I did my best to be patient.

Christmas passed, then the New Year. One night in early January, Jofre appeared for supper. On this particular occasion he lingered in the doorway, pale and shaken, unsmiling; even when Rodrigo came running to greet him, he did not bend down to lift the child, as was his wont, but absently laid a hand upon the disappointed boy's head.

'Husband,' I asked, concerned, 'are you unwell?'

'I am fine,' he said, without conviction. 'I need to speak to you in private tonight.'

I nodded, and quickly arranged for Donna Esmeralda to take the child early to bed, and for the other attendants, who usually served us at table and removed the platters, to set out the food and wine for us, then depart.

Once everyone had gone, Jofre opened the front doors and curtly dismissed the guards, then stood staring after them a time into the empty corridor; he returned and peered at the balcony, to make sure we were truly alone. Only then did he go to the table and sag down into a chair. The candlelight glinted off his closely-trimmed copper-gold beard, which failed to compensate for his weak chin.

He held out his goblet for wine; his hand was so unsteady that when I poured the ruby liquid into it, it sloshed over the rim. Once the goblet was full, he took a long drink, then set it down and groaned.

'My brother is the Devil Himself.' He leaned forward, elbow on the table, and clutched his forehead with trembling fingers.

'What has he done now?'

'He and Father are no longer satisfied with simply the Romagna. Cesare has moved down into the Marches, and taken Senigallia.' I had never been to Senigallia, but I had heard of it—a beautiful town south of Pesaro, on the eastern coast, with such soft, fine-grained sand the beaches were said to be made of velvet.

'Why are you surprised?' I interrupted acidly. 'Surely you have always known your brother's ambition is boundless. He would never be satisfied with only the Romagna.'

Jofre stared glumly down at his plate without touching the golden-brown leg of roasted fowl and chestnuts there. 'You have not heard, then, *how* he took the city.'

I shook my head.

'He called on all the *condottieri* of the Romagnol cities to ride with him.' These were the heads of the noble houses which had been defeated; they had been forced to serve as commanders in Cesare's army, leading their own men to do the Borgias' bidding. They had all sworn fealty—at the point of a sword. 'So they marched on Senigallia,' Jofre continued. 'The papal army was so mighty, the city opened its gates and surrendered without a struggle. But it is then that the tale turns ghastly . . . ' He shuddered. 'I cannot believe I share the same mother as this man; he is more treacherous than the Turks, more bloodthirsty than the one in Wallachia they called the Impaler.

'Cesare wanted more than the city as his prize. He invited all the condottieri inside the city walls, saying he wished for them to inspect the castle and sup with him, to celebrate the great victory.

'The commanders obeyed; they had no cause to expect anything but reward for their loyalty. But my brother . . . he ordered his men to surround them. The city gates were then closed, shutting them off from their own men.

'By morning, Cesare had killed every single one of them. Some strangled, others stabbed, or smothered . . . ' He laid his arm upon the table and rested his brow upon it.

I sat stone-faced across from him, trying to fathom the horror of what I had just heard. Proud, noble families who had ruled for centuries had been abruptly rendered powerless, broken. The Borgias truly controlled the Romagna at last.

He murmured into the crook of his arm, 'Father and Cesare had already selected new rulers; they were all simply awaiting word to seize command of each city.' He lifted his face and added miserably, 'cardinals die almost daily in Rome. Their wealth is being added to the Church's coffers, and all of it goes to fund the wars. Father will talk of nothing else. He is proud of Cesare, proud of the victories . . . I cannot bear it.' He began to shiver so violently that the plate beside him clattered. 'Now they are both so filled with arrogance, nothing will stop them. With Lucrezia gone to Ferrara, they cannot manipulate her anymore . . . and so their eyes have turned to me. Father made a comment to me yesterday about needing some of *our* wealth . . . for the wars. He spoke about Squillace, and other properties I have in Naples, and my gems and gold—how they might be of use to Cesare, and the Church. His tone was quite threatening. I have begun to fear for my own safety . . . Outside of my money, I am useless to them. What is to stop *me* from being their next victim?'

At his cowardice, I could no longer hold my tongue. 'Why do you tremble now, Jofre? Why do you show such surprise? Surely you have not been such a fool all these years, yet you chose to remain blind and deaf to all that has occurred around you! You know as well as I that Perotto and Pantsilea were innocents, slaughtered because they knew too much. You witnessed without comment the hanging of Don Antonio, Cardinal Sforza's guest, with your own eyes. You know the Tiber has been filled to overflowing for years with the victims of your father and brother.

Worst of all, you let Cesare murder your brother Juan, and my Alfonso, and did nothing to protect either! Do not complain to me, your wife—I live within the walls of a prison, with women who all were violated by Cesare!'

He let go a tortured groan. 'I am sorry, so sorry for all that has happened . . . but what can *I* do?'

'Were you a man, you would free me of this,' I said softly, harshly. 'Were you a man, you would long ago have taken a blade to your wicked family's throat.'

His brow was furrowed with worry, but his gaze was fierce; and his voice was very low as he confessed, 'Then I want to be a man now, Sancha. I want to be free to go to Squillace, and spend the rest of my days there in peace.'

So clear was his intention, so vehement his words that I fell silent. Here was the means I had been awaiting; but I had to be sure of Jofre's steadiness. I would have chosen a more strong-willed accomplice. Yet the longer I gazed into his determined eyes, the more certain I became that this was my opportunity.

At last I said quietly, 'I can help you, husband. I know of a way to stop the terror. But you must forsake the Borgias and swear your loyalty to me alone, to the death.'

He rose from his seat, moved swiftly to my side, then knelt and kissed my slipper. 'To the death,' he said.

Summer 1503

XXXVII

Jofre and I agreed that he would have to steel himself, and wait for Cesare's return from the wars. Were Cesare to hear of his father's death, he would ride into Rome and appoint his own pope, one that would yield to his bidding even more easily than his father had. We could not strike at Alexander alone.

Our wait seemed interminable, as Cesare slowly continued his campaign in the Marches.

One morning, however, brought hope. I woke to the distant sound of thunder; but when I rose and threw open the shutters, I looked out upon a cloudless, sunny sky.

The thunder sounded again. It was not, I realized, an approaching storm, but the echoes of faraway cannon. I left Donna Esmeralda asleep—she was beginning to grow a bit deaf—and dressed myself. Then I lifted Rodrigo from his cot and set him down.

Hand in hand, the two of us walked out into the antechamber, and I opened the doors. I had only one guard by then—a new one, Giacomo, a soldier of barely seventeen summers, who loved chatter and gossip almost as much as Donna Dorotea, and who knew I could be trusted.

Giacomo stood not at my doorway, but at the end of the corridor, staring out over the balcony at a point in the far distance. He was lean and tall, and the tension in his long limbs, as he stood with his back to me, conveyed mild alarm.

'Giacomo!' I called. 'I hear cannon!'

He whirled about, at once embarrassed to be caught leaving his post. He returned immediately. 'Forgive me, Madonna. It is Giulio Orsini and his men. The Holy Father has been imprisoning Orsini's relatives, so Don Giulio is leading a revolt. But there is nothing to fear. The Pope has summoned the Captain-General and his army'—and here he lowered his voice and eyelids slyly before adding—'if he can be convinced to come.'

For months, Cesare could *not* be convinced to leave his wars; the Pope was forced to make do with the few soldiers who had not marched with their Captain-General. Alexander could no longer rely on the support of the Roman nobility, who were mistrustful and bitter owing to Cesare's treatment of the *condottieri* at Senigallia. Why should they fight for a pope liable to murder them afterwards?

Giulio Orsini's strength and support swelled rapidly. One evening, Jofre looked meaningfully at me over the supper table, while Donna Esmeralda poured the wine.

He cleared his throat nervously, then said, with feigned casualness, 'His Holiness has grown quite desperate for assistance with the Orsinis. In fact, I learned today from the Cardinal of Monreale that Alexander threatened Don Cesare with excommunication if he fails to obey the papal summons and return to Rome. Cesare is reluctant—fuming, according to the cardinal—but today, Father received word that he and his men are coming.'

I reached across the table and clasped my husband's hand; Jofre's grip was surprisingly determined and strong. If Esmeralda found anything odd in the look of complicity I shared with my spouse, she said nothing.

. . .

In the heat of summer, months after the Pope's initial call for him, Cesare at last led his army into Rome. For two weeks, he remained inaccessible, encamped with his soldiers in the Roman countryside. But Orsini's small army was no match for the vast papal horde; the rebellious nobles of Rome were swiftly slaughtered. Jubilant, Alexander ordered all the cathedral bells to be set ringing.

After the victory, my husband arrived for his evening meal. Rodrigo ran to the door the instant he heard his uncle's footsteps; when Jofre entered, he lifted the boy high into the air, which made the child squeal with pleasure—then he abruptly kissed Rodrigo and set him down. Despite the boy's repeated pleas, Jofre could not be coaxed into playing this night, and I asked Esmeralda to put Rodrigo to bed early.

A small table had been erected out on the balcony so that we might enjoy the summer evenings while dining. As a pair of maidservants set the platters down, Jofre called for a goblet of wine. One of the servants fetched him one, and he drank the better part of it in a single swallow.

I rose from my chair in the antechamber and went over to where he stood. His gaze was distracted, roving; he had trimmed his beard that day, and none too steadily, for on his cheek was a small cut, marked by freshly dried blood.

'You bear news, husband,' I remarked, in a voice too low for the women on the balcony to hear.

Our attention remained on the servants, but I listened keenly as Jofre replied, 'Cesare is eager to leave Rome as soon as possible and return to the Marches. But Father has convinced him to stay for a victory party—a luncheon to be held tomorrow in Cesare's honour, hosted by Cardinal Adriano Castelli. It will be held outdoors, in a vineyard.'

'Arrange to sit between the Pope and Cesare,' I said softly.

'Then you need only ask the wine steward to let you deliver their full goblets to them—as a token of your honour and esteem. Make several toasts.' I paused. 'When the maidservants leave, I will bring what is required.'

The servants fretted overlong with the table arrangements, but at last they departed. I went into the bedchamber, where Donna Esmeralda sat sewing as young Rodrigo slept.

'I must retrieve something from my closet,' I whispered; she nodded and went back to squinting at her needlework while I opened my armoire.

The open doors blocked Esmeralda's view so that I was free to open a secret compartment in the closet floor and withdraw a box. Within rested the jewels from my suite in the Palazzo Santa Maria, as well as the vial of canterella. I had previously emptied a tiny container of clear glass which had held precious Turkish attar of roses, a gift Jofre had given me years ago.

I took a single ruby and the two vials, then returned the box to its hiding place, soundlessly shut the armoire doors, and retreated. Throughout the entire transaction, Donna Esmeralda never glanced up.

Out in the antechamber, Jofre was pacing. He had already poured himself more wine and had drunk most of it.

'You will have to contain yourself better,' I chided, 'if we are to succeed.'

'I will, I will,' he promised, then threw his head back and finished off the contents of his goblet.

I eyed him uncertainly, but said nothing. Instead, I handed him the ruby. 'In case a bribe is required.'

Then I went over to the oil lamp and held both the emerald and clear vials up to the flame.

At the proper time, the strega had said. I was never more convinced that this was finally the moment.

The green glass glittered with reflected flame. I thought of sunlight dancing off the waters of the Bay of Naples; I thought of freedom.

Inside, the powder was dull, silvery blue. *Beautiful, beautiful canterella*, I addressed it silently. *Canterella, rescue me . . .*

I thought of the moment I had killed the young soldier who had threatened Ferrandino's life. I had felt no guilt then; I felt no guilt now—only a cold, hard joy.

Keeping my hands steady, I unstoppered first the empty vial . . . then, with exquisite care, the one containing the poison. Jofre peered over my shoulder, his breath coming in short, nervous gasps, and craned forward.

'Stand back,' I warned. 'If I spill it, I do not know whether it will kill if inhaled.'

He obeyed, watching silently as I poured the powder from the larger container into the smaller. *Only a few grains*, Lucrezia had said; I never asked how she had acquired such experience. I gave Jofre hundreds, thousands—a third of the vial, enough to decimate the papal army.

I sealed both vials then, and handed him the smaller—half clear now, half greyish blue. He pocketed it in an invisible hiding place in his tunic.

'Why not give me all of it?' His voice held a trace of wounded petulance.

'Because if we are discovered,' I replied evenly, 'we will need some for ourselves.'

He blanched at that, but recovered himself and nodded.

I slid the emerald vial into the hiding place beneath my bodice. 'In the meantime, I shall keep this on my person, at all times, so that if we are captured . . . '

He nodded again, this time emphatically, to indicate I need not finish the thought.

We both turned to stare out at the balcony, where supper beckoned.

'I haven't the stomach for it,' Jofre said.

'Nor have I. I'll call for the servants to take it away.'

He turned to go; I caught his hand and said, 'I have little faith in God. But I will pray for you.'

He smiled faintly at that, then of a sudden seized and kissed me. It was not the requisite, habitual kiss of a husband long married to his wife, but that of a young man for the woman he passionately loved.

I drew back, overwhelmed, still in his arms; in his eyes, his face, I saw the shy, apologetic young boy of our wedding night.

'I am sorry to have disappointed you, Sancha,' he whispered. 'I will do so no more.'

In that way, we parted. I kept my promise; I prayed for him throughout that sleepless night, with my hand pressed to my heart.

The following day—that of Cesare's luncheon—passed with torturous slowness. I did not hear from Jofre that night; I had not expected to, for the canterella needed time to do its work.

But on the second evening, when Jofre failed to appear and give his report, I began to grow distraught. By the third evening, I was shaken. Had he betrayed me? Had he been detected, and captured?

I sat up the entire night in my antechamber, contemplating whether to make use of the green glass vial clenched in my fist.

In the hour before dawn, exhaustion finally overcame me. I staggered off to bed and dozed restlessly.

I woke in my bed to the most improbable sight: at first, I thought I was dreaming. Beside me, Donna Esmeralda lay motionless; Rodrigo slept quietly in his crib.

Leaning over me stood Dorotea de la Crema and Caterina Sforza, both in their nightgowns.

I blinked, but neither apparition disappeared.

'The Pope has been poisoned,' Dorotea hissed. 'Cesare, too.'

I sat up grinning, revived by a wave of jubilation. 'Are they dead?'

'No,' Caterina said; her pale face was radiant with joy. My heart almost stopped as she uttered that solitary word; she continued, 'But they are most seriously ill, and fearful of further attacks. Our guards have left.'

'Giacomo is gone?' I calmed myself. Rumour said the canterella sometimes took days to do its work. If the guards had left, this was an excellent sign that they did not expect His Holiness to survive.

'Gone,' Dorotea gloated.

I hurried to my closet and slipped on a tabard.

'They attended a party,' Dorotea said happily. 'The following evening, Alexander was stricken by a fever. No one thought anything of it—it is, after all, the hottest part of the summer, with everyone suffering from such illnesses—but *then*, yesterday morning, he showed all the symptoms of the canterella. And Cesare is sick, too. My guard said it was poisoned jam. But no one else at the party has fallen ill yet. It's possible the poisoning didn't even occur there.'

'Come look,' Caterina urged, gleeful as a child, and clasped my hand. She led me downstairs to the loggia—the building deserted, without a jailer in sight—and we looked across the piazza and down the street, at the Vatican.

The gates were closed, barred by a row of armed soldiers.

Caterina leaned so far forward over the balcony's edge that I feared she would fall, and caught her arm. She brushed me away impatiently. 'Let me be.'

'What are you doing?' I demanded, and she, with the sweetest, purest smile I have ever seen, replied:

'Listening for the bells.'

The following midday, as Donna Esmeralda tended Rodrigo while I packed my things in the bedchamber—trying to soothe myself through this hopeful act—Jofre appeared in the doorway. His shoulders were bowed by an invisible weight, his face haggard. He bore no good tidings; my grip on the folded velvet cape in my hands, which I had been about to place in my trunk, tightened.

'Donna Esmeralda,' he said. 'I need a word with my wife, alone.' His words sounded thick as a drunkard's—but it was not wine that slurred his words, but fear. His mouth was so dry, his tongue cleaved to his palate and teeth.

She nodded and took little Rodrigo's hand. As she moved by us, she cast a glance my way. She was no fool, my old nurse: on her round, wrinkled face was an expression of perfect understanding. She had no doubt noted Jofre's anxiety and my restlessness, and related them to the poisonings at the Vatican.

Her shrewd gaze held not reproach, but approval.

As soon as she had left with the child, I stepped up to Jofre and ran my hands over his shoulders, down his arms. His tunic was damp; he trembled faintly. His brown eyes were red from lack of sleep and slightly wild; upon his moustache, drops of sweat glistened.

'Speak, husband.'

Distractedly, he ran his fingers through his curls. 'They are not dead. I fear they are getting better.'

'What happened?'

'Nerves,' he replied, so ashamed he could not look at me. 'I—I spilled the powder. Almost all of it. I took the glasses of wine behind a tree, but I could not manage them and the vial. . . . Only a trace was left.'

'How sick are they now?' My questions were terse, urgent; there was no time to comfort him.

'Father is worst off. Sometimes he doesn't know where he is, or who is with him. But the retching, the bloody flux have stopped, and he was able to take some broth this morning. At the party, he took his wine neat—Trebbia wine, very strong—but Cesare poured some of his out after I brought it to him, and mixed it with water. He is sick as well, too weak to leave his bed—but not so bad as Father. He begged me to sit with him. He will recover, I know it . . . I finally excused myself, saying that I had to rest.' He reached out and clutched my arms suddenly for purchase as his knees buckled; I dropped the velvet cape in my hands and helped him over to the bed, where he sat.

He covered his face with cupped hands. 'I have failed you, Sancha. Now we will have to poison ourselves . . .'

In the face of his weakness, I might have grown angered, but instead I felt unnaturally calm. A conviction as unreasoning and mysterious as faith gripped me; I knew beyond doubt that Jofre had helped me take the first steps towards fulfilling my destiny. It remained for me to complete it.

'No,' I proclaimed forcefully. 'No harm will come to us. I require only a little more of your help. Tell me their situation. Are they guarded?'

Jofre shook his head. 'The only guards remaining now circle the Vatican. The rest have fled, as have most of the servants . . . But if they hear that Father and Cesare are improving, they might return.'

'Then we must work swiftly,' I said. 'Who is with them now?'

'Don Micheletto Corella was sitting with Cesare . . . ' Jofre grimaced with hatred. 'Not out of loyalty. He waits like a hawk, ready to strike the moment Alexander dies, or Cesare worsens . . . and then he will steal whatever treasure and power he can. Father is alone except for the chamberlain, Gasparre, who truly grieves.'

For an instant, I was perplexed. Destiny required that the fatal blow be delivered by my hand—but Jofre could hardly take me past the guards as a visitor to the Borgia apartments without arousing suspicion.

I stared beyond the unshuttered window, at the tiny, distant bodies moving out in Saint Peter's square, at the dark waves of heat rising from the cobblestones. It was summer, the time of Carnival, and I found myself suddenly transported to another vineyard, another party, where I had sat between Juan and Cesare, and had been intrigued by the appearance of a costumed guest.

I moved over to the black velvet cape I had dropped on the

floor, and lifted it from the marble. It was hooded; it would hide my hair. I turned to my husband.

'I need a mask,' I said. 'One that will cover my face completely, and a courtesan's gown. The gaudier, the better.'

Jofre stared, uncomprehending.

My tone grew impatient. 'You know such women. You can find such things. Hurry; we have until the sun sets.'

The mask Jofre brought was beautiful: leather cut and tooled to resemble butterfly wings, bronzed along the edges, and painted deep purple and blue green. It covered but half my face, revealing my lips and chin, so my resourceful husband had found a matching fan made from peacock feathers. The satin gown was bright, dazzling scarlet, cut immodestly low—nothing I ever would have worn. I asked Esmeralda to take a bit of fabric from the hem and create a small pocket—'as you did for my stiletto.' She complied without question; nor did she say a word as she helped me into the courtesan's gown, then watched me tie the mask in place, and cover myself with the black cape. Once I drew the hood over my hair, and spread open the peacock fan to hide my lips and chin, my disguise was complete. Only one thing remained: I slipped the vial containing the rest of the canterella into my gown.

Jofre gaped at me with open lust; I was at once flattered and jealous, for his reaction reminded me of all the whores he had taken during our marriage. I stifled my anger and proffered him my arm.

'Let us walk together, Don Jofre,' I said coyly. 'I am of the mood to take the night air of Saint Peter's piazza.'

He tried to smile, but was too sick with fear; I noticed that he carried his dagger that night, sheathed at his hip, in case our efforts again failed. I held his arm tightly, comfortingly, as we walked out of the unguarded, silent Castel Sant'Angelo.

Given the gravity of what I was about to do, my senses had the peculiar keenness I had experienced during madness: each step

Jofre and I took rang and echoed with excruciating intensity. There were few passers-by on the bridge, no doubt because most were at home, afraid of the crime and unrest prompted by the death of a pope. I watched the faint lights from the palazzos and the boats play off the dark waters of the Tiber; never had it smelled so swampish and foul, so redolent of a decade's worth of rotting flesh.

Once we crossed the bridge, we entered Saint Peter's square. The year I had come to Sant'Angelo—the year of Jubilee—it had been filled to overflowing with pilgrims; now it was empty, save for a few stragglers.

My heartbeat quickened as we approached the Vatican gates, where tired, surly-looking young soldiers eyed me warily; there were fewer now than there had been at morning. My grip on my fan tightened; I held it closer to my face. But upon recognizing Jofre, the guards immediately bowed and opened the gates without a challenge.

For the last time I ascended the steps to the papal palace.

It pained me to move through those familiar halls; the air was heavy with treachery and grief. When I entered the Borgia apartments, the surfeit of gilding and decoration no longer seemed breathtaking or glorious, but sinister.

I passed the Hall of the Sibyls, scrubbed clean of blood and restored to its previous luxury since I had last seen it; I averted my eyes, and summoned all the coldness in my heart.

'In here,' Jofre said, and led me to the Room of the Saints, the scene of much celebration. Now it had been turned into a hospital of sorts. A great bed with a canopy had been brought in; tables held basins of water and cloths, as well as flasks of water and wine, a goblet, and medicines. True to Jofre's word, Alexander had been abandoned save for Gasparre, who sat sleeping in a chair at the pontiff's bedside.

In the middle of the bed—beneath the brilliantly coloured fresco of Lucrezia as the sagacious Saint Catherine—lay the Pope. His skullcap had been removed, revealing a bald crown and a fringe of dishevelled white hair as fine and downy as an infant's. He wore only a linen nightgown; sheets had been drawn up to cover his spindly legs and half his round, protruding stomach. He too dozed, though his eyes were slit open; the lids were puffed and blackened; his complexion was grey, and his cheeks sunken, giving him a skeletal appearance.

I let go of Jofre's arm. He went over to Gasparre, put a hand on his shoulder to rouse him, then whispered something in the startled chamberlain's ear. I know not what he said; I was only grateful that my husband's lie worked, for Gasparre rose and left the room.

I turned to Jofre. 'Husband,' I said. 'Perhaps it would be best if you went, too.'

'No,' he replied firmly. 'I will see you safely out of here.'

I went over to the table and set down my fan, then poured a small amount of wine into the goblet. While Jofre watched the entrance, I withdrew the green vial, and poured half its contents into the liquid, then swirled it. It was a massive dose, enough for fifty men, but though I was cold enough to commit murder, I was not cruel. I desired that Alexander go quickly, not that he suffer.

When I was satisfied it was ready, I nodded to my husband.

He moved away from the door, sat on the edge of his father's bed, and put a gentle hand on the old man's arm. 'Father,' he said.

Alexander's eyelids flickered; he gazed up at his averred son in confusion. 'Juan?'

'No, Father. It is I, Jofre.' Tears gathered in my husband's eyes; his face contorted with sudden grief. Holding the goblet, I moved behind him.

Alexander blinked and recognized me at once despite the mask that hid the upper half of my face. 'Sancha?' His voice was weak, reedy, but held a trace of good humour; he seemed pleased to see me. 'Sancha, you have come to visit . . . Is it the season for Carnival already?' It was as though he had forgotten my brother's murder and my imprisonment. He spoke to me as he would have to Lucrezia, seeking feminine comfort. 'Sancha, where is Juan?'

I stepped in front of my husband. 'He sleeps, Holiness. As you should, too. Here. This will help.'

I held the cup to his lips; he drank, coughing at first, but then recovered, and managed to take several swallows. As I pulled the goblet away, he grimaced. 'It is bitter.'

'The most efficacious medicines always are,' I replied. 'Now rest, Your Holiness.'

'Tell Jofre to stop that crying,' he said peevishly, then sighed and closed his blackened eyelids.

With the back of my hand, I reached down and stroked his weathered cheek. The skin was soft, thin as parchment.

I sighed, too, and with the outflow of breath came a long, piercing pain in my breast, like someone withdrawing a sword. I knew then that I need accomplish no more: the canterella and I had both served our purpose.

'It is done,' I whispered to Jofre. 'Without him, Cesare has no power. We can go.'

But Jofre took the sleeping pontiff's hand and said, 'I will stay with him.'

I kissed his head in reply, and left him there. I had intended to return at once to the Castel Sant'Angelo . . . but strangely, my feet sought a familiar path, up the stairs, on a journey I had made surreptitiously, at night, so many years before—to Cesare's apartment.

The doors to both the inner and outer chambers were open. I kept the fan close to my face; I expected to confront Micheletto Corella there, and had prepared the alibi that I was a courtesan friend of Cesare's, so enamoured of him that I had to reassure myself he would recover.

But the suite was empty, save for the man upon the bed. Corella, fittingly, had deserted his master.

Cesare was naked and moaning, his long legs and torso tangled up in the linens; his feet were dark purple, swollen to almost twice their normal size. A single taper burned on the nearby table, but even that feeble light pained him; he squinted and clutched his head in agony.

I entered silently and stood before the bed, uncertain why I had come. I had never seen the man so helpless, or deserted; either servants or Corella had taken advantage of his condition, for his tapestries, fur rugs and gold candelabra were all missing. Any item of value, in fact, had been taken; only the gilded ceilings and frescoes remained. Yet I felt no pity . . . only amazement that I had ever loved a man so wicked, amazement that I had been so fooled.

At last his tortured gaze—black, shadowed eyes in a ghastly white face, framed by dark hair hanging in damp, tangled strands—fell on me. He struggled to cover himself, to regain some dignity despite his weakness; he tried to lift his head and failed. I understood why it was not necessary to kill him: it was greater torment for him to survive, stripped of power. Without the backing of the papacy, none would remain loyal to him. With his cruelty, his treachery towards his own men, he had hanged himself—just as surely as King Alfonso II had swung from the great iron sconce in Sicily.

'Who are you?' he rasped.

I spoke from behind the fan, my voice muffled. 'You are undone,' I told him. 'Your father is dead.'

He let go a groan—not of grief, but of great inconvenience.

'Who is it?' he demanded again. 'Who speaks?'

I lowered my fan, drew back my hood, and lifted the mask to fully reveal my face; I showed him a regal haughtiness worthy of my father at his coronation. Bereft of supporters, he was no more than a whimpering coward.

'Call me Justice,' I said.

XXXVIII

I moved swiftly down the staircase and returned to Jofre; he sat, shoulders slumped with guilt and grief, beside the motionless form of the Pope. I glanced at Alexander: his eyes were half-open now, dulled and sightless, fixed on a far-distant spot beyond the walls; his lips had been forced open by his violet-black, swelling tongue. His great broad chest had at last fallen still, and rose no more.

Around us, two servants—a man and a woman—were busily stuffing exquisite gold-threaded tapestries into a sack; others, I knew, would soon join them, and Alexander's quarters would soon be as bare as Cesare's. Yet neither I nor my husband made any move to stop them.

I took Jofre's hand. His own remained limp; he did not return my grip, and I let his fingers slip away from mine. He spoke in a tone devoid of feeling, his gaze fixed on the body of the man who for so many years had owned him as son. 'Gasparre has gone to tell the cardinals, and make preparations. Someone will come to wash him, then take him for burial.'

I stood silent for a time, then said gently, 'I am going home.'

He grasped my tacit meaning and turned his face away. I understood from the gesture that he had decided to return to Squillace; from that time on, we would live apart. He was not strong enough to remain with the one who had lifted the final dose to his father's lips, not strong enough to live in the presence of our shared guilt.

I leaned down, placed a gentle kiss upon his head, and left him.

By the time I arrived once more at the Vatican gates, most of the guards had fled; those few who remained let me pass without jeering. An odd silence fell over them at the sight of me, as if they sensed my power.

I walked through the gates onto the cobblestone piazza of Saint Peter, unafraid of the darkness despite being a woman unarmed. My spirit felt light—like Rome, the Romagna, the Marches, finally free of the Borgia curse. My brother's ghost had been avenged, and could rest at last. Ironically, Cesare had finally given me those things he had promised in the heat of love: my native city and a child.

In the distance, on the other side of the Tiber, stood the Castel Sant'Angelo, with the Archangel Michael spreading his wings over the stone keep; several of the tiny windows—those of Cesare's madwomen—glowed yellow. I smiled, knowing that Rodrigo and Donna Esmeralda awaited me there.

Behind me, the bells of Saint Peter's began their dolorous toll.

I stepped onto the bridge and crossed the dark river; this time I smelled only sweet brine. My heart was already in Naples, where the sun gleams off the pure blue waters of the bay.

AFTERWORD

The details of Pope Alexander VI's viewing and burial are particularly gruesome. After his death, his body was washed and clothed and, following custom, put on display in Saint Peter's so that it could be visited by the faithful. But as it lay in state, the Pope's body swelled monstrously and blackened, becoming so frightful in appearance that it was covered. The people began to murmur that Alexander had been possessed by the Devil, or had at the very least sold his soul for temporal power. Accompanied by a small group, the body was swiftly carried away for burial—to the chapel of Santa Maria della Febbri, where Alfonso of Aragon had been taken only a few years before.

The actual interment was horrific: Alexander's corpse was so swollen it failed to fit into the coffin, and was literally beaten into it with shovels. A great stone was placed atop the grave to keep the lid in place.

Although he eventually recovered, Cesare was resoundingly abandoned by all who had previously supported him. The treacherous Don Micheletto Corella confronted the Pope's Treasurer at knife-point, and made away with most of the papal funds; King Louis deserted Cesare at once. Friendless, with countless enemies in Italy and no support in France, Cesare was arrested by King Ferdinand of Spain. The monarch had been lobbied for years by Juan's wife, who publicly accused Cesare of her husband's murder. Cesare eventually managed to escape, however, and distracted himself by fighting in minor skirmishes.

As for Sancha, she succeeded in returning to Naples with her nephew Rodrigo, while Jofre returned to Squillace to rule. Curiously, Cesare brought the Roman Infante, Giovanni—his and Lucrezia's illegitimate son—to Sancha in 1503, asking that she raise the boy; one can only speculate that Cesare still had affection and respect for her. Sancha acquiesced to his request and took care of the two children, surrounded by the surviving female members of her family. Unfortunately, she died shortly thereafter of an unrecorded illness. Historians disagree on the year: some list it as 1504, others as 1506.

Interestingly, Cesare died not long after: in 1507, in Viani, Italy, while serving as a mercenary, he unwisely rode so far ahead of his own troops that he was immediately surrounded by the enemy and killed. Many considered his death a suicide.

Lucrezia remained in Ferrara and bore Alfonso d'Este four children. Towards the end of her life, she became increasingly religious, and took to wearing hair shirts beneath her glamorous gowns. In 1518, she joined the Third Order of Saint Francis of Assisi. She died in 1519, after giving birth to a short-lived baby girl.

Jofre returned to Squillace. Upon Sancha's passing, he married Maria de Mila and produced many heirs. He remained at his estate until his death in 1517.

Historians have speculated for centuries as to who actually poisoned Alexander VI and his eldest son. The mystery has never been solved.

Sancha of Aragon and the Borgias provided delicious nuggets of history. Here are some recorded facts which are included in this novel: the madness of Ferrante I and Alfonso II of Naples; Ferrante's 'museum' of mummified enemies (yes, he talked to them); Alfonso II's witnessing of his own daughter's marriage act with Jofre Borgia; Alfonso II's abandonment of Naples and theft of the Crown treasure; Savonarola's prediction that Pope Alexander VI was the Antichrist; the Pope's lewd conduct with women, including his fondness for dropping chocolates down women's bodices, and his love for his teenage mistress, Giulia; Lucrezia's unwed pregnancy and her incest with her father and brother; the murders of dozens of cardinals and nobles by the Borgias; the filling of the Tiber River with literally hundreds of bodies during the period of the 'Borgia terror'; the hanging of Cardinal Ascanio Sforza's guest; Cesare's murder of his brother, Juan, Duke of Gandia; Cesare's acts of rape and barbarism during the war; Don Micheletto Corella's murder of Alfonso of Aragon in the Hall of the Sibyls; Sancha's arrest and subsequent mad preaching from the Castel Sant'Angelo tower. I have omitted mention of numerous other murders to spare the reader redundancy.

From the pen of critically acclaimed author

JEANNE KALOGRIDIS—

more irresistible historical novels filled with danger and passion...

AVAILABLE WHEREVER BOOKS ARE SOLD

Download reading group guides at www.ReadingGroupGold.com.

St. Martin's Griffin